ILL FATE

MONZELLA SMITH

Order this book online at www.trafford.com
or email orders@trafford.com

Most Trafford titles are also available at major online book retailers.

Printed in the United States of America.

ISBN: 978-1-4669-2138-2 (sc)
ISBN: 978-1-4669-2140-5 (hc)
ISBN: 978-1-4669-2139-9 (e)

Library of Congress Control Number:2012905225

Trafford rev. 03/20/2012

 www.trafford.com

North America & international
toll-free: 1 888 232 4444 (USA & Canada)
phone: 250 383 6864 ♦ fax: 812 355 4082

PROLOGUE

kye Rainwater had always been different, seeing things that others could not see. She was fully aware of the many immortals; vampires, werewolves, witches, shape shifters; living in their small valley town, but they did not know she could see who they were. When some of the immortal's loved ones started disappearing or turning up viciously murdered, she could see the tension and upset building among them toward the humans. They started to prepare to take revenge. Somehow Skye knew it wasn't humans that were responsible for this. It is now up to Skye to come forward and convince the immortals to work together with the mortals in order to find the real killers. In a horrifying battle for both mortal and immortal, where something evil lurks, Skye will be taken down a path that will not only reveal secrets about her past that she was unaware of, but will also challenge her physically and mentally, leading her to question who the true enemy is.

ILLUSION

It's right in front of me.
It must be there.
But now it's gone.
Something's look like they're made of gold.
When it should be obvious it's junk.
It's an illusion.
It makes me think.
It's an illusion.
It makes me hope.
I long for it to be real but,
It's an illusion
The first time you deceive me, you got me.
The second time you deceive me, will make me despair.
The third time you try, You better watch Your back.

-LeVae Smith

PREFACE

I was overwhelmed with awe. I reached out to stroke the beautiful feathers on its neck, lost my balance and fell. I could feel my stomach churning and twirling as I fell so fast. I could see the ground coming up at me at break neck speed. Tree limbs flashed past me. The birds that had checked on me at the top of the tree began to circle around me. It was a stunning sight. They flew so gracefully. If they could do it, then so could I. I looked up at the blue sky above me, searching for my condor. Then there she was. Sailing beside me as I plummeted toward the ground. I couldn't even think of the impending death that loomed below me. I just wanted to reach out and touch her. Her feathers were so alluring. They looked like silk, like the blouse my mom had given me to wear today. I stretched out my fingers wanted so bad to hold on to her, to feel the comfort of her heart beat, to fly like her. I knew I had to be only several hundred feet from the ground, but I didn't care. I was determined to hold her before I died.

CHAPTER I

IT BEGINS . . .

It was after midnight. The mountainous background with black pine tree fingers grasping at the pale moon, foretold of ominous doom. Natalie had never been out so late hunting, but she had lost track of time following a shady man to a cottage where he attempted to break in the window of a little girl's room. He slowly approached the house and had the window half way open when he felt a hand grab him by the neck and yank him to the ground. Startled, he turned to hit the person who assaulted him.

"What the hell?" he yelled. As he raised his fist, he stopped just as he noticed it was a young, beautiful lady. Her skin was pale but glistened like pearl in the moon light. He groaned, "Give me a break!" She raised her hand to his face and waved one finger at him. She whispered, "Tsk, Tsk. I don't think so."

To his horror she suddenly grew fangs. Mesmerized by not only her beauty, but the sight of her fangs, he was frozen. He was unable to fight back as she pulled his head back and lowered her mouth to his neck. Natalie finished him off and left his body lying there.

She took the form of a bat and flew back into town. She landed and returned to her vampire form. As she began to walk home through the woods, she suddenly felt something following behind her. She turned to confront him, fully prepared to fight, fangs bared, crouched to jump, when something stronger than her grabbed her by the throat. She lashed out with her nails trying to claw out his eyes. He grabbed her arms, dangling her in mid air. She pulled up her legs and started to wrap them around his neck. He released her arms and before she could hit the ground, he grabbed her by her legs, again hanging her above the ground.

Somewhere from deep inside him he let out a deathly laugh. As she watched in horror his whole body suddenly began to shake and convulse. Where he stood was now a black as oil, shimmering void with glowing orbs suspended in the place his eyes were.

She stared unbelieving, cursed, and started fighting again. Desperately grabbing at the black cavity, she was unable to touch anything. All she could feel was an intense nothingness, a malevolent presence, a feeling she had never experienced before in all her years on this Earth. With another morbid laugh, he pulled her legs apart, ripping her in half, down the middle. He turned his back and started to walk away.

The only thing going through her mind was the agonizing pain, the loss of blood, and the fact that if she were to ever make it home she'd have to take time to mend and feed again to get back her strength. Never before had there been anyone, mortal or immortal, with strength enough to do this to a vampire. With a body like granite, what could possibly toss her around like a rag doll? She had to recover and warn the others. She thought she had a chance, but then he turned back around and shifted forms again taking on the appearance of a man. Her thoughts were of how ugly he looked, and that there was a familiar smell about him. Her and her brothers and sister had run across this smell before when they were out hunting.

She managed to reach into her pocket and pull out her cell phone. She pushed the speed dial to call her brother. She saw his name flash across the screen of the phone, *Shinu,* and started to yell for help. Just then the evil man-thing leaned over her body and whispered, *"Nana` se`ew kooshdaneit wa.e`!"* She recognized the language and just as she started to say something to him, he reached down and ripped out her heart. Blackness slowly consumed Natalie. Shinu's voice trailed off in the background, "Natalie?"

. . . .

For a long time now, Sadie had not been able to bare any children. Sadie and her mate, Thomas, had been nervously anticipating the birth of their third pup. For nine weeks she took it easy, resting a lot. Now tonight, the night of the new moon, their long awaited child was to be born. Nervously, Thomas paced back and forth outside the house as Dr. Whitcraft took care of his wife. He had kicked Thomas out because he was making Sadie even more frantic.

His second in command, Natasha, was inside to help Sadie through the delivery. Along with Natasha, Emily Silverstein, the packs newest member, sat on the bed beside Sadie wiping her head with a cold towel. Natasha's brother, Elliot, paced just as nervously outside with Thomas.

Thomas was mumbling and praying under his breath. He turned to Elliot with a look of dread. Trembling he said, "Births of a new pup are one of the hardest things our women must endure. I should have just stayed satisfied with the two pups we have already. They are beautiful, but both female and they have married and moved on to another pack. She insisted we try again for a male pup. Now I don't care what it is. I just want them both alive and healthy. What if . . . ?"

Elliot placed a hand on his shoulder and said, "Don't even think like that. They will be fine. We are all aware that for generations our pack has lived on through your lineage. Your male pup will become leader of this pack. It is only natural and expected that you and Sadie try. Have faith. Everything will be . . ."

He trailed off as a blood curdling howl emanated from inside the house. Before Elliot could stop him, Thomas bolted up on the porch, almost falling over the patio furniture, and inside the house, transforming into his wolf form along the way. He was up the steps in three bounds. Throwing the door open, he practically knocked over Dr. Whitcraft on his way to his wife's side. Sadie lay there, drenched in sweat, and covered with blood from the waist down. Her hair was plastered to her pale face. He changed back to human form when he saw there was no danger and knelt at his wife's side.

Stroking her hair, he laid his head on her chest thinking the worst. As he began to cry, he heard her heart beating, very slow and shallow, but still beating. He raised his eyes up to meet hers and a smile slowly crept across his face. Sadie brought up her hand and gently caressed his face, saying, "Do you honestly think I'd leave our son to be raised alone by his worry-wart father?" She gave him a bright loving smile as recognition crossed his face. Stunned he whispered, "Son?"

She shook her head yes, and he let out a howl that would wake the whole town. Standing quickly he looked around for his new pup. Emily was holding him, cleaning him off and wrapping him in the blanket that had been passed down through Thomas' family. She proudly smiled and handed him to his father. Thomas held his son, hugging him and crying, "Thank the gods! Nanuk, my son, you will one day lead our great pack!"

Natasha worked diligently on Sadie cleaning her up. When she finally made a sound, Thomas jumped a little startled and said, "Natasha! I am so sorry. I almost forgot you were here too. Thank you so much. For all you have done and are doing for my wife." He turned and looked at Dr. Whitcraft, smiled and said, "Doc. You are a miracle worker!"

Dr. Whitcraft nodded and stepped aside revealing a young girl standing beside him. She looked drained and soaked with sweat. He motioned to her and said, "My dear boy. You're welcome. But, I can only take credit for the delivery of your son. My daughter, Amber, has to take credit for saving your son and your wife's lives."

Thomas handed the pup to his wife and walked over to Amber. He hesitated and crying again he said, "You, you're a healer! Oh, god bless you. My family will be forever in your debt."

Amber hugged him back, and with a weak laugh she replied, "You're welcome. No need for debts. Just invite me to all his birthday parties. But please do not be afraid or alarmed. I had to save them. So they are now a part of me as I am of them. They now have a little touch of my magic. We will always be connected. At any time they need me, I will know and I will be here for them as well as you."

Thomas released her and let out a small howl that sounded a lot like a laugh. He smiled and said, "I could never be afraid or alarmed. You are always welcome. You are a member of my pack now. We all will look out for you like you were one of our pups."

They all smiled, cried and hugged. After all was well and Sadie was doing well, Thomas took Nanuk outside and introduced him to the pack that had all been anxiously waiting. They all let out howls of joy.

• •

Skye woke suddenly from a deep sleep. She looked around her room half expecting someone or something to be there. After she was fully awake, she walked to her window, pulled back the curtain, and opened the window. Outside she could hear a painful howl. Silently, to herself, she felt an impulse to reach out to them with her mind and strength. She whispered to herself, "I give you my strength and power to do what must be done." She felt a tug, like something drawing on her inner force. After a short while, and after feeling completely drained, she could hear the howls fill the night air. But, this was no ordinary howl. Skye knew a new pup was born. Not just any pup, the pack leader's heir. They had finally had a son. She closed her curtains, but, left the window open. Their howls always soothed her or warned her of danger. Either way, she loved to hear them. Smiling to herself she returned to bed.

Two weeks had passed and Nanuk was already growing into a strong and handsome pup. He had already mastered alternating between his human form and wolf form with ease. Thomas knew it was early, but he was playing hunter and prey with Nanuk in the woods. The sun was high and daggers of golden light filtered through the branches and leaves. They had been laughing and playing for a few hours now and Nanuk had become very good at hiding.

Thomas figured it was time to quit and rest since he was still so young. He called out, "Nanuk, son? It's time to return home and rest."

He listened for the familiar padding of his son's paws on the soft grass, but heard nothing. A sudden eerie feeling crept up Thomas' back. All his hair stood on end and he instantly changed into his wolf form. Something was not right. There was an air of something wicked hanging over the woods. More worried now, he began circling the area where him and his son were playing. Nanuk was nowhere in sight. That eerie sense of an evil aura hung in the air, thick, then slowly dissipated.

Panic set in and Thomas began frantically searching and yelled, "Nanuk! Son! No more hiding. Come out please!" He found the spot where Nanuk was last. He could smell him strong right there by a tree. Another odor hung heavy there too. The odd evil odor and evil presence he had felt several minutes ago, oozed from the same spot where his son last played. Nanuk was gone. Thomas howled out in anguish.

That was not the end of the chaos that weekend. Several other vampire, werewolf, and shape-shifter children and loved ones disappeared or were found mutilated.

CHAPTER 2

THE MEETING . . .

It was a typical Monday morning at the school. Everyone was gathered outside, in their individual cliques. I pulled into the parking lot, turned off the engine in my car, and turned to open the door and get out, when I noticed one small group seemed out of place.

Standing off to the side of the building was an adult male, Emily Silverstein, Amber Whitcraft, another boy, and another girl I only recognized as a junior. What was odd about the gathering was that the adult male was a werewolf, Emily was also a werewolf, Amber was a witch, the boy was a warlock, and the other girl, also a werewolf. I was born with the gift of sight. I am a seer. Very rare now days, but, according to my mom, there used to be a lot of us. They seemed to be in a serious conversation, not so much mad, but worried looking.

I hadn't realized that I had slowed down and was staring over at the group. I over heard just a little of the conversation. Something about a lost pup. Before I could stop myself, I gasped in shock and dropped my backpack. Bending down to pick up my things, I wasn't thinking when I whispered, "Oh god! Not the new pup." It dawned on me at the last second that werewolves had keen hearing and probably heard everything I just said. I tried to cover for my idiotic slip up, "Not my new book." They all turned when they heard the noise and stared.

The adult male looked at Amber and asked her, "Do you know who that is?" Amber and Emily answered in unison, "That's Skye. Skye Rainwater. Why?" He rubbed his temples, and said, "Not sure. I could have sworn I just heard her say something about the new pup. Anyway, Amber, please come by the house after school as soon as you can. Sadie is so sick over this." He headed back to his car and drove off, but not before he got a good look at me as he passed.

Moving on I entered the building and noticed other oddities. There was a crowd standing around Shinu Takai. Not only were there the usual smart kids that followed him around, but a few other kids as well. Again, like a lost, mutated zombie, I slowed down to listen. One of the smart kids was telling Shinu they were sorry he lost his sister, Natalie.

Before I could catch myself I again mumbled too loud. I keep this up and I'll need a muzzle just to get through the day. I knew Natalie. She graduated last year and was supposed to be heading off to college this fall. I just have to keep my thoughts to myself. *Come on Skye. A vampire? You know they can hear a pin drop on a bed of feathers in Australia when they're standing in America.*

I just headed on to my first class, wondering to myself, *What the hell is going on? Something isn't right. I should have felt something, picked up something.* I was so deep in thought that I hadn't noticed that I was being followed. When Shinu spoke, I thought I would have a heart attack right there in the hallway. That would really raise my popularity status. He snarled, "What do you mean you should have felt something? And, and just what are you? And why can I hear you now? And what do you know?"

We were at the door to our class when I was finally able to catch my breath. Startled, I said, "I should have felt you behind me. We can talk after class. I think it's about time. Ok?" He nodded yes, but still looked at me like I was one of the undead with pieces of my flesh dropping to the ground leaving a bloody trail.

His face was like stone. I could feel the anger and confusion pulsating off him in heat waves, directed right at my back. He sat four seats behind me in history, and I could still sense him through the other students directly behind me.

Class seemed to go on forever. I couldn't concentrate for nothing today. One reason was due to Shinu, the other was the strange things that were happening. Reaching behind my neck I rubbed it, *I swear he's going to give me a sun burn on my neck with all the heat he's throwing at me.* Suddenly I heard his voice in my head. *Maybe I should just burn your head off!* Ok, now I was really getting irritated. *Get out of my head Shinu Takai, son of Renji and Sue Lin Takai!*

I knew better then to address him like that, but I was getting very agitated. I wanted to take it back just as I thought it. I was just so upset, confused, and worried that I spoke before I thought. I always did that. That just made Shinu's temper flare even more and I thought I would have a fight on my hands. Not that I'd win. But, I could do some damage. I had trained with my dad my whole life to fight. We both stood at the same time and faced each other. He flipped his desk when he stood up. Shinu stared at me like he could rip me in half, which he could easily do. I tried to give him a look that said I am so sorry. The whole class stared in shock at us and the teacher stopped mid lecture.

Mr. Johnson was a little perturbed and yelled, "Mr. Takai and Miss Rainwater. I can sympathize with your loss Shinu and I have no clue as to what could be wrong with you, Skye. But you both interrupted me. Office. Now!" Shinu grabbed his things and pushed past me and almost knocked me on the floor. Grabbing my things, I followed him out. Once we were in the hall he stepped right up to me, eyes flaring, gritting his teeth and growled, "I think you'd better start talking fast Skye Rainwater, daughter of, of, . . . damn!"

Shinu started pacing in the hall trying to calm down. By the time he had managed to cool down, I had already started toward the office. He walked off after me and blurted out, "Hey. We need to talk. All school year you have just been another person at this school. Now all of a sudden, it's like you popped out of thin air as, as, as something. Why now? Why now that something's going on? Who are you, really? What are you?" Turning around and stopping right in front of him, I was calm which is odd for any normal person coming face to face with an angry vampire. Smiling, I said, "We have exactly twenty minutes before next class. Mr. Johnson forgot to give us our pass to the office. We can stand here and argue, go to the office, or go in the band room and talk real quick."

Once again Shinu pushed past me, knocking me off balance, but, not to the floor. He walked to the door of the band room and held the door open. Smiling again I couldn't help myself. I said, "Thank you. Such a gentle man." He laughed, and snorted back, "Oh. I'm not being a gentleman. I'd just rather not have you at my back. What kind of person or whatever makes a vampire mad and then just calmly faces them as if nothing's wrong?"

Shaking my head I said, "We'll get to that. Long story short, I am a seer. I have always been a seer. My mother is one and her mother. We can see things and sense things that normal humans can't. It's hard to describe. I can see the *form* of immortals as they assume a human persona. But, I can also see beneath that outer layer and see the true inner *form.* That's the only way I can describe it. The only other way I can think to say it is that I can sense who you are. I can see every vampire, werewolf, witch, and shape-shifter in town. Everywhere I go. The reason you and no one else know what I am is because my mother was taught to hide it and her mind, and she taught me. I can always tell or feel when one of you is around me, even if you were to sneak up on me. I've always been able to sense it. So, today when you snuck up behind me, it threw me off and I got defensive. Sorry. And, no one, human or immortal, has ever been able to get in my head. So, once again, I got defensive. Why you and why now? Something is wrong. Off. This is not right. The deaths and disappearances. I can't put my finger on it."

The bell rang and startled the mess out of me. I guess I had drifted off. He was sitting there looking lost and still skeptical. He gave me a smarty-pants look and said, "R-r-ight. So now what?" I stood up and headed for the door. I gave him a smarty-pants look back and said, "Now we go on to our next class before we get in trouble again. I have to figure this out. I have to finally talk to the others, and we all have to talk, together." Shinu frowned and replied, "Ooo. Might not be a good idea. But, who knows. See ya. You still aren't off the hook. I have more questions." He started to turn and head out the door when he paused and waited for me to go out first. Laughing I went out the door and said, "That whole back thing, huh?" He followed and smiled, a little.

. . . .

School went on as usual that day. I still couldn't shake the feeling that something strange was going on. Something that would ultimately change our town, if not the world, if I wasn't able to figure it out in time.

The rest of the day seemed to melt together in a mushy mass of gibberish. After school I headed out to my car with Stacey Ritennour following me out. Believe it or not, she is a cheerleader and one of my closest friends. She's also the mayor's daughter and only child. She was babbling on, as usual, about Jaye, the quarterback and the upcoming football game. She liked him, but had long ago accepted the fact that he was not interested in her and never would be. I just listened and nodded. She went on, "Anyway, Jaye gave in and told me I'm like a little sister to him. Can you believe it? A little sister! I guess that's ok though. He has always looked out for me like that. I wonder who he is interested in? She has to be gorgeous, and smart, and not here. Know what I mean? So, I guess I'll talk to you later. Hey are you listening to me?"

Snapping back to reality, I answered, "Oh. Yeah, Jaye, little sister, yadah, yadah. Sorry. Just thinking. Yeah. Hey, call me later?" Stacey said sure and took off across the parking lot to the other cheerleaders, who were already piled in to her convertible, waiting on her. Walking on to my car I noticed someone leaning on the hood. When I got closer I could see that it was Amber. Some of the Goth kids were standing there talking to her. Amber looked up and saw me heading toward them and turned to her friends and said, "I'll catch up with you guys at the coffee shop in a few, K?" They nodded and left.

Stopping at my car door, I unlocked it, and turned to Amber. I smiled and said, "Hi Amber. You need a ride somewhere?" Amber just looked at me puzzled. Amber had a dark, penetrating look in her eyes, which were an uncanny grey. The dark makeup she always wore didn't help keep her from looking menacing also. She had a tendency to wear all black. Today was no exception. But, this time she wore a violet blouse under her black lace vest, a black long, flowing skirt, and under that, the black, lace up stiletto boots she always wore. She was a stunning black girl with tiny little braids that hung down to her waist. She was petite and short.

She cocked her head to the side and stared at me, then said, "I don't quite get you. I don't know what to think. There's something there, but . . ." Smiling, which I seem to have done a lot of today I replied, "I can give you a ride and we can talk." Amber hesitated and then decided to get in. She was silent for a few minutes, then she demanded, "Ok. Talk."

I started the car, looked over at Amber and smiled again. Closing my eyes, I let out my breath, and dropped my head for a few seconds, meditating, before looking up again at her. Amber had a shocked look on her face and her mouth was hanging open. She started to speak, then closed her mouth again and just stared, like she recognized me. Not only from school, but of look like she knew me from somewhere. Finally, as we were pulling out of the parking lot Amber began talking, "You're a seer. You've been hiding it all these years. It's like, like you just lifted a blanket off yourself. Then I assume you know what I am?"

I smiled again. We had made it almost all the way to the restaurant, which s where I knew she hung out, when I pulled over. I finally said, "Yes. A witch. How much do you know about seers?" Amber had turned sideways to look out the window, trying to avoid looking directly at me.

After another uncomfortable few minutes she answered, "I know you can see things, like immortals, ghosts. Now I wonder why you've hid it all these years. And why were you eavesdropping on us earlier? How much do you know? How do I know I can trust you if I tell you things? How the hell . . . ?"

Amber took one more frightened look at me and jumped out of the car and took off running toward the restaurant. I sat there for a few minutes gathering my thoughts, shocked at Amber's abrupt behavior, I said to myself, "That went well." Turning the car around, I decided to head home. There was a lot to talk to mom about.

· ·

When I got home I didn't go in right away. I had to think for a while before I asked my mom the many questions I now had. I decided to go into the woods by our house where I often went to get away and meditate. The trees weren't thick here. They spread apart, sparse in many areas, reaching out to the mountains like a swath of plush, green carpeting. The grass was still green now and the flowers were still in bloom.

Here, in nature, among her beautiful creatures and glorious plants, I could think, breath clearer. My mind was free to grow, reach out, expand. I found my spot I always sat in. It was tucked in between two fallen tree trunks. The grass was plusher here, almost like a pillow. I could see clear through the trees to the sky, where I could watch the birds soar in and out of the clouds. I often wished I could fly with them. I thought that if I could, it would open up a whole new world to my mind's eyes.

As I sat down, I looked up in time to see a crow. I knew it was the same crow I always saw. For as long as I can remember there was always this crow. I could never tell if it was following me, or just coincidence. But, for some odd reason, I always felt safer with him up there, circling around me, like my own personal guardian angel. The sun reflected off his feathers and a beautiful flash of blue melded into the sleek black of his feathers. As he circled back around, the sun once again hit him. This time a brilliant, deep burgundy melted into the black. I closed my eyes, slowed my breathing, and began meditating. I swear that each time I've done this I could hear the crow, not cawing as a normal crow call, but I could hear a soothing melody, a sweet song. I imagined that if I could hear angels sing that this would be what their song would sound like.

After laying there for I don't know how long, I came back to reality. I didn't come out of my meditation the way I usually did, slowly, with reality and my other world slowly pulling apart. Something snapped me back just as I felt close to an answer to the odd things that were now happening. As my eyes adjusted to the remaining sunlight, I felt someone standing close by. I jumped up and almost hit my head on the branch of the overhanging tree. As I turned around, Amber came morphing out of the trees.

I brushed the grass and dirt off myself, smiled and walked over to her. I said, "So, is it my turn to run?" Amber twisted her face, mocking me, and said, "Only if you feel the need to. I just want to talk now. Sorry for the rude behavior earlier. You just really creeped me out, which is hard for anyone to do, considering who I associate with. I spoke to my mother and aunt. They explained that one day I would find a part of me that has been missing for years. That with you being a seer might mean something. They just didn't get how you all managed to keep it hidden all these years. They said witches always know when seers are in the vicinity."

Amber came closer to me and sat down. She patted the ground, offering a seat. She smiled and said, "Please, sit with me. Now that I'm calm, I want to see something." I sat down facing her. We looked at each other. Something odd happened next. Suddenly I felt as if a warm breeze washed over me and I was surrounded by hundreds of butterflies, fluttering on my skin. As if they were brushing me with soft rose petals. The air also had a faint scent of roses. Then I felt as if I was sitting across from my sister, even though I had none. It felt like I'd known her for years, centuries, but we had only known of each other since junior high school when her and her family moved back here.

Amber must have seen the look on my face. She had the same look on her face. For no apparent reason, I felt like I wanted to hug her. At the same time I was feeling that, Amber must have to, because before we could both react, we reached out and hugged each other. The hug was also like two sisters seeing each other for the first time in years. I hadn't realized a tear was slowly rolling down my cheek. I reached up and wiped it off, looking at my wet hand in disbelief.

We couldn't speak for a long time. We just sat there staring at each other. Finally my crow friend flew overhead again and let out a familiar caw, bringing me back to reality. Amber was the first one to speak. "Did you feel that? I nodded, still in shock. Amber said, "That was what my mom and aunt were talking about! That's what they tried to describe to me. But, they didn't say it would be that intense. They just said that when I found *you* I would know. Not a rush of something so strong, so powerful it makes you cry. I have to tell them about this. Did you feel the same thing, or was it just me?"

I was still in awe, but able to speak now. I said, "Yeah! I have never felt anything like that. It's like I know you, like you are my sister. Like we have always been connected over time and space, but had been separated. Like now we are finally together. Did you smell roses, and still smell them a little, or was that just me?" Amber look shocked too, and said, "Yes! Now what?"

I stood up, again, and offered my hand to help Amber up. I said, "Now we go to my house and talk to my mother. If anyone has a little clue to what's going on, she will or at least will know where to point us." We walked back to my house, smiling at each other. Over head, my crow soared into the clouds and out toward the sunset.

···

When we got to the house, my mother, Lily, was standing outside looking toward the woods. Lily was technically 42 years old, but she looked like she was 20. I've always thought she looked like an Indian goddess. She has high cheekbones and the perfect nose. She was average size and her eyes are a deep brown, almost black, which goes perfectly with her deep caramel complexion, which I inherited from her. Her eye lashes reminded me of long, black feathers that constantly seem to flutter in an alluring manner. Her hair is silky, jet black and falls down the middle of her back like a sinuous waterfall.

Every time she gets up and gets dressed, she leaves the house looking like a perfect model. Perfect outfit, perfect hair, no make-up needed. Today was no exception. She smiled when she saw Amber and me walking to the house. Once we were up to her, she hugged Amber and said, "So, you found us? You have always been with us, a missing part. Like that last piece of a puzzle that's been mislaid. I felt you when you two awoke the past. Come in. You both have questions."

We both looked at each other, shrugged and went in. My grandmother was in the kitchen, waiting, with cups of tea. She came over to Amber and cradled her hands in her own weathered hands. Grandma is a short woman, husky for her stature. She told me she was 110 years old, but I always had a feeling she was older than that. She is very wise and always knew everything I was thinking or doing. I was never able to get away with much mischief with her around. She looked no older than 60. She was still beautiful for her age, with flowing silver hair that reached down to her butt. She continued to wear the traditional Indian dresses and moccasins. Today she added her shawl, which she hand weaved, that resembled a flying hawk.

She smiled at Amber and I and said, "I never thought I would live long enough to see you return and unite with your sister in nature. You two were always meant to stand together, work together. Amber, now your most inner strength, power, is awake and now ready to use. Skye, your power is now in full form. Together, you two will do great things. I'm rattling. Have a seat. Drink some tea."

Once again we looked at each other, lost, but excited. We sat down and grabbed a cup of tea. After a few drinks, I was the first to talk. "I guess I don't need to introduce Amber to you. Mom, there is something strange going on. Shinu's sister was killed. We all know it's hard to kill a vampire. And, Amber, sorry for eavesdropping today, but I heard something about the new werewolf pup disappearing. I was awakened the night he was born. I knew it was the heir to the pack that was born, by their howls. I can, most of the time, understand what they are howling about. For me, their songs are beautiful, mysterious, and sometimes a warning. I just don't know your connection to him, the new pup."

Amber took another sip of her tea and said, "You know quite a bit. I wasn't aware of Shinu's sister. I'm sorry to hear that. Their kind doesn't speak to our kind often. Many of our relatives used to hunt vampires and werewolves, but most no longer do that. They are still a little leery of us. The werewolves, on the other hand, have gotten past that. My and my family's coven are healers. My family, the women in my family, are very powerful. My father is a doctor. The night Nanuk, the pup of the pack leader, was born, my father delivered him. I was there to observe. To see a werewolf pup born is unimaginable.

Anyway, once he was born something went wrong and the pup stopped breathing and the mother stopped breathing. My father did all he could, and I just felt compelled to do something. Up until then, I had only learned basic healing techniques; scrapped knee, broke bone. Before I knew exactly what I was doing, I had brought them back to life. My mother says that's something I shouldn't be able to do until I have gone through training, possibly ten or twenty years

17

down the road. But, suddenly I felt a rush of . . . power and something whispered in my mind . . ."

She paused, set her cup down slowly and stared at me. Simultaneously we said, "I give you my strength and power to do what must be done." Everyone grew quiet and stared at the two of us. I broke the silence first saying, "That was you? I felt someone needing my help. I just opened my mind. I was so tired right after that, but I felt relief too. That's when the howls began and I knew the pup was born, but that's all I knew."

Amber got excited again and said, "I knew I felt a surge of power from somewhere. I didn't know how I did it. I was drained afterward. It was you who guided me? We didn't even really know each other then. You didn't know I was there. How?" Amber looked just as confused as I felt.

My mom smiled and tried to explain it to us. "Remember how I said you, Amber, were a missing piece for us? You were a missing piece of Skye. Together you enhance each others powers. In the woods you two finally joined, completely. Back when the pup was born you two didn't know much of each other, but that connection was still there. Even though you weren't connected yet, there has always been a thin thread that has held you two together, pulled on each others powers and strengths. That night Amber, you really needed that extra boost of power to heal them. Your powers called upon Skye's powers. That's how you bypassed, in a way, the years of training. Your powers worked together as one to heal."

After another long pause of silence and just looking at each other, my grandmother broke the trance we seemed to have fallen in to when she said, "Oh dear! Amber, I think it's kind of late. Your mom will be worried about you. Especially with all the odd disappearances. Skye, why don't you give her a ride home and your mom and I will try and see what we can figure out about what's going on. Amber, I trust we will see you again?"

Amber smiled at my grandma and mother, which I very rarely see her do, nodded yes and we headed out to my car. I looked up out of habit to see if my crow was still circling around. Nope. I hadn't realized it had gotten that late already. The sun had set and the first light of the moon was dimly illuminating the ground. I turned to ask Amber for directions to her house and noticed she had gone into some sort of daze. Her eyes were eerie, glowing silver and she was staring off in the direction of the moon. I asked, "Amber? What's wrong?" I was getting worried now.

She stood there for what seemed like forever, then in a haunting voice she said, "It's the pack. They found one of theirs dead. Can you please take me by there?" Worried now too, I said, "Yes. No problem. Get in and I'll go tell my mom." I ran back in my house. Before I came back out, my mom handed me a medallion and told me to wear it around my neck. She said something about it helping the werewolf pack to except me quicker. I put it on and ran to my car. Amber was already strapped in. I asked, "Where to?"

Still in a trance, she quietly said, "Head back down this road. Just before you get in town, there is a trail to your right. You'll take that trail through the woods. At the end of the trail is a road to the left. Their houses are all back there."

As I watched the road I couldn't help but think about all the events that happened today. It's strange how things just seem to be falling apart, but at the same time, something inside me finally feels like it's coming together. I couldn't help but think that something big was about to happen. There's something more in me that I know is there. Has always been there. But, I could never put my finger on it. I've known for years that I had a purpose, something I am supposed to do.

As we drove, Amber kept her eyes glued to the road. I swear that if her eyes were any more day-glow silver they would light up the whole inside of my car. I couldn't hold back anymore. I inquired, "What's up with your eyes? They're like, glowing and silver instead of the usual odd grey." Once again she smiled. Still odd, but I could get used to it. She looked over at me and answered, "They do that when I pick up a strong psychic connection to the pack now. They never did that until the night I saved Sadie and Nanuk's life. I think it's because once a witch heals someone they take on some of their power and vice versa. The werewolf's eyes glow when they are in that form. I can now see for miles and smell for miles."

We reached the turn off and I suddenly felt the urge to talk. She was being so open with me now. I chattered, "Cool. I've always admired you. You seem to be so confident. You have many friends, even though you tend to gravitate to the Goth kids. I think it would be so cool to be able to heal people, physically. I can heal people emotionally and mentally, but to take away physical pain . . . ? Amazing. Not to mention your snazzy outfits. You make black look chic. Speaking of which, do you own anything bright colored?"

I couldn't help but laugh at myself that time. She laughed too and said, "My mom asks me that all the time. I tried yellow once. It hurt. My friends thought I was sick or dying. I'll never forget the look on one of my friends faces. I swear she turned paler then she already is. She said she thought she'd have to do a séance on me. We still laugh at it."

We talked like this all the way to the pack's village. It was nice to finally have someone to talk to about the immortal world. She had me pull over at a beautiful, large Victorian style house. The porch was a wrap around and there was a swing mounted near the door and a large picture window. I saw a pretty woman standing in the window looking out. She moved and opened the door. When she stepped out I could see she was wearing a striking, long, satin, flowing dress. She carried herself like I'd imagine a queen and had a smooth, stealthy gait. Her face was stunning and her eyes were a hypnotic light brown. She looked as if she had been crying.

We stepped out of the car and when she came over to hug Amber I felt a sudden rush of recognition wash over me, again like a warm breeze. I had forgotten about the medallion my mom had given me that was hanging around my neck. I could feel it pulsating and getting hot. I reached in my shirt and pulled it out. As I touched it, I faded back in time.

I was standing there physically, but no longer standing there, in my mind, with Amber and the lady. I was in a wood from centuries ago. I could see a pack of wolves running through the trees. The head wolf was large, had blue grey fur, and very muscular. His eyes were ice blue and glowing. There was only about ten of them in the pack. They were chasing after another wolf. All I could see of him was his fur which was black as oil and standing on end. His eyes were glowing red. The vision shifted and it was another time. In this one, I was still in the same wood, but there were now cabins where some trees had been cleared.

In one of the cabins a woman lay, covered in sweat and barely breathing. There was a man there with her. There was an old medical bag sitting on the floor next to the mat where she lay. The man held a baby boy in his hands and was chanting something when another man entered the room. He stopped abruptly, cleared his throat, and nervously handed the man the baby. Standing outside the cabin was a dark figure, black as oil. He vanished and the vision shifted to the present. Now I was standing in a room in *this* house. Again a woman was lying on a bed. I sensed a dark presence outside the house. She was fading. Amber approached her. There was brilliant light surrounding the lady, the baby, and Amber.

I was abruptly thrown back to myself where I stood in front of Amber and the lady. I blurted out, "Sadie!", before I knew it. I knew her! I felt connected to her too. I was so glad to see her. Again? Impossible! I knew her from another time. But there was no way possible! I was only 17. How could this be? It had to be an effect of the medallion. I could only stand there in shock.

Sadie was the first to speak, and bow? "Skye Rainwater?! As I live and breathe! It is you. By the gods, it's you! You look the same. It has to be you. You have the medallion. Only you can wear it. It has to be you! Skye Rainwater." With that, she bowed again.

Now Amber and I stared at each other. Something compelled me to walk over and lay my hand on her head. As I touched her I was once again flooded with images. These weren't of the pack. It was of an ancient Indian tribe, centuries in the past. My tribe! They were dancing around a fire. There was a young lady sitting at the head of the circle, sitting on the ground. She was telling a story. Just as I circled around the flames to get a look at her, the vision changed and I was looking at another time. In this one, there were cabins. Again, I saw the young lady standing in the center of a group of tribe's people, talking. I moved to look between the people to see the young lady and finally got a look at her. It was . . . . me!

CHAPTER 3

THE NEW BEGINNING . . .

t was like something, or someone inside me had just woken up after years and years of sleeping. When I was finally able to move, I looked from Amber back to Sadie. I had so many questions, but only one came out. I asked, "Sadie, my dear, how long has it been?" After standing quiet for so long, Amber finally was able to speak. She said, "I am so totally lost. You know each other, but not from now. From the past? Skye, how old are you? I mean, I know I'm 17, but technically I'm 300."

Sadie smiled a calm smile and looked at me as if asking permission to explain. I nodded to her and said, "Go ahead." With another bow of her head she began, "I haven't seen you in over 300 years. But, stories of you, of your tribe, go back at least 500. I remember you before I was even married to Thomas. I was a young pup infatuated with the handsome heir of the pack. I remember going to you to talk about him. I just knew I was not right for him. I thought I was not strong enough, brave enough, or able enough to lead. I will never forget what you told me, and to this day I live by it. You said, 'You are only as brave or as strong as you think you are. Your mind is a power house. Tap into it and you will be the leader this pack needs.'"

Sadie motioned for us to follow her to the backyard. We followed. She continued, "Shortly after that, wars broke out and . . . and much of your tribe was lost, as was many of our pack. We fought alongside your people, but the white man won out. We searched for you for many years. Word got out that you had been killed. Things slowly began to fall apart. Shortly after that, Thomas and I married. Like you knew would happen."

She turned and looked at both of us with more sadness in her eyes. I could feel a heavy burden. I could tell that Amber felt that same sadness. Sadie went on again, "We will have more time to catch up. For now, one of the pack has been killed. It's so horrible. The men are out by the body. They were waiting on Amber to see if she could do anything. I know they will all be just as shocked and happy as I am to see you have returned, Skye Rainwater. They are in the back of the woods by the creek."

Amber and I headed out through the trees. I was still so confused. Lost but found. I could feel some of my memory slowly returning. But, there still were so many holes to fill. As we got closer, I could feel a faintly familiar evil presence. It clung to the air like thick tar. It was almost suffocating. I almost choked on it. I had to stop and catch my bearings before I could move on. Amber must have felt it too. She stopped right beside me, grabbed her stomach, leaned over, and hurled.

When she could breath again she looked at me and asked, "What in the name of the gods is that?" I shook my head and said, "I'm not sure, but it's something vile. It's gone now. Let's get to them." After walking about another half mile, we finally reached the edge of the woods by the creek. There were six men standing around a body lying on the ground. Two other men flanked them on both sides further out in the woods. I could feel that they were scared and nervous.

Amber quickly ran and dropped down beside the body that lay on the ground. As I got closer I could see that the poor werewolf, a young female, had been half way between transforming into her werewolf form. Her top half had fully turned to werewolf and her lower half was still her human form, what was left of her lower half. Her legs had been ripped off and thrown off to the side of her body. There was blood splattered everywhere.

That couldn't have been what killed her. Werewolves heal quickly, and even if her legs had been separated from her body, all she would have had to do was put them back in the approximate place and lay still and wait for them to mend. She may not have been able to ever walk or run right, but she would have lived. No. Something else had killed her. I knelt down beside Amber hoping to understand more. Thomas stood behind Amber and hadn't really noticed me yet. He was talking to her, saying, "Amber. Is there anything you can do? Is it too late?"

Amber lowered her head to listen to her heart. She closed her eyes and placed her hands just above the werewolf's body. Her hands began to glow a phosphorescent pink at first. Suddenly she started to shake all over. The glow changed to a putrid green and she jumped to her feet. She started to drop to the ground. She looked at me and tried to speak, but a gurgling sound escaped her mouth. I ran to her, grabbed her hands, and closed my eyes. Before I knew what I was doing or saying, I started chanting this mantra, *"Your mind is strong. Your will your own. Your mind is strong. Your will your own."* Then I started yelling at her. "Damn it Amber! You are not dying! It's all in your mind! It's a trick! Do not fall for it! *Your mind is strong! Your will your own!"*

Slowly she came around. She began breathing again. She shook her head and stood up straight. She said, "She wasn't killed by her legs being pulled off. Someone poisoned her. It's not any normal poison I have ever come in contact with. It's tricky. It's from a witch." I knelt down by the woman's head and leaned over to smell her mouth. Amber was worried and tried to stop me. She yelled, "Skye! No!"

I looked up to reassure her that I was ok and said, "I'll be fine. It won't affect me. I don't know why, I just know it won't. It smells and feels so familiar." I stood up and now faced Thomas and the others. I said, "Thomas, I am sorry. There is nothing we can do." Thomas was looking at me with his mouth hanging open in disbelief. The other guys were staring too. Thomas was the first to speak. "When I seen you earlier today I could of sworn you looked familiar, but I couldn't feel you. It can't be! By the gods, it can't be!"

They all looked at me and simultaneously they bowed their heads. Thomas spoke again, "Skye Rainwater! You have returned!" He raised his head first and in one bound he was in front of me, hugging me. His voice wavered as he said, "We've missed you so much. Where have you been? When did you return? What's going on?"

In spite of the grotesque scene before us, I was so happy to see him and the others. I couldn't help but smile. I said, "I am just as lost as you. All I can tell you in short is that it began with Amber. She came to my house and first woke something in me. Then when we came here, when I came close to your wife it woke up something in my medallion that woke up something in me. I still don't have my full memory yet."

I looked back at the poor lady on the ground. Amber was pulling a sheet over her body to keep anyone from coming in contact with the poison that was still in her system. I turned to Thomas with questions of my own. I asked, "Who was the young lady?"

He lowered his head, sad, and paused before he said, "She was Natasha's soon to be sister-in-law. She was to marry Dakota tomorrow. They were so in love. The first time he seen her he told me he was going to marry her. They had been inseparable. Tonight they finally separated so he could have his bachelor's party and she her bachelorette party. He hasn't returned yet and doesn't know."

Thomas turned and talked to the other men. After he gave instructions to them as far as what to do with the body, Thomas, Amber, and I headed back toward the house. We were silent most of the way back when I spoke up first, "And how is Natasha and her family handling this?" Thomas shook his head in despair. Sadly, he said, "Not well at all. They think it was a human who did this, so they took off toward town to sniff around. They want to see if they can pick up a scent."

I turned to Amber and inquired, "Did that poison seem familiar to you too?" Shaking her head she answered kind of spacey, "Somewhat. It's like I ran across it in the past somewhere." She turned to Thomas and asked, "No word on Nanuk, Thomas?" After a moment of sorrow he was able to answer her. "Not yet. He just vanished into thin air. Or at least that's what it's like. I feel he's still alive though."

We had finally reached their house. Sadie was sitting out back on the patio talking to someone. I knew it was another werewolf, but couldn't see who it was until we got closer. Emily Silverstein. She stood up abruptly and started to leave. Sadie reached out to stop her, but Thomas spoke up first. "Emily. It's ok. This is . . ." She cut him off, rather hostile sounding. She positioned herself in front of Sadie. She was guarding her and I think on the verge of changing into her wolf form. She snarled, "I know who she is! I don't know what she is! You were listening to us this morning, and now you're here? I suggest you speak fast before I rip you to shreds."

Yep. She was changing. I stepped back with my hands in the air, like I was under arrest. I hadn't got all my memory back yet, but I remember you don't want to confront a wolf that had recently been changed. They were out of control, quick to anger, and very protective of the ones who take them in and care for them. I calmly said, "Calm down. Look. No weapons. I'm not the enemy."

Once she was under control, we all sat down. After about 15 minutes and four cups of tea, Sadie had managed to get Emily to chill out. I don't know what she put in the tea, but she sure mellowed out fast. Between Thomas, Sadie, Amber and myself we tried to catch Emily up to speed. She started to understand, but still didn't seem to want to accept it, yet.

She stared at me so intense I could imagine her fangs sinking into my neck. Following several more moments of silence, she decided it was safe to talk to me. "Sooo . . . you're not the one who took Nanuk or the one who killed Elaine. And after hundreds of years of being supposedly dead, you return, but still don't have back all your memory. And you're not Skye Rainwater, the odd girl at school, but Skye Rainwater, the seer?"

I smiled at her blunt responses. I couldn't help but think to myself, *I'm not the oddball.* You *are the strange one at school.* I said, "That pretty much sums it up." She continued to look at me skeptically.

We all talked for a little while longer. It was very late when Amber and I finally left. She directed me to her house and we chatted like old friends all the way there. Before she got out she turned to me. I noticed her eyes were no longer day-glow silver, but back to their normal odd grey. She asked me, "So now what's our next move?"

I hadn't had time to think things out but, I said, "Well. We can't just suddenly become buddy buddy over night at school tomorrow. But, we can talk in passing. And I have a feeling I need to arrange for several key immortals to meet so we can discuss this more. Before anyone innocent gets hurt. It's not the humans. That much I know. And if we don't convince the others of this quick, it could get ugly fast. I've already had a brief run in with Shinu. He already knows I plan on getting people together."

Amber agreed with me and said, "Sounds like a plan. You do remember that vampires and werewolves are natural born enemies? The ones around here just choose to keep their distance and the peace. Shape-shifters are kind of neutral. They get along fine with everyone, so we shouldn't have trouble there." She looked at her watch and startled she said, "I'd better get inside. Mom's probably freakin. It'll be hard tomorrow acting like we really don't know each other after today."

I reached over and hugged her and said, "Same here. You're like the other half of me now. We'll figure it out. Good night." She got out and waved good bye and ran to her door. Her mother was waiting there for her. I headed home. I needed to get some sleep but, I also needed to talk to mom and grandma first.

Ill Fate

When I got home, my crow was circling over the house. His graceful body was silhouetted by the moon that now hung high and full in the night sky. He circled one more time, let out a caw, then vanished into the darkness.

CHAPTER 4

THE FINAL MEETING . . . .

I was so not ready for school Tuesday morning after the long day and night before. It was about 5:00 a.m. when I finally laid down to sleep. My mother and grandmother filled me in on so many other things, but my full memory was still not back. They explained that that would happen in time, at the right time.

Basically they summed it up like this. When our tribe came under attack, they all feared that there was one person behind it all. The men that attacked us knew too much and were specifically searching for me. When my people would not give them the information they wanted, they began burning down everything and killing everyone they could catch. My parents knew they were looking for me and took off before they could get to me. They covered our trail, told no one where we were, and learned to hide their gift of seeing. They also did something they never wanted to do. They hid all my memories, of who I was, from myself. They had to do it in order to keep me safe. It was of dyer importance that I live.

So, after the excitement of the day, the news that I was being hunted, and the sad wails from the werewolves throughout the rest of the night, I couldn't sleep well. I drug myself out of bed, showered, and threw on something I pulled from my drawers. Once I was in my car and half way to school, I woke up all the way and noticed the something I had pulled out of my drawers and put on was my "I love Hippies", tie dyed t-shirt and my red flannel pajama pants.

There was no way I was going to school like that. I'm already viewed as strange; this would just confirm their suspicions. So, I was just going to be late for my first class. I'm sure Shinu would be glad I wasn't there. Then he wouldn't have to keep an eye on me and make sure I was never behind him. I had to laugh at myself for that thought.

I was only ten minutes late for class. Shinu wasn't there. When I asked one of his genius friends, they told me, "Not that it is any of your affair, but Shinu's family is burying his sister today. Now if you don't object, I would like to attend to the remainder of Mr. Johnson's address on pre-dating the brutal attacks of ancient knights." And with that, he stuck his nose in the air and turned back around in his seat. I hadn't thought about the funeral. I would have to try and catch up with Shinu later.

School progressed as usual, slow. It was funny how things looked and seemed a little different today compared to yesterday. Yesterday I was just an unordinary teenager, with an unusual gift or seeing immortals, ghosts, and spirits. No big deal. Now today, I feel as if I have to somehow set things straight and ultimately save mankind and immortal kind and return things to their unusual but normal order.

As I was thinking these things and heading to my usual lunch table to eat, I raised my arm to wave to Stacey; who was already standing there, most likely to tell me something about Jaye before she headed on to her usual table; when I was unexpectedly pulled by my waving arm across the cafeteria and out the lunch room doors.

I didn't have to look around to know who it was. I could feel her now. Before I turned around I said, "Ok, Amber. What's wrong?"

When I did finally turn around, she was flanked on either side by Emily, the same warlock boy from yesterday, and the other werewolf girl, also from yesterday. She frantically said, "There's been a situation. You remember when Thomas said that Natasha and her family thought they had an idea who did it and they thought they were human?" I nodded my head and that feeling of trepidation suddenly drenched me in sweat.

Still panicky she went on, "Well they caught who they think it was. They have him, now, in the woods and are refusing to let him go until they speak to you. Thomas filled them in on your return. They only trust your judgment."

I looked at all of them, and then lower my head to think. I had just started rubbing my temples and moaning, something I often did to help me think, when Jaye busted thru the cafeteria doors. He looked worried and shocked when he seen us standing there. He looked at me first and very seriously asked, "Are you ok Skye?"

I guessed it had to look strange. First I'm standing in the cafeteria getting my lunch, and then I'm pulled out by Amber, who is never seen talking to me at school. Then for him to come out and see them all facing me in a group and me with my hands on my head. That could look like they had jumped me. I had to chuckle a little at that. It was also surprising for Jaye to come to *my* defense when he usually only said hi to me whenever we crossed paths. I answered quickly to put him out of his misery, or concern. "I'm ok. They just needed to talk to me."

I don't think he believed me. He shook his head and nodded ok, but he still stood there, behind me, as if guarding me. I spoke up again in an attempt to get him to leave so we could finish talking. "I'll be fine. Emily just has a family emergency and she knows my mom, and she was asking me my advice when . . ."

I was shocked when he put his hand on my shoulder and even more shocked when images began to flash to me from his touch. I could see the sky. Beautiful blue sky with white fluffy clouds soaring at me. I could see images below me of the ground, trees, flowers, fields. Suddenly, I seen myself lying on the ground, in the woods, in my secret spot I often go to think, by my house. I saw black velvet feathers with shimmers of deep blue and deep burgundy.

Then I knew. The images faded and I turned to Jaye. I could only stare in disbelief. My mouth was hanging open for I don't know how long before Amber spoke and brought me back to reality. "Skye? What's wrong?"

I was finally able to speak. I was still looking at Jaye and still somewhat lost and dazed, but, I managed to get out, "You're a shape-shifter." He quickly pulled his hand off my shoulder. In shock he stammered out, "H-how do you know that? I mean, what are you talking about?"

I didn't have time to explain the whole thing to him right now, so I gave him a quick run through ending with, "Please don't freak out. I'll tell you more later. But, for now I really have to help them with this family emergency. Can we meet and talk later, please?" All I could do at that point was plead with him. I really didn't want or need him to run and hide from me now.

He finally decided after standing there looking disoriented. Clearing his throat, he looked a bit upset when he mumbled, "Ok! This isn't over yet. We'll talk. Everything better be ok." He turned and headed back in the cafeteria.

I turned back to look at everyone and they were looking back at me with puzzled looks on their faces. I hunched my shoulders and changed the subject. I said, "Ok. So, obviously this can't wait until schools out. I have to have an excuse to get out of here." Amber spoke up first again, "Done. My mom has already called in and gave them some excuse for all of us to leave. We're ready to go so we'll meet you there, ok?"

With that, they all turned and rushed down the hall. With all that had just happened again so fast, I had forgotten I was still holding my tray of food. As much as I didn't want to go back in the cafeteria after my unexpected departure, I had to take it back. I pushed open the door and started to walk my tray to the trash to dump it when

Stacey and Jaye cornered me this time. Stacey whispered, "Hey. Is everything alright? It freaked me out when Amber, *Amber* of all people grabbed you. I thought for sure it was some Goth thing. Then Jaye ran out."

I laughed to cover for the apprehensive feeling I was picking up from several people from the room, most of which were from the immortals. I said, "I'm ok. There's been a family emergency. I have to take off, but I'll call you later Stacey. Talk to you later too, Jaye?"

Stacey grabbed me and hugged me. She is always so dramatic. She nodded yes and sauntered back over to her table of anxiously awaiting cheerleaders, surely anticipating the latest gossip. Jaye stood there for a minute before he said, "You sure it's ok? I can follow if you like." I smiled again and said, "I'll be ok. How will I find you later?"

This time he smiled and said, "Don't worry. I'll find you."

Before I could ask him how he was going to find me, the bell rang and the guys from the football team grabbed him by the arm and pulled him out the doors. I was left to wonder. But, that could wait. I had a more pressing issue to worry about. I headed out.

CHAPTER 5

REVOLUTION....

n my way to the woods, I had very little time to think. One way or the other it was up to me to pull things together. We have to all talk about what's going on. This was just a prelude to what was inevitably approaching. If the werewolves jumped this quick, I could imagine the vampires would make their move too, soon. This was going to call for some working together, putting old issues aside, and excepting that we all had to work together. This included the werewolves, vampires, shape-shifters, witches, and some humans. That latter part I knew was going to be next to impossible. I already had some humans in mind.

I made it to the woods and got out my car to head to where they were waiting. I knew where they were because I could feel them. I looked up and there was a crow, my crow, circling above the tree tops. I could see it was the same crow that's always been there, wherever I was by the color and slight variance in its graceful flying. I just moved on. As bad as I wanted to stand there and watch him do his loops and dives, I had to save this poor humans life.

As I got closer I was met by Amber. She seemed anxious and worried. She said, "Oh! Thank god you got here so quick. They were about to give up and skin him alive. I'll let Natasha fill you in. This way."

We walked a little further into the trees. Here the trees were close and thick. Great place to hide an unsuspecting person and no one can hear or see them from the road. I approached Natasha first. She moved closer to me, smiled with teary eyes, and bowed her head to me. She was so upset she could barely speak without her voice shivering with anger and hurt. She said, "Madame! I didn't believe them at first when they told me you had returned. I miss you so much. I never thought we'd see you again." She grabbed me and hugged me. I wrapped my arms around her and she let go and began sobbing so hard it was hard to hold her up. I knew she was finally letting go of her sorrow for her soon to be sister-in-law's death, Elaine. Hugging her I received more images from my past. It was like looking at a T.V. show. I saw myself sitting on a log and watching Natalie train when she was a young pup. Another flash and she was a little older. We were sitting around a fire talking about her place in life. I was telling her that she would always be the right hand to the next great pack leader and remain there as the right hand to his pup. I could see and feel her excitement and happiness. More flashes and in each she was always walking beside me asking questions and relying on my guidance. I snapped back and hugged her tighter. I said, "Oh, my dear Natasha. We'll find him or them. But, this is not him."

She looked up at me with both doubt and respect. She straightened up and took back on her commander stance. She asked me, "Skye. If I may speak freely. We followed a scent we picked up near my sister's body. It led us to him. He was cowering in his house with the lights off and a bottle of whiskey. He's refused to answer any of our questions. We offered him his freedom if he would just tell us what he seen or a quick and painless death if he confesses. He's said nothing. He just sits there, shaking, like the coward he is!"

I couldn't help but feel a little sorry for the poor guy. I had seen him many times over the years that we had lived here. He was a hunter. Mostly kept to himself. In town the folks say he eats whatever he hunts and never buys any meat from the local market.

I went over to him and sat down on the ground where they had him tied to a tree. I looked in his eyes and saw nothing but fear. He was almost in shock. I knew that if he was to go into shock there would be no chance, anytime soon, of getting any information from him. I looked to Natasha for answers. I asked her, "How long have you guys had him tied here?"

Natasha's brother spoke up, "We took him some time around 3:00 a.m. We made it here from town in maybe five minutes and tied him then. We've been questioning him since." I looked at my watch. First of all, it took a good thirty or forty minutes to get here from town, by car. So that would mean they ran with him in their wolf form. That would send him into shock. Next, it was already 1:30 p.m. This meant that he had been tied here for almost twelve hours; I'm sure with no food or water. And, if he was drunk when they took him, he could be almost dehydrated.

I looked to Amber and said, "Amber. Is there anything you can do to bring him out of shock? And, Natasha, I need some water for him. He's almost dehydrated, and if I'm going to get anything out of him, he's going to need help and water." She nodded yes and motioned for her brother to give some of the water he had in a pouch to him.

I scooted over and let Amber sit down beside me in front of him. She raised his head up and looked in his eyes. She then placed a hand on each side of his head and closed her eyes. After a few seconds there was a yellow glow radiating from her hands. I could feel the power emanating from her. His face now had a healthy pink tint to it, his eyes were no longer bloodshot, and his cheeks were rosy. He took in a deep breath. Amber moved back and reached for the pouch of water. She handed it to him and said, "Here Lester. Drink this."

He took the water and guzzled it down. How Amber knew his name was a question I had to ask her later. For now, I had to question him and save his life. I said, "Lester. You'll be ok. I just need to ask you some questions. I know you want to get out of here and the sooner you cooperate, the sooner you can be back home with your bottle of whisky."

He nodded yes and I went on. "Last night there was a young lady killed in these woods. We know you were there. They smelled you. I know what you seen last night and early this morning has scared the crap out of you. But, if you don't start talking now, there's nothing I can do to save you from the horror that awaits you. So talk."

He looked at me with wide eyes. I could again see the fear in his eyes. But, he started babbling and like water running over a water fall, he spilled his guts. "I was just out a huntin' as I always do. I had just follered a deer in twenxt these here trees when all of a sudden this girl came runnin'! She looked like she went a saw a ghost. I started to see iffin I could help her when this big ol' black thing came a runnin' hind her. Wasn't no man though. It was big and black as oil! It growled summin' like *Love can't survive* or *Love will die.* Then it grabbed that poor little girl, or at least I thunk it was a girl! She was a girl, then she changed afore my eyes. She was half a wolf! So I thunk. I just started runnin'. I was so scared I wet myself!"

We all looked at him in revulsion and shock. After a few minutes of just gawking, I spoke up, "He's telling the truth. He was in the right place at the wrong time. We now have a little more information than we had before. Let him go. First though, we have to do something to erase his memory of everything from last night until now. Any ideas Amber?" Amber motioned for the warlock boy to come over by her.

The boy who had been silent until now bowed his head to me then answered, "Hi Skye. I'm Dave. I suppose you already know I'm a warlock. My powers are not that strong yet, but I can do a basic mind wash." Dave was a tall, thin boy with bright red hair and freckles across the bridge of his nose. Looking from Amber back to Dave I asked, "Then after that can either of you put him to sleep long enough for Natasha and her brother to take him back to his house?" They both nodded yes. I turned to Natasha and said, "Then that's the plan. I'm sorry to run off, but I have to speak to Thomas."

We all agreed and I started to leave when Emily grabbed my arm and asked, "Can my friend and I catch a ride with you? We came with Amber, but I want to talk to you." I shook my head yes and we headed to my car.

Once we were in the car I started talking first. "So, who is your friend? I'm Skye." The young girl shyly answered, "I'm Tania. I'm a freshman. I found Emily after her family was killed in that big house fire last year." She stopped and looked at Emily a little worried and apologized, "I'm sorry Em. I probably said too much." Emily smiled at her and shook her head no. Before I could ask Emily anything she started talking. "When my whole family was killed last year, I didn't want to live. I left the hospital and went back to my burned house and tried to kill myself. Tania found me and took me to her mom. Her mom took me to Thomas, who in turn saved my life by changing me. I would have died if it wasn't for him and Sadie.

It took until recently for me to understand and except that I needed to live. I have a purpose. I still don't know what that purpose is, but I have an important one they told me. So, here I am. I know I haven't been too friendly to you and it's because I thought you were a fraud and out to get Thomas and Sadie, so I jumped to the defensive. Everyone I've talked to that knew you from the past told me to trust you and talk to you. So, when we get a chance, can we talk, please?"

I could feel the relief in Emily once she let it out. I smiled and said, "Sure. Anytime. First we have to work on this problem. I have a feeling it's not going to stop. More then just the pack has been hit. Shinu lost his sister, so I'm assuming the vampires are going to have questions. I'm afraid all immortals are going to lose loved ones before we find out and stop whoever is behind this. I have to talk to Thomas first. Thank you for opening up to me."

We drove on and talked a little more about school and our pasts before we got to the pack village. By the time we made it to Thomas' house, Natasha and her brother were already back and telling Thomas about Lester. I couldn't believe how fast they traveled.

I couldn't help but feel at home now around Thomas and Sadie. I felt warm and fuzzy as old memories slowly surfaced. I hugged Sadie and said, "It's good to see you again. I'm sorry it's under these circumstances. I have to talk to you and Thomas about things from the past. If you can't recall or were too young then, are there any elders still with you that may be able to help me?" Thomas answered me first, "Any way we can help we will. There is one left from when my father was young. We call her grandma. She's blind now, but still gets around and is as feisty as ever. What do you need to ask us?"

I turned to Sadie first and said, "Yesterday when we met again for the first time in years, I had so many flash backs of the past. Some were with me from way back and some were without me from after I was gone until now. In one of the new memories there was a doctor who delivered Nanuk. Who was he?" Sadie and Thomas looked at each other and Thomas answered me, "That was Dr. Whitcraft. He is the only doctor in town who knows about us. He has been all of our doctor for as far back as I can recall."

I went on. "That's Amber's father, right?" They said yes and I continued. "Ok. In another vision I saw you born Thomas. There was a doctor there too. He looked like Dr. Whitcraft, but younger. Could that have been him then also?" Thomas thought for a minute before he answered. "I recall my mom telling me that Dr. Whitcraft delivered me and saved me. Something about me not breathing. I guess he has been around for some time now."

I suddenly felt a little uneasy but shook it off and hid my concern from them. I said, "That could explain the chanting I heard in the vision. I also sensed, not so much as seen, but sensed a dark figure outside the cabin during your birth. And again at the birth of your son. Hmm. Now, back even further, I saw the old pack when it was much smaller then yours. The head wolf had bluish grey fur and ice blue eyes. Like your eyes Thomas. They were running, no chasing another wolf. He was black as oil and appeared to be running for his life. Do you have any idea who that might have been?"

Again Thomas sat thinking for a while. His eyes got wide as some memory must have crossed his mind. He answered, "The head wolf you described had to be my grandfather. And the black wolf they were chasing, I really couldn't tell you. There were stories told from long ago of a wolf that became so evil he turned black as oil. It was a werewolf urban legend of sorts. It went like this,

> *Damien Wick was an angry lad.*
> *Never happy with what he had.*
> *He wanted money, he wanted power.*
> *But in his cave he'd whine and cower.*
> *He tried to take the baker's wife,*
> *Got chased away with a butcher's knife.*
> *He tried to take the banker's cash.*
> *Had to run away in a dash.*
> *When he lost all hope to ever rule,*
> *His bright idea made him the biggest fool.*
> *So he sold his soul to the Fair Queen,*
> *And that was the last of him we seen.*

That was just the poem that went along with the story of the greedy wolf. We grew up thinking of it as a way to teach us, or scare us into not being greedy and power hungry. You don't think it's a true story do you?"

I sat and thought for a moment before I answered. I didn't want to stir up an urban legend to scare everyone, so I said, "No, but it may have something to do with it. The one you call grandma, would she be up for a visit?"

They both stood and headed for the door. I followed. I still couldn't shake the feeling that somewhere buried in my mind was the answer to what was going on. We walked across the camp area and as we reached her door she opened it and stepped out, grabbed me and hugged me and said, "Why Skye Rainwater! The stories are true! Come in, come in! It's so good to see, well touch you again. I remember when you were just a little thing. But, we'll have time for that later. All of you come in and have a seat. What can I do for you?"

Once again I had the feeling I knew her from my past. We all walked in and sat down. Her house was so mixed matched. The furniture did not match in color. The decorations had no theme, and the throw rugs were every color of the rainbow and then some. But, her house was so comfortable.

She was a short, stocky woman. Her grey hair was curly and cut to shoulder length. Her iris' in her eyes were almost white, but they had the warmest smile. Her skin was weathered looking but felt soft as silk. I couldn't help but feel like a little kid who wanted to run and jump in grandma's lap, get a big hug and kiss, and wait for a plate of cookies. I could tell that Thomas and Sadie felt just as comfortable as I did. They were both smiling like little kids too.

I hated to put a damper on that happy feeling, but I had to get more information. I said, "I'm sorry to disturb your peaceful afternoon, but I just have a few questions." She smiled at me as she sat down in an old rocking chair and nodded, "Yes, child. However I can help." I continued on. "In a vision I had yesterday when I came in contact with Sadie, I saw about ten wolves running after one wolf, black as oil. Do you know who that wolf was?"

She hung her head down in dismay. A worried look crossed her face before she began her story. "The urban legend of the wolf pack about Damien Wick is not an urban legend. Oh, some of the extra scary parts in the story were added later to scare children. But the main parts about him being power and money hungry, all true. He tried several things to gain wealth and power.

He was jealous of all who loved, had money, and had power. That jealousy led to his demise. He was eventually chased out of the pack and banished from these lands after he tried to kill the heir to the pack. That baby boy, your father Thomas, was the only boy your grandmother was able to bare. She had all girls until your father.

Oh, the pack was overjoyed. The tradition of your great-great grandfather would continue on. Our pack had always gone on and grew strong because he first started turning over lead of the pack to his heir. This pass down of power has made our pack strong, happy, and very large.

Damien did not like that. He felt he had every right to fight the head for the position of pack leader. They tried to reason with him, explain that our pack didn't work that way. They even told him he should go and find another pack that did find its head by challenge. He wanted our pack and no other. He did all kinds of evil things to discourage us.

We thought we had finally won him over and had convinced him to stop his foolish ranting and raving about. At one point he had settled down. But, peace didn't last for long.

He then began terrorizing the humans there and killing off their livestock and some of their people to try and turn them against us. He figured that if the humans turned on us, he could gain favor with your father by fighting by his side faithfully against the humans. He would try and tell us we couldn't trust the humans, that we should sever ties with the humans before they slaughtered us.

When it didn't work he turned to the fairies. He had heard that the queen fairy would grant anyone's wish if they were willing to do for her. We never seen or heard from him again. Now that last part has been hearsay. He could have easily gone to another pack. I'm sorry dears, but that is all I remember."

We had sat there mesmerized listening to her story. We thanked her and I let her know that I would return to talk to her again. Once we were outside I spoke to Thomas and Sadie. "I'll have to talk to my mother and grandma next. We are going to have to all talk this out soon. I will be back in touch with you. Be well and watch out for everyone in your pack. Tell them to try not to go out alone for any reason. Try to stay in groups. It may be harder for whoever it is to attack like that." We said our goodbyes and I headed to my car.

....

I took my time heading back to the car. I needed to think things out, so I just walked around the woods for a little while. As I was circling back to my car I heard a familiar caw above me. I looked up and there he was, the crow, circling above the trees. As I watched, he descended. It looked as if he was taking a head dive right at me. Before I could move he slowed down right in front of me and hovered there for about 10 seconds before he morphed into a human.

I froze. By the time I could speak he was laughing at me. Besides being in shock I was now infuriated that he had nerves enough to startle me and then laugh. "Damn it! Jaye? It's been you this whole time? It's been you that's followed me, watched me? Then you scare the crap out of me and laugh?! How dare you?!"

I raised my fist to punch him but he stopped my fist before it could connect with his chin. He was strong and quick. He was still laughing at me. He started laughing so hard he had to let me go and doubled over holding his stomach. Watching him crack up I couldn't help it. I started laughing too.

He finally slowed down and was able to say, "You should have seen the look on your face. Were you scared of me?" Now that he thought I was scared of him I was furious again. I started yelling before I could stop myself. "I was not scared of you! I thought the crow was hurt and falling! I didn't want *him* to get hurt!" With that I was too angry to keep talking, or rather, yelling, so I turned and headed on to my car.

Jaye followed, of course. He pulled my arm and turned me around to face him. He had managed to stop laughing and took on a serious look when he said, "I'm sorry Skye. I should have warned you before I came at you like that. Yes it has been me, but, please let me explain."

I calmed down now. I took a deep breath and answered, "Ok. I shouldn't have gotten so mad. I'm sorry too. I really need to go to my mom and grandma and talk to them, but if you want to ride along and explain, that's fine." It had just dawned on me what time it was. Once again I looked at him skeptically and asked, "Hey. You're supposed to be in school still. What are you doing here?"

We had reached the car and were getting in. Jaye stopped and looked down at the ground before he said, "Again, I'm sorry. I followed you. Right after you left the school. I was afraid Amber and her group was up to no good." We got in and I started the car. Before I could protest him following me he continued, "I've seen her and her family late at night some times. I don't know what they are or what they are up to. I just know they're hiding something. So, when she yanked you out of the cafeteria and then I seen them all surrounding you, I thought they were trying to hurt you. So, I followed, but kept my distance. I didn't see or hear everything, trees are pretty thick up there, but I did see some freaky things."

I had to think before I said my next words. I didn't want to jeopardize things before I could get things organized. I also had to know about him first. So, I said, "So. Would you tell me how long you've been following me? And, have you heard anything about the recent murders?" That should work.

He sat there thinking for a while, then began to ramble on. "Well to be perfectly honest, I've followed you for a long time. Years. Actually, centuries. Let me back up. I am not stalking you, and I don't really know what type of immortal you are, if you are one. I first saw you when you were about six. You were lost in the woods. I was worried because you were really hurt and sick, so I led you out. There was something different about you that fascinated me. So, from that time on, I just sort of ended up where you were. Not on purpose. It's been more like I've been drawn to you. Any way, I'm not stalking and I'm not always there. About the murders? I've only heard very little. I think you need to fill me in on what's really going on, and just what are you?"

Starting again from the beginning, I filled Jaye in as much as I knew to the present. That whole conversation took us all the way to my house and we sat in my car finishing the discussion. I tried to end it with an answer to his question, but I was still stumped as to who or what I was. So, I just said, "As far as what or who I am, I am still trying to figure that out. A lot of my memory is returning, but there are still gaps. My mom and grandma said it will all come back to me soon, when the time is right. I'd like to know more about your shape shifting, and why I was never able to sense you."

Jaye was avoiding the subject in a discussion, and a sneaky, suspicious, but cute little smile consumed his expression. After a moment of silence and him staring me in the eyes, I could feel myself blush. Luckily I didn't have to respond when at long last he answered me. "Well, you have to get in there and talk to your mom. There is quite a bit to figure out in a short time. We'll talk again, soon."

And with that, he opened the car door, looked back at me and gave me an endearing smile, stepped out, and with a quiver that traveled down his whole body, he changed into a crow again. It was odd watching his transformation. After the quivering, he sprouted silky black feathers starting from the top of his head and layering down his body. At the same time, he went from his six foot height to no more than about twenty inches, spread his wings and soared to the sky.

As amazing as that was, and as bad as I just wanted to stand there and watch him circling around above me, I knew I had to get inside and talk to my mom and grandma. With a sigh, I headed in the house.

CHAPTER 6

THE INVITATION . . .

Mom was cooking dinner when I got in. The smell of tomatoes, onions, beef, beans, and many other spices wafted out the door as I stepped in. I hadn't even noticed how ravenous I was until that mouth watering aroma wrapped me in a warm and comforting blanket of drooling hunger. I walked through the living room and into the kitchen. Grandma was sitting at the kitchen table looking through some rather old and tattered looking books. Mom looked as stunning as ever dressed in her casual yet dressy suit with her apron on. She didn't even look away from the pot she was stirring and poking at when she said, "Hi Skye. Dinner will be done soon. How were things today?"

I sat down at the table next to grandma and gave her a kiss on her cheek. I said, "Well, I'm stuck trying to figure out what my next step should be. I've now met more of the pack and Jaye, the quarterback from school just revealed his true form to me. He's a shape shifter mom. A crow. You remember me telling you about the crow I've always seen, or was always somewhere near me? It's been him all along. I haven't gotten him to tell me his whole story yet. And I'm stumped on how he's managed to hide himself from me all theses years. I can sense other shape shifters. As a matter of fact, shape shifters stick out to me more then the other immortals. Sometimes I can even hear their thoughts. Always have. But, never him. That's another story though."

I paused long enough to try and look at the books grandma was looking through. The writing in them was some old language. I couldn't quite make it out. I turned my attention back to mom and said, "I also met an elder from the pack that told us a story of Damien Wick."

She looked up from her cooking and grandma closed one of the books and looked at mom. They both appeared a little shocked and worried at the mention of his name. Grandma was the first to speak after a few seconds of silence. "Yes. We've heard of him. We know the story the pack tells their little ones. But, we've had our run in with him ourselves. Lily, you want to tell her yet?"

Now I was really curious and a chill ran down my back, leaving my hair standing on end on the back of my neck. I was afraid to ask, but I did. "Ok. What are you two talking about, or do I want to know?" Mom turned off the pot and came over to the table and sat down by me.

They both looked grave. I was starting to think this was a part of my memory I didn't want to wake up. Mom took my hand in hers and began with, "I am so sorry sweet heart." Worried, I asked, "What are you sorry for? I highly doubt you had anything to do with that creep."

She bowed her head, sighed and continued. "Our tribe had gotten word of Damien and what he was trying to do. When the pack decided it was enough and voted to run him off, they let us know. Some of our strongest tribesmen joined the chase. Your father was among them. He was one of the first to volunteer because he was the strongest in our tribe and knew if it got bad he could be the one . . ." She paused there and turned pale. I could see she was struggling with whatever it was she was about to say next. She went on in kind of a whisper now. "He would have the strength to kill Damien."

Now I was really worried and confused. I sat forward, anxious and asked, "Why was dad so much stronger then the others?"

This time grandma stood and went to the stove. She bent over and pulled something from the oven. The silence was now killing me. But, before I could yell and tell them to go on, grandma spoke up. With a sigh she simply stated, "The cornbreads done. The chili has simmered all day. I don't know about you two, but I'm famished. We will eat and finish this conversation after dinner." When she spoke, we obeyed. No one ever spoke back to her, so mom kissed me on the cheek, rose from her chair, and got our bowls and plates ready. I got our glasses and got the milk out.

. . . .

Dinner was wonderful, as usual. Grandma made her special "Peace" tea and we all sat in the living room. Mom started a fire in the fireplace. It was nice and cozy now and the tea was helping to take the edge off the nervousness that was emanating from all of us. This time I started off the exchange. "Please go on. Why was dad the strongest?"

After taking another sip from her cup, mom sat it on the table, exhaled noisily and continued where we left off. "As I was saying, your father was the strongest . . . he was the strongest because he was a shape shifter. A Kodiak bear. If the chase got out of control or violent we all knew he could handle Damien with ease. Or at least, that was what we had planned on.

None of us knew Damien had somehow got a hold of poison. It was a special poison that only effects shape shifters. It was meant to lock a shape shifter in their human form forever, never allowing them to change back into their animal form. It's harmless to humans or other immortals. Your father had outrun every werewolf and caught up to Damien first.

Damien turned on him and the started to fight. Damien was too strong in his werewolf form so our father changed into his bear form. They said he fought for a good fifteen minutes. When Damien was almost defeated they said he changed back to human form, pulled a bottle from around his neck on a rope, and shoved it into your father's mouth.

They said he stumbled backward, and fell dead. You see. If the poison is given to a shape shifter in a small dose, the can no longer change. If too much is given, they die. I can't say for sure if Damien knew that, but he is still the one that killed him. They said he staggered around, pleased with himself, and then vanished.

When word got back to us, you were standing in the other room listening. We didn't know you were. You took off running, yelling *No! Not my daddy! I'll save him! I will mommy!* You were no more then six. You were so fast we couldn't catch you. We searched for three days and nights. We had started to think you were dead, when suddenly you came home. You were staring at the sky and mumbling something about a crow.

You had been lost for three days. You hadn't eaten or drank anything. You were all cut up, we guessed from the trees and bushes. You were dehydrated, incoherent, running a fever, delirious, your arm was broken. You were almost dead.

We went to Dr. Whitcraft. He did all he could do, but you were still going to die. That's when little Amber came in the room and walked over to you. She looked at you for a few minutes and asked your name. You whispered *Skye. Where's the crow?* She laughed, said your name, and said she would save you. All I remember is seeing a bright pink light cover you and Amber. When the light faded you two were sitting there, hugging each other and laughing and crying. She saved your life. From that point on you were inseparable. So you see; we know about Damien because he took your father from us, and, in a way, almost caused your death."

After that long story, all I could do was sip my tea and look from my mom to my grandma in awe. Once again, more memories began to flash before my eyes like a movie. I could see myself playing with my father in a field. He was a man.

Another flash and I was riding on his back, him in his bear form. I was laughing and giggling. Another flash and we were in the woods again, this time he was on his knees in front of me talking, no, instructing me. He put his palms on the ground and changed into a bear. He said, no, growled to me. I closed my eyes, got on my hands and knees, and slowly changed into a bear myself! I was so excited I began bouncing around, jumping up and down and wrestling with my dad.

Another flash and we were climbing in the trees. He was teaching me to climb. I could feel the sun warm on my fur. I could see the ground and feel myself getting dizzy. Another flash and I was running through the woods, lost. I fell down a cliff into the water. I tried to changed into my bear form, but couldn't in the water. I made it out the water, changed into my bear form and took off running again, with a limp. My arm was broke.

Another flash and I was lying on the ground, human again, crying. I was hurt and so hot. Lost. I heard a crow caw above me. I remember asking the crow if he knew where my home was. He circled around and cawed again. He landed on the ground beside me, twisted his head sideways, looked at me, cawed again and took to the sky. I followed.

Another flash and I was sitting on a bed hugging a little girl. Flash, and the little girl and I were playing together in a field. She was teaching me magic. When we held hands that magic grew stronger. Whatever we were doing, I could hear her saying I was doing a good job, learning magic fast.

When I finally came out of my daze of memories I felt a tear running down my cheek. Grandma was standing in front of me with the teapot in her hand. She must have asked me if I wanted more tea. I nodded yes. Mom was sitting across from me on the table holding my hands and crying too. She asked, "Skye sweetie? More memories returning?"

I nodded to her12. I was afraid that if I tried to speak now I'd just end up bawling like a baby. She left it at that and just hugged me. After holding her for about five minutes, I was finally able to talk. "I can shape shift too. Amber and I became best friends. She taught me some of her witchcraft. I know some spells and magic and Dad and I were close. I miss him so much."

I started crying again. This time both grandma and mom held me while I wailed and let out all the years of built up hurt and loss. I was completely drained and my eyes were puffy and red. Grandma got up first and with a little chuckle she said, "Well now. That was a ride. I'll make my "Energy" tea. You have some questions for us."

In all the events that took place since I came home I had forgotten that I needed to talk to them about what's happened and what I should do next. I spoke to both of them, "Mom, grandma. I really feel like things are going to get worse before this is over." I filled them in on today about Lester and the werewolves thinking it's the humans. I told them that I still hadn't heard anything from the vampires since Natasha's death. But, that I didn't think they'd let this go quietly.

I thought for a moment before I said, "I really think I should somehow call a meeting with all immortals, and it may be a long shot, but I feel I need to include a few select humans. What should I do and how do I go about this?"

Grandma returned from the kitchen with the tea pot and one of the old books she was reading. She poured our cups and sat down next to me. She was smiling and sighing with relief as she flipped through the book and stopped at a page that had a tattered old letter in it.

The envelope was brown from old age and the paper was practically falling apart. She turned to me and handed the letter to me. It had an ancient wax seal on it. She handed it to me and said, "Here you go dear. We have been waiting years to give this to you. When we had to take your memories to save your life and run, Shaman Rose gave this to us. She said someday, there will come a time when we need to give this to you. It will lead you to the answers you seek when there is a time of great despair. I think this constitutes as great despair."

I gently cracked the seal on the letter and carefully pulled out the paper from inside. It also was very fragile. I looked at the letters and at first they looked foreign to me. It too was in an old language like the pages of the books grandma was reading. I started to ask her to read it to me, when I took a second look. This time the letters were as plain as English.

The letter said,

> *Skye. My dear child. You have been given great gifts as well as great burdens. The day has come for you to finally know the whole truth. By you reading this now, I know a time of great despair has come upon us and only you can save us all from a tragic end. You are cordially invited to consult with me.*
>
> *Sincerely,*
> *Shaman Rose, August 5, 1900*
> *Yakutat, Alaska*

I looked up at them in shock. I said, "It's an invitation." That was all I could get out. I was shocked at the date. It took me a few minutes to read over the invitation again, and then I finally asked, "So who is Shaman Rose? How does she know me?"

My mom put down her tea cup and her face lit up so bright with admiration when she said, "She is a very ancient and very wise Shaman. She is such a beautiful person with a beautiful spirit. If it wasn't for her I would have lost you at birth. She taught me and your grandmother all we know. She taught you. She is very special. We have all been waiting for this day!"

She and grandma seemed giddy with excitement after I read the letter. I wasn't sure what all this meant, but I had a feeling I'd be finding out soon. Tomorrow was Friday, so they instructed me to wait until Saturday to go see Shaman Rose. The trip would take three hours driving. All I could think of was that I needed to remember how to change back into a bear like my father had taught me. It would probably make the trip shorter. Plus I was anxious to rekindle any lost memories. I had tomorrow after school. We cleaned up and turned in.

. . . .

Across town Lester was sitting at his kitchen table. He had a bottle of whiskey, his shot gun, and a cross. He was shaking all over, as if he had just seen a ghost. He reached down and picked up his glass of whiskey and tipped it up to his lips. His hand was quivering so much little droplets of the alcohol spotted the front of his grey t-shirt.

He was facing the window in his kitchen that was right above the kitchen sink. His eyes were wild with fear and glued to the window. He stood up and poured himself another full glass.

He picked up his shot gun and the cross and went from the kitchen into his living room. He had already shoved his couch in front of the door and was just checking to make sure it was still there. He nudged it to reassure himself that it was stable then turned and headed back to the kitchen.

On his way through he paused long enough at the table to tip his glass back and drain it. This time he dribbled a line of the liquid down the front of his shirt. Brushing it off he cursed the whiskey and then refilled his glass, again, and headed down the back steps to check that door also. He had it blocked with his tool chest.

Satisfied that he was safe and sound, he sighed and headed back up the steps. Once again he turned up his glass. He was still shaking and this time lost half his glass down his shirt. "Damn it! Chill it Lester. You're ok. I dare you to try and get in now! Come on in if you can you bastard!"

He took a deep breath, laid down the cross and this time he tipped the whole bottle of whiskey up to his mouth. He still cradled the gun in his arm.

After draining the bottle he sat it on the table and headed to the refrigerator to get more whiskey. His legs trembled and he was so inebriated his legs almost gave out under him. He took out the bottle, cracked open the lid and turned that bottle up to his mouth.

Before he could swallow the first mouthful a hand came up over his head and grabbed the bottle from his hand. His body lurched forward. He caught himself before he could fall face first into the refrigerator. He could feel his whole back turn cold and the hair on the back of his neck stood on end. His stomach turned and dropped as if he was on a downward descent on a Farris wheel.

He was afraid to turn around and face whoever the intruder was. But, he thought to himself, *Lester. Yer a man. You bess be seein' who just came in and face 'em like a man. Asides, you got yur gun.*

He slowly turned around. Instantly he began to sweat. His shirt was now drenched with not only whiskey, but beads of perspiration. As he turned he saw that he was not in his kitchen alone anymore. There was not only one intruder, but there were four. They were not ordinary people.

There were three men and one woman. They were pale; their hair was slick jet black. They all wore black t-shirts, black jeans, and black biker's boots. Their angry eyes glowed a fluorescent red. Their black lips curled back from their teeth revealing sharp fangs.

The one that grabbed Lester's bottle from his hand was holding it suspended over Lester's head. He was the first to speak. Angrily he yelled, "So. This is how the guilty wash away their remorse! Whiskey is known to deaden the senses, but in your case, nothing will deaden the pain and fear you are about to experience! But, we can be somewhat humane about things. We'll give you; oh I don't know, two minutes to explain to us why you associate with werewolves and who mutilated our sister's body! Begin!"

Now Lester was shaking so badly he could barely hold on to the shot gun as he raised it up and aimed it directly at the man thing that was just speaking. He pulled the trigger and being that he was very drunk, he almost lost his footing.

After the smoke cleared he expected the man thing to have a big hole in his chest and be lying on the floor in a puddle of blood. Instead, he was still standing there. The only hole he could make out was a hole in his black t-shirt, square in the middle of his chest.

He leaned over and began heaving and lurching as his stomach churned. He held his mouth trying to keep in the remnants of today's meals along with the gallon of whiskey he just ingested.

He was still holding on to the gun when he rose up. He took aim again. But, before he could pull the trigger, the female thing stepped forward, grabbed the barrel of the gun, twisted her wrist, and completely bent the barrel of the gun down into a contorted 'u' shape. This time she spoke up, infuriated. "Come on! My brother was just civil enough to ask for an explanation and you reward his kindness with a shot to the chest? Not to mention you ruined his good t-shirt! We smell the werewolves on you! So don't deny it. Start talking before I shove this gun up your butt!"

Lester could not figure out what they were talking about. All he could think was that he never knew werewolves existed. He tried to think about all the events of the last few days and couldn't remember anything significant. Last he could recall was hunting in the woods a few nights ago, and then ending up back at home.

He opened his mouth to speak, but could only get out, "I, I, I. There ain't no surch thin as a werewolf. G-git out my house!" They all looked at each other and laughed a hideous, otherworldly laugh. Lester froze and turned pale himself. His whole body shook as if an earth quake had erupted from inside his body. All he could think was *Run!*

He ran toward the living room. One of the other man things, which he now figured out were vampires, suddenly appeared before him out of thin air. He was the quiet one. He had an evil, sadistic smile on his face as he said, "Hhm." The other vampire that questioned him first called out from behind him, "So you know nothing! Yet you drink and flee as if you were guilty! I can reassure you that our sister didn't cower and flee when your friends tortured her to death!"

With that, the quiet one grabbed Lester by his neck and dangled him above the floor. He struggled to get his feet to grip the floor so he could try and run, but the vampire was too strong. The vampire carried him back into the kitchen effortlessly, as if he were a mere puppy.

He stood Lester in the middle of them all. Lester tried to push his way through them, but it was like hitting a brick wall when he slammed against each one of them. The first vampire that spoke spoke again. He was irate and shaking all over from anger when he snarled, "Our sister suffered great pain before her heart was ripped from her chest! Since you refuse to speak up and tell us what we want to know, you will also suffer great pain!"

He raised his hand up to his face and rubbed his chin as if in deep thought before he went on. "You'd be surprised at how much pain a human can endure before they die." The female vampire stepped forward and punched Lester in his left side sending him flying backward into the refrigerator. When he hit he could hear his ribs crack with a sickening snap.

The next male vampire reached down and picked him up under his arms, held him up at least three feet off the floor and then slammed him down, feet first. Lester could feel every bone in his feet and ankles pop. His knees buckled as a hot flash of pain and agony engulfed him and he lost his battle with trying to keep down the contents of his stomach.

After heaving and gagging for a few second he raised his head up a little. The vampire that had picked him up by his neck when he took off running for the living room now took his turn. He grabbed Lester again by the neck and fluently lifted him up and again suspended him in mid air. He smashed down again on the floor, causing Lester to land on the side where his ribs had already been cracked from the female vampire. He lay there, on the brink of oblivion and spotted the bottle of whiskey lying under the table. Even knowing that he was going to die, the thought that went through his mind right then was, *Man! I'd love a swig of that right 'bout now.*

CHAPTER 7

LOST MEMORIES FOUND . . .

h how I dreaded going to school this morning. I just wanted to stay home and rest and practice changing. But, I knew better. I slowly got up and got ready. After eating breakfast with mom and grandma, I drug myself to my car and headed to school. I made it all right, with the right clothes on this time. When I pulled up, Amber and Emily were waiting for me near the parking lot.

I got out and waved to them. I was actually anxious to talk to Amber and I was surprised to see Emily. I figured they would have their burial ceremony today. They both walked over to meet me. Emily spoke to me first. "Hey Skye. Did you get to talk to your mom last night to figure out what to do next?" She sounded kind of worried. When I looked at her closer I could see that she looked a little disheveled. Her hair was a mess and she had dark circles under her eyes. It worried me some. I said, "Yes. I have to first go meet a lady out of town. Then I should have the next move. Are you ok? You look a little worn."

She gave me a faint and tired smile before she answered, "Yeah. Just tired. I ran patrol last night. Don't worry. I wasn't alone. I thought I saw something so, me with the brave act, decided to follow it. I should have caught the scent before I got that far, but I was too excited. It took me all the way over the next two counties."

I was curious to know now what she had been chasing. I asked, "What was it?" She threw her arms up in the air, leaned her head back, and rolled her eyes. Then she lowered her head and was shaking it like she was embarrassed to say, but she finally let it out, kind of loud, "A damn moose!"

I almost couldn't contain my laugh, but I managed to just chuckle a little before I got out, "I am so sorry. Needless to say, it must have taken you most of the night to get back."

She nodded yes. We looked up in time to see other kids staring at her. I guess she yelled that kind of loud. Amber had been standing there kind of quiet until she tried to open her mouth to say something and burst out laughing. She leaned over, holding her stomach and bellowed out a deep hearty laugh. I had never seen her laugh before. This was like that smiling thing in my car the other day. I hadn't seen her smile much before then. Now Amber was laughing?

Emily pushed Amber and she almost fell over, off balance from laughing so hard. Emily was a little upset now and gave Amber an evil look when she said, "That's ok. Laugh all you want." I went ahead and changed the subject to spare her more embarrassment. I said, "Amber. We have got to talk today some time. I had both the saddest and the coolest memory recall last night." Amber said ok and we headed on up to the school.

As we got closer I spotted Stacey. She waved and came running over to me. Amber and Emily walked on. Stacey bounded up to me and hugged me then stepped to my side and held my arm in hers as we walked toward the doors. She asked, "How are things? I was just a little worried. You never called." I was about to answer her when

Jaye popped out of nowhere on my other side. He smiled at both of us and in his deepest most mature voice he said, "Ladies."

Of course, Stacey blushed and said hi. I looked at him and he winked at me and asked, "See ya after school?" I was a little surprised he asked me in front of Stacey, but I said sure and he ran off ahead of us. When I looked over at Stacey her mouth was hanging open. I tried to give her my, I'm-shocked look, but it didn't work. She gave a sneaky type smile and said, "So. Is this why Jaye has always refused my advances as well as every other girl in school? Because he's after you?"

She was way too amused and eager for gossip. I continued acting oblivious and said, "You know what? I'm as lost as you. He just started saying more to me then just hi yesterday. When I know more you'll be the first I tell. Ok?"

She laughed at me and said, "Oh my poor innocent Skye. Don't you know that when guys are interested they don't say much at first? Any way. Let me know. Later. I've got to get to class." She kissed me on the cheek and sauntered off back to her group.

First class was history. I wondered if Shinu would be back in class today. Just as I was thinking that, a voice popped in my head. *Boo. Don't you know if you speak of the devil, he'll pop up?* I turned to look behind me. I swear I had just passed his locker and he wasn't there. But, sure enough, there he towered over his roadies. He winked at me, smiled and nodded.

I decided I'd just try a whole conversation in my mind this time with him. I knew it had been years or centuries since I had tried. *You know it's not good to sneak up in people's minds like that. Especially if they are slowly getting back their memory and found out they hold great power.*

Even though we were communicating in our heads, I could still hear him behind me laughing. *Oh! So now you're even brave enough to* threaten *a vampire?*

This was getting interesting. I answered jokingly, *That's not a threat dear. Just a warning. You don't know who you're messing with.*

Smiling, I turned around to see the reaction on his face and smacked dead into his chest. Now I was startled. "What the . . . ? How do you do that? I have got to learn how to do that."

He smirked and held the door to our history class room open for me. He made sure his back was against the door and I entered first. He said, "You first, of course. When you tell me all about you, then maybe I can teach you."

Throughout class we talked back and forth in our minds. I filled him in on what I found out about myself and that I still had more to remember. He told me he had always heard about a person like me, but that it had always been told as a myth. That there had not been anyone like that for centuries and that most had forgotten the tale and wrote it off as a fairy tale.

By the end of class he finally trusted me, as far as who I was. But, on the way out the door I could tell he was still leery about having me behind him. He stepped aside and followed me out the door. I laughed. He said we'd talk more, later, and headed off down the hall.

....

The day went on as usual, except for the occasional student who had never really paid much attention to me before, would now nod as they walked pass, as if they knew who or what I was. It was much like the way Sadie and Thomas first acted when they saw me, again. I guess somewhere buried in my memory it is possible that I may know some of them or at least know of them.

I went on to the cafeteria. This time, I didn't expect anyone to pull me out, but anything's possible. I walked in and as usual, Stacey smiled and waved from her group across the room. I headed for the line and got my tray of food. As I was leaving the line a young freshmen boy walked up to me, shook my hand and nodded slightly. He leaned in close to me; I had to lean down some because he was quite a bit shorter than me; and whispered, "Madame, I was so glad to hear of your return and the return of your memory. You probably don't remember me yet, it's Wesley, but if there is anything I can do or get for you, please don't be afraid to ask. I am at your service. Again."

He seemed quite peppy and happy. I could sense he was a shape shifter and could tell from his almost stark white hair and little eyes, and the way he scampered around the cafeteria that he must be one of the white weasel family.

I went on to a table near the doors where no one was sitting. I needed a moment of thought alone. Suddenly, out of nowhere again, my mind was invaded. *You thought you had a moment to think. What did weasel boy want? That little rat is always taking someone's pencils or pens or other things and running off with it. Better check your hands. If you had on any jewelry, it's probably gone.*

As I looked up, once again, he just popped up and sat down at the table with me. All I could do was grin and say, "You are really getting a kick out of invading my thoughts aren't you?" He snickered at me and leaned on his elbows and stared me in the eyes and said, "Yes. Yes I am. It's so cool how easy it is to talk to you. And it doesn't matter where I am, I can just tune into you, like a radio dial, and Bam! *You are now listening to W-SKYE. Broadcasting from the other side of the school.*"

I had to laugh at that one. Just as I was about to reply, Jaye gracefully approached the table too. He smiled and said, "Hey Skye. I just wanted to make sure Mu Shu Gai Pan wasn't giving you a hard time." Shinu raised his hand up into the air as if to dismiss what Jaye had just said. With a grin he replied, "I was just saying hi and leaving. Skye. We will talk again. I'll let sparrow boy talk to you now." He reached over and took my hand and kissed the back of it.

I could not believe that I could feel myself blush. I looked up at Jaye. If at that moment he had adorned his feathers, I could picture them rustling and his wings frantically flapping. He stood eye to eye with Shinu, crossed his arms, and nodded a catch-you-later at him. Shinu drifted away.

Jaye pulled out the chair and sat down in front of me. He looked at me for a while with his head tilted to the side. Then he took a deep breath and said, "Sorry about that. I just wanted to make sure you were ok. Never seen Shinu talking to you before." I shook my head yes and gave him a reassuring smile. I said, "Yes. I am fine. How do you and Shinu know each other?"

He sat back in his chair and sat his hands on the table. He answered, "We've known each other for years. We aren't enemies. We've kind of developed this kind of competition thing, for fun. We race in the air a lot. Of course he's a bat and can fly into small spaces, leaving me behind a lot. We see who can eat the most bugs. We see who can hit a tree flying at full speed and are able to stand up immediately after impact. Kid stuff like that. He's cool, to a point."

I really had to laugh at that one. After I caught my breath I had to ask him, "Are you watching me or following me?" He leaned forward again and took my hands in his. He looked me in the eyes and with a very serious expression he said, "Skye. I swear I am not following you on purpose. Maybe we'll find out soon what the deal is." We both could only stare at each other for a while. Before either of us could speak the bell rang and startled us both.

We jumped up and I flipped my tray off the table. Before it could hit the floor Shinu was there again and snatched it out of the air and handed it back to me. Jaye turned toward Shinu and patted him on the back and said, "Good catch. I was about to catch it Egg Fu Yung. I'll see you later this evening Skye." Jaye slowly walked toward the door keeping an eye on Shinu.

Shinu snickered and patted Jaye back hard on the back. He said, "Thanks pigeon boy. If you need me Skye, just think about me and I'll hear you." He turned and drifted out leaving me standing watching as they both walked off pushing each other back and forth down the hall.

After school Amber met me at my car. Emily and Tasha were with her. I smiled and waved to all of them. I asked, "Hey. You guys need a ride?" Emily answered, "Tasha and I are just going to run home. I need the fresh air to wake me up. Amber we'll see you later for dinner right?" Amber smiled at them, gave them a hug and answered, "Without a doubt. I'm looking forward to it. Skye, I would love a ride. Besides, you have some exciting news to tell me, right?"

After a moment of recall I said excitedly, "Oh! Yes I do." I turned back to Emily and Tasha and said, "I'll talk to you too sometime this weekend. I have a road trip to take to find some answers." This time Tasha spoke up first. "Have a safe trip. Let us know if you need us for anything. You know, like . . . moose tracking . . ." Emily punched Tasha, lightly, glowered at her and took off running toward the woods. She said to Tasha, "Let's see if you can catch this moose tracker."

With that, they were gone. Amber and I got in the car. As I pulled out, I had to blurt out my news. I was too excited. "Guess what? My dad was a shape shifter. A Kodiak bear. And I can change into one too! I haven't tried yet, but I'm going to practice before I have to go out of town. And the best part of my past I remembered is . . ." I had to pause there. Amber was on the edge of her seat waiting to hear more. I could see her eyes gleaming with anticipation. After a few seconds she yelled at me, "Come on Skye! What?!"

All the emotions of my memories came flooding back to me all at once, while I was looking at my long lost best friend. It had been years, centuries, and the missing time ached in my chest. Amber sat there in awe. I could tell she didn't know whether to cry with me, or comfort me, or if the news was good or tragic. I had to pull over to the side of the road.

After gaining back a little control I finished what I was saying, "Amber. You saved my life when we were little girls. You and I became inseparable. You taught me some of your magic. We played together, got in trouble together. I've missed you so much and didn't even realize it until my memory came back to me. Oh, Amber! That's why we seemed so attached and didn't know why the other day."

Amber had started crying herself, but she held her head down and was twiddling with the strap on her back pack. I was concerned so I asked, "Amber? What's wrong? Aren't you happy we're back together again?" She looked up at me with confusion, longing, and anger all at once. Then she snapped at me, "Great news Skye! I've looked for you all these years. I had given up! And now you expect me to just open my heart and except that you really are *my* Skye? I've seen some pretty good tricks over the years. Including a stupid fairy that had me completely convinced that she was you. I almost gave up my life for that fraud! But, she didn't have the answer to the one secret you and I shared. And that's how I caught her! So, now, you tell me, Skye Rainwater! What is the one secret we kept between us and swore never to tell anyone else as long as we lived?"

I looked at Amber, who was now very furious and skeptical. It didn't come to me right away. I had to think. My memory was slowly returning, but not all of it. Amber looked back at me, now angrier, and said, "I knew it! That's why I didn't let myself get too attached this time. You fake! You jerk! You are so full of . . ."

I cut her off because it finally came back to me. So much so, I started laughing and couldn't stop. I was finally able to tell her the story. I began, "We were in the woods. Way in the woods. I was showing you that I could climb all the way to the top of one of the tallest trees. Half way up I chickened out. I couldn't get down. You tried to help me with one of the spells you weren't suppose to be able to do yet, or allowed to try.

It was a levitation spell. You were too young still and your parents had warned us both that if it was done wrong, it could blow up whatever you were trying to levitate. We panicked because I wasn't suppose to be climbing those trees yet, nor were we suppose to be that deep in the woods.

So we both decided that it would be better to try the spell and get out of there than to call my parents and get in trouble for being there. So, I closed my eyes, waiting to explode, and you tried the spell. I didn't explode, but it burned the fur off my butt. I fell out of the tree and landed beside you. My butt was on fire and I scooted around in the grass trying to put it out as you ran around me crying and apologizing.

I wasn't mad. I was dying laughing. I changed back to human form and we headed back. You snuck some salves from your house and we tried to heal my butt before our parents found out. I still have a scar on my butt."

Now she sat there staring at me with mixed emotions. I could tell she couldn't believe I knew our secret, but she wanted to. So, I turned sideways in my seat and pulled down my pants. I knew the scar was still there, as bright as day. I just never could remember where I got it, but knew I couldn't tell anyone.

When I pulled my pants back up and sat back down straight, I looked over at her. Her mouth hung open and tears were streaming down her face. All she could get out was, "Skye? My Skye? My sister? It's really you!" She grabbed me and hugged me so tight I thought I'd choke before she let me go.

The rest of the ride to her house was filled with laughter and tears, happiness and sadness. We talked about all the things we remembered together growing up, and then she filled me in on what happened after I left. I also told her how things were on my end.

Before we got to my house, Amber called her mom and told her the good news. She sounded just as excited as Amber and I. I could hear her scream from Amber's cell phone when she had to pull it back from her ear.

Once we finally made it to the house, we jumped out, ran inside, said hi to my mom and grandma, told them that Amber was now sure of who I was, and then we ran out the back door to the woods. I was too anxious to try changing. Out of habit I looked up in the sky, half expecting Jaye to be there, but then I remembered he had practice after school today. That's why Stacey and her crew weren't outside after school.

We headed to my favorite spot and sat down to catch our breaths first. Amber sat in front of me and asked, "Do you remember anything our dad had taught you about changing?" I thought for a little bit then answered, "Not a thing. I don't know if I should think *change* or think *bear*. Maybe I should think of a bear, close my eyes and think of a bear."

So, I closed my eyes and thought of a bear. I tried concentrating real hard. That only resulted in a head rush. It also brought images of Jaye to my mind, which didn't help me at all. Why was I thinking of him now? I guess it was because he always seemed to be there, like a guardian. I pictured him soaring above me. It brought to mind freedom. Being able to soar like that would be exhilarating.

That must have ignited something because suddenly my legs changed into bear's legs. Then just as quickly, they morphed back. Amber's eyes got big and she held her breath. She asked, "What was that? You almost did it. What were you thinking about?"

I was a little embarrassed to tell her, but she has been my best friend for centuries. I replied, "Ok. Don't laugh, but I was thinking about Jaye. I pictured him flying free in the air, circling above me and . . ." Confused she asked, "Jaye? Jaye, our quarter back? Him flying? Is there something you'd like to explain to me?"

I had completely forgotten that I knew about Jaye now, but that no one else probably did. I said, "Ok. Jaye finally revealed to me that he was a shape shifter. A crow. And not just any crow. He has been the crow that has followed me or at least turned up where I was, for centuries. It turns out that he was the one who found me when I was lost and hurt after I ran away to find my dad, and led me back to the village."

She just sat there looking at me with that trade mark skeptical look. She said, "Sounds like bird brain is a stalker. Sounds fishy. I'll have to have a talk with him. As a matter of fact, I do recall a crow was always around you when we were growing up. At that time I didn't think anything of it."

I had to laugh at her being protective. I smiled and said, "Ok. But for now, I have to figure out what I need to think of to change." This time I tried to think of all things that change; a worm into a butterfly, a tadpole into a frog, a funnel cloud into a tornado, a werewolf.

Then I thought, ah ha! A vampire into a bat, or whatever they chose to change into. Big mistake. The first person that came to mind was Shinu, and there he was in my head again. I had forgotten he told me to just think of him when I needed him.

There was no way, any way I could possibly think of, he was way across town and picked up my thoughts. Of course he answered. *So. We're only out of school an hour and you're already thinking about me. And yes, I am across town. I'm still at school. I had some research to do and stayed over. How can I help you My Lady?*

I groaned and shook my head. Amber looked at me curiously. I said, "It's Shinu." Surprised, she asked, "Shinu? Where?" She started looking around. I smiled. I had to explain this one too. "Well, I'm sure you know Shinu's a vampire."

She replied, "Yes. And . . . ?" I went on trying to reassure her it was alright. Smiling I said, "Well, we discovered that once I let my guard down that I was a seer, we could talk to each other, quite clearly, with our minds. I know vampires have the ability to read peoples minds or influence them through their minds, but not mine. This is different. We can talk like we are face to face and, at will, read each others thoughts. I was trying to think of things that change and I happen to think of vampires changing into bats, or whatever. He told me today that if I needed him to just think of him. Well, I didn't intentionally think of him, specifically. So, he popped in my head."

This time Amber just laughed. Shinu replied back, *Popping in your head is a rather intrusive way to describe it, don't you think? I prefer to think of it as tuning in to you. Much nicer put that way. And why is Amber laughing? Yes. You think it, I see it.*

Before I could answer him Amber said, "First you're stalked by a crow and now you're being invaded by a bat. You're developing quite a following."

Once again, before I could respond, Shinu cut in, *So you're thinking of pelican boy first, then me? I'm jealous.*

This was exhausting. I had to answer him back or he'd never leave me alone. *Ha ha. Shinu, my dear, you will always be first, in my head. Any way. Long story short, I was trying to change into my bear form. Yes, I just found out last night that my father was a shape shifter, a Kodiak bear. He taught me when I was young how to change, but it's been centuries. So, I was trying to think of things that change.*

He was really getting a kick out of this. I could hear him cracking up laughing in my mind. *So our dear sweet Skye is a teddy bear. How cute and cuddly. I knew there was more to you. Try this. Picture yourself running free through the woods, as a bear. You have to see yourself as the bear. Let me know how that goes. Once you change I may not be able to tune into you anymore.*

I told Amber, "Well he gave a trick to try. So, here goes. Wish me luck." I closed my eyes and thought of myself running free through the woods we used to play in. I could feel the wind blowing past me. I could feel the elation of running on all fours, free. I saw myself as a bear. The bear my father used to be. I kept thinking I'm a bear, I'm a bear.

Slowly I could feel myself changing. My legs became heavier and warmth spread up from my toes to my waist. My whole body began to quiver and I could feel myself getting thicker. My arms grew heavy and I dropped to all fours. My head grew heavier and before I could control it, I let out a growl. I had changed.

Amber stood up, shocked, and placed a trembling hand on my shoulder. I came up to her shoulder and I was on all fours. This was fantastic! I felt so free. I still had my own mind and could still think like a human. I was so sure that when I changed I would think more like an animal, but my thoughts were my own.

I turned to face Amber. I was so excited I just started chattering away at her. I was telling her how I felt, that I was ok. That this was so cool. But, she just looked at me confused and smiled and said,

"Oh Skye. I'm so happy for you, but, I don't speak bear, yet." Then she started laughing.

I hadn't realized that I was growling at her. I started laughing, or rather growling, and rolled over on the ground. I took it that she knew I was laughing because she joined me on the ground rolling around with me, and laughing.

As I was getting up and trying out my new-old form, once again there was a little voice inside my head. *So, either you haven't figured out yet how to change, or there's something strange going on here. Have you managed to change yet?*

That had me puzzled too. I answered back though, thinking I was hearing things. *Um, didn't you say that once I changed you wouldn't be able to hear my thoughts? And yes, I am big, fluffy, and quite intimidating.*

There was at least five minutes of silence before he responded again. *Well I'll be. You have changed. Yes quite intimidating, but I don't understand how I can still read you loud and clear. Fascinating. I have never before heard of such an anomaly.*

This time I not only heard him in my head, but I could smell him too. I knew bear olfactory senses were acute, but there was no way I could smell him all the way here from the school. I started sniffing around. Amber followed as I drifted off. She asked, "So, what is it Skye? Honey, a picnic basket, a bucket of fish?" I wish she could understand what I was saying right now. All I could do is give her my best dirty bear look and think to myself, *Ha ha. Good bear jokes.*

Suddenly Shinu stepped out from behind a tree I was heading for. He had a big grin on his face as he replied, "I thought it was very funny. Hello Amber. It seems your furry friend didn't take so well to the bear jokes. Sorry for intruding, but I had to see for myself. I still can't believe you are in your bear form and I can still hear you. I'll have to ask my parents about this one."

Amber looked at me and then at Shinu, every bit as confused as we were. She asked him, "So you can hear her still? That is unusual. Skye, do you ever remember being able to talk to anyone before when you changed?" They both looked at me. I thought for a few seconds and answered, *Not that I can think of. No one else besides my dad and other animals.* Shinu interpreted for me. He told her, "She said no one. Just her dad and other animals."

Amber went on, "When I get home I can research it. I'm curious now. There has to be some sort of a connection between you too. First the odd mind link, then, being able to maintain that link while in animal form. I'm sure my mom or dad would know. So, can you change back?"

I looked to Shinu and before I could think it he gave me the answer, *Now, just think the opposite. See yourself as human again.* I did as he instructed and sure enough, I felt that familiar quiver again and could feel myself getting lighter from my head to my feet. I changed back. I stood up straight and had to drop to the ground immediately. I was overcome by a wave of dizziness and nausea. I managed not to hurl.

Amber and Shinu both stepped to either side and helped me stand back up. They both asked in unison, "Are you alright?" I shook my head a little and when I was finally able to clear my head I said, "Yeah. Just got dizzy all of a sudden. Guess it's been awhile. I'm ok now."

Amber continued to hold on to my arm as we walked back toward my house. I said, "We could ask my grandma. She might have an idea." Shinu hesitated and asked, "Will they be alright with me? I mean, I don't want your parents freaking out about a vampire hovering over their daughter who is as pale as a ghost and dizzy. Looks fishy. No pun intended."

This time I had to laugh and said, "They won't freak. They know more about me then I do and they've felt right at home around any immortal. With all the concoctions my grandma keeps in her fridge, I wouldn't be surprised if she has a wine bottle full of blood, just in case company comes over."

We laughed together and headed in the house. Shinu still hesitated on the porch. I called out, "Mom, grandma? I have a guest to introduce you to. Come on in Shinu. No need to be shy. They don't bite, hard." I laughed. He didn't. They popped their heads out the kitchen, smiled and entered the living room. Shinu slowly came closer to the door. He still looked hesitant as he said, "You should know Skye, that I cannot cross the threshold until I am invited in by the head of the house." My grandma spoke up quickly and excitedly. "Oh my dear boy! Do come in. Have a seat. All of you."

I could tell Shinu was more at ease now. I had forgotten that he would need inviting in. We all sat down on the couch. My mom sat in the chair and grandma flitted around straightening up. She always did when we had company even if it was spotless. When she finally settled down some she turned to us to ask, "Would any of you like a drink? I just brewed a pot of my rejuvenating tea. And for you Shinu, I have a special drink if you'd like?"

Both Amber and Shinu looked at me. I giggled and said, "I told you so." I turned to face grandma and said, "I'd love some. I really need it now. I did it! I changed, with help from Shinu." Amber smiled and finally spoke up, "Yes ma'am, please. I'd love some tea too." Shinu surprisingly answered, "I am a little thirsty and very curious as to what you would have for me to drink."

Grandma seemed excited. A little too excited. I looked at my mom who was shaking her head and smiling. She asked me, "So. You were able to change?" Now I was the one excited. I sat forward and said, "Yes! It was so cool! But, I don't know how long it would have taken me to figure it out if it hadn't been for Shinu. Speaking of Shinu . . ."

Just then grandma came back in the room toting a tray full of drinks. One drink stood out from the rest. There were four coffee mugs and one wine glass with a very dark red liquid in it. Grandma smiled and said, "Drinks are served." She sat the tray on the table. We all grabbed our mugs and Shinu his glass. He closed his eyes and sniffed it like a wine taster would do before he said, "Magnificent bouquet. Where did you get this?" With that, he turned the glass up to his lips and downed it.

Grandma chuckled and said, "Well. Back when I was still a young lady, I had a very dear friend who happened to be a vampire. He helped me out of a lot of jams and vice versa. He gave me that bottle and told me one day it would come in handy. I guess he was right."

Shinu leaned his head back on the couch, stretched, and got the goofiest look on his face I had ever seen him have. He smiled a really big grin and slurred, "T-that wus ex, ex, excellent. Thans you Madame."

We all chuckled. I broke the hysterics up to finish what I was trying to say before we got our drinks. I continued, "As I was saying, Shinu helped me. But that's not the strange part. For some reason, we have been able to speak to each other clearly with our minds ever since I let my guard down. Not just that, but we can read each others thoughts, and he told me earlier today that if I needed him for anything to just think of him."

I looked back over at him. He was coming around a little and shaking his head to clear it. He leaned up and said, "Wow! Good stuff. Thank you Madame." That started us all to giggling again. He looked shocked and asked, "What? I was just being polite."

We'd have to tell him later how it affected him. I went on, "So, I was trying to think of things that change to spark me to change and thought of a vampire into a bat. That brought Shinu to mind and he answered. He was still at school. We were here. Our thoughts connected that far apart. Then he helped me to change and told me that once I changed he may not be able to connect to my mind. He said generally, once in animal form you have an animal's mind and you can't connect."

Shinu was finally able to contribute to the conversation, coherently. He added, "At least, that's what we've all been told for centuries and nothing has ever proven that theory wrong, until today. Even after Skye had changed to her bear form, I could still read her mind loud and clear." Amber had been sitting there quiet, thinking, but now she asked, "Could there be some reason behind this sudden connection?"

Mom spoke up first, "It is possible. I really can't say. When you make your trip tomorrow Skye you can ask Shaman Rose. I'm sure she'll have some idea." Shinu and Amber looked at me with questioning stares. I hadn't had time to tell any of them yet, so I explained, "Grandma gave me an invitation that was given to her to give to me years and years ago. I have to go meet her tomorrow."

After talking for a while longer and downing more tea, Amber and Shinu excused themselves to head home. I offered Amber a ride, since Shinu could easily fly home, but she said she wanted to walk. She had some spells she wanted to work on, on the way.

Shinu stopped at the door on the way out and turned to mom and grandma and bowed his head. He said, "It has been a pleasure meeting you. Thanks for the hospitality and the fine *wine*. Sayoonara, Skye. Remember. Just think of me when you need me."

Even though I was the one walking him out the door, he gestured for me to go first out the door. I smiled. He left and I stood there for several minutes just thinking and breathing in the fresh air. From a distance I could hear the familiar caw that I now know is Jaye.

He sailed through the sky floating elegantly over the tree tops. This time he didn't dive down and scare me like the last time. He drifted down and changed to his human form before he hit the ground.

I was once again amazed at how graceful his poise was for a football player. I smiled and asked, "Well, hello. How was practice?" He grinned and walked over and sat down on the porch. I joined him. He chuckled and said, "It was . . . interesting. You know Chuck and Buck?"

I nodded yes. I knew they were shape shifters as well, but they were moose. Jaye went on, "Paul was picking on them again about them being big and dumb. They didn't take that so well and the both went after him, one on each side, and head butted him. Needless to say, they broke his rib and he passed out. Thank goodness they were in human form or they would have run him through. They are so hot headed. Any way, they're suspended from the next game. Benched, and they're our best line backers."

All I could do was laugh. I could picture them attacking poor Paul. I said, "They have to learn to control their temper." He nodded his head in agreement and said, "I tell them that all the time. Goes in one ear and out the other. Oh, and get this. The cheerleaders were practicing their pyramid, right. And Jessica is always the one on top. She's the lightest and you probably already know that she's also a shape shifter, an Eagle.

Their in the middle of their routine and it's time for her to climb up top. Well, she didn't climb up. She must have been distracted because she basically flew to the top. Luckily no one noticed too much. She at least pushed off the bottom girl, but never touched the others and landed on top. I could tell she realized she goofed because she blushed, big time."

He really had me laughing. It was nice to just sit and laugh like this for a change. He must have sensed I felt the same way because he said, "It is so awesome to finally have someone to talk to like this and not have to cover up what I'm talking about. So, how was your day?" I took a deep breath. I wasn't sure if he remembered me from so long ago as a Kodiak bear, but I went on to tell him about all that happened. He seemed kind of perturbed when I mention Shinu and his being able to get in my head, but he maintained his composure.

He spoke up after a pause in my running my mouth. He said, "You know. I do remember you as a bear. I didn't know if you remembered though. I flew with you a few times when you'd take off running full speed through the meadow. Again, not stalking. Speaking of which, I was trying to tell you at lunch that I asked my mom about that. I was curious about it too. She comes out with this."

He pulled an old, very ancient letter from his pocket and showed it to me. I'll be danged if it wasn't the same type of letter my grandma just gave me last night. Same seal and all. I sat there in shock before he cleared his throat and went on, "Anyway. I read it. It's some sort of invitation from my Great Grandma. I'm going up to meet her this weekend and get some answers."

I was still in shock and couldn't speak yet, but I managed to reach in my pocket and pull out my invitation and show it to him. He took mine, surprised also, and looked up at me and said, "Wow! What do you make of that?"

I just shook my head and hunched my shoulders. I was just as floored as he was. I said, "Maybe my grandma would know. Would you like to meet my mom and grandma?" He smiled and said, "Sure." We stood up and went inside. Mom had started on dinner. Sometimes I swear she used to be a chef centuries ago. Our house always smelled like a gourmet restaurant.

We walked toward the kitchen together. Mom was the first to turn around and spotted Jaye. Her face lit up like a Christmas tree and she walked over and hugged him like he was a dear old friend. To my surprise Jaye responded with a warm hug back, like he knew her too. He said, "Lily! You look more and more beautiful each decade. It's so good to see you and your mom again. How have you been?"

Now I was really lost. First of all, how long had they known each other? Did they know he had been following me? What else were they hiding from me? Before I could say anything Mom explained, "We've known Jaye ever since he saved your life when you were six. He was always somewhere around you. We thought we'd never see him again when we had to go into hiding."

I felt a little better. I shrugged and said, "Makes sense. Greetings aside, can you tell us anything about this?" I handed her my letter and Jaye handed her his. She looked over both of the letters and said, "Oh my. I'm really not sure what to make of this. I mean, I have some idea, but not quite. Once again, this is something to ask Shaman Rose tomorrow."

Grandma had been quiet for a while now, but finally decided to leave her books to come over and hug Jaye also. She smiled at him and said, "My dear boy. We can never thank you enough. Well, it looks like you two were meant to come together at this precise time. Why don't you both go together tomorrow? That would ease some of my worry about you going alone Skye."

We turned to each other. As hard as I tried not to, I blushed. I swear this blushing is getting out of hand. I said, "Well that's up to Jaye. Would you like to go together?" He smiled. I could tell the idea made him happy. He said, "I think that's a great idea. I could use some company." So, that was settled. We would head out early in the morning. This was going to be an interesting road trip.

CHAPTER 8

EPIPHANY...

Jenna, Michael and their young calves were out grazing in their favorite spot. They usually go out for breakfast at the local restaurant, but decided they wanted to get some exercise and shake off some of the excess fur they were accumulating lately. There were only a few bison shape shifter families in the area, but this morning it was only them out.

They had just finished up and Jenna called for her two children to head home. Michael had already headed back. She called out, "Tania and Grant, it's time to head back."

Grant galloped back and joined his mom, but Tania stayed out. She called back, "Mom, if it's ok, I'm going for a swim first. I'll be there soon."

Jenna was hesitant, but decided she was old enough to take care of herself. Besides, she was 16 now and she had to let go soon. She said, "Ok. But, just for 15 more minutes, then come on in." Tania answered back, "Ok. Be there in a few." With that, Tania trotted off toward the creek. She loved to bathe there. The cool water felt good washing away the grass and leaves and dirt that would accumulate in her fur whenever they decided to go grazing.

She had just stepped in the creek when she heard a rustling in the bushes surrounding the creek. Shyly she said, "Hello? Anyone there?" Her brother was 12 and ornery and would often try and scare her. Impatiently she said, "If that's you Grant, I'll hold you under water until you turn blue."

There was no response. She thought to herself, *Must have been a squirrel or something.* She kept right on bathing. Once again there was a rustle from the bush, but this time she caught a glimpse of something black shuffling around. She got out of the water and sniffed around the bush where she seen it. Being a bison she felt she was big enough to take on whatever woodland creature decided to mess with her.

Not seeing anything there, she moved further on into the trees. Unexpectedly out of nowhere a black figure materialized out of thin air right in front of her. Whatever the thing was just floated there in mid air, shimmering in and out. It looked like an oil spill just levitating in thin air.

Tania sniffed at it and the putrid odor stung her nostrils. She flinched and stepped back. She shook her head, snorted, and turned to run. Something wasn't right. She was suddenly overcome with a feeling of terror. An immoral sensation made the air thick with tragedy.

She ran as fast as she could, but being so big and awkward, she couldn't coordinate darting back and forth. She was breathing heavy and running out of breath fast. She tried to call out to her family, but before she could open her mouth she was shocked by an abrupt burning sensation in her neck.

Since she was still in her bison form she couldn't reach back to feel whatever it was that stung her, so she tried to revert to her human form. She slowed down and concentrated, but only managed to change one arm that quickly changed back to her bison leg. She tried again and was able to change the top half of her body, but then altered immediately back again to her full bison form.

Whatever had hit her was not allowing her to change and now she was overwhelmed with terror. Now she was feeling dizzy and couldn't feel her legs. Before she could stop herself she dropped to the ground with a thud.

Her heart was racing and her eyes frantically searched for whatever was in pursuit of her. Once again, the black oil spill appeared in front of her. It slowly took on a form of a large man with red glowing eyes. It leaned down and looked her in her face. She snapped her teeth at him and growled.

It got down on its knees and lowered its demon red eyes directly into her eyes. A deep guttural laugh emanated from somewhere deep in the middle of the thing. Even though she was terrified of what he would do to her next, she built up enough nerve to yell at the creature in hopes that it would understand her. She growled, "You're the vile living thing that's been going around killing immortals, aren't you!?"

Another horrifying chuckle erupted from the thing. He snarled back and said, "You dare ask me if I am the one ridding this town of all the unholy, unnatural filth, even when you know you will die?"

Her whole body trembled with dread at that last statement, but she held her ground. She said, "The only *thing* that's unholy and unnatural filth is you!"

He threw his head back and growled, "Ha, ha, ha! So bold to be so young and innocent. I guess I could grant you one last wish and tell you." He sat down on the ground beside her and slowly pulled out a butcher's knife. It wasn't just any knife though. It curved back at the tip, almost forming a "j" shape. The handle had an ornate design on it. It almost resembled an ancient family crest. It was made of silver and the design rose up off the handle in a three dimensional fashion. It was a half moon with one star positioned at the lower point of the moon and another star set center at the back of the moon.

She was entranced by the knife. She was glad in a way that he decided to tell her who he was, hoping that if she could stall him long enough for her family to come looking for her. It went on with its story, "I have been here for ages, trying to clean up this misfortunate town. You see, it's not *right* for immortals to cohort with humans. It should never have happened.

Oh, I tried back when the natives of this land first thought it was *such* a good idea to befriend the werewolves. Hhm. I still remember dear old, let's call him Black wolf. He wanted power! He was brilliant! With some good scheming he almost succeeded in turning the werewolves against the humans."

He paused long enough to shift his greasy looking figure and take his knife and trace it along her side, drawing a little trickle of blood. She flinched.

He went on. "So, then later, he figured he'd try and turn the werewolves against the witches. Not an easy task. They had become very close. Sickening!

When the next wolf pup leader was born, he slipped into the cabin when the doctor had his back turned and poisoned the pup. If the werewolves thought the witch doctor had intentionally killed their new leader then a war would commence between them. But, he managed to remove all the poison with his limited witch craft before the pups father could enter. Filth!

Anyway. There was one person who kept everyone united. Damn her! Skye! But, her family left and she was never heard from again. So, if I can ignite a fire again, this time too big for anyone to extinguish, between all immortals, then I will finally complete my mission. Total control of the wolf pack! Without Skye, there can never again be unity among immortals. And if it means disposing of some to accomplish this, then so let it be."

Tania lay there in shock at what that hideous thing had just told her. She couldn't fathom how anyone could be so malicious. Trembling, she asked, "So, what are you going to do to me?" She had stalled as long as she could. No one was coming.

He then rose up, rather slithered, to what should have been his feet, and once again stood over her body. He snarled, "Oh, I intend to throw off our kind and lead them to believe it was a human that killed you. The more I turn the immortals against the humans, the more the witches will stand up for the humans. It is there "job" to protect human life. So, this will in turn start a war between the witches and the other immortals. Tit for tat, I let them do my job for me. Prepare to die foul shape shifter!"

• •

The night seemed to go by so quickly. I felt like I had just lain down and closed my eyes when the alarm went off. I drug myself out of bed and into the shower. That didn't help.

I thought it was going to take me forever to find something decent to wear, but mom came through. She had laid out a casually dressy outfit for me from her closet. I had to admit, it was very beautiful. It was one of her cream colored cashmere sweaters, a pair of navy blue slacks, and a pair of her three inch heeled, black leather boots. She even included some of her jewelry. I knew she just wanted me to look my best for Shaman Rose.

When I finally got downstairs, mom and grandma were already in the kitchen. Mom was making breakfast; French toast, eggs Benedict with Hollandaise sauce, sausage, bacon, home made biscuits, fresh squeezed orange juice, and grandma's wake-up-and-go tea. Stunned, I asked, "Mom. Are you cooking for an army? Toast and tea would have been fine."

I hugged them both and took a seat at the table. It smelled and looked so good. Toast and tea was no longer an option. I started to fill my plate up when I noticed there was another place setting. I asked, "Are you expecting company for breakfast?"

Oh no! Mom got one of her sneaky, scheming looks on her face and grandma giggled. Mom gave her one of those scolding looks and said, "Mom, stop giggling." Then mom turned to me and said, "First, you look so beautiful and it was the polite thing to do. It is so nice of him to drive you. That way we don't have to worry about you taking such a long trip by yourself. The least I can do is make him breakfast. Oh, and I packed you both a lunch too."

She smiled and gave me her innocent pouting look, so I couldn't be mad at her. She enjoyed cooking for others too much. And she was right to offer him something to eat before our road trip. I gave in and said, "Ok. I forgive you this time. When is he supposed to . . . ?"

Just then there was a knock at the door. I have no idea why I got nervous all of a sudden. My stomach felt like it flew up into my throat and I couldn't speak for a few seconds. Once I got myself together I answered the door. There he was. Why did he look so much better today then any other day? He had on a navy turtle neck sweater and khaki pants and brown oxford shoes.

I stood there for a minute when he said, "Are you awake yet? May I come in?" I snapped back to reality, cleared my throat and answered, "Oh. Yes. Come on in. Mom went overboard on breakfast, so I hope you're hungry." He smiled and walked in past me and said, "It smells wonderful! And yes, I'm starving. I just crashed last night before dinner and didn't eat. Thank you so much for inviting me."

My mom put on her prettiest smile and replied, "You're welcome. Sit down and eat all you want." Grandma pulled out his chair for him, right across from me. I really think she did that on purpose. I sat down too. We ate and talked through breakfast. I was surprised at how much past we shared. I was still slowly recalling most of my past. It seems like he was around quite a bit when I was younger. He knew a lot about Amber also. Boy, will she love to know this.

It was time for us to head out. We said our good byes, and I kissed mom and grandma. They wished us luck and we headed out to his car. Except it wasn't the car I was used to seeing at school. Nicely surprised I asked, "Is this your car too?" He walked around and opened the door for me, and answered, "No. This is my dad's. He figured it was safer and more durable for the trip. Plus it's more comfortable too." I got in. It was very nice inside as well as the outside. The interior was black leather and every surface was polished to a shine. It was definitely a luxury car. A Bentley is expensive.

When he got in he sat there and looked at me for a few seconds. I was really starting to feel nervous now so I asked, "Yes? Is something wrong?" He smiled and shook his head then looked away. Smiling he said, "No. You just look different. You look really nice today." I couldn't help but return the smile. He was just as nervous as I was. And I could tell it wasn't just because we were going to see Shaman Rose. I said, "Thank you. You do too."

He went on to explain that there were two temperature settings in the car. One for each side. I was grateful, because I am usually really warm. This, come to think of it, makes sense now. A bear is naturally warm with all that fur. We carried on small talk for part of the way. He told me about his past and the memories we should both share. I told him they should come back soon. That my mind was playing catch up and things hit me at odd times.

Speaking of things coming over me at odd times, I was unexpectedly overcome by a deep feeling of sorrow and loss. I couldn't breathe for a moment. I felt trapped, like I couldn't move or rather change to my human form. But, I was in my human form. The view of the car dash abruptly changed from the shiny black surface to a view of a field or meadow. I could see the grass swaying in the wind. Then there was a flash of something black and hideous. With that I was consumed by a feeling of emptiness and sickening evil bile. I could taste it. I thought I was going to lose my breakfast. I lurched and grabbed my mouth.

I could feel the car slow down and stop. I could also hear Jaye calling my name and feel him shaking me, but I couldn't break out of the trance.

•••

As he raised his knife in the air, Tania once again looked at the design on the handle. Suddenly she thought of Skye. She had remembered over hearing some of the kids at school saying that Skye was the great missing leader. That she would be the one with the answers to all that was wrong and would set it right. She managed to let out a laugh at that thought and suddenly felt at peace.

She watched as it shoved the knife deep into her side. He looked puzzled by her laughter with all the pain he knew he was inflicting. Smugly he said, "Poor dear insane child. You laugh though you know you are dying. Ha ha ha!"

He then pulled the knife through her flank. She not only felt the hot searing pain that began eating her alive, but could hear her own flesh rip and tear under the pressure of the blade. As the blood flowed from her, so did her last breath. And as her eyes closed and darkness swallowed her, she pictured Skye standing there, comforting her. She was gone now.

The black thing continued to carve out chunks of her body. He cut out filets to make it appear that someone had cut her up to get steaks and various other meat sections a human would eat. He threw those pieces in a bag, flung it over his shoulder, shimmered and disintegrated into thin air.

....

I reached out and tried to feel the grass to see if it was real. Before I could touch it I saw an object glimmer brightly in the sun. It moved and I could see, plan as day, a design on it. It was a knife! I was able to talk finally and frantically started yelling at Jaye.

I had to draw it. I don't know why, but I had to remember that design. I yelled, "I need a p-pen! I need a piece of p-paper! Please! Now!" He must have handed those to me because they were suddenly in my hands. I started scribbling as quickly as I could. I just knew that if I didn't hurry I would never remember it and it would disappear.

As I finished drawing it I felt a stabbing pain in my stomach. I screamed out in pain and the dash in the car slowly materialized back into view. The pain vanished, but the feeling of loss was devastating.

I started crying. Jaye reached over and grabbed me and held me while I tried to gain control of my crying. He finally let me go and asked, very concerned, "What was that and are you ok?"

I don't know how I knew it, but I answered, "Another immortal has been killed. A shape shifter. I don't know who or how I know it. She was in a field, near a watering hole, I think." He looked puzzled and asked, "And what was the drawing?"

In all my anguish I had almost forgot about the drawing. I looked down at it and said, "It was carved into the handle of the knife *it* used to kill her. I just knew it was important for me to remember it." I took a deep breath and calmed myself more. Jaye took the drawing and looked at it, puzzled he said, "It almost looks familiar. Like I've seen it somewhere before, but I can't put my finger on it. Hold on to it. Maybe my grandmother will know something about it."

I nodded yes and stuck the drawing in my pocket. I looked at Jaye. He looked worried for me, but also a little tired. I was too, so I suggested, "Why don't we just rest here for a little while and eat some lunch before we go on?" He smiled and said, "That sounds like a good idea."

We ate our lunches my mom packed for us and talked. It was nice just talking and reminiscing. I felt so relaxed with Jaye. He seemed to return the same feeling. We finished up and drove on.

• •

The rest of the trip was uneventful, which was fine with me. It gave me time to think of all the questions I had for Shaman Rose. I had a sense that many things would come to light before night fall. Some good, but others quite the opposite. I knew in every fiber of my being that this was only the beginning and that things would get worse before they got better.

I knew when we were getting close because there was an aura in the air. It almost felt like a blanket or force field of protection surrounding the whole area. It was cold outside, but it felt warm and inviting, as if summer had come. The grass was greener, the trees greener, and flowers in bloom. There were birds singing and I spotted more then one field animal scamper across the prairies. It was odder because we were heading further up into the mountains. Logically it should be colder.

Jaye turned the car onto a gravel covered drive and slowed down. I could feel the car begin to climb as if we were going up a steep hill. The closer we got, the more I felt I belonged here. It's hard to explain, but it felt like a nice, warm hug. I sighed and exhaled. Jaye smiled and did the same. He said, "I know. It feels breathtaking doesn't it?" I nodded yes and couldn't remove the smile from my face.

After about five minutes I could see a little cottage set back in the side of the mountain. Surrounding the front of the house were various sizes of evergreens and spruces. Off the left side of the drive, closer to the house was some sort of fruit tree. It was enormous. The leaves were huge, bigger then my head and such a luxuriant green it almost seemed iridescent. Whatever fruit grew on it were larger then my hand and also effervescent in color. The porch wrapped around from one side of the house to the other and had room enough for a table and chairs. There was also a porch swing. The banisters and whole porch were painted an energetic white. It appeared to glow in the dark shading of the trees. The house itself was a warm golden yellow. I felt at home.

As we pulled up and came to a stop a plump, but petite lady came out the door. Her smile was welcoming. Her silver hair draped all the way down her back and almost touched the porch floor. She wore a multicolored shawl that one could tell had been hand made. She was barefoot and very inviting.

Jaye stopped the car, turned it off, and got out and came around to open my door. He had the biggest smile on his face. His eyes were practically watery and he was tearing up with emotion. After he'd seen to me getting out of the car alright, he sprinted up the steps, so quick I barely saw him move, and grabbed his grandmother, sweeping her off her feet and into his arms. With that, I could see his body quivering from behind and knew instantly that he was crying. Not tears of sadness, but overwhelming tears of love and longing, like a child who had not seen their parents for years.

This made me overcome with emotion also and I had to swallow several times to keep from crying myself seeing him so happy. Once again I felt so warm and protected. It was a feeling of being swaddled in a blanket like a baby and rocked gently in a mother's arms as she hums.

I walked up the steps to the porch just as Jaye put her back down. She walked up to me and I bent over as she cupped my face in her hands. She smelled like warm butterscotch. She kissed my forehead and said, "My dear, dear Skye. You are as beautiful now as you were the last time I saw you. You have your father's strength, your mother's beauty, and your grandmother's wisdom. And oh, I can see that you have become more powerful than any of us expected! You don't know yet, but you are the only one who can save us all from impending troubles. Come on in children. We have lots to talk about, and dinner is done."

I followed them both in, in awe, of what she had just said. Jaye held the screen door for me. The inside of the house was just as inviting as the outside, even more. The house was furnished with antiques. All the colors complimented each other. There was an array of yellows and goldenrods, ambers and buttered rum. The ornate details in the wood that accompanied the plush couch showed a great deal of artistic endeavor and love went into the details. The legs and trim on the tables matched the detailed work on the couch. Even the picture frames had that same design.

One whole wall in the living room was covered from the ceiling down with pictures of many different people. All of them smiling. Their ages varied from babies in arms to the elderly. The other thing that seemed odd, but somehow right was that in each one of those pictures there was some type of animal posing with them.

I was mesmerized by all the faces in the pictures. Some way, many of them seemed recognizable to me. I walked closer to get a better look at them. I knew them. I don't know how, but some part of me knew them. As I stood there staring, my whole body began to tingle. I couldn't move. I was reaching out to touch one of the pictures that were the most familiar, when I noticed the picture right in the middle of all the others.

I moved closer to get a better look. There was a young lady, in old Indian clothes, surrounded by an assortment of people and animals. She was smiling and the ones around her were smiling at her, as if they were admiring her, no, looking to her for guidance. Even the animals seemed to gravitate to her. I moved even closer to see who this young lady was.

There was a thin film of dust on the glass and I reached to brush it off. I suddenly couldn't breathe. The face looking back at me from the picture was *me!* Abruptly I was consumed by a blinding white light. I could feel myself falling and saw a bright blue sky. Somehow I managed to turn over and face the ground that was quickly rising toward me. There were green fields and many trees. A pond, no, a lake of shimmering blue green floated below. I could feel my stomach twist and turn in anticipation of hitting the ground, but I wasn't scared.

The closer I got, the more intense the apprehension of colliding with the ground. All of a sudden, I was flying. I could see my wings. They were falcon's wings. I drifted gracefully down, but before I could touch the ground I was propelled into a sprint, running full speed across the prairie. I could feel the wind blowing past my ears at a great speed. I was on all fours. I could feel the strength in the muscles in my legs pushing me to faster speeds. Looking down at my legs, I saw gold and brown spotted fur. I was a cheetah.

I was running so fast I didn't notice the trees coming up quickly in front of me. But that didn't slow me down. I continued full speed, head on toward the trees. As the prairie turned into an immense wood I jumped at a tree and was suddenly changed again. Now I began to climb the tree. Not fast, but at a steady pace to the middle of the tree.

Once I stopped, I looked at my hands. No, not hands. I had paws. Big, bear claws. I came back down and jumped to the ground.

Once again I was off at a full out run. As I broke free of the trees I was racing toward the lake. I knew bears did ok in water, but a lake that deep? I didn't slow down. Again my stomach twisted with anticipation of the cold water and the fear of drowning. I dived in head first, and propelled toward the bottom of the lake. Then I was rocketing back toward the top, but I didn't surface. I continued to dart around under water, no fear of drowning. Gracefully I flipped and turned, shooting off to the bottom and back to the top. I curled into somewhat of a ball to get a look at myself. I was now a polar bear. I finally surfaced and trotted out of the water heading to the shore. I ran off again toward the prairie and as I hit the grass, my run turned into a slow and steady gait.

I could feel that I was much bigger and furrier. I continued to the prairie and could feel the big difference in the size of my body and head. Turning I was able to make out that I was now a bison. On I walked in the direction of what appeared to be a gathering of people and animals. The closer to the crowd I got, the lighter I felt. I had once again changed, this time, I was human.

The whole scenery around me slowly faded into a golden haze. I blinked my eyes and finally focused. I was now lying down on a soft couch. The multi-colored shawl that Shaman Rose was wearing when we got there was over me. A couple more blinks and I could make out Jaye's face and Shaman Rose's face. Jaye was pale and the first to speak, "Are you alright?"

I tried to sit up, but the feeling of euphoria and wonder still made me a little dizzy. I lay back down and tried to shake my head to reassure Jaye I was ok. All I could manage was to stroke his cheek. He closed his eyes and let out a breath he must have been holding for a while.

He brought a cup of some warm liquid to drink up to my mouth. It also smelled like warm butterscotch. He lifted my head for me and I took a sip. Closing my eyes briefly, I could feel it slowly warming my whole body. I felt a little more stable and asked, "How long was I out?"

Once again Jaye answered first. "A little over two hours. I was so worried. You went from pale to bright red, to hot then cold and pale again. I thought for sure it was something you ate in the car on the way here. Or something from your vision earlier. Needless to say, you had me scared. Grandma was calm the whole time, reassuring me that you were ok and that it would pass on its own time. Of course she wouldn't tell me what was wrong."

She smiled and chuckled a little. Then she said, "You, my dear, have just had a very strong and very deep past life regression. What brought it on sweetie?" I wasn't sure, so I just explained to them about how the pictures were familiar. I told her the last thing I remembered was looking at the picture in the middle.

She got up and walked over to the wall with all the pictures and looked at the one in the middle. Nodding her head, she returned to the couch where I was now trying to sit up and said, "Oh. I see. You found a picture of you. Many, many centuries ago."

Now that I felt more stable, I took the cup from Jaye and downed the rest of the drink. I told them about what I seen and felt. Shaman Rose was ecstatic and Jaye was in shock. Which is what I was in as I recalled everything that happened to me. When I was done I said, "I have so many questions for you I don't know where to start."

She smiled at me and stood up and said, "My dear sweet child. In due time. After that, you must be famished. I know my Jaye is. He refused to eat until he knew you were ok. Come children. Let's eat." We headed to the kitchen. The food smelled wonderful. I felt like I hadn't eaten in centuries after that ordeal. We ate and talked about the present for now.

CHAPTER 9

ENLIGHTENMENT . . .

After we ate I called my mom and let them know we made it alright. I briefly explained to her the epiphany I had. They were anxious to see what Shaman Rose had to say about it. I promised to call before we headed back. I had to call Amber and tell her a quick synopsis too. She said she wishes she could teleport there to be with me. Her exact words were, 'I should be there for you. I know Jaye is cool and all, but he doesn't know you like I do. I knew something was up. I could feel it. You'd better call me back right after you talk with Shaman Rose!' I couldn't help but laugh at her. Jaye called his parents also.

We all gathered in the yard off the side of her house where there was a pile of wood already set up in the fashion of old counsel meetings from long ago. Shaman Rose led the way. We all sat to one side of the pile. She raised her hands, mumbled something in the old language, clapped her hands above the pile and it instantly started to burn. Jaye and I looked at each other in amazement.

She sat down on the ground and motioned for me to sit beside her. Jaye gave me his hand to help me down and then he sat on my other side. Of course I got defensive and said to Jaye, "I am quite capable of sitting down by myself, thank you." He laughed at me and came back with, "Well you do seem to be kind of faint and spacey lately." I raised my eye brow at him in a chastising manner and snapped, "Ha, ha."

Shaman Rose broke us up before he could get me with another come back. She chuckled and said, "So. Tell me about the vision you had on the way here. Jaye tried to explain it to me while you were out earlier." I gave her every detail of what I had seen and felt. I then reached into my pocket and pulled out the drawing and said, "This is the design that was etched into the knife handle it used. It's etched into my brain now."

She took the piece of paper from me and studied it. After a few moments of silence, except for the crackle of the fire, she finally spoke. "Intriguing. I have encountered this same design long, long ago. It's been so long though. I don't recall where. I'm curious about something." She reached over and touched my arm. I could see her whole body tremble a bit, but not too convulsive. After she regained her composure she looked at me, very seriously and said, "My child. I mentioned before that you are more powerful then any of us anticipated. It's so rare. It's so odd. I need to see something."

She motioned for us to scoot back from the fire some. She looked at Jaye and said, "Now Jaye. I will hold her hand from this side. You hold her hand from your side. But hold on tight. And whatever you do, don't let go! Got it?" Jaye nodded yes and grabbed my hand. More like he put my hand in a death grip. She had me worried and I asked, "What is this all about Shaman Rose?"

She took in a deep breath and let it out before she spoke. "You possess a very potent power. One that has not been around for centuries before *I* was even born. I remember my mother telling me stories of an ancient warrior who had that power. The same power I feel in you. The same power I know you have but are unaware of.

He was able to transfer his visions into others so that they could see and feel the same thing he did. He could also shape shift into any and every animal at will. He could hide his identity from everyone who tried to enter his mind. But at the same rate, he could enter anyone's mind at will. He knew great magic. Magic that even topped the greatest witches and wizards. But, I can always tell you more about him another time. This is more urgent that we try this now."

Jaye looked at me concerned and inquired, "Are you sure you're up for this? I mean, after all you've been through today, can you do this now? Whatever it is grandma is going to ask of you?" The intense look in his eyes and worry made me tear up some. This crazy bird really did care about me. He wasn't just picking on me a little bit ago. I had never intruded in his mind before, but I felt compelled to. I touched his cheek and concentrated on him. I looked in his eyes, smiled and said, "You really do care. Thank you. I'll be fine. You are right here with me." He seemed to relax some and kissed my hand.

I turned and faced her now and asked, "So what is it you want me to do?" She patted my hand and said, "I want you to take us into your vision you had in the car. You have the power to recall it in every detail. We need to see what you saw and feel what you felt. As I understand it, once we are in it, you won't feel us holding your hands, but we are still here, in the present, holding on to you. This will keep us all grounded. We won't be lost in that world as long as we hold on here. You have the ability, deep in your mind, to keep us tethered here. It is up to you to not only show us, but to bring us back once it is over. All you have to do is split your thoughts. One part will be in the vision. The other part will remain here. Do you feel like you can do this?"

I thought for a few minutes. I knew I was up for this. I had to be. There was something very wrong going on and it was up to me to try and figure it out. I had to be strong. Somehow, I felt as if I had done this before. Right now I couldn't tell when or where, but, I knew I could do it. I let them both know I had the feeling I had done this before and reassured them it would all be ok. They nodded ok.

I took a deep breath and let it out several times. Before I knew what I was doing, I opened my eyes, looked into the fire, and shouted, *"Ohta us-ara see-mioota!"* I felt the three of us shot down a tunnel of bright light. The colors were so vivid, almost blinding. After traveling through the tunnel, we stopped abruptly and were standing in the field I saw earlier in my vision.

This vision began, *We were standing in a field or meadow. We could see the grass waving in the wind. There was a flicker of something black and hideous. Shaman Rose spoke up first, "Oh my! That feeling. It's so dark, evil." Jaye said, "I can taste it. It's sickening." Once again, I felt like I was going to throw up. I turned their attention to the bison that lay helpless in the field ahead of us. Kneeling over her body was the black, evil thing. Only now it wasn't just a shapeless blob, but the shape of a man. He raised his knife in the air. Excited about this moment I blurted out, "See! Look at the knife! There it is!"*

In the yard at Shaman Rose's house I kept an eye on both of them. I never let go of their hands. I concentrated on the warm heat radiating from the flames that licked at the ever darkening sky. Looking up from the tips of the flaming fingers that reached toward the heavens, I could see so many beautiful, twinkling stars. Looking back at my comrades I was tempted to reach out and stroke Jaye's cheek again, or brush back the hair that had fallen in his face. But I held fast to their hands that both seemed so still and so distant. But yet, I knew they were alive and well, with me in some other time.

Back in the vision, *Tania raised her head up and looked at the knife that was plummeting toward her. Jaye spoke again directing a question toward me. He asked, "It looks as if she's smiling. What is she looking at?" We all looked a little closer. Suddenly I materialized in front of Tania. I was kneeling beside her and stroking her fur.*

How could this be? I wasn't in that field with her. I was in the car with Jaye at the same time she was being murdered. Yet and still, I was there beside her. Comforting her in her time of despair.

Again to the vision, *She laughed and then was gone. We stood there, hand in hand, in shock and completely helpless to save Tania's life as he plunged his knife into her. The contemptible creature momentarily looked puzzled by her laughter. "Poor, dear, insane, child. You laugh though you know you are dying. Ha ha ha!"*

Back at the bonfire I cried finally. I wasn't able to cry and release my anguish of her loss earlier in the car with Jaye. But, here, alone now, except for the outer shell of Jaye and Shaman Rose, I cried. I took comfort only in the fact that even though I couldn't save her, my spirit was there to comfort her.

Returning again to the vision, *We stood and watched, as he carved chucks of flesh from her carcass. The contemptible black thing continued to cut. It looked as if he was covering his tracks by making it look like someone had cut her up to get steaks and various other meat sections to eat. Putting those pieces in a bag he flung it over his shoulder, shimmered and fragmented into thin air.*

Back in the yard again I said, "Ohta us-cama bata-acu mi." With a flash of bright orange light and a shot down a tunnel, I felt a part of me return and I felt whole again. I shook Shaman Rose's hand and I could see one small tear roll down her cheek as she blinked and opened her eyes. I then turned toward Jaye and shook his hand. Nervously I said, "Jaye? Please be alright." His eyes fluttered open and I could see his face turning red. I was just relieved that I was able to do it again and that they were alright.

Shaman Rose nodded her head to let me know that she was ok and that all was ok. I could let go of their hands now. I reached over and hugged her. She returned the hug only deeper and not so much as a thank you, but it felt more like a humbled hug. I looked in her eyes and smiled as if to say it was alright, then turned to Jaye. His color had turned back to normal. I hugged him too. He returned my hug and whispered to me, "I'm so sorry."

Shaman Rose was the first to speak. "Well now. After a journey like that, I think we could all use a drink." She reached beside her and pulled out three glasses and a teapot. It was more of the warm buttered rum she had given me earlier. She poured us all a glass. It tasted so good and comforting. Once again, she spoke. "Now Skye. I knew you could do it. I was a little concerned at first, but you did it perfectly. We are all fine. That was tragic. God rest her soul. I saw the knife. One could only wonder what his plan was next. But, when we saw you there?" Jaye interjected, "Yeah. What was that about? She was in the car with me, but we all saw her there with the poor girl." I corrected him, "Tania. Tania was her name." He rubbed my back. I guess he could feel my sorrow. He said, "I apologize. Tania. How was it possible for her to be there too grandma?" I was curious too. I face her and said, "Yes. I was wondering the same thing. I didn't know her, per say, but I had seen her before in school. Only a few times in passing. I didn't even know who or what she was. I felt something though. The same prickle feeling I get down my back when I come in contact with others I know are shape-shifters."

She took another sip of her rum and scratched her head, then said, "Of all the stories I've heard, I've never heard of one being able to separate there conscious from their subconscious mind unknowingly. If you are doing and have been doing the things you have so far without full awareness of your subconscious, imagine what you can do once we awaken that part of you. And thank you for allowing us into your vision. That is something so few have ever been permitted to do."

I was even more curious now, so I asked, "Why would someone not want to show another what they have seen if it will help?" She bowed her head to me as if in shame then paused before she answered. Jaye looked at her curious too. Keeping her head bowed she answered me, somewhat unsure of herself, "I'm am deeply sorry child. I really didn't think you could do it, take us into your vision so I saw no immediate need to tell you. But, once you did it; and so smoothly I may add, like you've done it all your life; it was too late for me to have you turn back. When a person allows someone to see their visions through them, they are allowing them into their mind and their thoughts and feelings about the person they allow in.

It doesn't expose all their inner most thoughts and feelings. It's like opening a window just a crack. Only a little air can go out. So, once in your vision or minds eye, you released some of your subconscious feelings and thoughts to us about us. We now know some of your deep thoughts."

For a moment I was confused. Then it dawned on me. More like, it hit me like a brick. I gasped in shock and looked at Jaye, who was now turning red again. I could feel myself turning red too. I thought to myself, *Oh my god!* I had never admitted to anyone, let alone myself, that subconsciously I had always been attracted to Jaye. All these years throughout school, I knew Stacey had it bad for Jaye, but secretly, I had a crush or an unexplained attraction to him. This must mean he picked that up from entering my vision. That would explain why he was so red when he came too. He wasn't upset; he was blushing from my innermost thoughts!

I couldn't look at him right now so I turned to Shaman Rose and asked, "So what secrets did you see? And don't worry. I'm not mad. A little embarrassed, but not mad." She bowed her head again and answered, "Thank you so much. I felt like I betrayed you. Yet, you aren't mad. You are such a humble child. That alone will get you very far. You do not remember yet, but you knew me when you were a little girl. You used to always sneak off, when you were suppose to be learning your lessons, and come and see me. Back then you lived in the village with your family and your people. I lived deep in the forest where I could train and meditate better. Your parents wanted you to not bother me all the time, telling you that I needed time alone to study and help others who *really* needed my help." She smiled and laughed at the old memories before she went on. "But, you were stubborn. You would sneak off when no one was paying attention. You would hide behind trees and watch me for long moments at a time before I'd pretend to suddenly find you. We'd sit and chatter. You said you loved my tea. I thought all these centuries that you had only been sneaking to see me because I would always give you tea and treats. But, in your vision . . ."

She gave me an admiring smile and a tear trickled down her cheek. She finally rose up her head and placed her hand on top of mine. Then she went on, "In your vision I finally saw the reason for your visits and I also saw that there were more than I was aware of. You were watching me all those times learning from me. You admired me and thought I was the greatest person in the world, next to your parents, and that you longed to one day grow up and be like me."

With that, she let go with full out sobbing. It wasn't tears of sorrow, but of respect and feeling honored. I couldn't help but hug her again. Only this time I opened my mind, my inner most mind, when I hugged her. As I held on to her I could hear a loud click and a snap like a giant lock was being cracked open. I was abruptly slammed in my mind's eye with a flood of memories. Memories that had been locked away. It was like opening a flood gate and watching all the water pour out. I finally remembered everything and everyone from my past. Past events flashed by. People that I had known flashed past me like a projector set on high speed. Things I've done, places I had been, quickly played out in my head. I don't know how long I held on to her, but it seemed like forever as the centuries played out in my mind.

When I was finally able to let go of her, I pushed back and looked at her. I couldn't help but laugh. Happily I said, "Oh Shahma! That's what I used to call you. I remember. Because when I was one or two I tried to say Shaman Rose but it came out Shahma. So that's what I called you from that point on. Oh, I remember mom and dad were upset at me for calling you that. They said, 'You must show her respect. It was fine when you were little, but you are bigger now.' But, you loved it and insisted on me calling you that. How could I be mad at you? Oh, it's so good to see you again. It's been so long! I missed you so much! I know my mom and grandma locked my mind up for a reason and I'll ask you about that in a few. First . . ."

I turned to Jaye. I could see the anticipation in his eyes. Before I could say anything he grabbed me and said, "It's about time you came back! You don't know how hard it's been trying to hold my tongue and not tell you everything. You missed so much when they had to take you away." I embraced him more tightly. I said, "Now I know why I was so drawn to you all these years. We grew up together. You were always there watching out for me. We even got into so much trouble. Amber! She was always there with us too!"

Just then my phone rang. It was Amber. I had to let go of Jaye to answer. As soon as I hit the answer button and before I could put the phone up to my ear, I could hear her screaming and crying in the background. She was able to speak first. I was bawling. "I felt it! I felt it when the lock broke! You have all your memory back! I've missed the real you for so long! My mom said don't call and bother you, but I couldn't wait. I'll let you go though. I just had to tell you I felt it too! Can't wait 'til you're back. Bye sis!" And with that, she hung up before I could get a word in edgewise.

Shahma stood up and waved her hands at the fire and it went out as quickly as it lit. She smiled and said, "Let's retire inside. We've had a long night and need our rest. In the morning there is much more to come." I stood up and headed toward the house but Jaye caught my arm and said to Shahma, "Grandma, we'll be in, in a bit. I want to get some air and stretch some." She smiled a sneaky smile and nodded before she went on her way.

Jaye took my hand and lead me toward the forest beside her house. He stopped when we were about center of the trees. Looking up there was a clear spot. I could see the moon and stars. Jaye took a breath and started talking, "You know. To say it was hard not to say anything to you was an understatement. Your grandmother ran me off from your house so many times. I used to just circle around to make sure you were ok. And even though it was killing me not to remind you about the past, about us, I kept quiet."

He paused and just stared up at the stars for a while. He was still holding my hand. I broke the silence as more of my memories slowly came back to me. I said, "I seem to remember flying with you. When I close my eyes I can feel the wind in my wings. I can hear you beside me, soaring and diving among the clouds." I paused this time and closed my eyes. I could see us high in the sky, no care in the world, just free to fly and be.

I felt an ache in my chest as more vivid memories played out in my mind. *Jaye and I had just landed high on a hill. We sat there for a while just looking up at the sky. He turned to me, looked me in my eyes, and stroked my face with his hand. I looked in his eyes and a flood of longing and emotions filled my heart. He spoke first, 'Skye. You know how close we are. We have been with each other for so long. Watching out for each other. I need you to know how I feel about you right now.' He paused and leaned in to kiss me, but stopped. He started to speak again, 'Oh Skye . . .'*

Out of nowhere my mom and grandmother came running toward us. Jaye never got to finish what he was trying to tell me. They rushed me off, apologized to Jaye and that was the end of my memories from that time until the present. I had to ask him, "What were you going to say to me back then, so long ago. We were on that hill after we had been flying around all day. You were going to say something but my mom and grandma interrupted and pulled me away. That's when they locked my memories away."

He turned to face me. That same look was in his eyes from long ago, except this time there was a tear in his eye. He cupped my chin and tilted my face up to his. He whispered, "I waited so long. I prayed the day would come when I'd get the chance to tell you. Now I don't know how you feel. With all that's going on, I don't know if this is the right time either. But, if I wait, it may be too late." I couldn't breathe. I was holding my breath this whole time. I let out a breath and said, "You have to tell me no matter what's going on now. There may never be another chance. We don't know what the future holds. We never know what may change later. Just have faith and say it."

He sighed, paused, and sighed again. Finally he said, "Skye, I love you. Always have. I've always known we were meant to be together. Always knew there was no me without you. Even when your mom had to take you away, I waited until I found you. Even then I stayed near you. I had no choice. All that time when Stacey was basically throwing herself at me, I couldn't see anyone but you. I love you."

That was all it took. I was bawling like a blubbering baby. I embarrassed myself crying like that. What was wrong with me? I can control myself better then that. What a wimp I am. I even leaned into his chest and balled my fists in his shirt holding on to him tight as I whimpered uncontrollably. When I was finally able to pull myself together I looked up at him. He looked scared, worried. Why not? I just broke down on him.

I managed a smile, took a deep breath and spilled my guts like a bag of rice with a gaping hole in it. Once I started, I couldn't stop. I began, "Back then I dreamed of hearing those words from you. But I just went on enjoying being with you even if you didn't feel that way about me. So many times back then I wanted to just blurt that out to you, but stopped myself. At school all these years I had to listen to Stacey babble on and on about you. I walked with her and watched her drooling over you year after year. You seemed to show no interest in her, but I thought it was just your way. I've felt we knew each other more than just at school. There were times when I told Stacey I didn't want to go to your games, that it was just guys bashing each other, and then I'd sneak to the game and stand outside the fence to watch you play. Making sure you were ok, or didn't get hurt. I knew the crow that was always there meant something. Look at me blathering on."

I stopped, put my hand to his cheek and, after all this time, professed, "Jaye, I love you too. Always have." That was all it took. Then it was his turn to bawl like a baby. After we were able to control our sobbing he kissed me. It was the most beautiful moment of my life. It had been a long and informative day. I felt, enlightened.

CHAPTER 10

COMPREHENSION . . .

We sat up talking all night. When we woke up to the smell of breakfast sausage cooking in the kitchen, we were sitting on the couch and I was leaning against Jaye's chest. Stretching, he looked down at me, gave me a kiss on my forehead, and said, "Good morning. You get any sleep? When you finally dozed off you were fidgeting all night." I smiled up at him and said, "I did. Surprisingly. That was the best night of sleep I've had in a long time. You sleep?" He brushed a piece of hair out of my face and smiled back at me. He said, "Yeah. I did. Best night of sleep for me too.

From the kitchen Shahma called out, "Well. Good morning children. Better get cleaned up. We're in for a long day. Lots to teach and lots to figure out. Breakfast is almost finished." Jaye offered me his hand when he stood up to help me up. "You go first. I'll go up when you're done." With that I headed upstairs.

It was just as cozy upstairs as it was downstairs. The whole décor up here was antique also. The same wood carving encircled picture frames, table legs, and chairs. Walking past what had to be her room

I noticed the large bed. The head board had that same ornate design in it. There were two other rooms also. I assumed they were guest rooms. They were beautifully furnished and as I thought, all the wood in there was decorated with the gorgeous wood carvings. My duffle bag was in one of the rooms and Jaye's must have been in the other. I grabbed my bag and headed down the hallway. I'd have to ask her who had done those for her. It must have taken that person a long time. And they had to be so artistic. I found my way to the bathroom and freshened up. Once again, mother came thru. She had packed another pretty outfit for today. The blouse was a silky, chocolate color with gold buttons. The jeans were black, but had intricate golden thread patterns on the pockets and at the cuffs of the legs. I decided to put my hair up in a bun. I figured we'd have a lot of work to do today and keeping my hair back may help.

I headed back downstairs. Jaye was standing in the kitchen pinching at whatever she had fixed for breakfast. They seemed to be in a deep conversation. I cleared my throat so they would know I was there and said, "Sorry if I'm interrupting. The bathroom is all yours now." He gave Shahma a warning look before he turned to me and kissed me on the cheek and dashed up the stairs.

Now I was curious. I asked, "Everything ok?" She motioned to a chair for me to sit. Smiling and patting me on the shoulder she said, "Just Jaye being a typical worry wart. He doesn't want me to put too much on you today. Sit. I've made eggs, sausage, bacon, biscuits, fresh squeezed orange juice, and waffles with maple butter syrup. Take your pick. Get a full belly. I have a feeling you'll need it."

Smiling warmly at me, she turned and went back to cleaning the kitchen. I was starving. I had planned on waiting for Jaye to come back down to eat with him, but I took one bite of the waffles and couldn't put it down. By the time he came downstairs; I was stuffing my last piece of sausage in my mouth and laughing with Shahma. She had been picking on me about how much and how fast I was eating, asking me if my mom ever feed me.

I was just commenting on how I usually don't have much of an appetite when I heard Jaye bounce down the steps. He took a seat by me and finished my sentence for me. "Grandma, she never eats. It's a rare occasion at lunch at school if she eats one slice of pizza." He laughed and elbowed me, gently, on my arm. I couldn't help but smile at his comment. I replied, "So. Does this mean you've been stalking me at school?" He smiled and turned a little red, again and answered nervously, "No, no. I just happen to be in line before or after you each time at lunch and noticed that." I had to let him off the hook. I said, "Just messing with you. You usually eat enough at lunch for both of us." He got me back with, "So that would mean you're stalking me." We all laughed and finished breakfast.

· ·

Back in town, the old butcher at Moe's Shop was beginning to set up the show case for the day. Saturday's were usually a busy day for him. This was the only fresh meat butcher shop for two towns over. So, people from town and out of town would travel there to get their fresh meat, or fish, for their Sunday dinners and most of the time, for the week. He was waiting on the last delivery truck to come in. This was one of the local trucks. A couple of the guys from town had their own meat business and had been selling the old man fresh meat from their hunting trips. He never worried about anything coming in bad. They had always been on the up and up, so he had worked with them for seven years now. Plus they had been inspected and certified by the state food board.

They were running a little late and he was beginning to worry. People would start pouring in soon and he knew he wouldn't have enough meat unless they made it here. Checking his watch one more time, he started to head back in the storeroom and call them when the truck turned in.

Relieved, he wiped his forehead as if to show the driver he was sweating from worry, and waved. The truck pulled up to the door and the driver got out. The old man was smiling and his smile faded a little when he saw that he didn't recognize the driver. He approached him slowly and asked, "So. Where's Jerome?" Before the stranger answered, Jerome got out of the passenger's seat and walked around the truck. He explained, "Here I am Ronny. Just training a new driver. Me and the misses are finally taking a vacation this year and I needed a driver to cover for me and the fellows while I'm gone. I need them out a huntin'. Didn't want to pull them in. This young'n came into town 'bout a month ago. He's just been doin' odds and end's for us, so I figured he can keep my truck runnin for us while we're gone. Ronny, this is Tucker Craft. Tucker, this is our old friend Ronny we been a tellin' you 'bout."

Tucker shook his hand and nodded his head in a form of respect, "Sir. I've heard a lot of good things about you. I'm sorry to throw you off. I'll just be driving for them until Jerome gets back. But, if you need help with anything else, just let me know. I'm pretty much a do-all handy man of sorts." Ronny shook his hand and felt a little surer of this new guy now.

The three of them worked together unloading the truck and filling up the freezer. There were the usual meats; deer, beef, pork, lamb; but there was additional meat as well. Bison. Ronny very rarely gets in any bison from these guys so he had to ask, "So, what's the special occasion? You all never bag bison 'til near winter. This is a delicacy." Jerome chuckled, "I know. Bob and Tucker here were out a huntin' deer when they ran across a herd of bison. They ain't never usually out in the open this time of year. So, they saw the opportunity. Bob went one way and bagged a few and Tucker went another and bagged one too. Just gives me more money to spend on the misses for our trip." They all laughed and finished up.

Back inside the front of the store they finished up business. Ronny paid Jerome for the meat shipment. Tucker looked around at the shop and commented, "You got yourself a nice place here." Ronny smiled with pride and answered, "It's been in the family for years. My great grandpa started the business and it's been in the family since then.

We get a lot of business here. Specially on Saturday's. People come from two towns over for Moe's fresh meat. Moe was my Pa." Tucker nodded and said, "That's just good business. I like shops like this. I'll put a bug in folk's ear back in town about your fresh haul of bison. You'll probably sell out today. Like you said, it's a rare delicacy."

Ronny thanked Tucker. They all shook hands again, then the guys left him to his work. He watched the truck pull out the alley and headed back in. He thought to himself, *Tucker was right. I'd better add that to the sign out front.* He first added some of the bison steaks to his display case, then ground some up and made burger meat to add to it too. After he had finished and cleaned up, he headed out the front door of his store. The sign was a simple dry erase board propped up on wooden legs about waist high, and set in front of one of the store windows. He took out his trusty blue marker and added to the top of the list of today's specials, **Fresh Bison!!** Ready to open for the day now, he went back in, turned on all the lights and flipped over the 'OPEN' sign.

As the first customers entered the shop he thought to himself again, *Yep. Today will be a good day.*

⋯⋯⋯⋯⋯⋯⋯⋯⋯⋯⋯⋯⋯⋯⋯⋯⋯⋯⋯⋯⋯⋯⋯⋯

After breakfast we all went out on the front porch and sat down. It was beautiful out again. The sun was peeking through the clouds and traces of the blue sky were bleeding through the white. I noticed many little forest creatures were lingering around the yard and in the trees, and many birds had gathered in the trees also. Jaye sat close to me and put his arm around me as Shahma started to talk, "According to what I know and the regression you had yesterday, it looks as if you are what is called a *Shoo-atee*, one that can change into many animals. This is a rare gift. You should be able to do this with great ease, but first, we must open up your subconscious and make that *one*, with your conscious. To do this, you must let go of all you know and believe to be true and embrace what seems to be impossible. In your regression you said you began out by falling from a great height then changed into an eagle. The falling was not only literal, but it also meant leaving behind what you know, to except what you don't. This morning will be a test of your mind."

I was getting a little nervous. Jaye must have sensed it. He tightened his grip around me. Curious, he asked, "What kind of test are you talking about grandma?" She took on a serious look then went on, "You have lived somewhat domesticated for many years and have lost touch with your inner spirit. You will have to experience a shock to awaken your inner spirit. That will then combine your conscious and subconscious minds."

Now, I was worried, but couldn't say anything. Jaye sat forward in his chair and grabbed my hand and asked for me, "So, what kind of shock does this have to be? If this means she can get hurt, I think we'd both agree that it's not worth it. Grandma, I just got her back in my life." I was so overcome with love for him. I was finally able to speak, "Jaye. I'm sure Shahma knows what she's doing. She has been in this business for centuries. I have always trusted her and I still do. Whatever it will take, I will do. I just know that something very wrong is about to escalate and I have to stop it." He nodded ok.

Shahma now took my hands in hers and looked me in my eyes. She stated, "I see that you are serious about this. You are ready to do this. All you have to do is let go. Clear your mind of what you think you know and open up to all the possibilities there are in this world and others. Believe in your heart and trust your inner senses."

She stood up and walked to the edge of the porch. We joined her there. She made a few clicking animal noises and a few chirps. With that, all the little and rather large animals I had seen, including a few bears, drifting around the yard gathered in a group at the foot of the steps. She went on to explain, "As you can see, I have asked many of my friends to join us today. They are here to not only help you if you need it, but to protect you from any harm. They are ready and willing to sacrifice their lives to save yours if need be. They are here, to catch you if you fall."

Jaye stepped forward in defense and anxiously exclaimed, "Fall?! What do you mean fall?" She looked up at him and gently patted his back. She said, "Don't be afraid grandson. You will be there too. To help guide and protect her. She must fall, as in her regression, to wake her spirit. You too, must let go. Now. Are you ready Skye?" I nodded my head yes.

We followed her off the porch and into the forest. The animals followed also. As we walked, she talked about time long ago, about how the people used to be in tuned with the world and their surroundings. She spoke of the great many Shamans before her and again of the great leader from long ago that had the same powers she says I now have. All was quiet as she continued on. Even the animals seem to be listening. I closed my eyes and listened to her words. They drifted not only in my ears, but also my mind, encircling it with many beautiful pictures from long ago. I breathed deeply and let my mind go back to the past. I concentrated on her stories. I could hear the drums of the past beating and they danced with everything in nature.

I opened my eyes again and the forest had changed. I could see so clearly. Everything seemed vibrant. Colors swirled in and out of each other forming shades of hues I had never seen before. Again I took a deep breath and let it out. I could hear every sound around me. Not only the sound of Shahma's voice, but the sound of every thing around us. I had to stop for a moment and admire the beauty of this new world. I could feel Jaye tense again beside me, but I reassured him, "I'm ok. Do you see it? All the colors? Every little creature down to that ant climbing up that tree trunk?" I sniffed in. "And all those smells. I can smell the mountain goat climbing up the side of that mountain." I pointed across the lake. "I can smell the sweet scent of the lilies blooming in the prairie over there." I was getting excited now! This was so cool! I continued, "I can smell the fish in the lake, the crabs, and the lobster! I can hear every bird and the flutter of dragon fly wings! It is so beautiful!"

I kneeled down on the ground and held my breath as I placed both hands on the ground. Quietly I let my senses flow through out my whole body. All was suddenly quiet. All that is, except for a pulsating sound and feel beneath my hands. I could feel the beating heart of the forest, the trees. And as I let myself feel the life pulsing around me, my heart began to beat as one with the forest. I felt so exhilarated! How could I have not felt this before? It was life changing.

I was now ready for whatever test Shahma had for me. I stood up and hugged Jaye. I said, "Its okay. I will be fine." We kissed. A long, passionate kiss. To him, he was probably thinking I was saying goodbye. To me, I was just saying I will be fine. We let go but Jaye kept his arms around my waist as I turned and faced Shahma. I could feel his heart racing against my back, but mine beat slow and steady, still in tune with the forest. "Ok Shahma. I am ready. What is this test?"

She inhaled and let out a long breath. A small bird lit on her shoulder and nuzzled her cheek. She smiled and gently stroked it's head. She explained to me, "She says the others are ready to go. They are in position to help you if you need it. As I said before, you said you were falling in your regression. You have to do the same now to awaken that within you. It appears that you have already awoken some of the spirit within you. In order to fall, with enough distance to give you time to connect, you must drop from a great distance. We are in the middle of this great forest where the heart is. I believe that is what you felt Skye, when you kneeled to the ground. Tell me. Did you feel the heart of the forest beating?"

I couldn't help but smile as I said, "Yes! It's alive and it feels too. My heart is still in beat with it." She beamed with happiness, "Good! You will need that connection. This is not only the heart of the forest, but it is also home to the tallest trees. I already know you know how to change into your bear form. You are to use that form and climb as high as you can in the tree.

Once you can't go any higher as the bear, change back to your human form and climb even higher. Once on the highest branch, stop, breathe deeply and concentrate on your spirit. When you feel even the slightest connection, jump. Remember to let go of all you think you know. It is in you to shape-shift into whatever you set your mind to. Don't think about the fall. Just find your subconscious. It is there waiting for you to open it. Now go child."

I looked at Jaye one more time and gave him a quick peck on the cheek. I ran toward the tree I could feel calling me and before I got to the foot of it, I morphed into my bear form. Without looking back I began to climb. Even through my bear paws I could feel the beat of the heart in the tree. I could hear every living creature whispering to me, *You can do it Skye. Reach within your heart. You can do it Skye.* It was comforting. As I got higher I could feel the air change thinner. My breathing picked up, but somehow stayed on beat with the tree.

It seemed like it had been a long time before I had gotten as high as I could as a bear. I sat on a branch, caught my breath and morphed back to my human form. I felt a little light headed and thought I was going to fall backward, but there was a small nudge in the middle of my back and I felt little paws tickle my side as whatever it was scampered up to my shoulder. It was a raccoon. He rubbed his head against my neck. I was no longer dizzy. It felt good having him comfort me.

I looked out toward the tops of the other trees, afraid to look down instead, and I could see many other raccoons gathered on the surrounding trees looking back at me. I had to laugh. I spoke out loud, "Shahma was right about you all looking out for me. Thank you. I'm ok." Just then a little chipmunk poked his head out from behind my leg and ran up me and into my blouse. He stayed there with his head popped out. Again I had to laugh. I told the raccoon that had saved me from falling that I was ready to go on now. He nodded his head yes, and scampered back down the tree. My other audience stayed in their spots and watched. I figured that one was going down to let Jaye and Shahma know I was ok.

With my new little friend nestled in my blouse collar I started climbing again. A few times I stumbled and almost lost grip. I could feel the chipmunk quiver nervously and laughed, "Hey. I'm supposed to be the one scared." She reached her little paw up and patted me on the chin. I went on.

Now that I was near the top I could feel the tree sway some and knew it was letting me know this was the spot. I leaned on the strongest branch behind me and slowed my breathing again to the pulse of the tree. "Ok Sansha. (On our climb up she told me her name) You can go back down now and let them know I made it to the top." I said with a reassuring smile. She nodded, pat my chin again, and disappeared back down my leg and down the tree.

I looked out across the sky thinking of Jaye and how at peace he looks when he soars through the sky. I closed my eyes and thought of how good the wind felt in my regression as I too flew among the clouds. After what I thought was a short drift back in time I opened my eyes and there were a multitude of various birds flying around me. There was a crow, but not Jaye, a few falcons, and eagle, and several little birds flitting back and forth around my head. The biggest one of all was a condor. I knew they weren't native to these parts, so he must have traveled a far distance for Shahma.

After acknowledging them all and thanking them for watching over me I spoke to the condor, saying, "Great condor. You are one of beauty, grace, strength and ancient wisdom. I am deeply honored to have you by my side for this journey. You must be very close to Shahma to have traveled this far for her." By my surprise, the condor spoke back to me, in my head, *Oh my dear Skye. You are named for the part of this world that you shall rule. Every part of nature is a part of you, but the sky is your domain. The birds are your people. I was not summoned here by Shaman Rose, I am your spirit. I am you. You have called upon me to guide you, to unlock your subconscious so you can do what must be done. When you fall, don't think of the fall. Look to me. Think of me and we shall become one.*

I was overwhelmed with awe. I reached out to stroke the beautiful feathers on its neck, lost my balance and fell. I could feel my stomach churning and twirling as I fell so fast. I could see the ground coming up at me at break neck speed. Tree limbs flashed past me. The birds that had checked on me at the top of the tree began to circle around me. It was a stunning sight. They flew so gracefully. If they could do it, then so could I. I looked up at the blue sky above me, searching for my condor. Then there she was. Sailing beside me as I plummeted toward the ground. I couldn't even think of the impending death that loomed below me. I just wanted to reach out and touch her. Her feathers were so alluring. They looked like they would feel like silk, like the blouse my mom had given me to wear today. I stretched out my fingers wanted so bad to hold on to her, to feel the comfort of her heart beat, to fly like her. I knew I had to only be a several hundred feet from the ground, but I didn't care. I was determined to hold her before I died.

Now only a few hundred feet from the ground I reached out one more time. This time I felt the silk feathers of her pelt and pulled her in to me. I held on tight and cradled her in my arms. I felt her life seeping in to me. I felt as one with her. Suddenly every sound ceased. Silence surrounded me. Darkness enveloped me. I was here and nowhere at the same time. Floating there in complete nothingness I could still feel the condor in my arms, but I wasn't scared. From inside me somewhere I yelled out, "Wee-tah ar-ray-un!"

There was an unexpected sound of glass shattering and a flash of bright light. Right before I collided with the ground; or rather, what should have been the ground, but was a massive heap of fur; I shifted into the form of a falcon. I cried out in triumph, which came out the call of a falcon, and shot off through the trees. I was flying! I had done it. I felt one-hundred percent whole. I flew up to the tops pf the tree and circled around up there for a few minutes with my bird friends. They all called out in their various chirps and whistles in congratulations to me or rather, welcome home.

I swooped back down, circled around Jaye and landed on Shahma's shoulder. I nuzzled her cheek and took off again. It felt so good to fly again. It had been so long. So many centuries had gone by since I was among my people, the birds. I flew and dived, swooped and looped. I looked around and there flying beside me, was Jaye. He had come and joined me up here. With my sight and senses so much clearer I could hear Jaye speak to me as a bird. He said cawed out excitedly, "You did it! I am so proud of you. I almost died back there when I thought you were going to hit the ground. I love you so much." I answered back, "I love you too."

But, that wasn't enough to just say it. I wanted to feel his arms around me. So I plunged back to the ground and right before landing I changed back to my human form. I ran over to Shahma and hugged her. That was all it took. I was crying again. She wiped off my tears and said, "You have done the almost impossible. I bow to you now, my leader." I kissed her on the head and turned just as Jaye was changing.

He ran to me before I could move and picked me up and hugged me. We were both crying so much we couldn't talk for a few minutes. After we were able to let go, I thanked all the animals for being there for me. I hugged the bears and told them I was especially thankful to them. They had formed a safety net of their own bodies to catch me if I hadn't been able to change. At that height and rate of speed I was falling at, some of them surely would have been hurt, if not killed from the impact.

I turned and faced Shahma again and said, "Now that I have joined with my spirit I want to see if I can still shift into any form at will." She smiled such a big smile, happy for me, happy for all of us. She nodded and replied, "You two go ahead. I will be back at the house fixing lunch. See you in an hour?" I nodded yes. She went on, "Good. We now have to finish our plans. Enjoy yourselves." She bowed to me again and headed to the house.

Jaye and I faced each other again. I couldn't help but smile ear to ear. He laughed at me then asked, "So what do you have in mind?" With a sneaky grin I said, "Just a little exercise. I will change into different forms while running. You have to try and keep up with me." He laughed again. He knew he was fast so he added a challenge to it for me. "Ok. We'll race from here to the other side of the lake. The loser has to wear a formal outfit to school on Monday." I was up for it. I shook his hand and said, "Deal. Whenever you're ready."

We stood side by side. He announced, "On your mark, get set, get ready," And I yelled, "Go!" We took off running. He was ahead of me, but not for long. I simply thought of my bear and suddenly changed into one. I took off. I heard him behind me yell out, "No fair." Then he changed into his crow and before I knew it, he was flying right beside me through the trees. The way he flew it was like there were no trees. He knew every turn, dip and dive. So, I figure my bear was too slow. I thought of a cheetah and I could feel my big body shrink to a sleek form and my big muscular arms shrink to smaller, yet just as strong, arms and legs. With that, I took off and gained ground on him. He was still right at my heels though. I ran in this form for a while and he kept up with me. From time to time he would swoop up in the trees and disappear, but soon caught up with me.

I could smell that we were getting close to the lake. I had to think fast as to which animal swam fast under water before I reached the shore. Ah ha. I had it. Right before I hit the water I changed into a penguin. They fly under water. I figured I had a chance to change before he broke out of the trees because he was a ways behind me. I could hear him laughing in my head as he flew out the trees, "Ok. Cute choice, but they are slow as molasses on land."

If I could have picked up a rock I would have thrown it at him. I dove in the water and took off. I couldn't see him due to the water above me, but I could sense where he was. He was a few feet ahead of me. I didn't know if it would work, but I had to try. I did not want to lose the bet. I shifted into a dolphin, got up my speed under water, jumped out of the water and shifted into a hawk. It worked! I shot off as fast as my wings could take me. I could see Jaye ahead of me, not by much, but close to the other shore. I flapped as fast as I could, but still didn't gain much distance. So, I figured I'd try and syke him out. "Hey! You're doing well. Oh my god what's that?" I took a dive for the water. Just as I thought, Jaye turned and headed toward me to see if I was ok. As he got closer I took off. If a bird could stop in mid air and stay suspended there, that would be what I had just seen Jaye do. Just the image of him made me crack up laughing.

Being new to this shape-shifting into other animals I didn't realize cracking up laughing while in flight would slow a bird down. Jaye regained his wits and soared past me. He beat me. I landed on the shore, shifted back to human and sat there, pouting. Jaye came over and sat beside me. He didn't rub it in. Thrilled with what I had done he said, "That was awesome! You have got this shape-shifting down to an art. Who would have thought of a dolphin jumping out of the water and mid-air, shifting into a hawk! Brilliant!" He leaned over and kissed me on the cheek. I couldn't be mad at him. I smiled and said, "Thanks." We sat for a while before heading back to the house.

CHAPTER 11

PLANS COME TOGETHER...

Ronny finished cleaning up for the day. Sure enough, it had been a busy day. The bison meat had gone good. He had just about sold out of all of it. There was just one last package left with filets, steak, and enough meat to grind up more for tomorrow for hamburgers. He thought about grinding it tonight so it would be ready in the morning, but decided to go on home and just come in early to do it.

He counted the register and finished his paperwork for the day. He made sure to check all the doors and all the freezer and refrigerator temperatures before he cut off the lights and left out the back door, making sure to double lock it. He got in his car and headed home.

The sun was just beginning to set. About fifteen minutes after Ronny left four dark figures crept down the alley toward the back door of the butcher shop. The tallest and stockier one, a male, approached the door. He began sniffing around the door. The other one, slimmer in stature and female, had dropped down and was sniffing the ground.

The tallest spoke first, "I can smell her still in here." The one on the ground said, "And I can smell the truck that delivered it." The third figure, a male, said, "Let's go in, get her, and get out of here before someone shows up. The fourth one was a younger female. She stepped up to the door and using a lock picking kit she unlocked the door knob. The top one would be trickier. She tried to pick it, but it wouldn't give. After several tries she got frustrated and just punched the lock right through the door. The bolt piece that went in the door jam tore right through the wood and metal that held it. The lock hit the floor with a clang.

They all crouched closer to the wall. The slimmer female cursed, "Damn it Emily! Are you trying to let people know we are here?" Emily shook her head no. "Sorry. I just got frustrated and impatient. Gotta work on that." They all ducked inside. It was dark inside, but they didn't need any lights. They could see just fine in the dark. Their eyes glowed as they began to sniff around and hunt. The tallest one was the first one to find what they were looking for. On the rack where he found it the packages were wrapped in plastic and placed in a tub marked **Bison Meat.**

He called them all over to where he stood. He spoke in a saddened whisper, "Here she is. Poor soul. I can skin whoever did this!" The other male spoke up, "We'll have time for that later, Elliot. Let's get her to her folks so she can have a proper burial. Then, we go find the sorry son of a bitch who did this to her!"

Elliot gently placed the packages of meat in a duffle bag, zipped it up, and headed for the door. The other male whispered to the other female, "Natasha. Go ahead and take some other meat. We have to make it look like a break in from a vagrant or someone, looking for food." She grabbed a few bundles of beef and pork and threw it in another duffle bag and headed for the door. Emily had already gone to the front of the store, in stealth mode, and fiddled with the register to make it look like they were looking for money too. The other male nodded in approval and they all left out the back.

After they made sure the coast was clear, they changed into their wolf forms and took off to return Tania, or what was left of her, to her parents. The journey from in town to the outskirts of town, where Tania's parents lived, was a short one for them. They took on their werewolf forms to get there faster. Her family was waiting outside their ranch when they arrived. Tania's mother was the first to see them coming. She could see that one of them was carrying a duffle bag in his mouth. She knew what it contained. She dropped to her knees and buried her face in her hands, and wept, convulsively.

Emily couldn't handle the pain she could see Tania's mother was going through. She headed off into the woods leaving the others to handle the family. Once alone, Emily began crying her own self. Natasha soon joined her and nuzzled her neck to comfort her, saying "We'll get whoever's done this. Be strong." Emily nodded her head. Natalie's skin rippled causing her fur to stand up on her flank as she caught a whiff of the smell she picked up in the alley. The truck had to be close. She raised her head and howled for the others to join her and Emily.

Once they were together Natasha told them, "I've got the scent of the truck. It's close." They followed her through the woods and out across the field in to another wood. She slowed and they did the same. About fifty feet in front of them there were two men sitting by a fire in a small clearing. The delivery truck was parked off to the side of the trees in another small clearing. It was running. Elliot spoke, "Either they are getting ready to leave soon or it's refrigerated. It has to run if it is. Bastards probably just offed someone else. No one hunts bison this time of the year. What were they thinking?" Emily answered that question, "Money. That was probably all they were thinking about. I saw the price of the other bison steaks in the shop earlier today. For old Ronny to charge that much to the public he had to of paid a lot to them for it."

They sat quietly for a little while behind the trees, listening to the conversation the men were having. Nothing out of the ordinary. No confessions on who did it. Just talk about where they would do their next hunting. They mentioned a Tucker Craft, but there was only the two of them there. Elliot cocked his head to the side trying to catch the scent of another man, but could only smell the two guys by the fire. Curious, he said, "Hhm. Tucker Craft must be one of their other customers somewhere. I can't pick up the scent of anyone else out here."

Just then the conversation took a turn. The turn they were hoping for. One of the men started rattling on about the bison he had pegged off. He laughed and talked about how easy it was to get the biggest one and soon spotted a medium sized one and got it too. All of the werewolves bristled their fur and made a spine tingling, guttural sound. The men by the fire must have heard them. They quit talking and jumped up from where they were sitting and raised there guns, pointing them toward the trees opposite the werewolves.

Elliot started to charge toward them when the other male stepped in front of him and snarled, "No! Not yet. We don't want them to run or shoot one of us. Wait until they sit and put their guns down." He was a little angry to have been stopped, but calmed and thought about it, "You're right Thomas. I just couldn't control it. That poor child. I can't wait to rip them apart!" Thomas thumped Elliot in the side as if to pat him on the shoulder. He said, "It's ok big boy. Patience."

As they all waited, the two men finally sat back down and placed their guns on the ground. The bigger one laughed, "Pathetic aren't we? Was probably the engine on the truck." They laughed at themselves and went on with their conversation. Little did they know that imminent death awaited them some fifty yards away.

As they patiently waited to attack the men, Emily began to think out loud, "We all realize this isn't going to sit well with Skye don't we? Going off like vigilantes." Natasha turned her head toward Emily and pushed at her with her snout. A little frustrated she snapped, "If you're having second thoughts, then maybe you should go on home.

They were wrong for what they did to Tania. We promised her family we'd take care of it. Skye isn't here right now." Emily lowered her head and tucked her tail, shamefully saying, "You're right. I'm not going anywhere. All of her friends at school were so sad. It hurt to see them all mourning."

Thomas rose up and the others followed suit. He stated, "Let's get this over with so we can go back and let her family have some piece of mind. I have to get back home and continue looking for my son. Ready?" With that, they slowly creeped out of the trees. Elliot went off to the right, Natasha to the left. Emily circled around and positioned herself behind the men, directly across from Thomas. He whispered to them, "On my mark."

They waited for his signal. He made a woof sound and they all bounded out of the trees, surrounding the two unsuspecting men. With teeth bared and hackles raised they kept low to the ground and closed in on them. Their eyes were blood red and streams of drool and foam coated their mouths. The sinewy muscles in their legs flexed as they continued to slowly pace back and forth. The men jumped up and stood still unsure of what they should do next. One of them stuttered out, "W-whoa boys. N-n-nice doggies. What the hell do we do now Bud?" Bud was shaking so violently he peed his pants and couldn't answer.

The werewolves continued circling and growling. Elliot was the first to jump. He flew straight at Bud's neck. Bud raised his arms to protect his face just as Elliot closed his jaws on him. He ended up grabbing his arm. The blood from Bud's arm shot out in streams. As Elliot bit down harder, he could feel Bud's flesh and muscles tearing against his fangs. He held on and began slinging his head back and forth with such force that it ripped his arm off below the elbow. The snapping sound of his bone echoed through the night.

With his snout now covered in warm blood, he flung his head and the gnarled appendage landed in the fire causing the flames to leap and turn from orange to blue. Pieces of his flesh still dangled from his mouth. Bud screamed in agonizing pain but managed to reach for his gun. Before he could get a grip on it with his one intact arm, Emily jumped in the air and landed on his back, knocking him to the ground. The force of the impact stifled his breathing.

He watched helplessly as she held him down with one massive paw. With her other paw on his gun, she snapped it in half. He turned his head and looked at the nub of his arm. To his horror the blood continued to gush out to the beat of his pulse. He could see the splintered remains of his bone and the shredded pieces of his skin.

At the same time, Natasha had backed the other guy up against a tree and lunged at his chest. The guy peed his pants and stepped aside just in time causing Natasha to hit the tree. She slammed into the tree hard enough to cause some of the loose limbs to fall out of the tree to the ground. A large chunk of bark broke free from the trunk of the tree. She whimpered from the hit, dropped back to the ground and lunged again at the man as he scrambled across the ground trying to get away.

He clawed at the dirt trying to pull himself away from her. To no avail, she grabbed him by the calf of his leg and ground her teeth into him. Blood splattered every where. She bit down harder and yanked her head up and away from his leg. A large chunk of the meat from his leg tore off into her mouth. The bone in his leg was now exposed. His pant leg was soaked, not only from him urinating on himself, but from the massive amount of blood that now pulsated out of his leg.

He screamed and called for help. Natasha spit out the chunk of meat she still held in her jaws and dug her long claws into his thighs, ripping through his jeans and into his tender flesh and drug him back toward the middle of the camp they had set up and stopped when she came up beside Bud where Emily still held him down.

Tears were streaming down both of their faces and blood continued to course out of them. The other man began begging, "Oh please. Don't kill us! Oh god help us!" Bud still hadn't gained back his breath yet and could only lay there sniveling. A dark red puddle of blood was forming below Bud's arm and under the other guy's leg. The air was filled with the smell of sweat, urine, and the sweet metallic aroma of blood. Natasha and Emily backed off the guys and stood off to the side of them allowing Thomas and Elliot to step in closer. They circled around and around the men, growling and gnashing their teeth as the men lay there helpless and begging, and praying.

Thomas was overcome with the sad images of poor little Tania lying helpless as she was being butchered. He recalled the look on the faces of her family as he handed them the packages, wrapped in plastic, of the remaining pieces of their daughter who had been brutally killed then sold at the butcher shop to be eaten by God knows who. Anger rose inside him so strong he began to tremble.

Clenching his teeth, he stopped right in front of the two men and glowered at them. His red eyes pierced through the men. He made up his mind to do something he had never done before. He changed back to his human form and kneeled down in front of them. The others were in shock but stood their ground.

Thomas still bared his teeth as he growled out to the men, "You think you are superior! You think humans rule and can do whatever they want to whomever they want! Arrogant bastards! That bison one of you killed over in Chilkat was part human. She was just a little girl and didn't deserve to die! Then you decided to carve her up, right there in the field, and leave her carcass to decompose. And to sell her to the butcher was just the icing on the cake! You don't deserve such mercy for what you've done, but you *will* die tonight. Oh yes. You will suffer before your last dying breath escapes your corpse!"

He stood back up and howled. The men watched, powerless to do anything, as Thomas changed back, right in front of them. With his head thrown back still howling, they could see his skin stretch as his bones grew and reshaped to that of a wolf. He fell forward on all fours and his knees bent backward to form his hind legs. His fingers clawed at the ground as they turned from human fingers to claws.

Thomas twisted his head back and forth as his neck stretched longer and thicker. His skull made sickening popping and cracking sounds as it reformed to a wolf's head. His ears grew to points and fur sprouted out of every pore in his skin. His nose stretched and his teeth grew to sharp menacing points. All during his transformation Thomas howled and growled, writhing in a grotesque dance.

It was the most horrifying thing they had ever witnessed. The two men were lying there in shock. They could not believe what they had just seen. Bud was speechless, but the other guy managed to mumble out something just before all four of the werewolves tore into them. "Please! It wasn't us! It was Tu . . . ." Before he could finish his words Thomas grabbed him by his head. His whole head fit inside his immense jaws.

He could feel the werewolf's tongue rubbing the back of his head as his teeth sunk in to his neck and held him there. He was still able to breathe and whimpered in excruciating pain. Elliot grabbed him by his legs. They pulled in opposite directions, whipping and yanking, trying to tear him in two. Natasha dashed over to help them out. She wrapped her mouth around his lower waist and bit clean through. He wailed out a gurgling screech as Thomas and Elliot held him suspended by his head and legs and gave one more tug and ripped him in half. Thomas then tossed his shredded body against a tree.

To his horrific surprise, the guy was still alive, barely. He was convulsing uncontrollably as his head bashed against the tree. His tongue protruded out of his mouth and nauseating gurgling noises escaped him along with a waterfall of dark oozing blood. There was one last hissing noise then his body stopped moving. With intense anger still pulsing through him, Elliot dropped his lower half there on the ground to get a better grip of a leg. He took it back in his jaws, flipped the torn and ragged extremities, and threw it up on a tree limb.

Natasha returned to Emily's side and started mauling Bud's chest. With her teeth clashing together she chewed through his ribs and sternum until she had reached his heart. Pausing only for a moment to watch the last beat of it, she plunged her incisors into it and ripped it from his chest cavity. Pools of blood coursed every where. Emily buried her teeth into his stomach. The taste of his blood excited her as all of her primal instincts suddenly took over. She masticated his flesh, digging in with not only her mouth but with her claws as well. A gnawing hunger and thirst consumed her every thought.

She had almost devoured his whole torso when Thomas came over to her side to calm her down. Unaware of whom he was momentarily, she lowered her head and flattened her ears, snarled and snapped at him while she still held on to a piece of Bud's meat, like a dog would do to protect his food from another dog. She finally recognized who he was and dropped the meat from her mouth and lowered her head in shame and turned to head back in the trees.

She had never felt such a primitive but alluring sensation in her life, yet she was embarrassed by how she reacted. Once she had gained control of her urges she looked back in time to see the other three rip the remaining parts of Bud to shreds. His head flew out of one of their mouths and rolled over to the edge of the tree where Emily stood. Although the look of terror in his dead eyes mortified her even more, she still couldn't shake the thrill of the taste of blood and flesh.

Once they had finished, they turned and headed back into the trees to get Emily and head toward Tania's house. No one said anything for a while. After several minutes had passed Thomas pulled back to where Emily slowly ran behind them and spoke to her. "Emily. It's alright. This was your first kill. It was to be expected that this would be how you react. As a young wolf it will take time before you can control the beast within you. We all had to go through it. It is a natural part of you. Cheer up."

He trotted off ahead back with the others. Half way there Emily heard someone calling her from the tree tops. She slowed to listen. She recognized the voice and told the others, "Go ahead. I'll catch up later. I just need some air. Need to be alone for a little while. I'll be fine." They hesitated, but understood. They sprinted off and were soon out of sight.

Emily was sure she recognized the voice, but remained on guard and in her werewolf form just in case she had to fight. Her hearing was extremely keen, but she could not hear any movement or smell anything. She cocked her head to listen for the first sign of anyone. Then out of the blue Shinu vaporized right in front of her. She lowered her hunches, sighed with relief and changed into her human form. Sighing, she said, "You scared the crap out of me. What are you doing here?" Shinu stood there calmly with his hands crossed behind his back. He looked at her and raised one eye brow, questioning, "The question is my dear, what are *you* doing here?" She became defensive and snarled, "None of your business! We had pack business to take care of. It's not nice to go creeping around spying on people!"

He smiled a sly smile at her and leaned closer to her and sniffed. He grinned and said, "It's kind of hard to miss the intoxicating scent of blood that now fills the air. My brothers first picked it up and wanted to come investigate. I recognized your scent and told them I would check. We were just heading out to hunt when it hit us like smacking into a brick wall of fresh plasma. Quite tempting. For them. I can restrain myself. I won't ask what you all were up to. Although I can guess. Probably the same thing I was going to eventually do myself. Except I wouldn't have made such a mess." He laughed at himself.

Emily was about to yell at him and plead the fifth, but decided she must look a mess. She was covered in blood. What better way to attract a vampire. She laughed at herself then slumped to the ground and began crying. Shinu quickly erased his grin and dropped down to the ground in front of Emily and held her while she wept. He rubbed her back and comforted her, "Its ok Em. The first kill is always the worst. Let it go. You did the right thing. Tania did not deserve that."

She sat there in his arms for a long time before she was able to control her sobs. She finally said, "Thank you. I needed that. Not only for tonight but for everything I've gone thru since before I was turned and after." Shinu helped her stand up and offered, "I have all night if you need to vent to someone. My brothers are long gone. I already fed this weekend anyway and I'm not hungry. So, if you want to go home and clean up and change, I'll meet up with you in a little while."

Emily chuckled. She hadn't noticed how bad she must look. "Ok. Guess I am a mess. Where you heading 'til then?" Once again he had a shifty, evil look on his face. He smiled a typical vampire grin when they're up to something and answered, "Well for one, I think I'll check out you guys' handy work." Emily felt both repulsed and intrigued. She shivered and said, "You are so . . ." Shinu finished, "Vampire? Yes. Yes I am. It's no shock. Violence is a part of me. I'm just curious as to what would happen to anyone that crossed you." Before she could come back at him, he vanished in a puff of smoke. She thought to herself, *The smoke was just for show. Smart ass.*

• •

Back at the house, Shahma had cooked lunch. I was once again starving. I had three bowls of her stew before I finally felt full. Jaye sat there watching me eat and smiling. I looked at him and asked, "What are you smiling at?" He laughed. "At you. You never eat. At least not like that. You are chowing!" I had to laugh too. I was kind of eating a lot for me. I said, "You're right. But in my defense. I have to use more energy shifting into each form than you do. So I have to replenish myself."

Shahma had been sitting there sipping her butter rum tea and watching us, listening. Smiling at us she said, "So, I take it you successfully shifted to other forms?" Jaye interjected for me. My mouth was still full. "Oh yeah grandma! You should have seen her. She makes it look so easy. And she doesn't have to stop to shift. She can shift as she's climbing, running, jumping. Let me tell you about jumping! I was beating her crossing the lake. She went in the lake a penguin but just as I passed her up, she jumps up out of the water, as a dolphin, and changes into a hawk. Mid-air! And almost beat me! I was impressed to say the least." She clapped her hands, "Wonderful! I knew you could do it. Did you win Skye?"

I almost choked on the piece of bread I was inhaling and coughed before I could answer. Jaye handed me a glass of water and pat me on my back. When I could catch my breath I answered, "I wish. Your grandson is extremely fast. Don't let him fool you. I had to use all I had just to keep up. He would have slaughtered me. I lost." I stuck out my lip. Play pouting. Then Jaye kissed me on my forehead, "It's ok. I think you'll look great in a formal gown Monday at school." Then he bent over, laughing so hard he had to hold his sides. I hit him in the back of his head with a spoon. It threw him off balance and he landed on the floor. I left him there and got up to clean up the dishes. He can be so rotten sometimes.

After we cleaned up the kitchen we headed to the living room. Shahma brought out another pot of tea and poured all our cups. She sat down in her chair and we sat on the couch. Jaye sat beside me on the couch. Shahma started the conversation, "I can see that you too have finally gotten back to where you were centuries ago. I have to tell you Skye. Jaye has been waiting patiently for years for you to return to yourself. Don't get me wrong. There have been other young women who have tried.

God knows they have driven me nuts. But, he only had one person in his heart, mind, soul. And he was not letting go of you. Many summers ago, after your mom had to take you away, he came here to spend the summer with me. I tried to get him to go have fun, but he wanted to stay here. You know all of these wood carvings and decorations throughout my house? He did it. He poured himself into it. When he wasn't out looking for you, he was here carving."

I couldn't help but be touched by that. Drying my eyes I looked at him. He was crying too. I touched his cheek and told him in his mind, *I love you so much. I'm glad you waited.* He leaned down and kissed me on top of my head. Shahma went on, "I could go on and on, but we have more important business to cover. We are all aware that something evil is going on right now. Something so vile and mysterious. I'm afraid it will get worse if we don't try and stop it now. You came around at the right time. Now, right before you were 'awakened' I had a vision."

She poured us more tea and went on with her story, "I was looking out upon the fields, the mountains, the forests. The clouds began to turn dark grey. The sky got darker and darker. Lightening flashed and in that flash of light an ominous black figure rose up out of the ground in the middle of a field. Trees withered, animals fell dead, birds dropped from the sky. He pointed toward another field and in another flash of lightening a pile of human corpses was momentarily illuminated. The darkness spread further, but was stopped by this blinding light. It was so bright, in my vision; I had to block my eyes for a moment. Standing in that light, was you." She paused again and took another drink before she went on.

She thought for a minute or two before she went on, "But the oddest thing was that you were not alone. It's not odd to say you were standing there surrounded by animals or humans. There was a majestic condor hovering right above you and multitudes of bird circling above the condor. And there was this presence in you. It spilled out of your chest and draped around you like a red silk blanket. But you were also flanked on both sides by shape-shifters, werewolves, witches, humans, and the oddest thing was, vampires!

My visions have never been wrong. It has never been heard of through out time that all these different creatures would ever be able to stand together and fight as one. Even the great leader I told you about from long ago was only able to unite the shape-shifters to stand and help him fight the demons of that time that were taking over. So, I meditated, prayed to the heavens and the elders of the past. I went on a sabbatical in the mountains. I read tea leaves, consulted with other Shamans, read bones. Every where I turned and everyone I talked to gave me the same answers. My vision was real."

We sat there again in silence for a little while, sipping our tea and thinking. Shahma finally went on, "It seems that in order to find out who or what this thing is and to conquer it, you have to unite all the creatures, alive or dead, to fight it together or we will be plunged into some sort of darkness no man has ever seen. I have a sickening feeling that this dark, vile entity that is here now, is only the beginning. It seems like a lot of me to ask you to try and bring these groups together. I'm sorry, my leader."

She looked sincerely sorry as she bowed her head to me, again. I hated to see her humbling herself to me like this. For so long I looked up to her. Now I am in a higher position then she is, but I still feel like I should bow to her. I knew she was just doing what was natural. I got up off the couch and kneeled down at her feet. I lifted up her head and kissed her forehead. I said, "Shahma. You have nothing to be sorry for. You didn't cause this. Besides, this means so many things make sense now to me."

I stood up and patted her on her shoulder, before I sat back down by Jaye. I explained, "Just in the past month or so I have acquired a variety of friends. It was like something inside me or around me woke up. You know Amber and I have been friends for centuries and just recently reunited. She is a witch. Jaye has always been there for me, the shape-shifter, and is introducing me to other shape-shifters. I finally reacquainted myself with the werewolf pack. Many of which remember me from long ago.

My best friend, for several years now, is human and her father is the mayor. He's been the mayor for years. So, he has many trusted friends in town and some of the surrounding towns. And, I guess the oddest ones from your vision, were vampires. And, you know, it's really strange because, I have always seen or sensed all immortals. I have also always been able to keep people out of my head unless I wanted them there. My friend, Shinu, can pop in my head whenever he wants to and vice versa. He said no ones able to pop in vampires minds unless they allow it either."

I had to pause. Just as I thought, there he was. Shinu asked, *You rang my dear?* I had to chuckle to myself. I asked Shahma to excuse me for a moment while I got rid of a pest. I headed for the kitchen and Jaye followed me. Jaye rolled his eyes and said, "Let me guess. The leech?" I rubbed his back as we leaned against the counter. "Yes. It's *Shinu*." I answered Shinu, *Not so much as called you, but was thinking about you.* Shinu snickered, *So the Sea Gull is not satisfying you? You need a big strong vampire. Hhm?* I was not about to justify his comments with an answer. We had too much to cover before Jaye and I had to head back. I simply said, *I'll explain things when we get back. I'm going to need your help.* I was just getting ready to tell him good bye when he interrupted me, *You might want to get back here soon. Do you know about Tania's death?*

Just the thought of it saddened me, again. Sadly I answered, *Yes. Unfortunately. I had a vision of it and of what ever the thing is that must be doing all the killings. What else has happened?* He hesitated to answer, then said, *There has been retaliation by some. The talk around the immortal circle is that humans are responsible and that someone needs to do something about it. I can't tell you who the some ones were. You will find out when you get back. Just hurry back.* He was gone before I could ask questions. And this time, he was blocking me from entering his mind.

I stomped my foot and Jaye bolted up straight and asked, worried, "What happened? I swear, if that parasite said anything to hurt you . . ." I calmed him down and said, "No. He's fine. There's just something going on there and I need to get back fast. He wouldn't tell me and he's blocking me from his mind. I just hate it when he cuts me off in the middle of a question."

We headed back in to the living room where Shahma was just finishing off her cup of tea by the window. I walked up to her and placed a hand on her shoulder. "I'm sorry I had to cut you off like that. That was Shinu I was talking to. He's my latest friend I was telling you about. The vampire. He says there's something going on there and I need to get back as soon as possible. He can pop in and out of my head when he wants to and vice versa. Which is odd because, he explained to me that normally no person, human or otherwise, is able to do that to vampires?"

She turned to face me. There was a strange look of concern on her face. She said, "That is odd in deed. Sorry I drifted off there a bit. Something is changing in my vision, but I can't quite decipher it. Any way. What is this vampire's full name?" I thought that was a curious question, but I answered, "Shinu Takai, son of Renji and Sue Lin Takai. Is there something wrong?" Now she looked stunned. She gasped and clutched at her throat. "Oh my! The Takai are a very ancient and very powerful sect of vampires. They date back before anything was recorded on their family. According to legend, their family has ruled all vampires throughout the Asian sects. As a matter of fact, it is said that they are the strongest of all vampires, second only to those in Italy. It is a good thing he is on your side. He is on *your* side, isn't he?"

I had to think about that. But, before I could answer, there he was again, *Boy, you really have a thing for me, don't you?* Then he was cracking up laughing, again. This time I spoke out loud, not noticing I was I said, "Ha ha. You have to stop doing that to me. You're going to make people think I'm losing it. Maybe I am. Wouldn't one go a little nuts with a vampire popping in and out of their mind at will?" I laughed this time. Although it was strange to have Shinu do this to me, in an odd way, it was also comforting knowing he was there when I needed him.

Oops. I thought before I thought about what I was saying. This was the ego boost he was waiting for. He said, *Aw. You do need me. Your turtle dove won't like that very much, will he? And, in answer to your question, I don't know why, yet, but I am drawn to you. There is this deep overwhelming necessity in me to help you in what ever way I can. You can tell your Shaman that I am bound to you. It's really quite endearing. It's almost like you and I were together in a past life. We'll chat soon, I hope?* I answered him yes in my mind and answered Shahma out loud, "Yes, he is on my side. He mentioned something about being bound to me. Do you know what he meant by that?"

She turned away from facing me and sat back down in her chair. I looked at Jaye. He looked just as puzzled as I was, but twitched a little when I said that. We sat back down on the couch. Shahma sighed, "Well. This is a true story not many speak of. Many, many centuries ago, when I was still a little girl, there was a beautiful young girl in our tribe that every warrior used to swoon over. She was the daughter of the chief.

Many men tried to win her over. Going on long hunts for rare and precious gems or the biggest and best meats to give her. Some worked to be the strongest and fought for her attention. Some strived to be the wisest. But none could woo her. She was not only beautiful, but she was very wise, very strong for a woman of that time, and she had a rare gift, not heard of in the women then. She was a shape-shifter. She could change into a hawk. She had sparkling, golden feathers and was the envy of several young women.

She would often disappear for days at a time and had her father worried. She told him not to worry, but on her last trip out of the village he decided to send his most trusted and stealthiest warrior out to follow her. He wanted to know where she was going. The warrior soon found her, many miles away. He was shocked at what he found out and returned as quickly as he could to bring the news to the chief. It turns out that the chiefs beautiful daughter had been sneaking off to visit a suitor. Not a suitor from another tribe, but a vampire. The chief was furious. He waited for his daughter to return and cornered her. He demanded to know where she'd been, hoping the warrior was wrong. She confessed that she had fallen in love with a vampire. Not just any vampire. Prince Shin Po Takai.

They had met by chance when she had injured her wing, and still in her hawk form, he mended it and placed her safely in a tree to rest. He returned each day, for four days, to check on her and to feed her. She stayed in her hawk form, afraid that he would kill her if he really knew who she was.

On the fifth day when he returned again to see if she was able to fly yet, she decided to reveal who she really was. He wasn't upset about being deceived, but more like relieved. He told her he had formed an uncanny attachment to her and was worried that he was developing feelings for a bird. They laughed and became good friends. They continued to meet and soon became fast friends. After a while, they began to fall in love.

The chief was angrier now. How dare a vile creature like a vampire seduce his daughter? It was not heard of. An Indian and a vampire. Vampires were there enemy. He demanded that she stay there in camp and he went out with his warriors to find and kill this vampire. Of course, she didn't listen and flew off to warn her love. She got there ahead of the warriors and her father.

Prince Takai and his warriors headed to face them. He had to let her father know how much he loved her. They all met and stood face to face, ready to fight, when the princess and Prince Takai confronted her father. Prince Takai told him the story of how they met and how he loved her enough to die fighting for her. The princess told her father she too was willing to die fighting for her love.

Reluctantly, the chief accepted this, warning them that it would be difficult for them to settle in the tribe. He would tell his people and they would have to except it because he was chief and they would obey. He wasn't sure if the medicine man and his family would agree to this either, but this was his one and only daughter's wish and he would grant it. They were soon married in a tribal ceremony in the village. Some of the tribes people could not and refused to accept their union and left. I remember the day they left there was a big up roaring. There was one Indian family and the medicine man and his family who tried to start a fight with Prince Takai and his warriors. Of course they lost the battle. The chief was outraged at such disobedience and banished them from the village.

Eventually the Prince and princess left the village to live with his family. She came to visit often. They also soon had children. The story goes on from there." Jaye had moved closer to me and was clutching my hand the whole time she told the story. He seemed tense during the story, but he looked at me and I felt he was just touched by it. There was a tear in one of his eyes. I kissed him on the cheek. He finally smiled. I was curious, so I asked, "Shahma. You never mentioned her name. What was it? The chief's daughter." She looked a little hesitant to answer me, but she answered, "Princess White Cloud Rainwater."

This time I gasped, "She was . . ." Shahma bowed her head again when she answered, "Yes my child. She was your great great grandmother." My head was spinning. The only thing that kept me grounded right then was my hand in Jaye's. I felt myself drifting back again toward another vision. I could see the village of old time. I could see the chief yelling at someone. But before I could get a clear picture, I felt Jaye shaking my shoulders and calling my name, "Skye? Skye are you alright?" I could see Shahma getting up and coming over to my side. I slowly came back to myself.

They both looked worried. Shahma handed me a cup of tea. Concerned she said, "Oh my child! You gave us both such a fright! This time you turned so pale. Your lips were blue as if you weren't breathing. We thought we were losing you." I shook my head to clear it. Then I said, "I'm ok. It was just the beginning of another vision. I couldn't see it all, or see it clearly. All I saw was an old tribal village and what I thought was the chief, yelling at someone before you guys brought me back."

Shahma shook her head, "My, my. You may have gone back to the time I was just telling you about. It may have been significant. There may have been some reason you went so far back. Maybe something to help with what's going on now. But, for some odd reason, this time you stopped breathing. That's not good. Not good at all. This means there is still some sort of block in your memories. None that your mom or grandma put there. No. No this is a very powerful block. One that could have only been put there by a very powerful witch or warlock. It's not safe for you to try and see that one again. Not without the right spell to break the lock. You may die trying to go back."

Jaye and I looked at each other in shock. He grabbed me and held me in his arms and pleaded, "Don't try again Skye. I can't lose you again." I felt so safe in his arms. I couldn't hurt him like that. Or myself. For the first time in a long time I really felt connected to someone passionately. I smiled, "I won't Jaye. Neither of you worry. I won't try again. We just have to figure out what's going on."

Shahma patted my hand, "Good. Now. It has all come down to this. There is something evil, dark, and vile that is causing all the problems around here. No one has any idea who or what it is. You have got to try and unite immortals and humans together to fight it. If something isn't done soon, I'm afraid this will be the end to things as we know it now. I'm sorry my child, but you are the only one who can do this. My visions never lie. It is in your hands now. Now I must warn you. Whatever this is that we are up against is very dominant and pretentious.

It may be right under your nose or someone close to you, or someone you thought was someone else. From my visions and what I've read in the paper lately, I deduce it is trying to first turn immortals against humans. From there, who knows? It seems that your friends, old and newly found, will be very powerful together. I will do what I can from here to find out more. I will be in touch with you. Both of you. You both need to get going." I hugged her again, not wanting to let her go. I sighed and said, "Shahma, you be careful." She chuckled, "Oh my sweet child. I will be fine here. This is hallowed ground. Anything of demonic descent cannot enter here."

• •

It was bitter sweet leaving Shahma. I could have stayed there much longer, but we both knew I had to get back home. For the first half hour of our drive back Jaye was silent. I think he was deep in thought. But, he worried me so I asked, "Jaye, are you alright? You've been so quiet." He finally smiled and rubbed my hand. He said, "I'm ok. Just a little worried about all of this. More so about you. I'd like to think that this will all pass and that things will be ok. We have so many years to catch up with and I don't want to lose you."

I unbuckled and scooted closer to him and laid my head on his shoulder. "You are not going to lose me. It will be ok. We do have years to make up for." I kissed his cheek and he seemed to relax a little bit. He then got one of his sneaky looks on his face and I asked,

"What are you thinking about?" He laughed and put his arm around me pulling me closer, "Well, first off, what are *you* going to tell Stacey? You know she's been after me for a long time now. And how do you think the leech is going to react to us being together? I think he has a thing for you." I had to chuckle, "*We* can tell Stacey together. We can tell her it just happened, out of nowhere. That neither of us ever thought about it, but it just happened. As far as *Shinu*, he doesn't have a thing for me. I'd know if he did."

We drove on. We talked and laughed, remembered the past and cried, all the way back home. He dropped me off, kissed me good night and headed back to his house. I had a lot to discuss with mom and grandma before I turned in to try and get some sleep. I had a feeling I wouldn't get much sleep tonight. What Jaye had said about Shinu replayed over and over in my mind too. I wondered.

CHAPTER 12

AND SO, IT BEGINS . . .

Monday morning the Sheriff's office was a buzz. Sheriff John Makepeace was questioning his men. The deputies had been doing their usual door to door check on the town elderly and had been concerned about Lester. According to the local bar tender, Lester hadn't been in to the bar in several days. Everyone in town knew he was at the bar at least once a day. When they got to Lester's house he didn't answer and there was a foul smell coming from inside. Needless to say, when they went in they found pieces of Lester throughout the kitchen. One of his men's faces was still green from being sick by what they'd seen. "Sheriff, it was awful! Poor guy didn't deserve that. Don't know what sort of man would do something like that."

Before they could finish giving him the details, Ronny came running in the door. "Sheriff Makepeace! Some scoundrel's done gone and broke in my shop. Busted the back lock clean in!" John rubbed his face and sounded very frustrated, "Anything gone Ronny?" Ronny caught his breath, "Yeah. My most expensive cuts of meat. Bison, filet mignon, a couple of rib-eye. They even stole my change from under the register for today's sales!"

Before John could answer either his men or Ronny the phone rang. He reluctantly answered, "Sheriff's office." He finished his conversation on the phone and slammed the receiver down. He turned back to Ronny and said, "Ronny, Steve'll take your statement. Meet him over at your shop. Ned, you and Brad come with me." They headed out the door and all of them got in John's car. John started the car and headed out to the outskirts of town before he told them what was going on. He explained, "That was Bud's wife on the phone. She said Bud and Francis never called or came home from hunting this weekend. They always go out for four days and return on Sunday night. She said the last place they said they were going hunting was at Anan Creek."

The rest of the ride was silent. None of the men knew what they were in for. Especially after what they had discovered at Lester's house. Once they made it as far as they could drive, they had to get out and walk the rest of the way. It was quite a distance from the road. They finally reached the woods and spread out to cover more ground. After about thirty minutes, John found the delivery truck sitting in a clearing. It wasn't running. He thought to himself, *The truck should be running. That's their meat freezer.* He pulled out his gun and slowly circled around the truck. He squatted down and ducked behind a tree when he saw heaps of something in another clearing and several crows circling over the heaps.

With gun in hand, ready to fire, he slowly crept from tree to tree until he got closer. Before he could make out what the heaps were he could smell the noxious odor of rotting flesh wafting toward him. He moved closer and to his horror the grisly scene played out in his mind. There were decomposing limbs strewn out all over the clearing. Lying by his foot was Bud's head. The eyes were still bugged out as if the last thing he'd seen terrified him to death.

A big black bug crawled out the corner of his mouth and various sizes of earth worms squirmed in and out of the opening of his neck. Dried blood was caked on his face. John walked on and soon found the top half of Francis' body. It had been ripped off and flung against a tree leaving it propped there as if it was just sitting down to rest. Worms oozed out of the bottom of his torso and multiple bugs were eating the innards that spilled out of him. His face was in the same contorted shocked look as Bud's. There were large bite marks surrounding his neck and dried blood was plastered in those wounds. His arms were suspended in an upward position as if he was trying to get whatever had grabbed his head, off.

John finally managed not to vomit long enough to call his men over to where he was. Looking around he saw an arm and a leg thrown here, a foot lying there. He looked up to see if his men were coming and noticed the bottom half of Francis was dangling from a low hanging tree limb. Bud's and Francis' shot guns were still lying on the ground by a log that they must have been sitting on when they were attacked. His men finally found him. Before he could speak, Ned turned and ran in the trees. Soon he was heaving, vomiting violently. Brad spoke first, "My God! What the hell happened here?"

John was shaking his head. He still wasn't sure he could open his mouth without vomiting himself. He covered his mouth and steadied himself and answered, "Looks to me like some wild animals got to them. But they had to be big in order to do this much damage. It had to happen quickly. They didn't even have time to grab their guns." Ned came back over to join them. He was pale green and shaking all over. Trembling he said, "I put in a call for the county coroner. Told them where to find us. Couldn't tell them what we found." John shook his head in disbelief and said, "Don't know if we need a coroner or animal control. Better put in a call for them too. Hate to leave you boys here, but as soon as one of them gets here I have to go and let Bud and Francis' wife know."

As soon as the other units arrived John nodded to his men and headed back to his car. What he had to do next was going to be the hardest thing he ever had to do in his twenty years as a Sheriff in this town. There had been wild animal attacks in the past, but every one of those victims survived. They may have been maimed, but they lived to tell about it or warn others where not to tread. But, never, had there been any deaths like this. Today was going to be a hard day. He hoped it would be the only hard day like this he had to face.

••

I didn't sleep well at all last night. I was up late with my mom and grandma telling them about everything from our trip. They were just as surprised as I was about the news of who Shinu was. They were ecstatic about me and Jaye and were worried about the vision Shahma had. They were saddened about Tania and feared what may happen next. Needless to say, we were up way too late. I also tossed and turned the rest of the night from dreams and visions. I still managed to roll out of bed in time to get ready for school. I was dressed and heading down the steps when I remembered the bet Jaye and I had. I cried out, "Dang it!" Mom called up, "Are you alright?" I answered sadly, "Yeah. I just remembered I have to change. I put on the wrong thing."

Back up the stairs I headed. Looking in my closet I couldn't find my dress I had bought for prom one day. Just as I was about to give up, happily, I found it. Mom had neatly covered it in a plastic bag and placed it at the back of my closet. "Dang it!" Well since I had to honor our bet I went all out. I had time to do my hair up in a fancy bun and perfect my makeup. I even pulled out my red pumps to match my red satin prom gown. The gown was low cut in the front; not too low; it had a string of ivory beads that trailed from my right shoulder, down around my waist and off to the left side of my gown, all the way down to the bottom. The gown was floor length and had a short train.

I packed a change of clothes in my back pack; jeans and a sweater and my sneakers. As I went downstairs my grandma was just leaving out the living room heading to the kitchen when she spotted me. I was hoping I could get out the door before either of them saw me. She took a double take and began hysterically laughing, "Either today is a special dress up day or you lost a bet." I lowered my head in shame and headed to the kitchen. Sorrowfully I said, "I lost a bet to Jaye." When I got in the kitchen mom was facing the oven making breakfast. She started talking before she turned around, "So, what will you have today? The usual toast and orange juice or are you going to . . ." When she turned she almost dropped the skillet she was holding. She didn't crack up laughing like grandma did, but she covered her mouth and laughed, none the less. She said, "Oh my poor baby girl. You lost a bet. You look so beautiful though. I should get my camera."

I waved my hands frantically. "No way mom! Please wait until actual prom night. Yes, I lost to Jaye. Today is going to be horrible!" She finally controlled her laughing, grandma too, and handed me a plate of eggs and bacon. She calmed down and said, "Well, at least you are honoring your bet. That says a lot for you. I think Jaye will be shocked and amazed." I shoveled my food down, still hungry from this weekend's excursion, and darted out the door before mom could sneak up on me with a camera.

It wasn't easy getting in my car in this get up, but I did it. I made it to school and was afraid to get out the car. I looked around and, as usual, there was Stacey, waving for me to come over. I was debating on whether or not to just turn around and go home when Jaye walked over to my car and opened the door. I turned as red as my gown when I looked up at him.

He was smiling, not a sneaky smile, but a wow smile. I could have sworn he was looking down my dress, but his expression begged to differ. "You look gorgeous! I almost don't want you to come in looking like that. Guys are going to drool all day. But, a bet is a bet. I can't believe you stuck to it. He leaned in and gave me a kiss on the cheek and helped me out of the car. I started to grab my back pack, but he took it for me.

He held my arm and escorted me up to the school. Of course, everyone was staring, even the teachers. It was embarrassing. The only thing that helped me keep my composure was Jaye holding on to my arm. It felt good. As we got closer to Stacey she ran up to us, overly excited and blurted out, "Oh my God! Why are you so dressed up? And, hi Jaye. What's up with this?" I guess there was no better time than the present to break the news to her.

We both opened our mouth to speak and ended up saying the same thing at the same time. "We're dating." We looked at each other and laughed. Stacey stood there with her mouth open before she said, "Oh my God! Well, if I can't have you then no better person than my best friend. I am so happy for you!" She hugged us both. "But, tell me what this is all about." She motioned toward my dress. I answered this time, "Jaye and I hung out this weekend. I told him I was a pretty fast runner. He challenged me. The bet was that the loser had to wear a formal outfit to school on Monday. And since Jaye is not in a tux . . ."

That, made her laugh even harder. She said, "You actually thought you could outrun Jaye? The all-star quarter back?" In my defense, Jaye spoke up, "Hey. She did give me a run for my money." Jaye walked us on up to the doors while Stacey gave us the third degree. He kissed me on my hand, "Ladies. I have to go that way. I'll see you at lunch?" I nodded yes and said later.

Stacey followed me to my locker still asking me question after question. She said, "I am so shocked! That is so cool though. I told you if he wasn't interested in me, even though I've thrown myself at him for years, that he had to have it bad for someone. I'm just glad it's you and not someone that will treat him like crap. Oh! I can't wait to tell everyone. See ya at lunch." She kissed me on my cheek and ran off down the hall.

I stood there for a while shaking my head and smiling, before I finally put my back pack in my locker, closed it and turned to head for class. I turned around and who would be standing there to interrogate me? Shinu. He had a big grin on his face as he said, "Well, well. This is a pleasant surprise. You look stunning!" I could swear he was licking his lips and yes, he was looking down my gown. Of course, I blushed. "Hello Shinu." He was so vampire right now I'm surprised no one else noticed.

He smiled, very seductively, before he took my hand and kissed it, "Kirai onnanohito. To what do I owe this amazing transformation?" I smiled, sighed, and explained to him about mine and Jaye's race and bet. At least I could explain the whole story to him, unlike with Stacey. He grabbed my arm and led me down the hall. Quietly he said, "So. You are what we call a shifter. I only recall one other. He was legendary leader from long ago."

I was surprised he had heard of him too, like Shahma. I asked, "You know about him too? Shahma told us about him this weekend." He continued, "Oh yes. As a matter of fact, I met him once. He was a very noble and honorable man. Very powerful. You are an extraordinary person. Sorry you lost the bet though. It would have been fun to pick on Jaye today. Being that he would have to wear a tuxedo I would have delighted in referring to him as a penguin in a penguin suit."

He cracked himself up with that one. Then he went on, "But to hear that you and bird boy are a couple somewhat saddens me. I guess you and I aren't meant to be." Again, there was that sneaky vampire look. So, I had to pick back, "Oh my love. If it wasn't for him, I would definitely be after you." We both laughed.

We had made it to our classroom door with everyone staring at us, or just me. I took a deep breath and paused at the door. Shinu had gone in and looked back at me, "Are you coming in?" I was so embarrassed, but managed a smile before I went on in. Mr. Johnson gawked and exclaimed, "Miss Rainwater. Either you have your days and times mixed up or this is some sort of juvenile bet. Do not distract my class or I will have to ask you to leave. Take your seat."

I sat down, not easily, and tried to make it through the class. It didn't help any with Shinu making snide comments all through class. At one point he said, *Your neck looks so appetizing from back here. So, exposed, so tasty.* Or my most favorite one, *You do look so delectable today. You sure the flamingo can make you happy?* I had to laugh at that one. This of course interrupted Mr. Johnson. He stared at me and inquired, "Is there something funny about my lecture today Miss Rainwater?" I was once again bright red. "No. Sorry Mr. Johnson." To Shinu I said, *You are going to get me thrown out of here. You are so flirting with danger.` Literally.* I had to smile at my own pun. He came back with, *Good one. I like a girl that's feisty.* I stifled my laugh this time. Fortunately class was soon over. Now I just had to make it through the rest of the day.

• •

By the time lunch rolled around I had been stared at, kids had whispered, and the guys gave me wolf calls. Many of them, literally. Some girls just rolled their eyes and made sarcastic remarks under their breath, but I didn't die of embarrassment. I was so glad to see Jaye. He was standing at the doors of the lunch room waiting for me. He had already got me a tray of food and found a table at the back of the cafeteria.

He kissed me and then pulled out my chair for me. He smiled and said, "So, I guess everyone knows about us now?" I smiled, "As a matter of fact, we are. Stacey made it around to a lot of people with the announcement. Cheer leaders sure can gossip. How has your day been?" Before he could answer, Shinu meandered over to our table. With a grin he said, "You two have room for anyone else? Or is this a couple's only domain?"

Jaye looked at Shinu then at me. I said, "I told him this morning. About this bet and us." Jaye smiled. His was somewhat devious. Messing with Shinu now he asked, "So you do realize that she is now off the market right, blood bank?" Shinu smirked, "Were you a little worried about me pelican boy? Don't let me ruffle your feathers. Besides, I may have another appetizer now." He pulled out a chair and sat down. All I could do was shake my head.

We went on to talk about things that happened over the weekend and what Shahma had told us about getting mortals and immortals to

146

work together. After a moment of silence Shinu spoke first, "Well my dear. This is going to be a challenge. The natives are restless and out for blood. Human blood. We have to do something quick. You weren't the only ones who had a little excitement this weekend." Before he could go on Amber came over to the table with Dave in tow. She looked at me and said, "I'm so glad you're back! I missed you." She leaned down and hugged me. "So, you lost a bet to Jaye. You look gorgeous though. Love the dress. May we sit down?"

I motioned for them to go ahead and sit down. I was now sitting between Jaye and Shinu. Amber was sitting on Jaye's side and Dave beside her. Looking at us sitting here, things just seemed to be coming together. I started to fill Amber and Dave in on what we had already told Shinu but she cut me off. "Ok. I don't mean to sound suspicious or anything, but I have to ask. Why is Shinu hanging out with you now?" She looked at Shinu and said, "No offense."

He didn't seem at all disturbed about it. In fact, he was still being facetious. He answered before I could, "Haven't you heard? Skye has taken a fancy to me and is debating on flitting about with birds or gallivanting with the more handsome and debonair undead. I personally think she should go for the latter." Jaye held his stomach and pretended to die laughing. "Oh you are so funny. I thought you mentioned something about another appetizer?"

Before Shinu could retaliate, another person walked up to join us at the table. Emily looked a little reserved, but she managed to speak as she was turning bright red. "Hey guys. I don't mean to intrude, but can I sit with you?" We all looked at her, surprised but pleased she came over. Shinu answered for us, "As I had previously mentioned an appetizer . . . Please. There's a seat by me, my darling." Emily turned an even brighter shade of red and timidly sat down by Shinu, who had got up to pull the chair out for her. She said, "Thank you. So, what's up?"

This time maybe I'd get a chance to briefly cover the weekend again. By the time I had finished my spiel, it was almost time for the bell to ring. I had to quickly throw in, "Are there any practices or club meetings or family business for any of you this evening?" They all looked at each other and one by one said no. I went on, "Good. We need to talk more and the sooner the better. Can we all meet at my place? Say, 5:00 p.m.? And don't worry about eating. My mom and grandma will cook enough stuff to eat to feed an army and will be hurt if you guys don't eat. Are we agreed?"

They all nodded yes. As the bell rang and everyone took off to their respective classes I added in, "Oh. Please don't be mad or afraid. I'm inviting Stacey too." Before they could protest, I shot out the doors and down the hall, which wasn't easy with five inch heels on. I looked back in time to see Shinu walking beside Emily down the hall and turn and wink at me.

. . . .

The rest of the day dragged by, as did I, now that I had traipsed around all day in a formal gown and five inch heels. Jaye will pay for this later. I had already texted Stacey and told her I really needed to meet with her at my house right after school and to plan on being there for several hours. She texted back, *Super!*, and that she was looking forward to spending some time with me. I was a little nervous about talking to her about everything, but it had to be done. I had to get humans on my side and who better to begin with than my best friend. All I could hope for was that she wouldn't run from the house screaming and never talk to me again.

On the way home I called mom and told her about our meeting. I told her there would be approximately six hungry teenagers invading our house at five and she was excited. She and grandma loved to entertain guests. I also let them know about my plans to tell Stacey everything. They were prepared for the worst.

By the time I pulled up our gravel drive Stacey's car was already there. She wasn't in it. That would mean she had to be inside. She had been to my house many times, so it shouldn't have surprised me that she would go on in. I guess it just threw me off due to my new found memories. Things just had more profound meaning to them now. I had to tell myself it would be alright. Just stay calm. It was going to work out fine. Even though I kept telling myself that, I just couldn't convince myself it was true.

I pulled on up and sat in my car for a moment before I got out. Taking a deep breath I walked in the front door. They weren't in the living room so they had to be in the kitchen. And, just as I expected, the smell of various dishes wafted from the kitchen. They had already started. I had little less then two hours to talk to Stacey, so I'd better get this going. Entering the kitchen the first person I saw was grandma. She was sitting at the table and Stacey was sitting beside her arranging cheese and crackers on a dish.

Mom was at the stove cooking. She turned to greet me with a big smile, "Hi sweetie! We were just telling Stacey a little history of the ancient tribes that used to live here. Surprisingly Stacey already knows a lot of the history of this town." Leave it to the two of them to help me break the ice to Stacey.

I loved them so much. But, I can't get all mushy right now. I don't have time. So I walked over to the table and snatched a cracker before grandma could tap my hand. She shook her head, "These are for the guests young lady." She gave me one of her big, loving smiles and pulled me down to plant a big, wet kiss on my cheek. I rolled my eyes when Stacey looked at me and laughed. "She did the same thing to me. So I figured I could at least help for now and eat later." Stacey said with a smile. We laughed. "Ok grandma. I have to steal Stacey from you now. Let's go to my room." Stacey thanked them both again for having her over and we trotted up the stairs.

When we got in the room Stacey jumped on my bed and made herself comfortable like she had done many times over the years. I stood near the door and began pacing, wondering how I would begin the conversation. Stacey watched me pace for a few minutes then stopped me, "Ok. Stop pacing. What's up? You look a little worried about something. Oh. This isn't about Jaye is it? Because you don't have to worry about me. I'm really happy for you guys. Besides. I was only obsessed with him all these years because he's the high school quarter back and I'm the head cheerleader. You know the old stigmata that the head cheerleader always dates the quarter back. I think you two will be great together. And besides that, I have found someone else to obsess over. Although I don't think he notices me. He's on the football team. A real lunk head, but cute."

Stacey can really talk. And if I don't cut her off she will go on like this for an hour. So I cut in, "This isn't about Jaye. And I really don't know where to begin with this. I don't want to scare you or lose you as a friend. But, I really need your help and the only way to find out if you can or will help me is to just tell you the truth." Stacey sat up straight and gave me a questioning look, "Skye. You know I'm your best friend and I will do whatever I can to help you. What is it?"

I took another deep breath and began. "You have to first promise me you will have an open mind. And if you don't want anything to do with me or what I'm about to tell you, you have to promise to never tell anyone." She promised so I went on. I guess the best way to begin is to see how open minded she was. "Do you believe in ghosts, witches, vampires, etc.?" She sat quiet for a moment before she answered me. I was really getting worried now. The silence seemed to last forever. Then she answered hesitantly, "You have to promise not to tell anyone. Promise?" I nodded yes and she went on. "All my life I have fantasized about meeting a vampire or being a witch. Hidden in the back of my closet are boxes and boxes of books on them. Some are science fiction stories and some are non-fiction. My mom says I'm obsessed with them. She used to tell me stories of how she could have sworn that she came in contact with vampires or witches or even werewolves ever since we moved here. I just figured she was trying to make me feel better about my out-of-this-world interest. Why?"

I was so relieved to hear her confession. I let out the breath I had been holding ever since we came in my room. So, I just blurted everything out. "Well you aren't strange. And it appears your mom was right. In this town there are more then just humans. Everyone sees them as human, but we are not." She cut me off. "You said *we* are not. Are you including yourself in the we?" I nodded yes.

She gasped and her mouth hung open. I continued. "I have always been what the tribe's people call a seer. I can see the other immortals around me and I have a sixth sense. I have visions. Always have. I'm so glad I don't have to explain terminology to you. In this town there are various shape-shifters. There are also witches and warlocks and vampires and werewolves. We keep it hidden well huh?" She bobbed her head up and down in agreement and her mouth remained open.

I sighed and continued to explain. "Jaye and I took a trip to see his grandmother, a Shaman, out of town this weekend. I found out I was more then just a seer. The Shaman told me I was what the Indians call a Shoo-atee, or one who can change into many animals. I can shape-shift into whatever animal I want. It turns out that I have a very old and rare power and that I am, for all intents and purposes, all immortals leader."

I paused again and sat down by Stacey. She was looking kind of pale now and her mouth was still hanging open. I gently closed her mouth and rubbed her back. "Breath Stacey. Like I said. If you aren't up for this or don't believe then you're off the hook." Stacey was finally able to look at me and the color slowly came back in her face.

She turned and looked at me, and then she punched me hard on my arm. I was ready for her to run screaming when she said, "I cannot believe you have kept this from me all these years! I knew there was something odd about you. That's why I was attracted to you as a friend. Because you are what I read about. And I didn't know it. You are so wrong! How could you not tell me, your best friend? If I wasn't a proper lady I would slug you."

With that, she hugged me, tight and said, "Of course I'll help you. Tell me what I can do, oh great leader." She laughed. I went on to tell her about what was going on around here and about the unknown evil thing we were going to have to face. "So where you fit in is I need a liaison with the other humans in town. I know not all of them, but I need as many as possible to help us fight this thing. We'll not only be saving our town, but possibly others. We don't know how far it's willing to go. And, we have to some how keep this in our town among our people. Human and immortal.

We can't afford to let the news of immortals living here among humans get out. We know that Skagway and Juneau have immortals living there too, but the humans are unaware of them. This has to stay our secret." She was so enthusiastic. "Count me in! I'm your girl. I know I can get my dad and mom to help. And I've overheard Sheriff Makepeace talking to my parents about his suspicions. Not in a bad way either. More like curiosity. Somewhat like me."

I was excited now. This did not go the way I thought it would and I was so glad about that. "Ok. Good. Now the others will be here in about thirty minutes. You know them from school so you'll get to know their true identity. They are somewhat leery, which is to be expected, so don't be offended if some of them aren't so receptive. I can warn you about one in particular. Emily Silverstein. She's a werewolf."

Stacey seemed even more excited now. "Oh cool! Is she an older one or a newly changed one?" That shocked me. I guess she has studied books on immortals. I answered, "A new one." I didn't divulge more than that. I wanted to see where she went with this. She went on. "Ah. I see. She's very testy then. Quick to anger and quick to change. Very protective of those she loves. Can you tell me who else is coming?" So I went on, "Shinu." She giggled and said, "You mean Einstein? So many girls drool over him. Let me guess, he's a vampire." I laughed and said, "You got it!" Then she asked, "What's his last name?" I said, "Takai."

Really excited now Stacey bubbled, "Oh my God! He's from a very old and very powerful family. I read some science fiction and some non-fiction on his family." I was shocked and curious, "Ok. Let's see who else you can figure out. Amber." She thought for a moment and answered, "I'd have to say a witch. But, I couldn't guess from what coven until I talked to her a bit. Betcha I could figure that one out."

Hmm. She was good at this, so I said, "Jaye." I could tell she had to really think this time. Finally she said, "I can't guess his. I know there's something about him though. Always have. He's fast on the field. He basically flies across the field. Let me guess. Some sort of shape-shifter?"

Again she amazed me. "You got it again! I am shocked. He's a crow." She fell over sideways on my bed laughing. "Oh my God! I have seen a crow somewhere around you for years now. I just assumed you were odd so why not. I would have never guessed that it was Jaye all this time. That explains a lot." I had to laugh at that one. "Well we better get downstairs and see if mom needs help."

I stood up to go out the room when she grabbed my arm and pulled me back in the room. Surprised I asked, "What is it?" She looked a little embarrassed, but she asked me, "I'm sorry. I didn't mean to grab you like that. But, can I ask you a favor? Please?" I said, "Sure. Anything." She jumped up and down clapping her hands like a little girl. "Good! Would you change into something for me, here? That way I can see and won't be so shocked if the others do it too. Besides, I am so curious to see it." Once again she made me crack up laughing at her. "Ok. I'll do something small and simple."

She sat back down on my bed and I backed up closer to my closet. I closed my eyes and thought of my falcon. I opened my eyes and everything around me shimmered. I could feel my body shrinking. My arms got shorter and I could feel my fingers grow longer and stretch out at my sides. My legs shrunk and my knees bent backward as my feet and toes formed talons. I shivered and could feel my skin sprouting feathers. My nose and mouth became one and curved down into a beak. My eyes shrank and my vision became extremely keen.

I spotted a chipmunk in a tree several yards from my window. Guess I was a little hungry. I stretched my body and let out a cry. Stacey jumped a little when I did that. Once again, her mouth was hanging open. She stood up and walked over to me. Before she got up she grabbed a sweat shirt I had lying on the bed and wrapped her arm. She extended her arm out to allow me to lite on it.

I flapped my wings and flew up to her then gently landed on her arm. She had the biggest grin on her face I had ever seen. She said, "Sweet! Can I carry you downstairs?" There was a little more time before the others got there so I bobbed my head up and down as close to nodding yes as I could.

She must have understood because she said ok and opened the door and headed downstairs. On the way down she chatted on and on about what she had read about immortals. Most of what she had read was true, some of it was so far fetched it had to be from one of her science fiction books. I'd have to remember to tell her that when I changed back. She went in the kitchen. Mom was setting the table up buffet style.

She didn't even look up when she said, "Oh good. I was hoping it would go well. I knew Stacey had an open mind." Stacey smiled and sat down with me still on her arm. She enthusiastically chirped, "Open mind doesn't quite cover it all. Long story short I told Skye I have always believed in things that are odd or strange to most. I always dreamed that it was true about immortals. Dream come true!"

Grandma stood up and came over to where Stacey sat and rubbed my head and gave Stacey a kiss on her head. "You are a good friend to my granddaughter. Watch out for her for me. And, I hope you have a little idea of what you're getting yourself into. After the meeting tonight I want you to stick around for a minute. I'll have something for you." She looked at me questioning, but answered, "Ok Grandma Rainwater."

Mom looked up from her work and cocked her head sideways listening, before she said, "The others are heading up the road. You may want to get changed back Skye." I raised my wings and took off back upstairs. By the time I had morphed back I could hear two cars turn on to our drive. I made it downstairs just as there was a knock on the door.

I yelled out to the kitchen, "Got it.", and opened the door. Amber, Dave, and Emily were the first to arrive. Behind them Shinu and Jaye were walking side by side playfully pushing each other back and forth. Jaye pushed him one more time and ran up to the door, grabbed me, and kissed me. I closed my eyes and melted into his arms.

When I opened my eyes again Shinu was standing behind Jaye making kissy faces. I laughed and rolled my eyes at him. "Come on in Shinu, you Do Do bird." Shinu cackled, "I think you just finished kissing the true Do Do bird." Jaye retaliated, "What's wrong mosquito? Jealous?" There was that teasing smirk again. "Of course not. I already told you I had my own delectable morsel." Just then Emily called out from behind Amber, "Hey! What did I tell you about referring to me as if I was a gourmet meal?"

Everyone, including my mom and grandma, turned to look at Emily. She's usually so reserved. No one expected her to be the one Shinu was interested in. And among immortals everyone knew vampires and werewolves usually didn't get along so well. So it was a shock on both levels. A good shock though. Emily shrunk back behind Amber and said, "Oops. Sorry guys."

Shinu came on in and walked over behind Amber to retrieve the poor cowering Emily. "There is no need to apologize. If you all must know, we started talking this weekend." Everyone congratulated them. That helped Emily feel a little better. Stacey was standing in the kitchen door the whole time just waiting for me to say something. As I walked over to Stacey, the tension in the room engulfed me. It was as if I were trying to breathe through a blanket of searing heat.

Everyone was looking at me, imploring with their eyes, whether I knew what I was doing or not. I could tell Shinu was ready for any opposition from Stacey or anyone who might be hiding and ready to attack. Emily looked like her ears had flattened to the side of her head, her nostrils were flaring, and I could have sworn I heard her growling really low. The others just seemed prepared to except whatever was to come.

I sighed and addressed them first. "You can all relax. I talked to Stacey hours before you got here. And as odd as it may seem, she fully believes in anything odd, unusual, weird, different, alien, and immortal. As a matter of fact, she is quite the scholar on each type of immortal. I was shocked myself. Oddly enough, after I talked to her and explained things to her, she was able to tell me what each of you are, except Jaye and Dave. I didn't ask her about you Dave. I even shifted into my falcon form in front of her."

My mom and grandma could feel that they were still not sure about accepting Stacey so grandma spoke up. "Stacey is very extraordinary. My daughter and I have known this for quite some time now. Sorry Skye. We couldn't tell you. You had to find out for yourself. I had a vision the first time I met Stacey. It wasn't quite clear back then, but as time went on, it made sense. Stacey, although not immortal, is one of us." The tension subsided and everyone began to smile now.

It was like the whole house let out a breath it had been holding. Stacey waved at them and said, "Hi. No need to worry about me. I'm a closet nerd when it comes to this stuff. Literally. I have boxes and boxes of books on every immortal known to man." I had to cut her off. Stacey would go on for hours. "Ok. If everyone is hungry, mom and grandma have prepared a buffet of various foods. You all have to eat something or you'll hurt their feelings. Shinu, you're excused from eating, of course."

I was glad to see each of them talk to Stacey while we were eating. Everyone sat around the living room. Even mom and grandma joined them. I stood back and ate while I leaned against the doorway. I needed a brief moment to observe and think things out. I think Jaye picked up on it. He remained in the living room picking at Shinu and chatting with Stacey.

Stacey seemed to be in heaven. I could understand how she felt. For her to read about and admire those of the unknown for years and finally get to be with them would compare to a person getting to meet a famous movie star they had always dreamed of.

These were my people. I had to come up with a plan and lead them in a battle I was not sure we could even win. They would all depend on me and rely on my judgment, not just in this battle, but in other aspects of their lives as well. I now have to explain to them that I was chosen as the leader of all immortals. Not only those that live here, but others as well. The more I stood and watched, the more clearly things came to me. At first I thought this was a strange pairing. How did all of them fit together? Then slowly everything came together like a puzzle and Stacey was that last piece I needed to see, to know what must be done. It was so clear now.

CHAPTER 13

THE ARRANGEMENT...

Later that evening at the sheriff's office, John was sitting at his desk looking at his computer trying to figure out what was going on in his town. He had read and reread the report from his deputies about what they had found up at Lester's place. The report said they had found Lester lying on the floor in his kitchen. There was a bottle of whisky on the table, partly empty, and he was crumpled up in a heap there on the floor. They also mentioned that they were not coroners but that it appeared every bone in his body had been broken. Then there was the ghastly scene over in the hunting grounds. He was getting a headache from thinking so hard.

One of the deputies, Brad, had been evaluating the two cases also. He got up from his desk and got a cup of coffee and walked back over to the sheriff's door. "Sheriff. I been thinking about all the cases that came in today. The mess up at the hunting grounds could be animal attacks. The break in at Ronny's could have been some drifter looking for food and money. Although he had to of had an expensive taste in food and a strong arm to just pound out the lock like that.

Now about Lester's. I don't know what kind of man nor beast could do anything like that. There was no sign of a break in either. So, if it was a who, then Lester had to of let them in. Guess we just have to wait for the forensics' report and the coroner's report before we can go jumping to conclusions."

John scratched his head and stood up from his desk. Walking past Brad he patted his shoulder and headed for the coffee pot. "I know. It's got me baffled too. It's been a long day. You should head on home. Keep your phone on though in case I need you. I'm going to hang around here a little while longer before I take off." Brad gave him a yes sir and headed out the door. John took an aspirin and went back in his office and faced the computer screen again. He had requested that the coroner and forensics department get back to him through email as soon as they had any kind of information and was hoping it had come in already. It had been ten hours since the investigation began. Being that it was now 5:00 p.m. they probably had already called it a night and it would be morning before he heard anything.

John needed an aspirin and someone to talk to. Whenever he needed to confer with someone or needed an outside opinion to help him pull cases together he always went to Mayor William Ritennour. They had become fast friends when he and his family moved there from the states. Once William took the position as mayor, John took it upon himself to get to know him very well. He wanted to make sure the person running his town was a good and upright guy.

It turned out that the more he visited him or went on fishing trips with him, the more they noticed they had a lot in common. Even as far as belief in the unexplained or supernatural. So when those cases came in this morning and he saw what had happened at the hunting grounds, his mind didn't go to a human as being responsible, but an animal. And not only any animal, a supernatural animal.

John headed to the front of the office where Maribelle was still manning the phones and looking out for anything suspicious. She looked a little concerned about something when she turned to talk to him. "Sheriff. There ain't been any really unusual calls. Just the norm. I always get calls from time to time 'bout someone's kid findin' a dead bird or raccoon, or squirrel. Heck, I've even gotten calls of dead moose. But the odd thing today is that there's been a whole lotta of those calls. I ain't never had more then two dead animal calls in one day. So far today there's been twelve. One was even a bear found down by the creek. Guess it's just been one of those days, huh?"

He rubbed his chin and thought before he answered. "Yeah. Looks like it. We may have a vagrant on our hands. I know you heard about the break in at old Ronny's shop. Maybe it's some teenager that wondered into town looking to stir up some mischief. Why don't you go on home too? I can handle things here. I'm sure Stanley's probably getting hungry by now." She chuckled and agreed. After she gathered her things up she waved goodbye and left.

John picked up the phone and called William. "Hey Bill. How's the family? Good. I need to talk to you. You got any time right now? Great. See you in a bit." He hung up the phone and waited for his friend to get there.

• •

After I watched my friends and family chatting and enjoying themselves for a while longer I walked on into the living room and sat down on the floor by the television. They all must have noticed me because they all slowly stopped talking and turned to look at me. I told myself again, *you can do this*, took a deep breath and began.

"Thank you all for coming at such short notice. I take it you enjoyed dinner?" They all nodded yes or made a comment about how good it was. I went on. "Great. As you all know, Jaye and I were called to visit his grandmother this weekend. She is a very old and wise Shaman. She had a very informative vision and disturbing vision. I have had several myself. We know that there has been a rash of very brutal killings lately. So far the targets of those murders have all been immortals.

And as Amber and Emily know, the newly born pup of Thomas and Sadie and the only boy they have had who is to one day take over the pack, has disappeared. There is something or someone behind all of this. It is an evil, vile creature and according to Shaman Rose this is only the beginning. I had some very vivid and disturbing dreams and visions last night. What I gathered from them is that this *thing*, for lack of a better name, is trying to turn all immortals in this town against the humans. In doing so, *it* is hoping to have an uprising of immortals to kill all humans. But there's more, *it* will then try and turn immortal against immortal.

I have no idea why *it's* doing this, but I'm afraid *it* will stop at nothing to accomplish this. While visiting Shaman Rose I had a past life regression and then with help from her and several animals I was able to finally break the lock that had been placed on my memories, for a good reason. I have been chosen as the leader of all immortals. My spirit rules the skies. I also found out that I am what is called a shoo-atee, which is one that can change into any animal.

Amber, my sister in spirit and long time friend, long ago helped to heal me when I almost died. In doing so, some of her powers were transferred into me. She also taught me some witch craft, so I also have that gift. Shinu, it turns out that we have a not heard of connection for a reason. Shinu informed me that he feels as if he is bound to me. And we are able to talk to each other through our minds. No one is able to enter a vampires mind without their permission, but I can."

Before I went on, Shinu interrupted me. "I was curious about that myself and consulted with my father. Let me go back just a little. For those of you who don't know; Stacey I now know you do know this; the Takai go back centuries upon centuries. We are the second biggest sect of vampires and the strongest. My father is the head vampire of parts of this country and Asian countries. Thus, he is the king, and due to the order of lineage, I am the Prince.

But, that's not what I asked him about. It turns out that many centuries back my relative; Prince Takai fell in love and married a shape-shifter. This, in essence, was forbidden. But they married anyway and had children. Prince Takai married White Cloud Rainwater."

Everyone gasped and looked at Skye. Jaye was the first one to say anything. "So, this means that you and bat man are somewhat distant cousins?" And then he laughed. He looked more relieved then amused. Shinu rolled his eyes and answered, "Yes robin, we are very, very distant cousins. That joining long ago bonded our two families together and thus has bound me to you, Skye." This time, my mom and grandma seemed surprised.

Grandma gasped and held her hand to her heart, and said excitedly, "Oh heavens! Now it all makes sense! Shinu, remember when I gave you that glass of special wine and told you that a very dear old friend, a vampire, had given it to me? And I also said that he was always there to get me out of trouble? I remember his name now! It was Naoki Takai!" She laughed joyfully and grabbed Shinu and hugged him. Everyone joined in with the laughter.

....

William made it to the Sheriff's office in fifteen minutes. John was surprised. He expected it to be at least an hour. He said, "That was fast." William got out of his car and walked up to the door. He was a tall and daunting looking, but was a kind and caring man. He towered over John at 6'6" and 250 pounds. His hair was an almost white blond. He wore glasses and a permanent smile that made him look like the perfect politician. John always thought he should be a senator or governor.

William would just tell him he preferred a more quiet life with his family. John was 5'11" and weighed 175 pounds. Being of Indian decent he bore a permanent tan. His hair was deep brown, almost black. William always told him he made a perfect Sheriff; fair, kind hearted, took the law seriously and loved his town. William stuck out his hand and shook John's. "It sounded urgent. How can I help you?"

They went on in and stopped to get a cup of coffee before they headed to John's office. He offered him a seat on his couch and John sat at his desk. He paused and then said, "I really need your opinion. I know by now you've heard about the recent murders and the break in at Ronny's. I gotta tell you. I went out and seen what happened to Bud and Francis. It was awful Bill. I never seen such carnage.

But, here's the odd thing and why I wanted to talk to you first. I'm not an expert forensics investigator, but I could swear those were wolf bites in what was left of them. And not just your normal wolf either. Much bigger. My men just think they were mauled by some bears. And according to their report every bone in Lester's body was broken. There was no sign of a break in. So you'd think whoever did this, Lester had to let them in right? There was a couch pushed up to his front door, not moved, and they'd had to have shoved their way in the back door, but there was a heavy tool chest shoved against that door. No windows were open."

William had moved up to the edge of his seat and was leaning forward deep in thought. He waited several seconds for John to continue. John sighed and said, "I know we've had our little talks before about unusual things and such. I've always believed that something odd has always gone on in this town." William questioned John, "So what are you getting at? In my opinion, if, and I stress *if,* there were such things, I'd say your murder scene in the hunting grounds was done by werewolves.

And *if* there were such a thing, I'd say Lester was killed by vampires. The break in at Ronny's may have been just some drifter. But, I heard the top dead bolt lock looked like it had been punched in, not hit in with something like a sledge hammer. Only something non-human would have the strength to do that. Now don't go quoting me John. You know as well as I do that, as far as we know, we may be the only ones that believe in such things. Did I hit it on the nose?" John nodded yes.

Before he could say any more his computer beeped, signaling him that he had new email. He looked up at William. "Well, this may be what I've been waiting for. The preliminary test results from the coroner and forensics." William got up and came over to John's side of the desk. Just as John thought, there were two new emails. One from the coroner and one from forensics. He opened the coroner's report first. It read:

This is just a summary of my report. It is inconclusive until I can do further testing. I hope this helps. The puncture wounds in Bud's and Francis' body were bite marks. Presumably from wolves. Every bone in Lester's body was broken, including various breaks in his skull. The force and trajectory needed to cause such damage would be equivalent to a person repeatedly jumping off a ten story building. I will have more for you in several days once the specimens come back.

He looked up at William. He had gone pale a little bit and was sweating. Trembling he said, "I'll open the next one." He clicked on the email from forensics and they read that one.

We have only processed a few of the samples taken from Lester's house and a few from the hunting grounds. The results from Lester's house were inconclusive. The only prints we found on the samples from the kitchen were Lester's. The samples from the bodies found at the hunting grounds showed traces of canine, or more specific, wolf DNA. We tested it twice to make sure we didn't make any mistakes. Again, this is not conclusive. There are more tests to be run. We will have a full report in ten days.

William had turned and walked back over to the couch were he slumped back into his seat. Stunned, he said, "I'll be. Could it be possible John?" John looked just as pale as William. He couldn't say a word right now. He was dumbfounded.

•••

I continued after everyone settled down. "Shaman Rose also explained to us the legend of one great leader from many many centuries back. He was also a shoo-atee, but he didn't have the other powers that I have. Hhm. Jaye. All these connections would explain why she said I was very powerful, more powerful then anyone she had ever met or read about or heard about. Sorry. Back to where I was.

My job, as your leader, is to unite each and every immortal and as many humans as we can, so that we can defeat *it*. It will not be easy. Earlier while we all ate I stood back watching each and every one of you. I was asking myself why you guys? Why did we all become fast friends? Then it came to me. I have to find a way to conquer *it*, but I can't do it alone. Behind every great leader are great assistants. Each of you has a purpose."

I had to stand up and pace a little. I was getting excited and more encouraged about what we had to face. I went on, "First, thank you all for accepting Stacey into our group. I can see that you all seem comfortable around her now. This brings me to you Stacey. Stacey, your role is liaison for us to the humans. I know not all humans will accept us and you cannot tell all humans.

Your job is to get those who will believe and listen and try to convince them not to blame the mortal animals or the immortals. Then you will have to arrange a meeting with them and us. I know this is a great burden due to the natural suspicions and disbelief they harbor, but I have faith in you." Stacey nodded in agreement.

I went on, "Jaye, in my visions last night it was revealed to me that your family are of royalty and that you and your family are the leaders of the shape-shifters. I will need you to get all the shape-shifters together and explain to them that it is not the humans and that we must all stand together in order to beat *it*. I know you will have no problem with that task." Jaye answered, "I will do all I can."

I continued, "Amber, you have seen first hand the tragic things *it* has done and know the depth of what we are facing. We go back so far. I will need your family's help and the help of anyone else in your coven that is willing. I want to also ask you to be my personal advisor. Not just for what faces us now, but from this point on."

Amber had tears in her eyes, "You are and have always been my sister. I accept."

Next I faced Emily, "Emily, I know you are new to your pack, but you are also very very strong for a young pup. You have a sharp edge about you and a deadly commitment to protect those you are loyal to. I can talk to the pack myself and let them know what is going on, so I don't need you to do that. I need you as my second guard and protector. Are you willing to pledge your loyalty to me?"

Emily smiled and seemed pleased. Hesitantly she said, "I don't know what to say? I'm honored, but I'm afraid that when you hear what I did, you won't trust me." Shinu put his hand on her shoulder, "Em. You do not have to do this now in front of everyone." She touched his hand, "Yes I do. Everyone will hear about it anyways. I'm sure it will be in tomorrow's paper and better for me to confess now to you Skye, than for you to hear about it from someone else later.

You know about Tania's death. This weekend Natasha, Thomas, Elliot, and I were called to her family's house. They needed someone to find where their daughter's body parts were and get them before someone ate her. They couldn't bare the thought of that. We tracked her down to Ronny's meat shop. We broke in and took what was left of her. We also took some other meat and money to make it look like someone broke in.

Once we returned her to her family they begged us to hunt down whoever had done this and kill them. They convinced us with tears and pain and played on our sympathy. They even threw in, what if it had been one of our pack and that immortals had to stick together." She sighed and hung her head down as she went on, "So, we tracked them out to the hunting grounds and took care of them. I lost control! Why would you want someone who can't even control their own selfish urges to guard you?"

She buried her face in Shinu's chest and sobbed. I couldn't help but feel for her. I went over to them and held her too while Shinu did. Comforting her, I said, "Shh. Even though I can't condone anyone running off and taking matters into their own hands, I understand.

I saw what that thing did to her on our way to see Shaman Rose but was helpless to save her. We were too far away. All I can say was that when it happened I couldn't be there physically but my spirit was there to comfort her. She died at peace. Because of her reaching out to me I have a clue as to whom or what we are looking for."

She tensed up for a moment then relaxed a little. I said, "I still trust you and I still need you. Will you reconsider and be my second guard, please?" She turned around and looked at me with awe and grabbed me and hugged me. Happier now, she said, "You are too kind. Yes I will. Thank you! Now I know what my purpose for living is!"

They both sat back down and Shinu kept his arm around her. "Now. That leaves you Shinu. You have probably already surmised that I will need you to ask your family to help us in this battle. You have suffered your own loss. I now know it was by the hands of *it*. In my dreams she fought back and stood her ground honorably." At the same time I spoke to him in my mind. *No need to explain. I know about your brothers and sister and the incident with Lester. They were more civil with him then I would have been if it had been someone dear to me and I thought it was him involved.*

He nodded in understanding. I proceeded out loud to explain his role. "I will need you to talk to your family and try and convince them to hold off on any attacks. Let them know that we are all working together to bring *it* down and that I would like to talk to them to come up with a plan. I also have one more request for you. Now that we know our history and understand the bond we share, I want you to be my number one protector and head guard from this day forward. That would mean that until you take over for your father, you will have to be with me quite a bit."

Obviously this was right up his alley. "I am at your beck and call, my lady." He bowed to me and gave me his devious smile and looked at Jaye. Then he even stuck out his tongue to Jaye. I shook my head and laughed to myself as I spoke to him again in his mind, *You are so ornery.*

It was getting late so I quickly summed things up for them. "Now that we have this much figured out each of you are to also get your strongest people together and arrange an army. Once I have had a chance to meet with the heads of each of your people I will need you to report to Shinu, let him know how many soldiers you each have and what each of their strengths are. He will then put everyone in order. We will all meet up and organize our search for *it*. Then the battle will begin. Is everyone in agreement with all of this?" Everyone said yes. I added, "First, it is imperative that each of you talk to your people quickly and stop anyone from going after the wrong person or groups now. Thank you all for everything you have done and will do."

Everyone, except Shinu, grabbed some of the cookies grandma had made for dessert and headed home. I asked Stacey to wait. Jaye gave me a quick kiss and whispered that he'd be back later tonight to see me then he changed and flew off. Stacey watched in amazement. "That is so cool! So what do you need me to do first?" We sat down on the couch while mom and grandma retired to the kitchen to clean up. I faced her and explained, "I need you to talk to your parents tonight. I don't know how much they believe in the unexplained, but I need them to know about this tonight.

While we were in the meeting I seen your dad and Sheriff Makepeace talking. They are pretty much convinced that all the murders are the works of something immortal. They think we are hostile so I need you to get them to see that we aren't. They want to do something within the next few days to try and stop us. If you need my help, please call me, tonight." She understood how important this was and hurried on to the door. She stopped and hugged me. "You are an awesome leader. I'm glad you are in charge and thrilled you are my best friend!" Before she left out the door, she went to talk to grandma. She was in the kitchen for about fifteen minutes and then she hugged me again and ran to her car and sped off.

I joined mom and grandma in the kitchen and helped them clean up. Mom was teary eyed. "You ok mom?" She put the plate down that she was washing and turned and took me in her arms and held me tight. Through sobs she said, "I am the proudest mom in this world. We knew when you were a baby that you were something special. Not just doting parents special, but born for a purpose. Your father would be proud of you."

Grandma came up behind me and hugged me too. "Have a seat sweetie. It's time we told you why we had to lock away your memories." Mom sat on one side of me and grandma on the other. Grandma began, "Back after we lost your father, things were pretty leery. We weren't sure if the one that killed him would find out about your growing powers and come and try to kill you too. It seemed to have calmed down for a long time then we got news that there was someone coming for you."

Mom sighed and took up where she left off. "I saw how close you and Jaye were becoming. You two were inseparable. You and Amber were also inseparable. The three of you were either all together all the time or at least one of them was with you at all times. I started to notice that you were getting interested in Jaye for more then just friends. I saw the googly eyes and the occasional holding hands and that was the signal I needed that we had to do something quick before it was too late.

The day we decided to take you and go we found you and Jaye sitting on a hill. He had his arm around you and I just knew he was going to kiss you. Once that would happen, it would be harder to protect you. You see. Love is the strongest bond between people and no matter how far you go or how much you try to make a person forget, when their love is as strong as you two would have had, there would be no keeping you away from him and you would be vulnerable.

So we stopped you just before you kissed and ran. We had to lock away your memories to protect you because you swore to us that no matter where we went you would go looking for Amber and Jaye. We also had to lock them away because you were growing too strong. Stronger then any of us thought you would. That kind of power is hard to conceal and whoever was coming after you would surely feel the pull of it and find you."

Grandma had gotten up and made us all some of her calming tea. She handed us a cup and sat back down and continued. "Oh how we hated to hide your memories. It hurt to try and explain to Jaye what we had to do. He protested and swore that he could protect you himself. Amber tried to come up with a hiding spell to mask your magic so you could stay. But we had to go, far away. So for most of your young life we stayed away.

We finally decided to come back and try again. You didn't remember anyone or anything from around here. This made us feel a little less worried about our return. Then wouldn't you know it? This crazy bird started hanging around. It was always sticking around here and following you. It didn't take long for us to figure out it was Jaye. We tried to run him off, but he was very persistent. He swore to us he would never tell you who he was if only he could just stay around and be close to you. Love didn't die.

Amber was so hurt back when we first left with you she built up her own wall against anyone who would try and get close to her. She threw herself into her magic and wouldn't let anyone in. When she first found out that we were back she tried to convince her parents to relocate. She didn't want to be anywhere near you if she couldn't have you back the way you were then. She even persuaded herself that this Skye wasn't even the real Skye. That we had come back with a substitute. As painful as that was to see we felt it would keep you safe."

Mom took over again. "Then we got the letters from Shaman Rose. One for us and one for you. She told us it was time for you to be released. That you were needed now. We had to do what she said. Before we could give you your letter an odd thing happened. You started to ask us questions about Amber. We tried to skirt around them.

From there you know what happened. You and Amber connected again. Like we said. True love has no bounds. Jaye's love for you and Amber's love for you. So we are so sorry we had to lock your memories away. Please forgive us." I hugged them both and cried like a baby. Everything that had happened before the weekend up to now went so fast and was so much to take in. I had to stay strong though. "I forgive you."

CHAPTER 14

UNITED . . .

tacey made it from Skye's house to her's in record time. She parked and ran in. She didn't see her mom or dad so she called out to them. "Mom? Dad?" She heard her mom call from upstairs. "I'm up here sweetie. Your dad ran over to the Sheriff's office. He'll be back later." Stacey remembered Skye telling her that her dad and Sheriff Makepeace were discussing the murders and were getting the wrong ideas. She made up her mind to go talk to both of them. "Mom. I'll be back. I really need to talk to dad now."

She ran back out the door and jumped in her car and took off toward town. She made it to the Sheriff's office just as her dad was shaking the sheriff's hand at the door and turning to leave. She flew into the spot beside her dad's car just barely missing it and jumped out. She ran up to the both of them, and said, "Glad I caught you. We really need to talk." Her dad looked worried. "Everything ok? I thought you were out at the Rainwater's house." Stacey answered, "Yes I was. The meetings over for now. Now I have something I need to do and I need to talk to you right now. Both of you."

They both looked at her suspiciously, but agreed to talk to her. She walked past them into the office and waited for them to follow her in before she closed the door. She turned and faced them and asked, "Sheriff Makepeace, is anyone else here?" He shook his head, "No. Just us. What's this all about?" She went on without answering his question. "Can we talk in your office please? I really don't need anyone else to hear what I have to say. At least not yet."

He agreed and they all headed in his office where she once again closed the door behind them. Stacey motioned for them to take a seat and paced back and forth. Her dad was really worried now, "Sweet heart. What do you need to talk to us about? What's got you so worked up?" She couldn't figure out how to say what she wanted to say so she just began, "I know you two were discussing the two murder cases earlier and I know you've come to the conclusion that the murderer has to be something not human. I also know that you were talking about trying to do something about it in the next couple of days.

I know too, that you may have figured out who has done these things. I know because Skye seen you two discussing this while we were in our meeting. Dad, you know I have boxes upon boxes of books on immortals; werewolves, vampires, witches; and that I believe they exist. You and mom have had little chats with me, at separate times that hinted to the fact that you too believe in the supernatural. What I have observed from you Sheriff is that you believe too. I was chosen as a liaison to the immortals in this town by Skye. Skye is what is called a Shoo-atee."

Before she could go on, John gasped and cut her off, "One who can change into any animal. They are rare. There has only been one in past recorded history. A man. He was a very powerful man that led the immortals of that time in a battle against some demon. How could this be? How do you know about this? What's going on?"

William looked at John in shock now too. He said, "Wait a minute. What are you saying Stacey?" Stacey was afraid to go on; afraid she may have just opened a Pandora's Box. She was not prepared for the

Sheriff to know this much about what she was there to explain. But, she knew she had to go on. Skye was relying on her to get the humans to work together with the immortals.

Even though she was unsure, she went on. "Skye just found out this weekend about being the chosen leader of the immortals. So here it goes. There are werewolves, vampires, witches, warlocks, and shape-shifters living in this town. They have been here for many years. They have lived in peace until something happened.

First let me say that, Sheriff, you are right about the murders. The hunters were killed by werewolves and I'm assuming Lester was killed by vampires. Assuming, because I have a tendency to listen in when I shouldn't and can read between the lines very well and put two and two together. But it is not entirely their fault. There is something evil, some contemptible thing that has slithered into town and is killing off various immortals and setting it up to look like humans have done it.

This, of course, has got the immortals, which are generally peaceful, going after the wrong people. Skye believes this demon thing is purposely turning them against us first and may eventually turn immortal against immortal." Stacey sort of drifted off behind the sheriff's desk and was now speaking to herself. "Now that I've said that out loud, there has to be something or someone that *it's* after."

After mumbling to herself she turned around and found both her dad and the sheriff looking at her amazed. Their mouths were hanging open and they looked lost. She continued. "I'm sorry if I lost you there for a moment. I just had an idea I had to talk out. Anyway. I know all of this sounds fantastical and you both must think I'm crazy or have been reading too many books so now I can't tell the difference in reality and fantasy, but it is real. Skye told me to call her if I needed her help. I really have to get you two to believe what I've told you."

Stacey's father was the first one to regain his composure and was able to talk now. "If in fact what you have told us is true, and you have been chosen as the liaison for the immortals to bring the humans together, who is arranging things with the other immortals?" John finally added his input in. "I need the names of these others and what kind of immortals they are. I'm not going on a witch hunt, I just have some theories of my own and if they match what you tell me, then I can begin to believe what you just told us."

Stacey had to catch her breath and think for a moment. Reluctantly she gave their names. She just didn't want to get her friends in trouble if they didn't believe her. "Amber Whitcraft is a witch. She is working with her coven and she was appointed advisor to Skye tonight. Shinu Takai is a vampire. He is convincing his family to work with the immortals and the humans. He was given the position of head guard and protector for Skye.

Emily Silverstein was recently turned into a werewolf. She was assigned the position of second guard. Jaye Crowe is a shape-shifter, oddly enough, a crow. He is heir to the royal lineage and is leader of the shape-shifters in this region. Each of them is responsible for getting their people to come together with everyone else. Skye was told by Shaman Rose that it is up to her to bring everyone together in order to fight this wicked thing."

Again John jumped up, anxious, and said, "Did you say Shaman Rose?" Stacey nodded yes, then said, "She is Jaye's grandmother and is the one that helped Skye discover who she is. Why?" John shook his head and he got up and started pacing around too. Thinking aloud he said, "My grandmother told us kids when we were little about a great and wise Shaman named Rose. She said she was many years old and had been the caretaker of our people for centuries.

She said she had visions and could heal the sick and she maintained peace and harmony among our tribesmen and the immortals. She said she moved away one day into the mountains. I was just a little kid and thought those were just bedtime stories shared among our people. If this is all true, then you have your work cut out for you Stacey. You can't do this alone. William, you know I'm not some wishy washy man and don't believe every whim that comes my way.

I believe your daughter and as sheriff I feel I have to help her. I knew something wasn't right here lately. Maribelle even said she had an increase in small time calls about various animals turning up dead. We're used to the occasional raccoon or even moose. But she said earlier that there had been a lot of other animals turning up dead. So what do you think Bill?"

William had been sitting there quiet the whole time Stacey and now John had talked. Now he spoke up. "I never wanted you to think your mom and dad was crazy Stacey. But we have always believed in these things. That's one of the reasons we hit it off when we first started dating. You're my daughter and I believe everything you've told us. I will also help you out any way I can. My baby, a liaison. You get that from me. I'm so proud of you."

He got up and hugged her. She felt so relieved she wanted to cry but she kept her poise. Her father asked, "So what now?" Stacey held her head up high. She was now feeling like she was living up to her appointed position. She said, "Now, we have to get as many humans as possible to work together with us. We have to tell mom first and go from there. Sheriff, I appreciate you believing in me and I will need your help."

He smiled and nodded, "I'll do what I can. I'd really like to meet Skye. You said you can call her and she'll come?" Stacey said, "Yes. Just tell me when you want to meet her." He looked at William and asked, "Bill, can we meet at your place tomorrow night say 7:00 p.m.?" William said yes. Stacey had accomplished her first step in a long line of many.

CHAPTER 15

THINGS COME TOGETHER...

When everyone left Skye's house, Shinu offered to give Emily a ride home. She accepted and said good night to Amber and Dave. Being the gentle man he is, Shinu opened the door for Emily and she got in. She had been looking at his car from the outside and once inside, she admired the inside as well. When he got in, she commented, "Nice car!" Shinu smiled, "Thank you. It's an Aston Martin Coupe. It was my older brother's, but he decided he'd rather have a Lamborghini.

So, I got the hand me down. One can't complain about a hand me down like this, can they? He had a gaudy deep purple leather interior in here. If you ask me, I think there's something seriously wrong with him. But, if you ask him, he's perfectly normal. I had it completely redone. I prefer a black leather interior." He started the car and drove off. "Let me know if it's warm enough in here for you. Oh. That's right. I don't have to worry about you being too cold, do I? Your people generally stay warm all the time don't they? It's all that fur."

She punched him in the arm playfully, but then ended up rubbing her hand afterward. "Ouch! I keep forgetting I can't punch you can I?" With a big smirk he turned to her and winked, "Tough exterior, but I'm as gentle as a teddy bear inside." Emily burst in to fake laughter. "Ha ha ha! You're so funny. Teddy bear my butt. You forget who you're talking to. There's a beast within you too."

He knew what she was referring too. After what she went through Saturday night, she was still coming down on herself and feeling remorse for what she did. He decided to change the subject to spare her feelings. He said, "So, congratulations on your position. I know you're new to the world of the immortals, so I'll explain why it's such a big deal. I've been around for a very long time. And being in a hierarchy and a prince I know how things work. A leader, like Skye, would never put a new and inexperienced person in such a high position, let alone any position in the royal brigade, so to speak.

It is unheard of. Those positions are given to those who have served under the leader for a long time and have gone to great lengths to prove they are worthy of that position. She obviously has great faith in you, and I can almost guarantee that she has had a vision about you to back that faith up."

Emily pondered what he had explained and was quiet for a little while. Then she said, "Thanks for explaining that to me. I was honored when she asked me, but I didn't understand the magnitude of her decision to choose me. I will do my best to show her she made the right choice." Shinu reached over and held her hand. There was an endearing look in his eyes. Smiling, he said, "I have faith in you too. And don't get me wrong. I'm not just saying this because I am growing an attachment to you, but because I can see the potential in you. If it was left up to me to chose who I would want to work by my side, I would have chosen you too." Emily looked at him and could tell he was sincere. She leaned over and kissed his cheek.

They rode on in silence for a while. Emily broke the silence first. "So do you think you'll have trouble getting your family and others to agree to fight with everyone? Especially with werewolves." She was referring to the fact that vampires and werewolves used to be mortal enemies in the past. Up until several years ago, they still didn't get along with each other.

But slowly they had finally started to accept each other and had been trying to get along. He answered, "It won't be a challenge to *command* them to join in and help fight. But it will be a challenge to *ask* them to stand side by side with werewolves and humans and put aside their differences. I don't want to use my authority over them, so I am first going to try and appeal to their hearts, so to speak. Skye knows that either way she will have the aide of the vampires in this fight."

They made it to the road that lead back into the woods where Emily lived with her pack. Shinu stopped his car and asked Emily, "Do you want to get out here and head on home or do you want me to drive you to your door?" His smirk gave him away. He was hoping she wanted him to go all the way to her house. He loved a challenge. She laughed at the thought of it, but was curious herself. "Sure. I can introduce you to our pack leader, Thomas." He put the car back in gear and drove on. Before they could reach Thomas' house, they were suddenly flanked on both sides by five werewolves, hiding in the trees.

•••

After we had finished our tea and chat, I went upstairs to rest and get my thoughts together. The meeting went well and all that remained was for me to get things planned out. Tonight's meeting was the first in many I knew I would have to conduct throughout my life and I was glad it had gone so well. I sat at my desk and took out a notebook I had kept for years that my grandma gave me one year for my birthday. At that time she told me I would use it one day for something great. I didn't know what she meant, but put it in my desk anyway and there it has sat until now. She must have known even back then.

I pulled out my special pen, given to me by my mom, and opened the notebook and started the first entry. Although I knew who I had chosen for each position I still felt the need to list them. I began from the top most important person, Shinu, my first guard. It was strange. I know my vision is now keener since my subconscious joined my conscious, and I know everything seems so much clearer and that I'm now seeing things I hadn't before, but this was odd. As I wrote his name, each letter lit up like a blaze of fire. When I finished writing it and his position the blaze went out and the letters on the page appeared burned on it.

I turned the page back to look at the other side to see if it had burned through. Nothing. And the page was cool to the touch too. I had to see if it would happen again. Below Shinu's name I wrote Emily and her position. Sure enough. Emily's did the same thing. Next I wrote Amber's name and advisor. Her's lit up and sparkled. Below her I wrote out Stacey's name and her job. Even Stacey's name blazed and went out.

Lastly I had to write out Jaye's name. I wrote down the 'J', and something tapped at my window. I closed my notebook and went to the window. It was Jaye, in his crow form. Speak of the devil. I opened the window and he flew on in. He shifted back to his human form and hugged me. "Hello sweet heart." I hugged him back and said, "Hey you. I know I asked you to come back tonight if you could, but why didn't you just use the door?" He pouted, "I thought this would be more romantic, but I can go if you don't want me here." Then he smiled.

I went over and sat on my bed and patted the seat right next to me, signaling him to come sit by me. I smiled and said, "Of course I want you here." I pulled his head down to mine and kissed him. He responded and kissed me back. I said, "I love spending time with you.

We do have years to make up for don't we? And, it's so nice to have you all to myself right now. No interruptions."

Just as the words came out of my mouth, Shinu popped in my head. I let out a sigh. Jaye thought I was upset at him. He asked, "What did I do? I didn't hurt you did I?" I smiled, "No dear. You are fine. It's Shinu." Jaye let out a frustrated groan. Shinu chimed in my head, *My Lady. I hope I'm not interrupting anything.* I took a deep breath and paused before I answered, *Not really. You do have impeccable timing though. How can I help you?* I could read his mind. He was in a wily mood, *Looks like it takes a vampire to do a bird's job. Anyway, you mentioned tonight something about having a clue to finding this thing. Would it be possible for you to bring it and meet me here at Thomas'? I need to run a thought by you and Thomas anyway.* I was shocked. I know that vampires and werewolves are trying harder to get along, but for him to throw himself in the middle of the biggest pack on this continent was brave, *You are at Thomas'? That's got to be a sight. Sure I can. I'll be there shortly.*

Jaye was looking at me patiently waiting. A little agitated he asked, "So, what did he want?" No mean or funny name for Shinu this time. Odd. I answered, "He's over at Thomas' camp. I guess he took Emily home, but he's still there and asked me if I could come. He asked me if I could bring the clue with me. I'm going to head on over there. It sounded important. I'm sorry Jaye. We'll have to get together another time."

I could tell he was disappointed. He let out a heavy sigh, "Fine. I know these things will happen and I have to share you. But, we will get to be alone real soon. I'm going to head back. I really need to get started talking to as many shape-shifters as I can. I already talked to some of the other crows. They are helping me to get the word out that I need to meet with them. I'll see you later, ok?" We kissed good bye and he flew back out the window.

I'd better let mom and grandma know that I have to head over to Thomas'. Before I ran out the door I looked back at my notebook. I'd have to ask grandma about that later. No time right now. So, I just put it back in my drawer. I grabbed the piece of paper I had drawn the symbol on and stuck it in my pocket. It would be faster for me to get there if I ran. After talking to mom, grandma was sleep, I left out the front door and shifted into a cheetah and took off.

....

Shinu grinned, "It appears we have company. We've been followed since I turned the first corner. Very good guards." Emily seemed a little perturbed about it. She said, "I know. It's Natasha, she's Thomas' second in command; Elliot, whose fiancé had to of been murdered by *it*; and three others. Security is tight since Thomas' son disappeared." Shinu was surprised. He inquired, "Disappeared? How strange. Wouldn't his son become leader upon his death?"

Emily nodded her head yes. Shinu then said, "Whoever took him knows this. There is a definite reason for his disappearance. I need to talk to Thomas." Emily was taken aback by Shinu's boldness, but also admired him more. She smiled, "Sure. I'll see what I can do once we make it to the house. I don't think they'll attack unprovoked."

They made it to the front of Thomas' house. Thomas and Sadie were standing on the front porch. Natasha bounded out of the trees and stood at Thomas' side, still in wolf form. Elliot stood at the front of Shinu's car also in wolf form. The others placed themselves behind the car ready to jump if need be. Emily and Shinu got out of the car at the same time. A low growl escaped Natasha's throat. Thomas waved his hand at her and said, "Calm down. He's with Emily. Good evening. Emily? Do you mind introducing us to your friend?"

Emily walked over to Shinu's side and held his hand. She calmly said, "This is Shinu Takai. He's a dear friend of mine from school. We've been up at Skye's house and have some interesting things to tell you. But first. Shinu would like to talk to you and Sadie."

Emily turned and looked at all the wolves directing her next comment to them, "He's a good guy. He's on our side." When none of them said a word or backed off any, Emily got angry. She stepped in front of Shinu, her eyes started to glow a fluorescent blue, she bristled up, and growled defensively. She was just a few phases away from changing into her wolf form. Her voice had dropped several octaves and she spoke through gritted teeth. "I said back off! Don't even think of touching him!"

The werewolves that had been standing behind Shinu's car slowly backed off and trotted off into the woods. Elliot stepped back closer to the porch and changed back into his human form. Natasha relaxed and sat down on her hind legs. Elliot raised his hands up in front of him as if to ward her off and said, "Whoa Emily! It's ok. We just wanted to make sure he wasn't that *thing*. We're good. We're good. Calm down. Don't go all crazy on us." Shinu rubbed her shoulders and whispered, "It's ok Em. I'm ok. They were just doing their job. I understand."

Emily slowly composed herself. She looked back at Thomas and lowered her head. "I'm sorry Thomas, Sadie." Thomas smiled and stepped down off the porch. He said, "It's ok Emily. I think we all know how you are by now." Thomas walked over to Shinu and stuck out his hand to shake his. Shinu shook his hand and Thomas said, "You must be a very dear friend in order for Emily to get that defensive of you. We can trust you then. Hi. I'm Thomas." Shinu bowed half way down, which was a symbol of great respect, and replied, "I like to think I am a dear friend. She is to me. And thank you for your trust. Do you have time to talk right now?" Thomas said yes.

They all walked back up on the porch. Thomas offered Emily and Shinu a seat. Natasha stayed in her wolf form and sat down on the floor next to Thomas. Sadie stood by the table and asked, "Can I offer you two anything to drink?" Emily said, "Yes, please." Shinu declined. Sadie went on the house and came back out with a tray, white mugs, and a pot of hot chocolate. There was one black mug on the tray too. Sadie motioned toward it and said, "I brought you something anyway, Shinu. Just in case you change your mind. We keep some around for any new pups born in our pack."

She seemed a little sad at her thoughts so Shinu tried to redirect the conversation. "Thank you so much. As we were saying, we were up at Skye's house. She called a meeting with us and a few other key people." He picked up the mug, sniffed, smiled and took a sip. It was blood. "Mm. Thank you again. Guess I did need it."

They all sat there and listened as Emily and Shinu explained what the meeting was about and what Skye had found out when she and Jaye went to see Shaman Rose. They told them about Skye's plan to get all immortals and any humans willing to fight together to try and fight this *it*.

As they were talking several of the others from the pack had drifted over to see who Shinu was. Some of them couldn't believe a vampire had come to visit and had to come see for themselves. They stayed and listened to them talking. Shinu continued, "During the meeting Skye mentioned something about having a hint that may help to find who this thing is. I completely forgot to ask her what it was. I'd like to share my thoughts with you and her too." Thomas started to get up, saying, "We can call her. You can use my phone." Shinu smiled, "No need. One of the new found things Skye and I share is that we can talk to each other, through our minds."

He smiled at them and called Skye, *My Lady. I hope I'm not interrupting anything.* After a brief pause she answered back, *Not really. You do have impeccable timing though. How can I help you?* He grinned deviously, *Looks like it takes a vampire to do a bird's job. Anyway, you mentioned tonight something about having a clue to finding this thing. Would it be possible for you to bring it and meet me here at Thomas'? I need to run a thought by you and Thomas anyway.* She was surprised, *You are at Thomas'? That's got to be a sight. Sure I can. I'll be there shortly.*

Shinu let them know what she said, "She said she'll be here shortly. She may have a bird trailing behind her too." Thomas gave him a puzzled look. Shinu smiled and explained, "Sorry. I was referring to Jaye. He's a shape-shifter. He is a crow. They are dating so since he was there when I spoke to her; I'm just assuming he may come with." Thomas signified that he understood.

They just sat and continued to chat about things that had happened lately. Shinu told them about the loss of his sister. They told him about the death of Elliot's fiancé. And the disappearance of their son. Emily and Shinu didn't even really notice when they had scooted their chairs closer to each other and were now holding hands with their fingers intertwined.

Thomas noticed and leaned forward in his chair to talk quietly to them. He smiled, "You two do realize you're holding hands, right?" Shinu and Emily looked at each other and then down at their hands. They looked back at each other and hunched their shoulders. Emily said, "Yeah. I guess we are. Why?" Thomas just laughed, but Shinu answered her, "I believe he is referring to what I was telling you in the car. About how, long ago we did not get along. And until recently, we didn't even associate. You and I dating would cause quite a stir."

Emily blushed and pulled her hand out of Shinu's. He took her hand back and held it in both his hands. "Em, I don't care if you don't care. I have become quite attached to you and if Thomas doesn't object, I would like to get to know you better." They looked at Thomas to see what his reaction would be. He burst out laughing, "I may be pack leader and my pack has to obey what I say, but I'm a more lenient and open leader and don't tell my people who they can and can't date. And there is no way I'd even attempt to anger Emily. She may be a new pup, but she is also the strongest in the pack. If she got mad, we'd be able to *eventually* contain her, but in the meantime, she'd cause quite a bit of damage to my camp. You two have my blessing. Just don't be surprised if, and when you do have opposition to your union."

• •

It was amazing how fast I could go when I was in a cheetah form. I made it to the edge of the woods surrounding Thomas' camp in five minutes. Driving it would have taken me at least ten minutes and another ten just to get up the road. I stopped there and shifted into a falcon. I didn't want to scare the patrol group Thomas had guarding the camp. Nor did I want to have to fight any of them.

I'm pretty sure they would win. I haven't had any practice using magic while I'm in animal form so I couldn't even use that against them. Although, I would have a pretty good chance of coming out alright. I have to remember that I can call Shinu any time I need him and he's fast.

Now as my falcon I soared and circled overhead. I could see the werewolves stationed at each watch point of the camp. They were paired in two and pacing back and forth. I circled around and gracefully fluttered down and landed on the ground right in front of Thomas' porch. Before I could change back, Natasha was right in my face growling and flaring her nostrils.

Everyone else jumped up when she darted off the porch and were standing ready to attack. Thinking fast I spoke to Shinu, *Shinu. It's me. Please tell them it's me before I become Natasha's dinner.* Shinu laughed and everyone turned to look at him, everyone that is except Natasha. He walked off the porch and came to my rescue. He grinned, "It's ok everyone. It's Skye."

The tension in the air eased up and Natasha sat down and lowered her head to me. I went ahead and changed back. Natasha changed at the same time. When we were both human again she came up to me and hugged me. It was quite a tight hug. I rubbed her back. "It's ok Natasha. You were just doing your job." She shook her head, "No. I was ready to eat you. I'm so sorry. I should have recognized your scent. I was just to busy trying to protect everyone. Please forgive me." I took her face in my hands, "You are fine Sweetie. I'd think something was wrong with you if you didn't do exactly what you did. We need more like you. I forgive you. Now, if it's ok with Thomas, I think you need a break." Thomas smiled at me and said to Natasha, "Go on Natasha. With Skye here now too, I'll be fine. Take a break." She bowed to me again and took off into the trees.

Shinu took me by my arm and led me up to the porch and to a seat on his other side. I addressed Shinu first. "Thank you dear. Hello again Emily. It's so good to see my two guards working together and so fast. Hello everyone." I directed my attention back to Shinu and Emily. "I trust you've both filled everyone in?" Shinu nodded, "Yes. I was just telling them you had mentioned you had a clue or something and they asked me to call you here to tell us about it."

Just then Sadie came out of the house with a tray full of drinks. She saw me and almost dropped the tray to get over to me. I stood up to hug her. "Oh, Skye! As always, it's so good to see you. I was elated when Shinu told us you went to see Shaman Rose and that while you were there you got all of your memory back. You remember everything now?" She clasped her hands together like a little child waiting for a gift. I could feel her excitement radiating off her. Excitedly, I answered, "I remember everything like it happened yesterday. I'm so proud of you! And sorry we have to put this off once again, but I have to show you all what clue I have."

Sadie sat down by Thomas and I sat back down by Shinu. I reached in my pocket and pulled out the piece of paper. I summed the vision I had up, "I hate to cut the vision I had short, but I saw Tania murdered and the thing that did it. This is the symbol that was on the knife that *it* used to cut her up." At the mention of Tania Thomas lowered his head in shame. I patted his hand, "Its ok. I know and I understand. I have a message for her family too. For now, I need everyone to look at the drawing and please let me know if any of you recognize it." I handed the paper to Shinu who then passed it around the table. When it made to back to me I handed it back to Emily. I asked, "Emily, will you please pass this around to the others standing here then bring it back to me?" She stood up and walked off the porch to the crowd that had gathered around to listen.

Emily finished passing it around and had returned to the table and handed me the paper when I turned to Shinu. "Shinu, you said something about you have something to discuss with all of us. What is it?" He leaned forward on his elbows on the table and focused on

Thomas and Sadie. He said, "I'm sorry to do this. I know it will be painful, but I need to hear about your son. I need to hear about what happened when he was taken, when, and where. I also need to ask you to tell me how your pack works as far as leadership."

Thomas looked at Sadie and pulled her closer to him to put his arm around her. He sighed and began, "Nanuk is our only son. The night he was born we almost lost him. If it wasn't for Amber . . . Two weeks later I was out teaching him how to hunt. He is so good at it. It was time to head back home and I called for him. He didn't come when I called him. I searched all over. I found the area where he was last. I could smell that he had been there, but he was gone. We all looked for hours and days.

The way I have always run the pack was passed down to me from my father and so on. When the leader has a son that son one day takes over when the father can no longer lead. Other packs decide who the new leader will be by a challenge. If a stronger wolf decides to challenge the leader they fight. Whoever wins becomes the head of the pack. I prefer to pass it on down through the family. And everyone in my pack appreciates and abides by that law. It keeps things more orderly for us."

Shinu sat and thought for a moment, then he said, "Hhm. I see. That's the way most, well almost all royal families decide their leaders, so there's nothing odd there. When he disappeared did you notice anything out of the ordinary?" Thomas thought back, "There was an odd smell around and very strong where I picked up Nanuk's last scent. I also felt very eerie, like something wicked had been there too." Shinu looked up from his mug at Thomas. Surprised he said, "When we found my sister there was something not right there too. A horrible odor. Try to think hard about everything around you right before he disappeared up to after. Anything small or insignificant." Thomas clasped Sadie's hand tighter as he tried to remember back. Upset, he said, "Damn it! I can't remember anything. I know it's there. I just can't remember."

I took Thomas' hand in mine. I had to try and help him remember. I said, "I will look in your memory to see if I can help you pull it out. It will be a painful memory. You will feel everything you felt the day he was lost. The heartache, the sick stomach. Are you up for it?" He looked over at Sadie and said, "I need to do this honey, but it will be hard on you too. Do you want to go inside?" She shook her head, "No. I want to be right here for you. I know it will hurt, but I have to be here for you." He caressed her cheek and said, "You are so strong. I love you so much. Go on Skye."

I turned my chair around to face Thomas. I took both his hands in mine and closed my eyes. I let out my breath and explained, "I will go into your subconscious mind to pull that memory out. I won't invade any other memory you hold in there. Just think of that day. Picture when you first got to the spot where you played."

Thomas closed his eyes also and let out a breath. I could feel myself floating through memory after memory. Pictures flashed past me like a view from a roller coaster. I floated on through blurry images zipping past me until I reached a scene and made a dead stop. *I was standing in the woods in a small clearing.* I spoke this part out loud, "I can see Thomas down on his knees crawling around with Nanuk. He grabbed Nanuk and threw him up in the air and rolled around with him." *I could feel the joy and intense love shared between them. Pride coursed through me.*

Again I spoke, "The trees look normal. The sky is clear, very clear and sunny. I can hear the birds singing and bugs chirping and hopping and climbing. A crow is flying overhead followed by several other small birds." *They flitted and played in the tree tops. I looked back at Thomas. He was now standing and explaining to Nanuk how to creep up on his prey slowly. He was telling him how to walk so softly that even the leaves on the ground wouldn't stir.*

Speaking again I said, "Nanuk wanted to go off just a little distance and hide and try to sneak up on his father." *Thomas laughed a joyful laugh, again proud of his son and said go ahead, but not too far.* I looked around again at the sky. Something had changed,

"The sky is getting darker. It's too quiet now. I can't hear the birds or the bugs. The trees are even still. Something smells and I can feel sadness, evil, despicable anger. It's so thick in the air I can hardly breathe."

I began to gag and choke. I could feel Shinu patting me on my back and I could hear Sadie stand up. I felt her near Thomas. I could feel Emily stroking my hair and rubbing my arm. *Thomas is calling for Nanuk now. He turns into a wolf and starts running through the trees. He's looking around and calling and calling. He arrives at a tree and sniffs around. Oh poor Thomas. I can feel the overwhelming pain. My heart felt like it was being ripped out of my chest. The feeling of just wanting to die right there was so strong. My stomach lurched.*

I could finally talk again, "Thomas has found the spot where Nanuk was last. The smell is worse here. I c-c-can't breathe. It's, its horrible! Such menacing evil. Such hatred and ferocious anger!" I can feel Sadie pulling at Thomas. She's crying. What is she saying?

I couldn't hear her anymore. *Where am I now? What's happening? Where's Thomas? Where's . . . Dad?* I screamed out loud, "Oh God! It's so dark! I can't see anything! So dark! No! Dada? Where are you? So cold! What do you want? Where's Dada? Mom? Don't touch me!" I had crawled off my chair and was cowering in the corner of the porch. I could feel myself curl up in a ball and lay down with my arms wrapped around my legs, but I couldn't reconnect to my conscious mind. I could hear everyone calling me but couldn't get back. Back in my subconscious I was in someone else's mind. How? I couldn't control what I was yelling out. "What do you want? Let me go!"

I could feel Shinu pick me up and hold me right there in the corner of the porch on the floor. He was rocking me and stroking my hair and back. I still couldn't connect with myself. Shinu was trying to find me. He was trying to get in my head. I have to let him in, but this other mind is so scared. It won't let anyone else in. *You have to let him in to help you. He has to talk to me to help you. Please.* Finally. I could hear him now. Shinu was finally with me. *Skye, you have to come back. We need you here with us.* I tried to answer him. I couldn't answer him in his mind.

Something was blocking me, keeping me from answering with my mind. I have to fight it. I told myself, you have to at least answer with your conscious mind. "It's so dark. Cold. The floor, no ground is hard rock. It's wet. It smells. It smells like, like salt. I hear water. The walls sparkle when he turns on a light. Dirt. He keeps feeding me stinky fish. Don't want fish. I feel feathers. Wanna go home to Dada!"

I could feel someone else's hands cupping my face. I suddenly felt warm all over. I could see a bright pink light flickering through my eye lids. *I was suddenly knocked backward. I was hurling thru a murky tunnel. I hit something. A flash of brilliant light and finally my conscious and subconscious reconnected.* I sat up straight and opened my eyes. Shinu was still holding me. Amber was right in front of me. She looked worried. Thomas, Sadie, and Emily were down on their knees on the porch floor behind her. I could see Natasha in wolf form pacing back and forth behind them. I reached past Amber and grabbed Thomas' arms. He looked at me with frantic hope and yelled, "Nanuk!"

CHAPTER 16

A UNITED SEARCH ...

Every body got up from off the floor and took a seat at the table. Shinu and Amber helped me up. I was still shaky and couldn't get my balance yet. Sadie went in the house to get me some water. Shinu still sat by me and Emily sat on his other side. Amber sat on my other side and held my hand. Elliot had positioned himself right behind me in his wolf form and Natasha also in her wolf form.

They both paced back and forth with their ears standing up listening for any sound. I looked at the driveway to the house and didn't see Amber's car. I was confused. I looked at Amber. She finally looked a little calmer. I asked, "When did you get here and how?" She put her hand on my forehead like she was checking my temperature. She said, "I got here an hour ago. Elliot came and got me. That was the first time I ever rode on a werewolf's back. He insisted. He said if I drove he was afraid I wouldn't get here fast enough. We got here in like five minutes."

Still lost, I asked more questions, "Why did they get you? How long was I not here?" Shinu answered me as Amber continued to check me out. She was taking my pulse this time. "You were gone for a little over two hours. Right after Thomas rejoined us from you reading his memory, you slipped somewhere else. After about an hour of trying to bring you back I told them to go get Amber. If anyone could reach you it would be her. She worked on you for about forty five minutes then you finally answered me. She should be completely drained. I never felt such strong magic before. I'm impressed."

I looked at Amber again and held back my tears as I grabbed her and hugged her. She squeezed me back. I said, "Thank you again for saving me. You are always there for me." Amber couldn't hold her tears back. She let them flow, "Don't ever do that to me again. I lost you once. Never again."

I looked at Thomas. He was visibly shaken. I thought back to all that had happened in my journey into his mind and everything clicked. I faced him and said, "Thomas. When I came back, you yelled out Nanuk. Were you still upset about your memories of that day?" He stared at me for a few minutes before he could answer. Then he said, "I don't know if you realize it, but you were no longer in my memories right after the part when I couldn't find Nanuk. I was going to ask you what happened. Then, when you started talking about a dark place . . ."

Once again he paused. I could see he was on the verge of crying. He went on, "When you said it was dark, you kept saying Dada, mom. At first I thought maybe it was a lost memory of yours, but then you said, 'Wanna go home to Dada." One small tear rolled down his cheek. He took a deep breath and finished what he was saying, "Nanuk calls me Dada. Could you have seen into Nanuk's mind? Could that be possible?"

A cold chill ran down my spine and made me shiver. Everything flooded back through my mind. I jumped up from the table and started pacing back and forth my own self now. I had to think before I answered him. I know I can go into the mind and memories of anyone and see their memories. I had never been able to see or feel what a person was doing at the very moment they were going through it. Could it be possible? Shahma said I was stronger than she realized.

Maybe, just maybe. I said, "Thomas, I don't want to get anyone's hopes up because this is the first time I have ever experienced anything like that. But, there's a possibility that when I was in your subconscious mind I somehow connected with Nanuk's mind. If your thoughts were on Nanuk's at the same time he was thinking about you or reaching out for you, there's a slight chance I connected with his mind."

I started to feel excited about the thought of Nanuk still being alive. And with the hints and clues that I picked up, there was a small chance that we may be able to find him. I had to go on cautiously. "If in fact that might have been him, we need to start looking for that place. Day time would be a better time to go traipsing about. I want to talk to Stacey and see who she's been able to tell about us.

I sent her to the Sheriff's office right after our meeting because I had a vision of her dad talking to Sheriff Makepeace and they were pretty close to putting two and two together as to who's been doing some of the killings around here lately. If they can accept us and are willing to help us in the battle we have to face, then who better to help us look? Thomas, I don't want to give you false hope, but whoever it was, needs our help." Thomas agreed with me.

I turned and faced Shinu. "Shinu, before all of this happened you were asking Thomas questions about Nanuk. What were you trying to find out?" He sat forward in his chair and said, "Oh, yes. I was trying to compare scenes with the one where we found our sister. By the time we got there it would have been too late to notice surrounding things. But the one thing they both had in common was the smell. There was this horrendous aroma lingering in the air. It had a substance to it too. Almost like the whole area was in a bubble of thick, choking smoke."

Emily asked him, "You also asked how our pack works. What were you looking for in that?" Shinu went on, "I have been around a long time and the one thing I've seen happen time and again in history was that, when it came to hierarchy, there almost always was someone jealous of the next one to inherit the throne. Many times they just begrudgedly accepted the fact that they would never have what they wanted. But there were times when some would not acknowledge it. They just had to have the power, rule the kingdom or what have you, and tried to take it by any means necessary. Could there have been someone in your pack now or in the past who may fit that description?"

• •

The streets in town were pretty much deserted. Besides the occasional car heading down the street, most likely heading home, there was no one in sight. In the alley behind the gun shop, though, there was a small crowd gathering. A band of raccoons were creeping along the walls and behind the dumpsters to meet up with the others that were standing at the back door to the gun shop. There were three hunched down and waiting. An additional six slowly advanced forward and joined them.

The biggest of the bunch stood up on his hind legs and shifted into his human form. In a hushed voice he asked, "Any of you see anyone coming this way?" The group squeaked. He replied, "Good. We have to be fast about this. He told us that we needed to get as many guns as we can and keep them from the mortals. He said they were the ones slowly killing off our kind while hunting." One of the raccoons that were waiting at the door with him stood and changed too. "Filthy mortals! Where do they get off killing innocent animals? They have never hunted simple raccoons, squirrels, birds. They even took out several chipmunks!"

The biggest one spoke up again, "Keep it down. I know we're pretty ticked off, but we can vent later. We have to get in here quickly and take as much as we can. Ready?" The other man nodded his head and reached in his pocket and pulled out a lock picking kit. The first man shook his head and laughed, "Where did you get that?" The other man answered with a sly smile, "I'm a raccoon, aren't I?" The first man nodded yes and motioned for two of the other raccoons that had been waiting at the door, to come on inside.

Once inside they changed into their human form. One was a woman, the other a younger man. The first man stayed by the door for a moment to talk to the rest of the raccoons. "I need two of you to change and move this man hole while we go in and start bringing things out. Three of you keep a look out at the east end of the alley and the rest of you keep a look out on the west end. We gotta move quickly and quietly. The rats are waiting down in the sewer for us to start handing the guns down. Move now."

With that, two of them shifted and removed the manhole lid. The others spread out and kept watch. Inside the gun shop the group began grabbing guns and ammunition and taking them out the door to the two men that had removed the manhole lid. They then handed the guns and ammunition down the hole to the rats that had shifted into their human forms. After a while of transferring the things, one of the rats called up and asked, "Hey, can you hold off for a minute? We have to go grab another cart." The men up top agreed and let the ones inside know to wait.

The woman that was with the group inside sat down on the floor and took a deep breath. She looked to the first man and asked, "Are you sure we're doing the right thing? I mean, I got a feeling it isn't the humans behind the killings. Something just isn't right. The humans have never just gone around killing for the sport of it. Not here anyway. They have always seemed to respect or cherish nature around here." The first man gave her a chastising look. "You heard what he said. He's never lied to us before or led us wrong. We've always followed him and I don't plan on questioning him now. If you don't like it, you can leave." She sat there and thought for a while, then said, "You're right. I just thought maybe we should discuss this with Lady Skye first."

He turned his back to her and went to the door. He leaned his head out to talk to the men outside. "Hey. They back yet?" Before any of them could answer one of the raccoons that had been standing guard on the east end of the alley came running back and quickly changed to human form. "Sheriff's on his way down the street. We'd better go." He took off and changed back into a raccoon. The others heard him and did the same. The two men that removed the manhole cover replaced it and changed, then scampered off toward the west end of the alley. The first man called back inside to the others, "Sheriff's on his way. Someone dump the trash and spread it out. Every body, change back just in case we don't get out of here.

As the first man stood at the door watching, the sheriff turned his jeep down the alley. He changed just as the headlights washed across him. He ran back inside the gun shop with the others and waited in a pile of trash for the sheriff to get there. Sheriff Makepeace pulled his truck up to the back door and got out. He shined his flashlight down the alley to look for anyone that may be hiding.

He saw movement behind one of the dumpsters. As he moved closer to see who or what it was, he put his hand on his gun ready for anything. Something small ran out and shot down the alley. He turned his flashlight in that direction just in time to see it was a raccoon. He shook his head and laughed at himself for getting all worked up.

Now he had to check on the gun shop's back door. He could see when he pulled up that the door was open. Once again he put his hand on his gun and slowly moved toward the door. Leaning against the wall outside the door he took a deep breath, pulled out his gun, and situated his flashlight in his other hand. His pulsed raced and he broke out in a sweat. He called out, "This is the sheriff. Come on out with your hands up!" He waited a few seconds but there was no response.

He heard a crashing sound and quickly turned around the corner of the door. He could see glowing yellow eyes in the beam of his light near the floor. He panned the area inside with his light and spotted three raccoons. One of them appeared to have his hands in the air and the other two were staring at him with bits if trash in their paws.

The sheriff lowered his gun and put it away. He wiped his face with his hands and leaned over to catch his breath. Laughing again he said, "Whew! Raccoons. Here I am ready for some big bad guy and I get raccoons. Go on fellows. You won't find much to eat here." He wasn't sure if they understood him or not, but they did turn tail and run out the door. As they ran off to meet up with the others the first raccoon asked the younger one, "What the heck were you doing holding your hands up?" He answered, "Well he said come out with your hands up." They all laughed and continued on there way.

• •

Before Thomas could answer one of the young ladies came up to the porch with the one they call grandma. She timidly said, "Excuse me Madame. I'm sorry to interrupt you, but grandma said she had to speak with you all right away. I was describing the drawing you brought for us to look at to her, because she couldn't see it very well, and I thought she was going to have a heart attack. That's when she begged me to bring her here immediately."

I thanked her and helped grandma to a seat on the porch. She didn't hesitate and started speaking fast and quietly. "I'm sorry to bother you all, but I'm afraid it isn't good news. Skye, my dear, that knife you saw in your vision belonged to Damien Wick."

Elliot and Natasha simultaneously growled and their hair stood up on their backs. Thomas pushed back from the table and jumped out of his seat. Sadie dropped the tray she was carrying back into the house and Amber gasped. With just the mention of his name I felt as if my stomach had been placed in a blender on high speed. My head began spinning and I felt like I was completely enveloped in a darkness that was slowly consuming my whole body. I must have drifted off again because Shinu was at my side again holding my arm. Worried, he said, "My, my. You look like you have been completely drained of blood. I didn't do it." Emily must have been right behind him because she smacked him in the back of his head and said, "Come on Shinu."

As much as I wanted to laugh at Shinu getting smacked in the head, I couldn't right then. Once I was able to speak, I said, "When you said his name I remembered a vague flash of that same feeling when I went into Thomas' memories. In the woods when Nanuk disappeared."

Shinu faced grandma and asked her, "Pardon me ma'am, but would you mind briefly telling me who this Damien Wick is?" Grandma jumped a little, but then walked up to Shinu and touched his face. She giggled a little and said, "Hhm. So it is true. There *is* a vampire among us. I never thought I'd live to see the day when another Takai would be around. We must talk another time. As for Damien Wick, he was an evil man. Power hungry. He wanted to challenge Thomas' great great grandfather to be the head of the pack.

The pack leader has never been chosen that way. It has always been handed down through the family. He did some very bad things back then to make his point, cause havoc, so many bad things. He was finally banished from the pack. Skye's father lost his life helping us to rid ourselves of this terrible creature. This was only since I was born into the pack. It is said that he goes back even further then that."

Everyone turned and gaped at Shinu now, because of what he had just hit on. I even had to look at him and said, "Shinu, sounds like you may have been on the right track." He winked at me, "I've seen it so many times before it just made since to me. More then someone just randomly running around killing and kidnapping." He faced grandma again and said, "Thank you ma'am. I would love to sit and talk to you some time. Once things settle down." She smiled again, nodded ok, and then the young lady led her back to her house.

Now that things seemed to be coming together we just had to figure out where to go from here. I motioned for everyone to come back to the porch so I could go on with the plans for now. "Well, first thing first. Whoever it was that I connected to needs our help. I will get in touch with the Sheriff and Stacey's dad tonight. Hopefully Stacey got through to them and they will be willing to help us out, not only with the battle to come, but with looking for this person.

It would really help us to have the sheriff working with us on this. He may even have an idea of where I was describing. I know tomorrow is school, but we really need your help Shinu and Emily and Amber. If you are willing to skip, it would be greatly appreciated. I think we should start as early as possible. Once I know something from Stacey, can I call all of you and arrange a time and meeting place?" Everyone nodded yes. "Great. I'll go now to Stacey's. Thank you all. Get some rest and see you in the morning." I left them all sitting there talking. It was good to see them getting along. I changed back into a cheetah and headed for Stacey's.

· ·

The run back in town didn't take me that long. Before I hit the edge of town I changed back into my human form just in case someone was out nosing around. There aren't any cheetahs in this area. I think I'd stick out like a sore thumb. I took out my cell as soon as I could catch my breath and called Stacey. She picked up on the second ring. She was so excited she didn't even let me say hello. "Guess what? I did it Skye! I got my dad and Sheriff Makepeace to not only listen to me, but to believe me too. They want to meet with you tomorrow night at my house at 7:00 p.m. Dad's downstairs talking to mom right now. I overheard them. She was ecstatic. She said this finally proves that all these years she hasn't been crazy or imagining things. Sorry I'm babbling. What's up?"

I had to laugh at her. This was typical Stacey. I said, "I am so proud of you. I knew I chose the right person for our liaison. Something's come up. It's imperative I speak to your parents tonight and to Sheriff Makepeace. Preferably a.s.a.p." Stacey paused for a few seconds then went on, "Where are you right now?" I answered, "About five minutes from your house." She said, "Ok. Give me a few and I'll call you back." She hung up. I stepped back into the trees to sit and rest a moment. I figured I'd try and call Jaye and let him know what was going on and see if he'd be willing to help us tomorrow. I know he would. I dialed his number and it went straight to voicemail. I left him a brief message and hung up. He was probably consulting with the shape-shifters. I hope all was going well for him.

After waiting about twenty minutes my phone rang. It was Stacey. I answered, "Please tell me its good news." I could hear talking in the background before she spoke, "Skye. Sheriff Makepeace was already on his way over here when I had dad call him. Seems there was a break in at the gun shop. Turned out to be raccoons. They all said they'd talk to you tonight. How soon can you get here?" Relieved, I said, "I can be there in five minutes." She said great and she'll see me in a few. I hung up. Now I wondered about that break in. It could have been just regular raccoons looking for food. I hope so.

I stood up sprinted to her house. By the time I got there the sheriff was already inside. I walked up the steps to her front door. Although her house was as familiar to me as my own I still felt a little apprehensive. I had to have faith in Stacey. I've been around all of them for years now. They all knew me. But I still couldn't shake the feeling that I was meeting them for the first time. I guess in a way I was. My stomach curled in a knot then untied with a snap.

I took a deep breath and rang the doorbell. As I was standing there waiting for someone to answer I kept telling myself, *You can do this. You know them. You have to do this. Everyone is counting on you to lead them. You're a leader, not a wimp.* Stacey opened the door. She smiled at me and I smiled back. Just looking at her eyes and knowing that she too was counting on me gave me the courage I needed.

Stacey walked ahead of me and led me into the living room. Her mom was sitting on the edge of the couch looking at me with a smile. Her father and Sheriff Makepeace were standing on each side of her. Neither one of them smiled, but they didn't look upset either. They looked more like little kids looking at Santa Clause and wondering if he was the real thing or not. Everyone stayed still, just looking at me, so I smiled and broke the silence first. "Good evening. Thank you for meeting with me on such short notice. Let me start by first apologizing for having to keep you all in the dark all these years. And, I have to ask, how much do you know and how much of it do you believe?"

That did it. They looked at each other and started talking it out amongst each other. After about a minute of chattering, Sheriff Makepeace was the first to speak up. "Stacey has filled us in some. We have always had some suspicion that there were more out there then just humans, but kept it to ourselves. For many years we talked about it on different occasions and wondered, what if. We have so many questions, which we hope to get answered eventually. But first, can you relieve our curiosity?"

I was thankful they didn't want to attack me. I smiled and asked, "Anything. How can I help?" This time it was Stacey's mom that asked, "Stacey told us you changed into a falcon in front of her to show her what you can do. Can you change for us? Maybe into some animal not native to Haines. Say, a kangaroo."

There was that look on their faces again. This time it was little kids waiting to see Santa make the reindeer fly. So I took a deep breath and changed. I stepped back from the coffee table first. I wasn't sure how big I'd get. I had never changed into a kangaroo before, but it couldn't be too hard. I closed my eyes and thought of all the pictures and documentaries I had ever seen on them.

I could feel my feet stretching out and getting longer. I scrunched down as my thigh muscles expanded. I could feel my body spreading out some and I could tell I was growing a tail. My arms shortened and drew into my body some. My nose stretched out and I could actually feel my whiskers sprout out of my face. My ears grew out.

I finally opened my eyes and looked down at myself. I actually had a pouch on my stomach! Looking down, I half expected to see a baby kangaroo looking up at me. Well, I did it. If I could talk to them now I would say, Tah-Da! I obviously shocked them because all of them, including Stacey, just stared at me with their mouths hanging open. I laughed. I couldn't help myself. Stacey's dad said, "Well I'll be a monkey's uncle! If I hadn't seen it with my own eyes I would have never thought it possible. I'll be damned. It's true. All of it! Can I touch you? I mean, to just see if my eyes aren't messing with me."

I nodded my head and wiggled my ears to let them know it was ok. He walked up to me, cautiously, and reached out and rubbed my head. His eyes got huge! He giggled and turned to the others, "Honey, you gotta come see for yourself. John, take a look." They each came up to me, timidly, and touched my head. Stacey had already seen me change before and wasn't so leery. She stood behind me and rubbed my back.

Leave it to her to break the monotony. "Oh my God! Skye you have a tail! If the house was bigger I'd ask you to jump around! You are so cool! Mom, don't I have the coolest best friend, ever? I told you guys. See I told you. You have to believe completely now. No mirrors. No magic tricks. She's a shape-shifter. Not just a shape-shifter, a Shoo-atee!" Stacey's mom shushed her, "Now Stacey. Calm down and stop rambling. She always rambles. Skye dear, you are amazing!" Sheriff Makepeace chuckled and patted me on the back. "Ok Skye. We really believe you. That's fantastic! You can change back now. We need to talk."

I changed back, which brought out more oos and ahs, and sat on the couch between Stacey and her mom. Her mom grabbed my hand and held it. She gave me an endearing motherly smile. I felt at ease now. We briefly covered what Stacey had already told them and I added a little more detail. I told them about what we were facing in the battle and how I was working on a plan to unite everyone to fight.

I also told them about the death of Natalie and about Nanuk missing. They each agreed we had to do something and I asked, "So, does this mean we can rely on you all for your help in any way we may need it?" Sheriff Makepeace answered me, "Skye. We will help in any way we can. I do have to say that I am the law and I do have to somehow bring justice to the men who lost their lives. With that, I have to ask for *your* help."

I nodded. I knew something had to be done. "I will take care of it Sheriff Makepeace. I myself do not believe in vigilantes. I understand and sympathize with their loss, but I will also do what needs to be done. As far as your investigation and closure to the cases, I will also help you to report the facts and solve the problem with as much truth to it as can be done. I know not everyone will believe in us, and that's great. Not everyone needs to know.

We need to keep it as much of a secret as we can. We don't need tourists and government finding out and causing all kinds of trouble for any of us, human or immortal. I need to protect my people and you yours. Can we agree on this?" The sheriff agreed and we shook hands. That was another relief.

Now I had to explain to them about what happened earlier at the camp. "We can wait to further discuss and investigate Shinu's theory, but we have to start looking for whoever it was I connected with. I have a gut feeling we don't have long. I didn't tell the others that because I didn't want to discourage them or cause an all out rush without order to look for them." Sheriff Makepeace paced around some and scratched his head for a few minutes. He sat down and closed his eyes in thought, and then he stood up and paced around again. He walked from end of the living room to the next, and then abruptly stopped when he was standing in front of a picture of him and Mr. Ritennour.

He looked at the picture for a few seconds then moved even closer to the picture. He turned around and looked at Mr. Ritennour and asked, "Bill, you remember that spot we went fishing at back last summer?" He stood up and walked over to look at the picture too. He nodded and said, "Yeah. That's where we found a massive amount of salmon. Boy, did we eat salmon for a long time that year. Why?" The sheriff came over to me and said, "You said in your, connection, that it was dark and cold, there was dirt, the walls shined when light hit it and something about stinky fish. When you were there, did the coldness feel like it was just outdoor winter cold or windy cold, or more like sitting in a freezer cold?"

I had to close my eyes and revisit the place. Just thinking about it made me shiver and Mrs. Ritennour moved closer to me and put her arms around me. I finally said, "I know it sounds weird, but it was more like sitting inside an ice cube, cold. Does that make sense?" He nodded. "Sure does. I think I know where we can begin our search tomorrow morning. Bill and I went fishing in a place last summer we hadn't tried before. It's real remote. Never seen anyone going out there for anything really. It was quiet. Lots of salmon.

They practically jumped in the boat. But that wasn't the odd thing. Right off the shore on the north end of the lake was a mountain like glacier. It looked like a glacier swallowed part of a mountain. There were some openings near the top. We just figured some animals had burrowed their homes in it. What you described fits that description. I could imagine that one of those holes is just hollowed out ice with some rock. That might be the shiny walls. And being ice would explain the coldness like being in an ice cube."

I was a little more encouraged with that news. I directed my response to all of them now, "Then it's settled. We can search there first." John interrupted me, "Sounds like a good place to start. But how do we get up there? Me and one of my men can spelunk. We can go down from the top. What about the others that will help? Oh, sorry. Stupid question, huh? Gotta remember who I'm talking to now." He laughed at himself. I laughed too.

We went on to discuss the time we would all meet and where, when I thought of another question for John. I asked, "In all our discussion I never thought to ask you about your men. Do you think they would believe us or even want to believe and work with us?" The sheriff got a sneaky look on his face. He said, "You just leave them up to me and Stacey young lady. My men believe in U.F.O.'s. Won't be too hard to get them to believe in you all." We agreed to meet at my house, since it was closer to the place he was talking about, and we'd get together at 6:00 a.m.

I thanked them all for their help and understanding and left. I walked to the edge of town and stopped long enough to call everyone and let them know that we have Stacey's parents, Sheriff Makepeace and his men on our side now. I told them to meet at my house at 6:00 a.m., and to be ready to do some swimming, boating and climbing. I also warned them that we need to stay on our toes and be ready to fight just in case. They said they'd be there.

I decided to change into a hawk to head home. I needed to feel the wind and clear my head. I talked to Shinu in my mind on the way. I told him about the meeting at Stacey's too. Of course, he got a kick out of me becoming a kangaroo for them. He said his older brother, Yusuke, and his sister, Hana, were coming to help us search. I told him good night and flew on.

The flight home was relaxing. I loved soaring in the sky. At night the stars zipping by were beautiful. It didn't take long flying either. I circled the house a few times before I landed and changed. I just thought I'd check out the surroundings just in case. Once inside I told my mom and grandma about everything from the time I left until now. They were excited too to hear that Stacey's parents and Sheriff Makepeace would work with us. And, as I knew they would do, they said they'd have coffee and muffins ready for everyone in the morning. When I headed upstairs I could hear them discussing the different types of muffins they would make.

Before I turned in I tried Jaye's phone again. I still got voicemail. I really hoped he was ok. When I finally laid down and dozed off, I once again tossed and turned in the throws of vision after vision.

CHAPTER 17

LOST AND FOUND . . .

Morning came too quick again. I drug myself out of bed and dressed for the hike and the weather. After I was dressed I checked my phone to see if Jaye had returned my call. Nothing. I was really beginning to worry. For now, I had to concentrate on our search for whoever it was I connected with, and then I'd try and find out where Jaye was. I headed downstairs. Before reaching the bottom steps the smell of coffee and various muffins drifted up to me. I could smell banana, blueberry, and strawberry, cherry and chocolate chip. I walked into the kitchen and was floored by the amount of muffins that lined the kitchen table. They must have gotten up early and started these. Leave it to mom and grandma.

They greeted me with a mug of coffee and kisses. Mom was dressed beautifully, as usual. You couldn't tell by the way she was dressed that she had been baking all morning. I complimented her, "Mom. You look as stunning as ever. No one will believe these muffins. Grandma thanks." They smiled back at me. Grandma motioned with her hand toward the table and said, "I think this should cover whatever taste any of them may have. I made plenty of coffee too. You'll all need as much energy as you can muster for this search. It will be a tough one. Today will end with happiness and sadness. My dreams only revealed to me that it will be a day of lost and found. I'm sorry, but that's all I can give you for now."

I hugged her. She always has something inspiring for me it seems. Grandma wasn't gifted with the ability to see visions, but many times her dreams have had hidden messages in them. I picked out a strawberry muffin and looked at my watch. It was 5:30 a.m. Soon people would be arriving. I grabbed my coat, my coffee and my muffin and headed for the front door. I needed to get some fresh air to wake me up and greet them as they got here.

I decided to take a quick flight around the area to just look out and try and speak to some of the other animals to see if they might have seen or heard from Jaye. I stepped off the porch and shifted into a hawk and flew toward the woods. I swooped between trees and over branches keeping an eye out in case I saw him coming. Flying higher and higher in the air I was able to clear my mind. The morning looked like it was going to be pretty good for our search. There were only a few clouds. The sun was rising and cast a breath taking orange and pink glow on everything.

I found the tree central to the woods and lit on one of the top branches and called out to any birds that might be in the area. Soon the air was filled with various kinds of my feathered comrades. Some continued to circle overhead while others lit on the branches surrounding me, above and below. After they had all settled I spoke to them, "My dear friends. I am sure by now you are aware of who I am." The trees rustled and the sound of a variety of chirps, caws, and whistles signified they knew and acknowledged me. I went on. "I will soon have to ask of all of you a great deed. But for now, I am just looking for information. I am looking for Jaye Crowe. You should all know of him. He is the leader of all the shape shifters in our area."

Before I could go on I noticed I was gaining more of an audience. There were now raccoons, squirrels, deer, bears, and other animals slowly gathering in the trees and at the foot of the trees. I was glad to have them there to hear. I continued, "I had asked Jaye to speak to all of you and let you know what we are about to face. There is someone or something beyond evil that is going around killing our kind and mortals. I don't have time to get into that now, but *it* has to be stopped and it is up to me to lead you all in that fight. Like I said, for now I am looking for Jaye.

I hope nothings happened to him, but will you all please keep an eye out for him and let me know if any of you find out anything? I greatly appreciate your help. Oh. I will be tied up all day looking for someone lost, but later or even tomorrow I will meet with you to let you know more if Jaye hasn't already covered that with you. I will let you know the time and place. Thank you for all your help."

All the birds chirped again or whistled and flew off. The other animals answered me with growls, squeaks, or barks and went on their way. None of them seemed to know what I was talking about. Now I wondered could something have happened to Jaye before he could speak to the shape-shifters. Later. I spread my wings and flew back to the house.

I circled around the house first and didn't notice anything out of the ordinary, so I shifted back right before I landed on the ground. I didn't see the sheriff and his men coming up the drive as I shifted, until I landed. They were a little early. I waited for them to park and greeted them as they got out. They were dressed in camouflage, but still had their badges on. I smiled and said, "Good morning. I can't thank you enough for your help." Sheriff Makepeace introduced me to his men. "Morning Skye. This is Brad. He's been with the force for nineteen years. He's my right hand man."

Deputy Brad removed his hat and shook my hand. "Ma'am. Good to *officially* meet you. You may know my boys. They're on the football team. The two biggest most hard headed boys on the team. Always fighting with each other or competing with each other?" I had to think for a minute. Then it dawned on me. "Oh my gosh! You're a shape-shifter! You and your family are moose! So good to meet you.

I would love to talk to you after we're finished today. Pleased to meet you. Oh my. Sheriff, did you know this?"

He chuckled and rubbed his forehead. "Well. I didn't know until I talked to him last night. Imagine my shock and relief. And this is Ned. He's our young rookie. He's been with us for two years now." Ned took off his hat and very clumsily shook my hand too. "So cool to meet ya. Gotta tell ya. I believe in aliens. Weren't a problem acceptin' you all. I seen ya change when we pulled up. So cool." I had to laugh at him. "Good to meet you too. Thank you for your cooperation. We can always use someone with enthusiasm."

I walked them into the house to introduce them to mom and grandma. Mom was at the door already, opening it. She greeted the sheriff first, "Hello Sheriff. Nice to see you again." I have never seen my mom light up like she did when he shook her hand. I could almost swear my mom was blushing. I'll have to give her the third degree later. Everyone introduced themselves and grandma led them into the kitchen for coffee and muffins. I went back outside to wait for the others.

Soon Thomas arrived with several from his pack. They were in their werewolf forms and were on foot. I recognized them all. I smiled, "Good morning. Glad you all came. Did Sadie stay with the rest of the pack?" They went ahead and changed back into human form. They were all wearing thin jackets, a white t-shirt, jeans, and hiking boots. Thomas nodded, "She can keep an eye on the rest of the pack while we're out. My other guards are standing watch also." Natasha, Elliot, Emily and Natasha's brother had accompanied him.

Before we could make it up the porch, Amber pulled up with Dave and behind them were Stacey and her family. Good. Almost everyone was here. I was just waiting on Shinu and his brother and sister before I introduced everyone. I think of him and there he was in my mind. *Sorry we were running a little behind. My brother couldn't decide what to wear. We will be there in about two minutes.*

I smiled. I told Thomas and his crew to wait on the porch a moment. I went to Amber, who was now out of her car, and hugged her. She was dressed in a long black trench coat, a black t-shirt, black jeans with lace down the legs and black high heel boots. I shook my head and said, "So glad you made it. We may need some medical attention today. Besides, I need your support. Nice outfit." She hugged me back, smiled and said, "What would you do without me? And thank you. Thought I'd dress down for this." I laughed and greeted Dave. He just had on a brown parka, black turtle neck sweater, brown denim pants, and hiking boots. I was starting to think everyone had gone shopping at the local shoe store and got the same boots on sale due to an over order. We shook hands and I excused myself to go say hi to Stacey and her family.

They were all decked out in camouflage hiking gear. It was odd seeing her father dressed like that and not in a suit as usual. I could sense a little hint of apprehension in her parents, but they smiled when they saw me. I smiled back and said, "Thanks so much Mr. and Mrs. Ritennour. I know this is kind of awkward at first, but I'll introduce everyone and then we'll go over our game plan." Stacey added her part in too. "Yeah mom, dad. You got me to help you out too. We'll be fine. You'll see." With another smile I told them to follow me to the porch also.

By the time I had shuffled everyone to the porch; mom, grandma, the sheriff and his deputies, were coming back out the house and joining the others on the porch. Before I could reach the first step, Shinu and his family vaporized out of thin air in front of me. Shinu had on a thin black jacket, a red t-shirt, black jeans and black hiking boots. He took my hand, bowed and kissed it before he said, "My Lady. So good to see you this morning. Let me introduce you to my siblings. This is Yusuke, my older and eccentric 'ladies man' brother, and this is Hana, my older and unstable sister."

I started to ask him why he called her unstable when Yusuke bowed to me and took my hand and kissed it too. He was wearing a burgundy colored suit. The suit coat came down to his knees. He had on a black silk shirt and tie, and black leather boots with somewhat of a heel to them. He had that same sly smile on his face that Shinu had whenever he was being facetious. Then he said, "It is a pleasure to finally meet you Madame Skye. My brother talks about you a lot. Of course you know our families are bound together and I am at your service anytime you need me, for *anything*." He kissed my hand again, this time he lingered there for a while, before he raised his head and winked at me.

I thanked him and turned to Hana. She had on a brilliant fire red blouse, kind of low cut, a lacey black vest that also came down to her knees, black slacks and black stiletto boots. I shook her hand and had to ask her, "So why does Shinu call you unstable?" She giggled. Her laugh almost sounded like little bells tinkling. She was also unusually perky for a vampire. "Oh, don't mind my little brother. He's referring to the fact that I'm not always in a good mood. I'm fine and very happy to meet you too finally. Shinu talks highly of you. Which is odd for him. He doesn't think much of any body really unless they're family. You are quite intriguing. I hope we get to hang out some time." I had to laugh. She was very interesting. I said, "I'd like that very much. Now if you all will excuse me, I have to get everyone acquainted and get our game plan in order."

I walked up on the porch and stood as center to the crowd as I could. Oddly enough I didn't have to ask everyone to be quiet. They all just stopped talking at the same time and turned to look at me. I cleared my throat anyway and spoke to everyone, "I'd like to thank you all again for coming together like this on such short notice.

Before I begin my mom and grandma would kill me if I didn't let everyone know that they have went to great lengths to make a variety of muffins and several pots of coffee. Everyone is welcome to go inside and help yourselves. They want to make sure everyone has something to eat and some hot coffee in them before we leave."

They both rubbed my back and kissed me on my cheek. I went on, "I will first introduce each of you and hopefully clear up any tension or apprehension. I know from my visions and from my feelings that everyone here will get along just fine. I will start with Thomas and his people. Thomas is the leader of his pack. They are werewolves."

I walked over to him to let them see who he was. Thomas took over for me, "Hello everyone. I am Thomas. This is Natasha, my right hand and first in command in my pack. This is Elliot. He is second in command. This is Dakota, Natasha's brother. And this is Emily. She's new to my pack. Don't let her size fool you though. She is a force to be reckoned with." Through out the crowd people said hi or waved and smiled.

I then went over to Amber and Dave. "I'd like you to meet Amber Whitcraft and her friend Dave. Amber is a witch and Dave, a warlock. You may all be familiar with her father, Dr. Whitcraft." Stacey's parents gasped, but not a bad gasp. Just one of shock. I continued, "Amber is my advisor and I guess you can say she is also our medical support. Their coven is healers. Kind of fitting that her father's a doctor, huh?" Again everyone said hello or waved.

I headed down off the porch and came over to stand by Shinu. "Next in our group is Shinu Takai, his brother Yusuke, and his sister Hana. Shinu is my first guard. I place all my trust and my life in his hands. They are trustworthy. They are vampires." Leave it to Ned to be the first one to burst out with a question. He asked, "Hey. I thought vampires couldn't come out in the day time."

Shinu and his family laughed. Shinu answered his question, "I'm sure you aren't the only one with that question. There are some who cannot venture forth in the sunlight, but many of us are capable of leading a normal life, or death, under the sun." That comment brought out a little laughter in some of them.

I walked over toward Stacey and her family and continued with the introductions. "I'm sure everyone here is familiar with the distinguished mayor of our humble town, Mayor Ritennour. This is his wife, Mrs. Ritennour and their daughter and my best friend, Stacey. They are human. Stacey is my liaison between us and the humans."

I walked back up on the porch and went over to the sheriff. "Last but not least, I know you all know Sheriff Makepeace. I will let him introduce his deputies and go on and explain where our search will begin today." After all my introductions I was ready for another cup of coffee. My mom must have sensed I'd need one because she walked over to me and handed me a fresh hot cup. I smiled at her and said, "Thank you mom." She just smiled at me and patted me on my shoulder.

Sheriff Makepeace had stepped to the edge of the porch and was now addressing everyone. "Hello everyone. Thank you for coming here this early in the morning. First, you all know me. This is my first deputy Brad and I just found out myself last night that he is a shape-shifter. He and his family are moose. And this is Ned. He's still a young'n so you have to excuse him if he asks weird questions. And yes, he and I are human.

Now on to business. Skye came to me with a vision or I think she called it a connection she made last night with someone that may be in trouble. The description she gave me as to where they may be is very close to a place me and the mayor went fishing at. It's over at a lake not far from here. Across that lake is a mountain iceberg thing. That's where we will begin our search today.

There are some caves carved into the face of the mountain iceberg. It won't be easy to reach. At least not easy to reach by humans. Me and Brad know how to spelunk, so we will hike up to the top and drop down by one of the openings. Whichever one of you can get to another cave opening will check that one. I know I saw a good four or five openings up high. There are some down closer to the surface of the lake.

We will take two boats out and whoever is in those will need to cover the surface level caves. I hate to even think of this part of our search, but we do not know if we will be confronted by an enemy while we're looking. For this, me and my men are armed. The mayor has his shot gun with him. I can assume that the rest of you have your own form of weaponry. All I can say is for everyone to be on guard. While those of us search the top caves, I would like to have someone stand guard at the top of the mountain."

Thomas stepped forward and said, "Me and my people can do that. I'm sure there is a way up the mountain thing from the opposite side." The sheriff nodded, "Good. As for the boats, we will need someone to stay in the boats to watch over the ones that check the caves at the lake level. Shinu spoke up, "Yusuke can take one boat and Hana the other. They can guard those going in and can also pop in and out with them to make sure they are alright." The sheriff smiled at Shinu. "Great. I think we'll go with another boat. Amber, can you and Dave ride out in that one? That way we'll have you close if someone needs medical attention." Amber grinned. She always felt happy when she was needed to heal someone. She replied, "Yes we can. I'd rather be close anyway."

Sheriff Makepeace finished off his part, "Good. That's all set. Skye, you have anything to add?" I had been thinking about my role in all of this and finally decided, "You covered it good sheriff. I will be around at the top levels and at the bottom levels. I remember the feel of the place vividly and may be able to pinpoint it. I will be in my condor form. Shinu, I want you fly with me. If I need to, I can always call on more of my people to help. Again, thank you all. Please eat and then we'll be on our way. We can all follow the sheriff to the location."

One by one or in groups they all drifted in and out the house getting some coffee and muffins. Stacey and her parents talked to everyone. It was good to see that they were no longer afraid to talk to the immortals. The sheriff and his men mingled too. Ned had a million and one questions for everyone. During the time that we finished up, Shinu and Emily drifted around the group together talking to each person. I'd have to tease them later about that. Once again, standing there watching everyone gave me a good feeling. I was watching my people get along with mortals. This was a good omen.

After about fifteen more minutes everyone got ready to go. Those in cars lined up behind the sheriffs' car. Thomas and his crew changed back into their werewolf forms and prepared to run beside the cars in the line of trees on the way. Shinu and his brother and sister joined me on the porch. Shinu put his arm around my shoulder. He said, "My Lady. We will fly with you to get there. Once there they will drop down to the boats and I will stay with you. Don't worry. I will stay with you at all times." I felt safer hearing that. I said, "Thank you Shinu." I kissed mom and grandma good bye and stepped off the porch to shift.

The condor I become is huge and I needed a lot of space to change and take off. Once in the air I felt better. Freer. The wind blew across my wings, rustling my feathers. Every muscle in my body relaxed and again I could think and see clearer. I could see everything around me. Every little creature on the ground and in the trees was easier to spot. I could see Thomas and his people running along in the tree line.

I followed along with the sheriff's car. Shinu and his brother and sister fluttered right along beside me at amazing speed. I knew with my wing span that just a few flaps and I'd cover a great distance. So I was worried that with them as bats, they'd have trouble keeping up with me. Nope. Amazingly they kept up with my pace.

So far the trip had been a quiet one, but I knew that wouldn't last long. Shinu had to ask, *So where is your parakeet?* I let out a loud cry, laughing. *I don't know where he is. I've been trying to get in touch with him since I left the pack's camp last night. I just hope he's ok.* He took on a serious mood. *Well, My Lady, I hope he's alright too. I'm sorry dear.* I eased his concern a little. *He should be. Thanks for your concern.* We flew on in silence, pondering what lay ahead of us.

••

The morning started out to be beautiful. Shaman Rose decided to have a cup of her favorite tea, butter rum, outside on her porch to enjoy the day. The birds were out in flocks, dipping and diving through the clouds and over the tree tops. Many of the little woodland creatures came out to eat and just dig around. Some drifted up on the porch with her from time to time to greet her. She fed them bits and pieces of the homemade bread she had baked last night.

She had been up all night. Many disturbing visions had kept her up and worried. She knew something bad was going to happen today, but the visions didn't show her who would fall victim to destruction. In one of them she was fighting against something dark, but all too familiar. She kept getting glimpses of the face, but never got a full view. In some of the visions she saw Skye standing at a crossroad with her head held down.

She had to decide which road to take, but each time she tried to take a step down one of the roads a long black chain that looked like snake skin would pull her back. In another vision she saw Skye standing amongst her friends and comrades. While they were turning to look at something in the distance, someone stabbed her in the back with a snake skinned dagger.

Whatever the day was to hold she knew she just wanted to enjoy what beauty there was left in it this morning. As she sat and rocked in her chair a sudden chill crept up her back. The sky was suddenly consumed with dark grey clouds. All the birds that had been flying around had gone and every little animal that had been scavenging about had disappeared. Out of nowhere a blustery wind began whipping the trees causing them to bow against its force. She stood up and clasped the amulet that hung around her neck. It was for protection against demons. It didn't comfort her and felt ice cold in her hand.

She stumbled backward and almost fell over the rocking chair she was sitting in when a wind lashed against the front porch. The force of it was so strong it shattered her picture window that led to her living room. She turned and gasped at the sound of glass cracking and tinkling to the ground. She took a deep breath and called out, "Who dares come on hallowed ground?" In a whirl of grass and leaves, a dark figure took shape in front of her. It stood about 6' 6", was dressed in a black cloak and had the hood pulled down over its head. She addressed him again, "These are hallowed grounds!

No demon may trespass here! Be gone if you know what's best for you!"

He just stood there staring at her from under his hood with glowing red eyes. He leaned his head back and let out an unholy, demonic laugh. He calmly said, "Hallowed ground. Hmm. Only keeps out those that have given their soul to hell or the vile slime that crawls out of the gates of hell. Me? I'm no demon. You might say I am someone near and dear to your heart that drips with sappy love and understanding."

He raised his hands up and held them out in front of him, palms out, and chanted something. The wind gushed again and wrapped Shaman Rose up in a bundle of leaves, lifting her up and suspended her in mid air. With a whip of his hands, she flew off the side of the porch and landed face down on the ground.

He laughed again and walked over to her limp body. She lay there for a few seconds and then pushed herself up. She levitated off the ground, turned toward him, raised her hands up and said, "Oona-ta-wanee!" He lifted his arms up to block his face just as sparks of electricity encircled his whole body and threw him into the tree in front of her house.

When he hit the tree a loud crack echoed through the air. He dropped to the ground on his hands and knees and instantly jumped up. The hood had almost come off his head. He pulled it back on and yelled, "Cursed old woman! If you wanna play, we can play." He chanted something again and vanished. She looked around wondering where he would pop up. She took a moment to catch her breath and was just turning around to head in the house when he reappeared right in front of her. He shook his finger at her, "Tsk Tsk. Can't let you sneak inside and try and ambush me, can I? You're staying right out here!"

Stretching his arms out to his side he conjured up another burst of wind. It encircled her and lifted her up above his head. He swirled his hands around in circles and she started twirling faster and faster in the air above him. He flung his arms toward the drive and the wind pitched her in that direction. She hit the drive with a thud and the wind was knocked out of her. She slid back a few yards and came to a rest on her stomach.

She raised herself up. The front of her dress was ripped into shreds and her knees were skinned and bloody. The palms of her hands were skinned also and bleeding. She looked back up toward the house. He was standing there, menacingly, staring at her with the most contemptible smile she had seen on anyone in a long time. He yelled out to her, "Well, well, well. Aren't you resilient?"

She lowered her head and slumped her shoulders. In a low voice she said, "I'm not finished yet." She mustered up all the strength she could and rolled her shoulders back. With her head still looking down she began chanting, "Oona-ta-wanee. Oona-ta-wanee ha! Oona-ta-wanee!" She yelled that phrase out one more time and then was surrounded by a blinding bright blue light. Bolts of lightening flickered and flashed from her hands.

When she looked up, lightening was flashing in her eyes also. She extended her hands out in front of her and pointed them at him as she took off running toward him. He started to run but was caught up in a twisting and twining web of electricity. His whole body began to spasm and contort with the electric charges that were being run through his body. He let out a scream between clenched teeth and writhed in pain. She flung her arms to one side and his body followed the current and smacked the tree.

She flung her arms in the opposite direction and his body followed that current and smashed against the railing on the porch. Raising her arms one more time she threw him in the air and then slammed him down on the ground with a force so hard the earth rumbled when he hit. His body lay there, lifeless. There were burn marks left on the tree and porch and ground where he lay and the smell of burning flesh drifted on the wind.

She took this as her opportunity to go in the house. Once inside she could hide until she regained her strength and get some of her potions to use on him. Most of her strength was gone, but she pushed herself to try and get away. She made it past him and had one foot on the first step when he reached up and grabbed her leg causing her to fall forward and strike her head on the porch floor.

The bang to her head made her see stars and she was knocked dizzy. He held on to her leg as he pulled himself up. He turned his head to crack his neck. Holding on to her leg still he slithered to his feet and looking down at her he hissed, "Fool woman! You fail to realize that I am immortal and you? You may be immortal, but you're a lower, weaker form. Good try though. You get an 'E' for effort. You are pretty damn powerful so I guess we'll have to do this the hard way!"

He lifted her up by her leg and threw her down on the steps. Her ribs cracked and blood flew out of her mouth with the hiss of her breath. He came around to the side of her that hit the steps and kicked her, hard. He grimaced when he heard that side of her ribs crack also. She yelled out in agonizing pain. He leaned his head back and belted out a loud and vicious laugh.

With all the strength he could build up he stomped down on her arm that was laying half way on the bottom step. The angle with which he stomped her arm, broke it in two places. One of her bones in her forearm broke through the skin. Where the bone protruded blood began to gush out and puddle on the steps.

She wailed out with more excruciating burning misery. She began to cry and ask, "Why? Who are you?" He cackled with amusement from her question and sat down on the steps beside her head. After sitting there for a minute, watching her sob in pain he took a deep breath and answered, "Where to start? I guess I can fill you in since you won't be around much longer. A brief history lesson maybe. My father fell in love with a beautiful princess many, many centuries ago. She, unfortunately, fell in love with a contemptible creature." He twisted his face like the next word he was about to say tasted horrible. He hissed out, "A vampire."

Even with all the torturous pain she was enduring she was able to recognize the story he was telling her. She gasped, "Princess White cloud Rainwater." He snarled and continued, "Yes! He never got over her you know. Even after he married my mother and had us kids he would pine after her day and night! He was so obsessed with her he didn't pay any attention to our mother or us kids. He would sneak off to find her in hopes that she'd ditch the blood sucker and be with him! Day after day, year after year, until my mother couldn't take it anymore, so she killed herself! Right in front of us kids! I never forgave Princess Rainwater for what she did to our family! So, I vowed to get revenge on her most prized and valued ancestor!"

She raised her head up. Tears streamed down her face and her eyes got wide with recognition, "Skye!" His laughter echoed through the trees. "You got it! Ding, ding, ding. And the prize goes to the crumpled up old lady bleeding to death on the porch of her own house. I'm growing tired of this drift back in time." He leaned over and grabbed her by her head. She reached up with her good arm and snatched his hood off. She could not believe her eyes.

Her lips trembled and her heart sunk when she saw who he was. He leaned in over her, giving her a better view, and growled, "I'll see you in hell old woman!" She started to say his name, but he placed his hands on both sides of her head and with a quick snap, he broke her neck. The last remaining light of life in her eyes slowly faded to grey and the last breath escaped her mouth with a whoosh. He stood up and whirled around in a gust of wind, shifted, and flew away. One black feather drifted down and landed in the open palm of her hand. Her hand clasped shut on it.

· ·

After flying a little further we finally reached the lake. The sun was up more and the day was going to be bright enough to see well. I looked over to the west sky and there was a bank of dark clouds developing out that way. I thought to myself, *Looks like Shahma may get rain today. Hope she's well.* Shinu darted closer to me and said, *Thinking out loud are we? If it will ease your mind, we can go check on her when we're finished here.* He was so thoughtful. I answered, *Thank you. We'll see how it goes here first. You know you can't go all the way there though, right?* He fluttered back away from me again and said, *I know dear. But, I can get close. I can have Em join us so she can go all the way to her house with you to guard you there.* I felt a little more at ease at that idea. *Sounds like a plan. Let's get to looking around here.*

I swooped close to the mountain iceberg thing and watched as Yusuke and Hana dropped down to get to the boats. As I circled around near the top of the mountain I was drawn into someone's mind again. I could hear Shinu calling me and I could feel myself falling, but I couldn't gain my senses. It was so dark and so cold in here. I felt so weak and scared. Something was in there with me. Something sickening and evil hovered over me. I snapped back to myself and caught myself right before I hit the water. Shinu was diving down to me and shot back up as I did.

He was frantic, *What the hell was that? I thought you were gone for sure!* I was out of breath but worried and anxious. I told him, *He's here! Whoever it is called out to me again. He's here for sure and scared. Something's with him! You have to tell the others to look out. Please. You can get to all of them quicker than me and let them know. I'd have to change each time and we don't have that kind of time. Go now!* He vanished quickly. I knew he could just pop in and out and get to the others. I continued to circle around looking out for any sign of trouble.

• •

The sheriff and the others pulled off the road. They all got out and headed to the lake. Yusuke and Hana flew down and changed back to their vampire forms. Once they had all gathered there Sheriff Makepeace spoke to them all. "Ok. I need Yusuke to go with Stacey and her parents in one boat and Hana to go with Deputy Ned in the other. Amber, you and Dave take out the third one. Thomas, how fast can you and your group get to the top?" Thomas answered, "Give us five minutes. We'll scout the area and we'll be waiting." They took off. The sheriff continued, "It's gonna take Brad and I maybe fifteen minutes to get to the top. The rest of you go and watch out for any sign of anything."

As they turned and headed their separate ways, Stacey yelled out, "Oh my God! Skye! She's falling!" They all ran closer to the lake to see what was going on. Skye was still in her condor form. She had stopped flapping her wings and was falling fast toward the water. They could see a small bat darting down after her. Right before she hit the water she started flapping again and gained momentum. Everyone let out a sigh of relief and continued heading to their destinations.

Sheriff Makepeace and Brad took off around the lake and headed for the mountain iceberg. Mayor Ritennour pulled their boat out in to the water with Stacey and her mom inside. Yusuke helped to push it out. They all then got in and paddled off. Shinu suddenly popped in their boat and startled everyone but his brother. He quickly announced, "I'm sorry to startle you. It's urgent. Skye said whoever it is, is here and in trouble. Something's with him. We have to be careful. Sorry but I have to warn the others." He popped and was gone. Yusuke giggled, "You have to excuse my little brother. He can be somewhat dramatic at times. We do have to keep an eye out though. I'm here for you."

Over on the shore of the lake, Deputy Ned was tugging at the boat to try and get it in the water. Hana laughed and said, "Why don't you let me do that. You go ahead and get in." Ned blushed and stepped into the boat as she pushed it into the water. He smiled, "I almost forgot you're a vampire. You all are pretty darn strong, ain't ya?" She just smiled back and jumped in the boat. Before they got further out, Shinu vaporized in their boat. Quickly, he explained, "Skye has felt something. He's here. The one we are looking for. Also, something evil. Keep your guard up." He vanished. Hana looked at Ned. He was holding his chest like he'd had a heart attack and was out of breath. She asked, "Are you alright?" He caught his breath and answered,

"Yeah. He just scared the crap out of me. Guess I gotta get used to that, huh?" He smiled.

Back on the shore Amber and Dave were getting situated to pull their boat out. Shinu materialized on the shore there in front of them. He said, "Skye just had another mind connection. He's here. The one we're looking for. Also, *it* is most likely here too. Be careful. I have to warn the others." He disappeared. Amber looked at Dave and asked, "Are you up for this? It may get ugly." He nodded, "I'm pretty much ready for anything." They got their boat in the water and paddled off toward the others.

Shinu circled around the lake and spotted the sheriff and Brad close to the foot of the mountain getting ready to head up. He flew down and changed. He told them, "Hey. Skye said the lost one is here for sure, but that's not all. Whatever that thing is, *it*, is here too. Be ready for anything." Then he was gone. The sheriff said, "We'd better hurry. Think you can give me a ride up?" Brad laughed, "Sure thing. I never tried it before, but I get bigger than a horse. I think I can handle you." He dropped down on the ground on his hands and knees and in a matter of seconds changed into a rather large moose. The sheriff climbed on his back and they took off.

By the time Shinu caught up with Thomas and his group, they were already at the top of the mountain. He changed and ran over to where they had gathered. He explained, "Skye connected again. He is here. Problem is, so is *it*. I don't know if we're in for a battle just yet, but be prepared if *it* tries to attack. I have to get back to Skye now." He took off. Thomas addressed his people, "Change back and stay in werewolf form. We'll be better suited to fight that way. Elliot, I want you to take the north side, Emily take the south and Dakota the west. Natasha, stay with me. We'll cover the front of the mountain facing the lake." They split up.

I had finally gained back full control of all my senses just as Shinu rejoined me. I asked in his mind, *Did you get to everyone?* Shinu flew in closer to me and answered, *Yes, My Lady. They are ready for anything. Do you have any idea which cave they should check first?* I had to think for a moment, but that didn't give me any clue. I said, *No, but I have a feeling it's one of the ones up top. I think we should continue to circle around up here.* He agreed.

I looked down and could see that two of the boats had made it to the foot of the mountain and one lingered back some. I knew that one was Amber and Dave. I dived down closer to the other two boats to watch out as they got their boat set for them to get out. Stacey must have seen me. She waved and I gave here a cry back. She waited in the boat with her mom. Her Dad was entering the cave with Yusuke behind him.

Over just a little further Ned and Hana had situated their boat. Ned got out and went in that cave. Hana stayed behind him. She looked up and nodded her head to let us know she had him covered. In the boat further out, Amber was watching everyone. I knew she was ready to handle whatever came up, but I was still worried about her. She must have sensed my unease. She looked up at me and called out, "I'm ok Skye!" I cried an answer back and flew back up toward the top.

I could see Thomas and Natasha pacing back and forth at the top. The others must be running scout at every side. Sheriff Makepeace and Brad had already put on their climbing gear and were scaling the face of the mountain already. They headed for one of the openings on the south end.

Shinu had circled around me and was now heading to the opening in the middle of the mountain. He flitted inside and was gone for quite some time. I was starting to worry so I called out to him, *Shinu Takai! You'd better be alright or I'll kill you!* I waited for an answer, but got nothing. I flew in closer to the hole. Just as I landed inside I felt an impulsive tug pulling me in further. Something was compelling me to go on. I shifted back and whispered for Shinu, "Shinu? Are you alright? I swear you better answer me." He finally came toward me, creeping slowly. His face was scrunched in an angry frown, his eyes were glowing red, and his fangs were bared. His fingers were curled and his nails had extended into claws. I could feel the tension and anger radiating off him like he was a furnace set on high. He looked like he was ready to pounce on me.

Something was wrong. I cautiously walked closer to him. I asked, "Shinu. What's wr . . . ?" Before I could get the rest of my words out my back felt like it was turning into ice, the air suddenly got thicker and harder to breathe, and there was a foul smell emanating from behind me. Shinu lunged toward me and threw me into the wall. I hit it hard enough to crack the rock and ice. A large chunk of the wall broke loose and hit the floor beside me. I felt a hot searing twinge in my arm. It wasn't severe pain. Just an annoying throb. Blood was gushing out of a gaping hole in my arm and I could feel that my arm was broken. But, again, it didn't really hurt.

I spun around just in time to see Shinu hissing and clawing and viciously attacking this huge black figure. It let out a guttural growl like a demon, twisted and writhed, then shot out the opening of the cave, leaving a trail of stench so bad I gagged and almost threw up. I ran over to Shinu who was standing there watching the thing leave. Anxiously, I asked, "Are you alright?" He turned and looked at me. His eyes were still glowing and his fangs still out. His eyes cleared when he looked at me. He yelled, "Oh hell! My Lady! I'm so sorry for throwing you. Am I alright? Are you alright?"

He began inspecting me and turning me around to check me at every angle. My arm flopped some and more blood poured out my wound. If a vampire could turn any paler, he just did. He gently held my arm and said sorrowfully, "Your arm's broken. You've lost a lot of blood! How are you still standing?" I looked down at my arm and touched it. I looked back up at him. He was really concerned. I felt fine. I said, "It's alright Shinu. You did it to save my life. Thank you. Besides, look. It's already healing." I could feel my bone mending itself and the break disappearing like it had never been there. My skin was sealing itself shut at the same time, and I could feel the blood pulsing through me as if it was replenishing itself. He rubbed his hand over my arm and his eyes got big, "What the . . . ? You're healing just like a vampire! Amazing!"

I smiled to ease his worry. Then I said, "We'll have to ponder this later. For now, I need to know if everyone out there is alright. Let's check, then I have to come back. He's here." He nodded ok and we headed for the cave opening. He vanished as I took a head dive out the cave. After I had fallen half way down I changed into a hawk and flew back up to the top of the mountain. I heard gun shots from the opening where the sheriff and Brad had gone in. I watched in shock as both the men ran straight out of the cave, turned around and continued firing as they plummeted down the face of the mountain. Just as I was about to fly over and try to stop their fall, they stopped abruptly and just hung there, still shooting. Their safety cords caught them.

So, I turned my attention to the top of the mountain where Thomas and his crew were standing guard. I could hear them howling and growling. I flew up faster and landed near Thomas. I changed back into my human form. Thomas' hair was standing straight up, his ears were laying flat on his head and he was quivering all over with rage. Natasha, Elliot, and Dakota were all standing there ready to attack too. I scanned the area and asked, "Where's Emily?" All of them pointed in the direction of the trees. I started to run to find Emily when Dakota changed back to warn me, "Don't get too close. Emily has a hold of it. You don't want to come anywhere near her when she's like that. Shinu headed that way already."

He must have gotten to the others and back up here when he heard Emily. I knew it was risky, but I couldn't stand here and wait. I ran for the trees. I got there where Shinu was standing back watching just in time to see Emily. Shinu held his hand up to stop me. He warned me, "You don't want to get any closer." I looked back toward Emily. She was enormous! I had never seen a werewolf that size before. Her fur was almost pure white and it stood up all over her body like porcupine spikes. Massive fangs protruded out of her mouth. Her eyes were iridescent green and extremely long claws extended from the tips of her immense paws.

She was spastically writhing and twisting, biting and clawing at the huge black thing. She rose up on her hind legs, towering up to the middle of the trees, and pounced back down on top of *it*, burying her claws in it. She opened her mouth and with a growl so loud the ground rattled, she took a hold of *it* and flung it across the woods. It smashed through several trees, knocking them down, and landed at least twenty-five yards away.

Emily was off and running in the direction she had just thrown *it*. I could hear it bellow out, "I'm not finished yet!" We followed, but by the time any of us got there, *it* was gone. The path of destruction Emily caused looked like several bulldozers had plowed through the woods, ripping up trees and digging holes.

Thomas and the others finally came over to us. I looked at Dakota, who was still in his human form. I said to him, "Now I see why you all stood back." That was all I could say at the moment. Emily was still in werewolf form and was panting and looking around. She still growled a low growl and every muscle in her body twitched and flexed, ready to attack again. Shinu shook his head, looked at me, and headed toward Emily.

She turned and was ready to snap at him, but he must have told her it was him. She stopped and dropped to the ground and lay her head down by his feet. Her breathing slowed as he rubbed her head and she calmed down and changed back to human. They sat there holding each other.

I turned to Thomas and told him I had to get back to the cave I was in. Whoever it was, was in there and needed to be found right away. I needed someone to go with me, so I told Thomas, "You can come with me." He looked a little puzzled. He asked, "How am I supposed to get down there? Wolves can't climb." I reassured him, "My condor is huge. You can ride down on my back. Just hold on tight." He was ok with it so we headed back to the edge of the mountain. I looked over at the others below. The sheriff and Brad had descended to one of the boats, and they were all heading to the shore.

I stepped back and changed. I looked at Thomas to give him the ok to climb on. He got up there fairly easy and held on. I stepped off the edge and spread my wings and tried to drop down as slow as possible so I wouldn't scare him. I sailed in a circle and headed in the cave. He had to duck as we entered. I landed and leaned down to let him off my back, shifted back and we headed further into the cave.

It was so dark in there it almost felt like I could reach out and touch it. We could see alright in the dark, but slowly advanced, listening out for any sounds. Without warning I was pulled again into the mind of the one we were looking for. I felt myself stumble and Thomas caught me before I could fall. He whispered, "He's here isn't he?" I could only nod my head yes. There was an unexpected turn and a sudden drop of the floor.

We both almost lost our bearings and hit the floor, but managed to stay up. We traveled in further, about another hundred feet or so and came to a wide open room like area. The walls and floor were covered in ice and there were piles of dirt spread out in several spots. I could smell and see fish.

I stopped and opened my mind, calling out to the lost person. I knew they were in here. I just didn't know where. I spoke in my mind; *Can you tell us where you are? We're here to help you. The bad guy is gone now.* Nothing. I turned to Thomas, "We may have to look all over this area. They may be too weak to talk or think now." He nodded and we walked around in opposite directions. It was freezing in here and the air was so thin and hard to breathe. I tried again to talk to them, *Please. We want to help you. Tell me where to find you. Tell me . . .* There he was! Right in front of me. There was a small hole in the wall at the floor and lying there in a ball was a little boy. His hair was all tousled and what little clothes he had on were shredded. His head was tucked under his arm and he was shaking violently.

I called Thomas over, "Thomas! Right here." He ran over to where I was on the floor and dropped to his knees. He looked at me and then very gently he reached toward the boy and touched his head. The boy turned his head slightly and looked up at us. A single tear rolled down his dirt stained face and he whispered, "Dada?" That was all it took. Thomas grabbed him up and began crying, wailing out tears of joy. He cried, "Nanuk! My baby! Thank heavens. Oh my boy, my boy!" I rubbed Thomas' back and cried with them. This had to be the most fulfilling moment in my life. I was overcome with love, appreciation, and relief.

I had to regain control of myself. We had to get him out of here quick and get him to Amber and Dave so they could help him. I touched the side of his neck to feel for a pulse. To my horror it was very faint. I jumped up and pulled Thomas with me. "Thomas! We have to get him out of here and down to Amber, now!" He shook his head to bring himself back to reality and looked at me in shock. "What's wrong?" I hated to tell him and see his heart rip back out of his chest, but I had to let him know how urgent it was. "Nanuk is barely breathing. We have to go now or he may not make it!" He stared at me in disbelief, but then turned and ran for the cave opening. I ran after them.

CHAPTER 18

FOUND AND LOST...

We made it back to the opening in a matter of seconds and without even thinking about how we would get him down, I changed back into a condor, Thomas cradled Nanuk in one arm, jumped on my back and held on with his other hand. I ran out the cave and dived as fast as I could and headed straight for the shore. I could see Amber and Dave pulling in their boat and cried out to them at the top of my lungs. My cry startled everyone else. I saw them all turn and duck. The sheriff and Brad drew their guns and pointed them toward the way I was flying. They must have thought *it* was back.

I dropped to the ground and landed softly, squatted down and let Thomas off. He jumped down, still cradling Nanuk and ran for Amber. He was still crying and yelled, "Amber! You have to save him! You have to save my little boy!" Amber and Dave ran over to him. Everyone else joined them and circled around them. Mayor Ritennour took off his coat and laid it down on the ground for Thomas to lay Nanuk on. Yusuke took off his suit coat and laid that over Nanuk.

Amber kneeled on one side of Nanuk and Dave on the other. She felt his head, looked in his mouth, and checked his pulse. Dave ran his hands over his body checking to see if there were any broken bones. They both looked at each other. I could see the worry and dread in their eyes. Amber looked up at me and said, "I need the fastest person here to go to your house and get some Wolf's Bane tea, now!"

The first person I thought of was Shinu. He had just made it back down to the shore with the other werewolves so I turned to him. I had gotten so tied up in what was happening that I didn't notice that I hadn't changed back, so I changed quickly and turned to Shinu, "Shinu, we need someone fast to go to my house. Amber needs Wolf's Bane tea, fast." He nodded to me and said, "That would be Hana. She's the fastest out of all of us. Hana, did you hear?" She nodded yes. He said, "Go quickly!" I watched as she ran and virtually disappeared in a blur of red and black streaks.

I turned my attention back to Amber and Dave. They were waving their hands over Nanuk's body. Multiple waves of yellow, green, and blue light was radiating from their whole body. They were each chanting spell after spell. Nanuk's color was quickly fading and I feared the worse. Everyone that was gathered around each began to hope and pray in their own way. Stacey and her parents were holding hands and praying; Brad, Ned, and the sheriff had formed a circle near Nanuk's head and were repeating an old Indian prayer for good luck; Shinu was holding Emily in his arms as she was crying; Dakota, Natasha, and Elliot had stayed werewolves and were pacing back and forth around all of us, watching out; and Yusuke had come to my side and had his arm around my waist trying to comfort me.

I had been so busy watching everyone and praying to myself that I hadn't noticed that I too was crying. Yusuke leaned down and whispered to me, "You did good Skye. It will be alright. You'll see. Hana's coming back now with the tea." I could only nod my head, afraid that if I opened my mouth I would lose it and drown in a sea of emotion. Just like he said, Hana suddenly appeared right beside me holding a thermos with the tea inside. She smiled at me and handed it to Thomas.

He opened the thermos and poured a little of the tea into the cup and held it out to Amber. She broke her chanting and took the cup. Dave continued and the light emanating from him grew brighter. She raised Nanuk's head up and put the cup up to his lips and speaking softly she said, "Here you go sweetie. You have to drink this." He opened his mouth a little and took a tiny sip. She gently laid his head back down and looked at Thomas. She explained, "He had a lot of broken bones. There was interior bleeding. We healed the broken bones and stopped the bleeding. He's practically starved. The tea will feed him the nutrients he needs to recover, but it's up to him to recover his mind. He's locked himself away and doesn't even realize he's here. He still thinks he's in that cave."

I knew what I had to do. But first, I could feel something was wrong. I looked up at the sky. It had turned grey. The mass of clouds I had seen over the west when we first got there was moving in over us. There was something familiar about the uneasy feeling that was slowly creeping over me, but I couldn't put my finger on it. I addressed everyone, "I can try and help Nanuk. Thomas I'll need your help. But I have to ask everyone to be on guard. Something's not right. Something or someone is heading this way and it's dark and evil. Please be careful, all of you."

Yusuke helped me down on the ground. I sat beside Thomas and took his hand in mine. I said, "You remember how you let me in your mind and I had you think of the day Nanuk was lost?" He said yes. I went on, "This time I need you to think of Sadie. He needs to see you and his mom in his mind. Talk to him the way you used to when he was still a baby. He needs to see you and Sadie and feel safe before he'll come back. I will go in to his mind through yours and talk to him too. Are you ready?" Before I closed my eyes I saw Shinu and Emily come over and stand behind me. The rest of them were pacing and holding their guns. The wolves had spread out and were covering the further areas.

I closed my eyes and focused on Thomas' mind. Once again I was drawn in through a tunnel of flashing lights of various colors. Blurred images of his memories flickered in and out of my mind. I finally came to an abrupt stop in one special place. There was Sadie sitting in Thomas' arms and Nanuk was in her arms. They were sitting on their porch and were both beaming with pride and love. Sadie leaned down and kissed Nanuk's head softly and they both sang a lullaby to him. It was a beautiful memory. The sun was shining and the birds were singing. I spoke to Thomas, *Good. Now just hold that memory and reach out to Nanuk now.*

I could feel him thinking about Nanuk now. He started singing that lullaby and thinking about nothing but Nanuk. Again I was pulled from Thomas' mind and thoughts and was slammed into pitch darkness. I could feel it was Nanuk's mind. He was blocking me and everything out. I had to get him to open up. I whispered, *Nanuk. Baby. It's me. I'm the one you talked to before. I'm here to help you go home. It's safe now sweet heart, but you have to let me in to get you out.*

Nothing. I tried using the same words again, but he still locked me out. I had to think. I started singing the lullaby Thomas and Sadie sang to him, and could feel him open up just a crack. In that little peek of light I saw his scared little face. Then he shut back down.

I didn't want to try this technique, but I now had no choice. It had been too long and if I didn't reach him now, I may never reach him. I had to scare him out. In the deepest and most frightening voice I could think of I said, *Now little brat! You have one chance and one chance only to run for it! I'll let you out of this cave, if, you can out run me boy! Oh yeah. If you don't leave, I'll kill you then I'll go and kill that pretty mama of yours too! Now, run!* That did it. He opened his mind. I traveled down a short tunnel in his mind. I saw memories of his mother's face, his father's face, and Emily's and Amber's. It was sunny here too, and he was happy.

Now I spoke to him in a calm and loving voice. *Hello Nanuk. I'm Syke. You're safe now baby. The bad man is gone and now I can take you to your father.* I could feel him smile and he reached for me with his mind now. I grabbed him and pulled him into Thomas' memories. He laughed when he saw his dad's memories and cried, "Dada!" That was all the recognition I needed. I quickly pulled the two memories apart, flew back down the tunnel of lights, and opened my eyes in time to see Nanuk sit straight up and reach for his dad. He was crying and saying, "Dada!"

I fell back, exhausted. Shinu caught me and held me. He was smiling, "You did it. You are a fascinating woman. Here. Drink this." I took the flask he handed me and smelled its contents first. It smelled so delicious. I had to ask, "And what are you giving me to drink?" There was that smile again, devious. He grinned, "It's a special brew my family loves. I have a feeling you will too. It will quickly revive you. You're really drained." I turned it up to my mouth and took a sip. It was heavenly!

I took another sip, handed it back to Shinu and got up. I felt 100% better. Refreshed, I said, "Thank you Shinu. Whatever it is, I love it. Now, how long was I gone and what happened here?" As I looked around, I noticed that the whole area looked like it had been hit by a tornado. Tree limbs were down, leaves were every where, and everyone looked disheveled. Shinu shook his head, "You and Thomas were gone for a little more than an hour. I was a little worried.

As far as here, it was like a storm set in. The sky turned almost black and a wind started blowing everything and everyone around. There was a figure in the middle of one of the gusts. It looked like a man standing in the middle of a whirl wind. Everyone stood their ground and fought it off. Amber and Dave shielded you guys with some sort of force field. Whatever it was finally gave up the fight and took off. Hana ran after it."

I was shocked to hear that. I said, "That doesn't sound like the thing we fought off earlier. I'm beginning to think we're up against two instead of one." Shinu agreed with me. "Yes. I agree. Just the aura alone was different in this thing. It some how felt familiar. I can't explain it."

I looked up in the sky. It was clear and beautiful again. The sun was directly above us, so it had to be around noon. I got everyone's attention. "Excuse me. I want to first thank you all for your help. Now that Nanuk is back with us, I think it best that we get going." Thomas stood up, holding Nanuk safely in his arms now, and said, "Before we go, I want to thank you all too. If it weren't for every one of you, I wouldn't be standing here holding my son. For us to all come together like this . . ." He broke off and started crying. He composed himself and went on. "For us to work together like this is a miracle in itself. I would like to thank you all by inviting you to my camp this evening around 7:00 p.m. for a cook out and welcome home party for Nanuk."

Everyone said you're welcome. They each came up to Thomas and shook his hand or hugged him and accepted his invitation. They then came over to me and hugged me. It was an astounding feeling. I told them I'd see them tonight. They all got in their separate vehicles, or changed into their individual forms and headed off.

I asked Shinu and Emily to stay behind. He said, "Of course, My Lady." Yusuke waited too. Before I could continue, Hana returned. She was visibly furious. She had a deep frown on her face and her fangs were showing. Shinu leaned over and whispered to me, "Remember when I told you she was unstable? Well you've seen her nice perky side and now you get to see her psycho side." He laughed at himself.

Hana walked over to us. With her teeth clenched she said, "That damn son of a b . . . Bastard got away! I almost had him! Damn it! He's fast. When ever I catch up with him I'm going to rip his head off, tear his guts out, and shove his head so far up his ass he'll be looking out the hole I tore in his belly! I did get a hold of him though. This is all I managed to grab out of the whirl wind." She opened her hand and showed us a fist full of black feathers. Odd.

Shinu laughed again, "Told you so." I could only shake my head. I wasn't about to make her mad. I said, "Thank you for trying Hana. That may be an important clue. I have a sinking feeling we'll get our chance. I know you've all done a lot for me already today, but I have to ask one more favor. I need to go check on Shahma. She's two towns over. It took Jaye and I a little over three hours to get there driving, but if we go in our other forms, we could be there in maybe thirty minutes. I shouldn't go alone, but if I have to I will."

Emily was the first to talk. "Madame Skye, there is no way I will let you go alone. I'm fine and ready for more. I'm in." Shinu grinned, "I'm always up for a road trip and I don't tire so easily. I'm your first guard so I can't let you go alone." I felt better. I said, "Thank you. Yusuke and Hana, you don't have to go if you have other engagements." Yusuke shook his head and said, "What, and miss out on a chance to be near you, lovely lady." He took my hand and kissed it. Hana smacked him in the back of his head and said, "Back off Romeo! I'm still fired up and I have nothing to do. So, I'm going with. Besides, I have to keep my brother in line."

So, it was settled. We got ready to take off. I decided to change into a cheetah for the first stretch of our run. Shinu and his brother and sister changed into rather large bats, and Emily, her werewolf. This time, she wasn't as large as she had been earlier today. I'm going to have to ask her about that later. We headed off west.

∙∙∙

On our way I looked up and watched Shinu, Yusuke, and Hana flipping and darting around. Emily ran beside me, keeping up my pace. I could see she was getting winded and I turned and headed off toward a lake. The rest followed suit. Once we got to the edge of the lake we both leaned our heads down and lapped up the refreshing, cool water. I guess I was thirsty too. Emily lay down and rested her head on her paws. Changing back, I sat down by Emily and leaned against her. I stroked her fur and could see that she was finally breathing normal again and not panting so much. Shinu, Yusuke, and Hana came down and joined us.

After a few minutes, Emily changed back too. Now was as good a time as any to ask Emily, "Can I ask you a question?" Emily looked at me a little apprehensive but nodded yes. I went on, "I've seen you when you're a werewolf and you're a pretty big one. But, back there on the mountain, you were huge! And I've never seen such green eyes on a werewolf either. Why is that?" Emily took a deep breath and thought for a minute. Then she said, "Well. Back after Thomas first changed me, I got scared and ran off. I just ran around for a long time in the woods, seemingly with no direction.

Then I stopped to rest and an older woman appeared in front of me. She had a kind face and smiled at me. We talked for a while and then she pulled out this amulet." She pulled it out of her shirt and showed it to me. She went on, "She told me I had great things I would one day do and that I was chosen to fill that role. She explained that I was a fourth generation werewolf that was given great powers.

She handed me this and said I had to choose the road I would follow. And that with this great power, many had chosen to do evil. She said I had to choose the right road and I would one day save the lives of many. Chose the wrong road, I would live a life of exile. Then she disappeared. I put it on and I could feel the power coursing through me. I have yet to learn how to control it though. As you saw earlier, I lose it quick."

I was moved by her story. It all made sense. I said, "Emily, you were meant to be by my side. I knew it from the first time I met you. I will work with you and teach you how to control your powers." We hugged. Yusuke joined us and hugged the both of us. Although he hugged me tighter and let his hand roam up and down my back, lingering too long down near my butt. He whispered, "I love to see two people so happy together. Touching moments like this make me . . ."

Before he could finish, Hana smacked him in the head, again. He looked at her rather mean, and then let us go. Shinu was laughing hysterically behind them. She turned and gave him a chastising look too. He instantly stopped laughing and jumped to his feet. I could see him mouth the words, *unstable* behind her. I had to laugh.

After ten minutes of resting we transformed back into our animals and headed on our way. As we got close I told Shinu, *We will be coming up on the area that surrounds her home. From that point on, all the ground is hallowed. You and your brother and sister won't be able to join us there. We won't be long. I just want to check up on her. Emily can go with me. I'm sorry you all can't go any further. Will you let them know and just wait around here for us? I can call you and let you know how it's going.* He answered me back, *I will let them know. Please be careful, My Lady.* I said, *I will*, and ran on ahead of them. Emily followed.

I couldn't quite remember where the line was, but I knew I'd feel it. The last time there was a wash of peace and warmth. We continued on. I waited and waited for that feeling, but nothing ever came, and I knew we were close to her house now. I looked up and they were still following us. Something was wrong. I called out, *Shinu, I don't know what's wrong, but we should be in the threshold of hallowed ground right now.* He said, *We don't feel any resistance or pain either.*

I looked up to the sky again and a multitude of birds had gathered and in one group they all swooped down to me. They fluttered frantically above me. Emily pulled away from me as I was surrounded. I slowed a little and asked, "What's wrong my friends?" They began chirping, whistling, and screeching all at once. Simultaneously they said, "Hurry my queen! Hurry! It's Shaman Rose!" They all flew back up and away from me. I picked up speed and called to Shinu, *There's something wrong with Shahma! We have to hurry.*

I rounded the corner of the drive to her house and half way up the drive I stopped. I shifted back and rubbed my eyes to see if I was really seeing what I saw. There were tree limbs everywhere. Leaves covered the ground. As I got closer, there were burn marks in the big beautiful tree that sat in her front yard. The picture window to her living room was completely shattered. All the lovely flowers that lined her porch were pulled up and flung every where. I walked slower now. My heart was racing dangerously fast and I broke out in a sweat.

Before I could take another step further Emily pounced in front of me and stopped me. She began to growl and her fur stood up. With her ears pressed flat she looked at me. In those emerald eyes I could see that she was telling me to stay back. Shinu landed in front of me and stopped me completely with his body. I tried to look around him, but he kept moving to block my view. Up closer to the house Hana and Yusuke were looking down on the porch at something.

I had to see. I had to know. Shinu turned and held me against his chest and gently said, "I am so sorry. I'm so sorry Skye. It's your Shaman. You can't see her like that. We smelled the blood way back there and were hoping for your sake it wasn't her. She suffered greatly but it looks like she put up a good fight. She should never have died that way."

I was more anxious now to go see for myself, but he wouldn't let me go. I could see around his shoulder that Hana and Yusuke had went in the house and brought out some blankets and were covering her up. Emily had gone up to the porch and was now back beside Shinu. She looked at me with her emerald eyes and I could tell she was crying. She whined and then changed back to human. She joined Shinu in holding me back and said, "That was the old woman that visited me that day and gave me my amulet." She broke down and cried more.

I was in shock now. I couldn't even fight them anymore to try and move to the house. It felt like my heart stopped beating and everything around me began to whirl and spin out of control. I couldn't even really think right now. Poor Jaye. How will he take this? I could feel myself sinking into an abyss of red, fiery hatred. Pictures of past memories flashed in my mind. Then, there was only blackness.

•••

Skye passed out in Shinu's arms. He told Emily, "Stay right here with her. I have to go and look around and see if I can find anything." Emily nodded her head, ok, and sat down on the ground and held Skye. She rocked her back and forth, cuddling her, comforting her and telling her to come back.

Hana had covered Shaman Rose's body up with a blanket and Yusuke picked her up and carried her in her house. He laid her on her couch and rejoined his sister on the porch. Shinu circled around the house and through the woods and popped back on the porch. He asked Hana, "Did you see anything unusual when you came up here? Anything at all." Hana nodded yes. She held her hand out to Shinu. "Yes. These were clutched in her hand." Shinu's eyes got big with shock. He said, "Black feathers. These are the same as the ones you grabbed back at the lake." Hana said, "Yes. And the scent is fairly fresh. He must have done this before he attacked us at the lake. Now what do we do?"

Shinu thought for a moment. He took out his phone and said, "I'll call Skye's mom. She'll know what best to do. I don't know the tribal traditions. But, I know her mom and grandmother will. We have to wait for Skye to come to before we can travel. We'll also have to tell her about the feathers." He called. Her mother picked up on the second ring. She said, "Hello Shinu. How are you and how did things go at the lake?" He briefly told her what went on and that they had successfully found Nanuk.

Then he asked, "Ma'am. I hate to be the bearer of bad news, but there has been a tragedy. Shaman Rose has been killed. My brother, sister, and I, Skye and Emily came here to check on her. It was the same person that attacked us at the lake. Skye has passed out. We didn't let her see the body. I don't think it wise to turn to the authority up here, considering. So I need to ask you what we should do now. We can't just leave her body lying in her house."

Skye's mother paused for a moment then began to cry. She said, "Hold on Shinu." She got her mother and put her on the phone. She said, "Hello son. Here's what you need to do. A Shaman is a holy woman and must be buried in a spiritual ritual so her spirit can go on to live in another. You must find a place around her house that looks like a place she cherished, like a garden or something. Dig the hole there. Her body has to be clothed in her ceremonial gown, headdress and shoes. Place her body in the hole, no box, no casket.

That way her body can return to the earth. If you can get her ready that far, we can take it from there. The ground has to be blessed and a special ceremony must be performed. You and your brother and sister cannot be there when we do the blessing ceremony. That will become hallowed ground, just around the house and in the yard. Skye should come to soon. My daughter and I will get Amber and we'll be there in a flash. Don't ask. Just wait for us."

She hung up and Shinu put his phone away. He looked back down the drive to see if Skye was up yet. She wasn't. Emily was still holding her and rocking. He turned to Yusuke and Hana, "Yusuke, I need you to check her closets and find what looks like it would be ceremonial clothes, headdress, and shoes and put them on the coffee table. Hana, I don't want to disrespect her, so I need you to get her dressed. I will dig the grave for her. Then we wait for Skye's mom, grandmother, and Amber to arrive." They both agreed and went about what they needed to do.

Shinu went back outside and walked around the house trying to find what would be a sacred place. It didn't take him long to find a beautifully arranged garden behind the house. There were flowers everywhere. He could tell she took great care of them. They were planted by color and they were large, gorgeous blooms. There was a small bench in the center and a large bird bath. He moved the bench and bird bath and looked around for a shovel. In a little shed near the house he found one and set about digging the grave. It didn't take him long.

He walked back around the house, looked in on Skye again, she was still out, and then went back into the house to check on Hana and Yusuke. Hana had already got her dressed and cleaned off the dried blood and dirt that was on her face and hands. She was placing the headdress on her head when Skye walked in with Emily holding her up.

∙∙∙

I don't know how long I was unconscious. When I opened my eyes Emily was holding me, rocking me back and forth and humming. I blinked to focus and asked, "Where's Shinu?" She pointed toward the house. I pushed myself up, with help from Emily and started walking slowly to the house. Emily held my arm to steady me. I looked over at her. She had a lost and sad look on her face. I said, "Emily. Thank you. It will be ok. We have suffered another terrible loss, but the one responsible for this will pay." I gave her a faint smile. It seemed to lift her up some.

We made it up the steps and into the house just as Hana was putting Shahma's headdress on. I looked at her lying on the couch and choked back my tears. She was wearing her ceremonial gown and shoes. I looked at all of them and a tear rolled down my cheek. I swallowed back the flow of tears and said, "Thank you all. How did you know?" Hana answered me, "Shinu called your mom. We are so sorry Skye."

She came over to me and hugged me. Shinu said, "Your grandmother told me what to do. We couldn't just leave her here. We know there are certain traditions, just like in our family, and I wanted to make sure we did the right thing. She also told me she will be here soon with your mom and Amber. I didn't think we should involve the authority, given the situation."

I went to him and hugged him. I kissed his cheek. Grateful, I said, "Thank you. You made the right decision." Yusuke was standing behind Shinu and he said, "Since we're giving out hugs . . ." I chuckled, and went to him and hugged him too. I smiled, "Thank you too Yusuke." He squeezed me tight and once again rubbed my back letting his hand trail to my lower back. This time I looked at Hana and stopped her before she smacked him again. He was fine. I could use some comfort. And as long as he didn't get carried away, I just enjoyed the hug.

He finally let go and Shinu went on, "I found a place out back that looked like it may have been dear to her and I've already dug the grave. Now she said for me to go ahead and lay her in it. When they get here my sister, brother and I will go and wait at the end of the drive."

We followed Shinu out as he carried her carefully to the back yard. Once back there Shinu placed her body in the grave. We all sat down and waited for my mom, grandma, and Amber to arrive. Soon, the birds started to gather around me. They perched on my lap and on my shoulders. Everyone turned and watched me in awe. I smiled at them to let them know it was ok. The little creatures all came and sat beside me too. Squirrels, chipmunks, raccoons all crowded around me. I looked behind me to the woods and I saw a few bears and a couple of foxes and several moose gathering at the edge of the trees.

I was filled with a sense of being one with nature. I cleared my voice and addressed all the animals. "My fellow beings. We have all suffered a great loss, but will soon celebrate her life. Shahma was a good person and good to us all. She was the meaning of love and gave us all a special part of herself. She may be gone, but she lives on in each and every one of us. Give praise and thanks for being blessed enough to know her."

Each animal cheered and applauded in its own way. The air was filled with grunts and growls, squeaks and peeps, shrieks and tweets. The bears and the moose pawed at the ground and bowed their heads to her memory. They soon went off on their way and we were once again bathed in silence.

After about ten minutes my mom, grandma, and Amber vaporized in front of us in a puff of smoke. We all jumped back unsure of who it was at first. Then when I saw them, I got up and ran to hug them. We all held each other for a few minutes then grandma looked in the grave and went over to Shinu, Yusuke, and Hana. She addressed them all, "Thank you all for all you've done. I'm sorry you can't stay for the ceremony, but this ground must be blessed." Shinu answered, "That's ok ma'am. We will be waiting at the end of the drive. Again, we are sorry about your loss." They turned and left. Shinu stopped to pat my shoulder and say, "Remember. You call me if you need me. Hallowed or not I'll be here." I thanked him again. We waited until we knew they were safely off the property and began the ceremony.

The ceremony was wonderful. Shahma was now laid to rest and all was peaceful again there. We cleaned up her house and front yard before we left. We all agreed that we would let Jaye know as soon as possible and let him handle the property the way he chose.

We walked down to the end of the drive to meet back up with Shinu, his brother and sister. They were waiting for us. We told them it went well. Emily asked my grandma, "Excuse me Ms. Rainwater, but would you mind telling us how you got here?" I could see that the others were wondering the same thing. She giggled then answered, "Well children. My daughter and I have had many centuries to learn much magic. We've been taught by some of the best witches and warlocks. This is but one of the spells they taught us, transportation." Everyone said oh and nodded their head like it all made sense now.

My mom looked at her watch then said, "Oh my. Amber, we have to get you back. You have to help Thomas set up the party. You too Emily. Do you want to go with us?" She looked surprised when she looked down at her watch too. She said, "Oh. I almost forgot. Yes, if I can please." They said yes and Emily went over to Shinu. She asked him, "Will you be there tonight?" Shinu gave her a teasing grin, "I have a date tonight. Didn't I tell you that already?" Emily growled at him and he leaned over and kissed her on the forehead. "You know I'll be there my little pup." She turned and walked away from him. She looked back with a serious face and said, "I told you to stop calling me little pup." She turned back around, looked over at me smiled and winked.

They vanished again in smoke. Shinu spoke to Yusuke and Hana, "I'm going to go back with Skye to make sure she makes it alright. I'll meet you at home. Let mom and dad know what happened today please." They said yes. I asked them, "You will be at the party tonight, won't you?" Hana was perky again. She grabbed me and hugged me and answered, "Of course we will silly. Wouldn't miss it for the world. See ya tonight." Then she took off flying.

Yusuke had to get in another hug. I squeezed him back this time and rubbed his back, letting *my* hand trail down his back and stop at his waist. He giggled, "Ooo. Now, now. You're a taken woman. Maybe you should think about ditching the bird and giving me a try."

This time, Shinu smacked him in the head. He said, "Hey. Back off brother. She is spoken for. Besides, if anyone gets first dibs, it's me." He laughed and winked at me. Yusuke blew me a kiss and took off. Shinu turned to me, "So, do you feel like flying or running?" I looked up at the sky. "I think I feel like flying. I need to travel without having to think. Flying is second nature to me. I don't have to think about it, I just do it."

I took off running, jumped in the air and changed into a hawk. He was soon behind me. He said, *Very impressive! What else can you do?* I was in the mood to play now. I had to let off some steam and actually enjoy myself for a little bit. So I flapped my wings as fast as I could so I could glide on the wind long enough to change into a bat. He laughed, *Very nice!* I flitted about for a little while like that then I took a dive and changed into a falcon and shot back up.

I was laughing this time. I said, *I've got a better one for you. Watch closely.* I flew full speed again until I was able to glide then I took another dive, this time for the ground. Just before I hit the ground I pulled up and flew along the ground, then I changed again. This time into a tiger. He swooped down and flew beside me as I ran. Surprised, he said, *My, my, my. You are incredible! To change mid-stream like that takes great concentration and power.* I roared for the heck of it, then said, *Thank you. You'll excuse me for a moment.* Shinu stayed flying along the path we were taking and I ran off into the trees.

All of this changing had me drained and hungry. I didn't want him to see me eat, but I had to grab something. Several rabbits, not shape-shifters, hopped about. I grabbed one and downed it. It wasn't much, but I had to eat something. I headed back to where Shinu was still traveling along. He flitted about around me then settled back to flying beside me. *You know if you were hungry, that's all you had to say. You are an animal after all.* He was laughing so hard at his own joke that he didn't see the tree looming up in front of him. I made a dead stop and watched as he smacked the tree and dropped to the ground. Now it was my turn to laugh. I rolled over and over on the ground, roaring and laughing.

I turned back to human and sat up. Looking over at Shinu, just laying there on the ground, I started to worry. He wasn't moving. I got up and ran over to him. I got down on my knees and touched him. Cautiously, I asked, "Shinu? Are you alright?" He didn't flutter or answer me. Now I was really worried. I touched him again and was just leaning over him when he changed back and scared the crap out of me. I jumped back and grabbed my chest. I yelled, "Dang you! You scared the heck out of me! I thought you were dead-er."

He burst out laughing and fell over backward. I jumped up, ran at him, changed into a panther, and landed straddle over him. I bared my teeth and snarled at him. He put his hands up and slowed down laughing. He said, "Ok. I give. I give." I changed back and got off him and laughed myself.

We sat there for a while smiling at each other. Shinu spoke first. "You are really someone not to mess with. I'm impressed, again. And it's not easy for someone to impress me." I looked at him and said, "Thank you. I'll take that as a major compliment. You're pretty amazing too. I hate to admit it, but you had me pretty scared back in that cave. You are no one to mess with either." He gave me a ha, "That was nothing. But, since we're back on the subject of the cave, it surprised me how fast you healed. I'm really sorry for throwing you so hard. I knew I had to get you out the way, though, before he attacked."

I thought for a moment, and then I said, "You know. I surprised myself how fast I healed too. It didn't really hurt that bad either. And what was that concoction you gave me?" He sat forward and inspected me for a minute. Then he said, "That drink. It didn't bother you in the least? Or upset your stomach?" I shook my head, "No. It tasted really good too. I never tasted anything like it. As a matter of fact, it tasted sweet and sort of metallic. It could be addictive. You know what I mean?"

He twisted his face, questioningly, "Yes, I do know. Here's another question for you. Can you tell the difference between the smell of human blood and animal blood?" Again, I thought first, and then answered, "Yes. Always have been able to. I figured it was normal." He shook his head, "No. It's not normal. Most humans can't tell the difference in the smell. I have to tell you something, and please don't get mad at me. You looked so weak today and you lost a lot of blood in that cave. I had a theory and tested it. That was a special blend of human blood in that flask. My family keeps a lot of it on hand for emergencies."

He stared at me a little, flinched back, like he was waiting on me to attack. Surprisingly, I wasn't the least bit disturbed by that. It made me more curious. I inquired, "That doesn't bother me. What do you think all of this means?" He rubbed his chin and said, "Well, your ancestor did marry a vampire, my ancestor. They had children, and so forth. But none of their offspring ever mated with another vampire. There is a possibility that some vampire DNA might have lain dormant for centuries and only manifested itself in you. When your memories were restored and you connected with your subconscious, it could have awakened that part of you long lost."

He pondered something else and continued, "You sure heal like a vampire and that was blood, human blood you drank. It revived you and it didn't bother you. I know all immortals heal faster and more completely than humans, but only vampires can recover so fast. Interesting." He got a sneaky smile and added, "I'm not going to go throwing you into any trees or off cliffs to test my theory though. Unless you want me to." I picked up a hand full of leaves and threw them at him and said, "No thank you. I know how hard you throw, first hand."

I stood up and started to walk in the direction of home. He got up and followed me. Once he was at my side he changed the subject, "I have to show you something. I didn't want to interrupt your ceremony so I waited. When Hana found your Shaman, she was clutching these in her hand." He reached in his pocket and pulled out some black feathers. I was astonished. I took them and smelled them. Surprised, I said, "These are the same feathers that Hana grabbed a hold of. It has to be the same person. But, who?"

We walked on for a while in silence. Shinu finally asked, "Have you heard from your pigeon yet?" I shook my head, "No. And I'm starting to worry. What if *it* got to him? Or this other guy? Hopefully I'll hear from him by night fall. I keep thinking maybe he went out of town to get in touch with other shape-shifters to help us out." Shinu nodded his head, but didn't look too sure. He said, "Yes. Maybe that's where he's gotten off to. There were times, if you think back, that he would be out of school for a couple of days. He usually said it was some family matter."

I thought about it and remembered that to be true. I said, "Speaking of school, I wonder if they thought it strange that we were all out today. Mr. Johnson won't be too happy when we come back tomorrow, will he?" He laughed, "No he won't. Well, we'd better get a move on. You really need to get some rest before the party tonight. I expect you to be dressed impeccably. I, of course, will be in my best suit." I smiled, "Emily will love that." I made goo goo eyes at him, ran off, changed back into a hawk and flew off before he could retaliate.

CHAPTER 19

CELEBRATION...

made it home in time to try and take a three hour nap. I first went to my desk and pulled out my notebook. I was curious about something, more like worried because I still hadn't heard from Jaye. I reread my list. All the names still flickered on the page as if they were on fire. I looked down to where I started to write Jaye's name and seen that I had only written the 'J' before I got interrupted. So I took out my pen and continued to write his name. Nothing. There was no spark and after I finished his whole name it disappeared off the page. I tried to write it again, and again it vanished. What did this mean? Had I already lost him? I couldn't think straight. I put the notebook and pen back in my desk and went to my bed. Shinu was right. I really needed some rest. When my head hit the pillow, I was out. No dreams, no visions. Just sweet, engulfing sleep.

Ms. Rainwater and her mother were sitting in their kitchen talking over cups of tea. Skye had just made it in and they'd sent her up to bed to rest. All was quiet, and then there was a knock at the door. Skye's grandmother got up and answered the door. It was Jaye. She was glad to see him. She said, "Oh Jaye. My boy. Skye has been so worried about you. Come in." He stepped inside and stood there. He said, "I had to go out of town. There was a family issue that couldn't wait. I'm sorry. I had to go so quick I forgot to let Skye know. She's probably furious with me." She shook her head, "Nonsense! She's just concerned and missing you. Please have a seat. I'm afraid we have some good and some bad news."

Jaye came on in and sat on the couch. She called for her daughter to come into the living room with them. Ms. Rainwater came in with a cup of tea for Jaye. "Here dear. You'll need some of mom's calming tea." Her mother continued after she sat down. "I'll tell you the good news. They found Nanuk today. He's alive and well, thanks to everybody. They are having a celebration tonight at 7:00 p.m. at the camp." She paused and looked at Jaye, sadly, and said, "The bad news is your grandmother, Rose, has been killed. It seems she put up a good fight, but in the end, she lost. We went up there and gave her a proper burial ceremony. I'm so sorry my boy."

She came over to him and gave him a hug. He just sat there in shock. He held the tea cup in his hand, mid-air, and stared into space. He didn't move. Skye's mother came to his side and sat down and held his hand. She asked, "Son? Are you ok?" Tears began to stream down his face. He moved his mouth to talk but nothing came out. Finally, he stood up and asked, "Where's Skye?" Her mother said, "She's upstairs asleep. She just got back and needed to rest before the party." He looked at his watch and said, "I have about three hours. I have to go to the house. I have to see for myself. I have to say goodbye. I'll be back. If Skye wakes up, can you tell her I'll be back?" They nodded yes. He ran to the door and out the door, changed into a crow and took off.

I opened my eyes and peeked at my alarm clock. I had been out cold for two hours and fifteen minutes. It felt more like two days and fifteen hours. I must have slept like a rock. It was both tiring and refreshing. I turned over to get up and found an outfit laid out for me. Mom to the rescue again. It was a gorgeous low cut burgundy silk blouse, black silk skirt with a split going up both sides to the thigh, and black leather boots that came up to the knee with thick souls. It was perfect. I went in the bathroom to shower and change.

Once I was finished in the bathroom getting dressed and doing my make-up, I headed back to my room. I was startled by someone sitting on the foot of my bed. It was Jaye! I ran over to him, "Oh Jaye! You're alright! You're alive! You had me so worried." I punched him in his arm. He slowly rubbed it but still sat there with his head down. I asked, "Are you alright?" He shook his head no. "Your mom and grandma told me about my grandmother. I went to see. I went to say good bye. I can't believe it happened. If only I had been here. Maybe I could have helped her."

He buried his face in his hands and sobbed. I rubbed his back, "I'm so sorry Jaye. I wish I had been there too. Her spirit's at rest now though." He leaned over on my shoulder and cried. After a little time of crying, he pulled me into his arms and began kissing me on my neck, then my cheeks, my forehead, then on my lips. It felt so good to kiss him. He whispered to me, "I'm so lucky to have you. I've lost my grandmother, but at least I have you to love and to love me."

He kissed me again and lay me back on the bed. I looked into his eyes. He was so upset he seemed distant. But, I knew he had to grieve. He started to kiss me again, then I put my hands against his chest and held him off. I said, "You don't know how bad I want this, but I have to get ready for the party still. You have to come too."

He sat up and then I did too. He turned his back to me and mumbled, "I don't feel much like celebrating. Why don't you skip it and stay here with me? We both need comforting and I want you to stay right here with me." I bowed my head then looked back up at him. He was so hurt. I wanted to stay here with him and just wash away everything that had happened by wrapping up in his arms, but I also knew I had to be there at the party. I pleaded with him. "Jaye. Please say you'll come with me. I have to be there. It's not only what I want to do, but it's my duty as everyone's leader to be there."

He sat quiet again. I could sense the tension and anger building inside him. He yelled, "Your duty! I want you here with me tonight. Just tonight. Then they can all have you there with them. I just lost someone dear to me and I want you here! I have a feeling that if you go, I'll lose you forever. I already lost you once. I won't lose you again!" I reached out to touch his shoulder, but he shrugged my hand off. Then very snidely he said, "If you care anything about me, you'll stay." I didn't know what to say. I didn't want to hurt him, but I knew I had to go.

Before I could answer, there was a knock on my door. I called out, "Yeah?" The voice that came back wasn't the one I expected. It was Shinu, "Knock, knock. Are you decent My Lady?" For some odd reason I felt relieved that he was here. I looked at Jaye, who was now turning red and answered, "Yes I am. Come on in." He opened the door and stepped in. Jaye turned and glared at him. Shinu being Shinu had a smart remark. "My, my. So the prodigal son comes home. Welcome back homing pigeon." Jaye jumped up from the bed and faced Shinu rather angrily, "Nice to see you too, blood sucker! Perfect timing, again!"

He looked back at me one more time and walked over to the window. He leaned down to open it and mumbled again, "You know what? Go ahead and enjoy yourself. Sorry for being such a sour puss. I'm just hurt and lashing out at the wrong people. I should be out hunting for the one who killed my grandmother. I love you." He raised the window then dived out. He shifted into a crow and shot off over the trees.

I stood there in shock for a moment looking at the window. Then I turned to look at Shinu. He looked surprised too. He asked, "What ruffled his feathers?" I hunched my shoulders and said, "Well, he did lose his grandmother. He was really hurt and wanted me to stay here with him and skip the party. I told him I couldn't and you saw the rest. I know he's hurting, but he doesn't have to get so bent out of shape."

Shinu agreed. Then he looked at me closer now. His eyes went from my head to my toe and back up again. "Wow! Stunning outfit. Maybe that's why he didn't want to let you go." I grabbed my little pillow and threw it at him. Laughing, I said, "Ha ha. Keep your eyes to yourself. Now. I do believe we have a party to attend. By the way. What are you doing here?" He took my arm and led me out the room. He answered, "I just had a hunch I should come and escort you to the ball Cinderella." I laughed and we went down the steps. Mom and grandma were ready to go too. They both looked astounding too. I said to mom, "You really know how to pick outfits. Thanks mom. Now, if we're ready to go, our escort is here." They smiled and we followed Shinu out the door. He helped us all get in his car, and we headed for the camp.

···

By the time we arrived at the party almost everyone was already there. As we pulled up to the house I saw Stacey's family's car, the sheriff's car, and Amber's car. We got out and started to mingle. Looking around at the faces of all those there I couldn't help but feel grateful. The way everyone came together and accepted each others differences was remarkable. Thinking back on times past, you would never have seen humans associating with werewolves, werewolves associating with vampires, or shape-shifters with any of them.

I walked on up toward the house with my mother and grandmother and Shinu excused himself so he could go and find Emily. Everyone was talking, or eating, or drinking something.

Grandma made a comment, "My, oh my! I would never have believed it if I hadn't seen it with my own eyes. Skye my dear child, for you to be able to unite all of these different people together is wonderful. You are truly a spectacular leader." She squeezed my hand affectionately.

The sheriff spotted us coming up and he came over to say hi. "Hello Skye, Ms. Rainwater." He shook our hands then turned to my mom and kissed her hand. He smiled at her and said, "Good evening Lily." His eyes practically sparkled when he said that. My mom blushed again and said, "Good evening John. I'm so glad you came." He looked at me and asked, "Skye, would you mind if I stole your mom for a little while?" I had a really big smile on my face and looked at my mom when I answered him, "Not at all Sheriff. You mind if I ask if Ned is here?" He answered me but still didn't take his eyes off mom. "He's patrolling with some of Thomas' guards. Probably driving them nuts by now with a thousand questions." I winked at my mom and she blushed a shade brighter. She held his hand as they walked off to meet the others that were there.

I turned to grandma and asked her, "How long have they been interested in each other grandma?" She giggled, "They have been watching each other for about three years now, but neither of them has ever made a move. I guess they both had their doubts about who each other was and were afraid to discuss it. That was until you brought humans into our world. So see, my child, you have not only united all of them, but you have also brought two people together that should have been together years ago."

I was shocked and happy for my mother. She has been alone ever since my father passed and that was centuries ago. I headed on up toward the house and grandma drifted off toward the crowd. Deputy Brad approached with three others. He smiled at me and reached out and shook my hand. He said, "Madame Skye, I would like you to meet my wife, Judy." I shook her hand and said, "It's a pleasure to meet you."

He pushed his son's forward toward me and said, "And these are my two boys. I'm sure you've seen them around school. Shake her hand boys." They both stood there looking down at their feet. They finally looked up at me and their eyes got big. They were checking me out. I watched as their eyes trailed down my legs and back up to my chest. Chuck, the oldest one said, "Hey Skye. I seen you around. Man you're hot!" His father hit him in the head, his mother gasped, and his brother, Buck, bent over holding his stomach because he was laughing so hard he couldn't breathe.

Chuck punched him and they ran off hitting each other. Judy looked at me. I smiled back at her and shook my head. She said, "I apologize for my bull headed son's. But, you probably already know how they are from school. You'll excuse us while we go round them up?" I let them know it was fine and I wasn't insulted.

I spotted Amber standing near the house with her parents and waved. I walked over to them and Amber hugged me. She asked, "How are you feeling? Did you get any rest? You look gorgeous! Have you heard from Jaye yet?" I had to smile at her concern. "I'm feeling fine. Yes, I took a nap and yes I heard from Jaye. He was upset, moody, and was torn up about his grandmother. He didn't feel like coming." Amber frowned, "That doesn't sound like him. But, I guess everyone grieves differently. You know my mom and dad." She directed me to them.

Her father said, "Good to see you again Madame. I always knew you were someone special. Now I know why. I did a thorough check up on Nanuk. He's recovering well. His broken bones are completely mended. There was no concussion and the arterial blood vessels . . ." Mrs. Whitcraft cut him off, "Now honey. I'm sure Madame Skye would love to hear all your medical gobble-dee-gook some other time. We are here to enjoy ourselves. I'm sorry. I can never get him to shut up. Please, go have fun."

We all laughed about that and I asked them to excuse me. I told Amber I'd have to talk to her later. She nodded and walked on with her parents. I headed up on the porch, finally, and found Thomas and Sadie. Natasha was standing on Thomas' side with a stern serious look on her face. She nodded her head in acknowledgement of me.

Nanuk was running around on the porch, with Dakota close behind him, playing tag.

Coming up closer to them, I could see both of them virtually glowing as they watched Nanuk. Their eyes sparkled with happiness. I embraced them both and held back tears, again. I could feel the joy radiating off both of them. We smiled at each other. There was no need for more than that. I turned and squatted down so I could talk to Nanuk. He was running from Dakota and giggling. He almost ran into me, but stopped. He cocked his head to the side and looked at me, frowning for a second. Then his little face lit up. He ran into my arms and just laughed and giggled even more. I laughed with him. He said, "You're the lady in my head! Thank you for mommy and Dada!" He leaned closer and whispered in my ear, "Don't worry. I won't tell your secret." He giggled again and ran off after Dakota.

Standing up, I turned to Thomas and Sadie and said, "He is doing so well. He whispered something about not telling my secret. Do you know what that was about?" As soon as I got the words out my mouth and looked at Thomas' face, I knew what he was talking about. I had forgotten that when I enter anyone's mind, I open up a part of mine to them. And by the look on Thomas' face, I could figure out what that secret was. This time, I blushed. The only thing I was thinking about right before I went into Thomas' mind was Yusuke, because he was comforting me after all that happened. I was thankful to him.

Thomas looked at me jokingly and said, "Don't worry. Your secret is safe with me too." Then he laughed. I had to laugh too. Thomas said, "We are getting ready to thank everyone." I nodded and stepped back down off the porch. I wanted to be down with the others when he spoke so I walked over to about the middle of the crowd.

Where I stood; Stacey and her parents, Shinu and Emily, and several of Thomas' pack were to my left. To my right stood; Amber and her family, my mom, the sheriff and grandma, Deputy Brad and his family, and Hana. It felt good to be surrounded by so many friends. Thomas began to talk and everyone quieted down. He said, "May I have your attention please? First, I'd like to thank you all for coming to help us celebrate the return of our son." Everyone cheered.

Thomas went on. "Second, I'd like to thank Madame Skye. If it wasn't for her, Nanuk may not be here right now. As I look out among all of you, I would never have believed it if someone had told me that one day, humans and vampires and werewolves and shape-shifters would work together. But you did. And because of you also, we have our son."

They all clapped and raised their glasses in a salute to each other. Just as I was wishing I had grabbed a drink to salute with them, a hand reached around me and handed me a glass. Then I felt him move up closer to my back and lean down and whisper to me, "You may need this if you're going to make a toast." I turned around to see who it was and just as I thought, it was Yusuke. He was dressed in an expensive looking black suit. His shirt was a brilliant ruby red. He had on dress boots. Even with my thick heeled boots on he still stood a good foot or more, taller than me. And just as I was thinking, wow, he wore something normal; I noticed the long black cape on his back.

I looked at his face and could tell he was looking down my blouse. I quickly said thank you and turned around. I could feel myself flush. I directed my attention back up to Thomas. He was saying something about all of us continuing to work together and something about everyone eating and enjoying themselves. Yusuke put his hands on my shoulders and stepped closer to me. He started massaging them, gently. I hadn't realized how tense I was until I started to relax. He leaned down and whispered to me again, "I told you, you did well. Look at everyone here. You should be proud. Relax."

He was right. I needed to try and enjoy myself for once and not worry about so many things. With everyone here, we should be able to handle whatever is thrown our way. I took a sip of my drink and was surprised that it was the same thing Shinu had given me to drink earlier today. I turned around to question him about it, but he spoke first, "Shinu told us about you and about how much you enjoyed the sip you had today. I thought I'd treat you to a little more." Again I thanked him and again I flushed. I turned back around. I don't know what was wrong with me. It had to be the euphoria of the night.

Looking over to my left I saw Stacey madly waving her arms at me. She was mouthing, *What's up with that*, and pointing at Yusuke. I had to laugh at her. I mouthed back, *Nothing at all*. She nodded her head to say ok and I gave her the thumbs up to let her know I was fine. When I looked to my right, Shinu and Emily were looking at me too, laughing. I gave them a back off look, and then smiled to myself. Thomas had already finished speaking and was now off the porch with Sadie by his side walking around and talking to everyone.

Now Yusuke was feeling really bold. He lowered his hands to my waist and whispered, yet again, "My, my you are looking quite succulent tonight. Give any thought about plucking the feathers of chicken boy?" My heart skipped a beat and I had trouble breathing. I half expected Hana to appear behind him and whack him in the head again, but when I looked down to where she was standing, she was being hounded by Ned. I was on my own. I turned my glass up and downed my drink.

When I turned around to face him, he kept his hands right where they were. I looked up at him intending to let him have it, gently, but I suddenly couldn't breathe at all. My heart was racing one hundred miles an hour and I felt light headed. Vampires can't use their powers on me to control me. Just like they can't sneak up on me either, nor get in my head, with exception of Shinu. So why did I feel like I wasn't in control of any of my senses. My mind was screaming, *Tell him to back off and let you go. And that you're a taken woman.* But, another part of my mind and my heart wanted to grab him and kiss him passionately.

He looked at me with those alluring eyes and I couldn't move. My stomach was abruptly invaded by millions of butterflies. I tried to speak and was only able to get out a breathless, "I . . . I . . . I'm with Jaye." He let go of my waist and put one arm behind his back and held my chin up with his other hand, and looked at me so deep

I could've sworn he was looking right into my soul, and said, "But what does your heart tell you?" I could feel myself start to close my eyes and purse my lips to kiss him, but gained control finally and stepped back from him.

I couldn't answer him now. If I opened my mouth, the wrong thing would come out, so I took one more step back and turned around. When I looked in front of me, Jaye was standing there looking back at me.

CHAPTER 20

REVELATION . . .

aye was standing there just staring at me. The look on his face was dark and ominous. He was dressed all in black and his eyes were red. I could feel the fury lashing off of him. Out of nowhere a wind began to pick up. He walked over to me and began circling around me. He had his arms crossed behind his back. He was looking back and forth at me and then at Yusuke. After a long, eerie pause, he finally said, "Well, well, well. What have we here? It appears that history is repeating itself." He stopped and stretched his arms out, one toward me and one toward Yusuke then went on. "Another Lady Rainwater again returns to a filthy blood sucker! What is wrong with you Rainwater's? Are you just predestined to wallow with unholy trash, or are you all just so weak you can't control the hold they have on you?"

I tried to go to him to calm him down, but he held his hand up signaling me to stay back. The anger in him was growing more and more and the wind was picking up and blowing harder. I could see Dakota grab Nanuk and run in the house with him. That was one relief. Everyone out there began to gather around us and look on to see what was happening.

Jaye clenched and unclenched his fist and rolled his head like he was cracking his neck. He clenched and unclenched his teeth over and over again. Now I was growing angry. I yelled at him, "What the hell is your problem Jaye!?" He snapped at me, "First of all, my real name isn't Jaye! My *real* name is Luke! Some of you old folks out here may remember my father's name. His name was Stephen Crowe." I could hear the wolf they call grandma gasp and yell, "No! It can't be." My grandmother stepped forward and said, "This isn't possible. You can't be his son. You have always been Jaye." Others from Thomas' pack gasped too and a hushed murmur began to rise from the crowd. They recognized the name.

Jaye leaned his head back and let out laugh so deep and dripping with evil that it could have come from Satan himself. I stood there in shock. This was Jaye. This was the man I had fallen in love with. This was the boy I grew up with and played with. This was the man, the crow that always followed me and looked out for me. How could this be?

After he finished laughing, an unnatural hush fell over the crowd and all creatures in the area. He smiled and walked closer to me. I backed away. He directed his answers to me, "I can tell you're thinking back and wondering. Yes, it has been me with you all these centuries. I have been your Jaye. The Jaye you fell in love with. Jaye, leader of the shape-shifters." He stopped talking again and stopped right in front of me. Yusuke started to come up behind him, but Jaye turned and held up his hand to stop him.

Yusuke backed off and he went on, "Let me give you all a brief history lesson. Long, long ago there was an Indian chief who had a beautiful daughter. White Cloud Rainwater. She foolishly fell in love with a vampire, Prince Takai! Oh, there were plenty other men in the village who pined over her, my father included, but she went to a leech! Some of the villagers did not agree with their princess marrying a creep like Prince Takai. But her father, the chief, blessed their union regardless.

Some of the villagers left. My father was one of them. Now the other men there soon got over there infatuation for Princess Rainwater and learned to accept her and her foul husband. My father, however, never got over her. He was obsessed with her. His obsession drove my mother to kill herself. I watched her die! I watched the last of her life flow out of her with her blood! That day, I swore to her as she died that I would one day get revenge on a Rainwater for what Princess White Cloud put her through!"

All around the crowd, silence still filled the air. The wind started whipping leaves and limbs off the trees. I could see the pack all change to their werewolf. Emily had dropped down to her knees and was changing fast into her large werewolf form. Shinu's, Yusuke's, and Hana's fangs had grown along with their claws and all of their eyes were glowing iridescent red. Their faces were contorted and fuming with hate. The sheriff, Ned, and Stacey's father had all drawn their guns. I didn't even realize they had them with them. Deputy Brad and his family had shifted into their moose forms.

Jaye started talking again, "Now, I couldn't just pick any Rainwater woman to kill. I had to pick the most prized of all the Rainwater women. So I waited. For centuries I searched and searched, then what do you know, a special child was born. Skye Rainwater. I watched you grow bigger and felt your power grow stronger. When you were old enough I befriended you. We were always together. As sickened as I felt about even being near you, I had to make you trust me and fall in love with me. But, you mother took you away before I could take my revenge. Again, I had to wait. Then you returned."

He turned around to look at the crowd and laughed again. He stepped a little closer to me again. I wanted to change, to take wing and fly away from him, but I couldn't in front of him. That would give him the advantage and he could kill me before I even changed. My skin crawled and every fiber of my being radiated anger. My conscious mind and subconscious mind joined as one again and I could see everything vibrantly, and could smell everything, and could hear everything. I could feel myself trembling with immense hatred for this man.

He had more to say, "You want to hear something funny? My own grandmother didn't know what I had planned. Oh I had her fooled too. She was so sweet and so doting over me. Just a bunch of icky, drippy, sappy, love. She took me in and consoled me when you left. I played the role of good guy and bided my time. Then, she began to have too many visions. She was getting too close to the truth and she was going to blow my cover. So, I had to get rid of her too. Oh, she put up a good fight, the old lady did. But, in the end, I won. I think you all know her. Does Shaman Rose sound familiar?"

That was it! Everyone gasped, and cried out, yelled and screamed. Some of the older ones that knew her dropped to their knees and cried. I couldn't contain my rage any longer. Before I thought it out I lunged at him. He was quick though. He side stepped me and then grabbed me by my waist, pulling my back against him, and held me tight him. He reached behind his back and pulled out a knife. It was a snake skinned knife. I could smell something on the blade of it. Some fetid odor wafted off it. He held it to my chest.

Everyone prepared to jump him, but he yelled, "Stop! This blade has been saturated with a spell that will kill her instantly. No trick, no chant, no power could bring her back. She will slowly writhe and twist, spasm and contort in a pain so profounding her mind won't even be able to wrap around it. It will slowly drive her insane and then after months of suffering, she will die! Kind of fitting isn't it? My father suffered the same ill fate. So, back off! She's coming with me so I can subject her to a life of living hell and torture before I sentence her to death!"

A wave of growls and howls, rumbles, screaming, yelling, and shouting broke the silence. A hideous, slimy cackle escaped Jaye's throat. He raised his voice above everyone, "What? What are you gonna do? Come on! I'll kill her right here!" I looked up in time to see Yusuke charge head on at him. He threw himself at Jaye's arm to try and knock the knife away. I watched Jaye as he raised his arm and thrust the knife deep into Yusuke's side. Yusuke was able to grab his arm and rip it backward before Jaye could plunge it in again. This gave me time to duck down out of his arms. Mom ran forward and flung out her arms. A bolt of lightening hit the knife dead on and whipped it onto the roof.

I had enough time now to change. I chose a lion. Not just any lion. I was huge. I let out an ear shattering roar and jumped on Jaye, knocking him to the ground. I pinned him there and leaned my head down so I could rip his head off. Before I could close my mouth on him, he vanished. I raised my head up and looked around. He was now standing in the middle of everyone. He waved his hands above his head and conjured up a gust of wind. Some of the wolves were tossed backward by the wind.

My grandmother ducked down on the ground, vanished in a puff of smoke, and reappeared behind Jaye. She thrust out her arms and lightening flew from her fingers and knocked him forward toward a tree. He turned and flung his arms at her then swirled them around. She was taken up in a whirl wind that rose higher and higher. Then he cut off the wind and dropped her to the ground.

He laughed again and screamed, "Two Rainwater's for the price of one!" I changed again to a condor and swooped over him. Before he could react and bring up another wind I dived and grabbed him and soared as high as I could. I drew my legs into my body and then with all my strength, I pitched him down toward the ground. By the time I circled back around and shot back to the ground. Shinu grabbed him from mid-air and clawed at his face and body. He howled out in pain, but managed to throw Shinu off him and into a tree. The sound of his body hitting the tree sounded like a boulder slamming concrete. I could hear various bones breaking throughout his body.

I dropped down and changed into a panther and pounced on his back before he turned back around. I dug my claws into his body and began ripping and tearing at his flesh. Somehow he flipped me off, bounced to his feet and kicked me dead in my side with a force that felt like a truck. I felt my ribs break. He ran off toward the trees. I could hear gun shots ringing out behind him.

I changed back to my human form. Holding my side, I tried to stand up, but fell back down. Hana popped up beside me and helped me up. Shinu was right beside her. He looked like he had recovered, but I asked, "Are you alright?" He nodded and asked me, "What about you?" I took a deep breath and stretched. My ribs had already healed. "I'm fine. Let's go get that asshole and finish him off!"

Before we took off I looked back to the field where my grandmother was laying. Mom was with her helping her up. She looked at me and gave me thumbs up, so I took off. As we ran through the trees I could hear him yelling and cursing and screaming.

I heard tree limbs breaking and the sound of rocks slamming against something. We rounded the corner in time to see Brad and his oldest son, Chuck, running head on at each other. Jaye was standing in the middle of the two of them staggering. They both hit him with there antlers. That was the sound I heard that I thought were rocks slamming concrete.

They backed up and were coming in for another hit when he regained his senses and whipped up a wind so strong it threw them back through the trees. Jaye jumped and landed on a limb high up in a tree. Hana ran to him and was up the tree and standing beside him before he could see her. She grabbed him by the neck and flung him to the ground. Again, before he could hit the ground, several werewolves charged at him. I could tell it was Thomas in the lead. He grabbed him with his mouth and they all ran past me heading back to the field in front of his house. Shinu said, "It's better to fight him in an open area. That way he can't hide in the trees. We both turned and followed the werewolves back. Mayor Ritennour and the sheriff were right behind me. They still had their guns drawn.

As we broke free of the line of trees I could see Jaye standing in the middle of the field. He was holding his sides and stumbling around. I could see and smell a great loss of blood from him. I joined them in the field and stood behind Thomas. The others started gathering around the circle of wolves too. I looked around and saw Stacey and her family, and Deputy Brad and his family. The others must be off getting healed by Amber and her father or out patrolling the area in case someone comes up.

I brought my attention back to Jaye. He was still laughing wildly. He yelled, "You all may be able to kill me, but that won't end the slaughtering around here! Oh yeah. I didn't mention this earlier did I? I haven't been working alone. Shinu, Hana, Yusuke. Yeah I know all your names! Your beautiful sister? That was his work. Sweet little Tania? His work. I had to hand it to him. The idea of selling her parts at the butcher shop? Classic! All the helpless little shape-shifters found dead or as road kill? Well, that was me. Kidnapping and torturing Nanuk? Him."

Thomas almost lost it and attacked him, but I touched his back to get his attention. Urgently, I said, "No. In a little bit. Let him finish blabbing so we can find out who else it is." He calmed down and held his ground. Jaye went on, "Who is he you ask? Well, he's one of your own kind Thomas. Damien Wick! Oh, he has big plans for all of you bastards!" He lowered his head like he had finished his spiel and started to slump to the ground when he popped his head back up and said, "Oh yeah! I almost forgot to take credit for another one of my fun kills. I did have fun with this one."

He laughed hysterically and then said, "That young girl werewolf. Oh what was her name? Elaine. She was tasty. I used a potion on her that stopped her from going full wolf. From there I had my fun ripping her pretty little legs off, one by one. She died screaming like a banshee." He threw his head back and howled in laughter.

Before I could open my mouth and give the command for them to kill him, Emily came sailing out of nowhere over our heads. She was in her giant wolf form again. Thomas gave the command to his pack to back off and I yelled to everyone else, "Get out the way! Run back as fast as you can!" I ran over and grabbed Stacey and headed for the trees. I put her down, checked to see if she was alright, and then returned to where Shinu and Hana stood watching.

When Emily jumped over everybody, she caught Jaye in her mouth. She was now flinging him up and down, slamming his body into the ground. The force of just his body hitting the ground left large pits in the dirt. She threw him up high in the air and jumped up and grabbed him in her mouth again. She twisted her head back and forth. Blood flew everywhere. I could hear all his bones breaking. She dropped him down on the ground and stared down at him. I could hear him whimpering in pain. She lowered her head and growled, "You dumb son of a bitch! This is for everyone out here!" She took his head in her mouth and ripped it off. I could see a little of his spine dangling from his head. She tossed his head way across the field.

I looked at Shinu, but he knew what to do next. He went to Emily to get her to calm down. It was over for now. He was gone. In all the excitement I almost forgot about Yusuke. I looked at Hana and asked, "Do you know where Yusuke is?" She noticed she had forgotten too and gasped, "Oh no!" We ran back toward the house where he first attacked Jaye.

This battle was over. I had lost a very dear friend. Someone I had always admired and loved. My mentor, Shahma. She was taken from me by the hands of someone I thought I knew. Someone I had always been close to. Someone I had fallen in love with. Jaye. How could I not know all these years? How could I not see? Maybe if I hadn't been blinded by love, Shahma and the others would still be here. Maybe if I had been more suspicious. Maybe if I had been there with her or the others, they would still be here. But, life doesn't thrive on maybe if's. I had to go on. I had to continue to protect those that were still with me. I also had to know about Yusuke, so Hana and I ran to the house where we had last seen him.

When we made it to the porch, Amber and her father were leaning over a body that was lying limp on the porch. I was so afraid to go any closer, but I had to know. Hana walked beside me. I reluctantly looked down. It was Yusuke! I could see the dark area in his side where Jaye had stabbed him with the dagger. His eyes were closed and he didn't move. Hana cried out, "No!", and turned her back. I looked to Amber and her father, pleadingly, "Can you do anything?" They both looked at me with dread. Her father said, "We did all the spells we know. We have never worked on vampires so we don't know what to do. I'm sorry Madame Skye."

This couldn't be true. He couldn't be gone. I thought back about the over powering feelings I felt for him right before it all happened. I thought of the butterflies. I thought of the breathless moment of wanting to kiss him. I thought about what might have been and leaned my head down on his chest, and cried.